EMPEROR
THE BLOOD OF GODS

Also by Conn Iggulden

The Emperor Series

The Gates of Rome
The Death of Kings
The Field of Swords
The Gods of War

The Conqueror Series

*Wolf of the Plains**
Lords of the Bow
Bones of the Hills
Empire of Silver
Conqueror

Blackwater

By Conn Iggulden and Hal Iggulden

The Dangerous Book for Boys
The Dangerous Book for Boys Yearbook

By Conn Iggulden and David Iggulden

The Dangerous Book of Heroes

By Conn Iggulden and illustrated by Lizzy Duncan

Tollins: Explosive Tales for Children

Tollins II: Dynamite Tales

* Published in the USA as *Genghis: Birth of an Empire*

To George Romanis

ACKNOWLEDGEMENTS

I am indebted once again to the talented group who read, re-read, argued furiously about and edited this book with me. In particular: Katie Espiner, Tim Waller, Tracy Devine and Victoria Hobbs – I thank you all.

The Roman World, 44BC

B l a c k   S e a

• Ancyra

I A   M I N O R

Tarsus
•

• Antioch

CYPRUS

Ctesiphon
•

Babylon
•

• Damascus

S e a

Euphrates

Tigris

Nile

'I am the most peaceable of men. All I ask is a humble cottage with a thatched roof, a good bed, good food, fresh milk and butter, flowers before my window and a few fine trees at my door; and if the dear Lord wants to make my happiness complete, he will grant me the joy of seeing some six or seven of my enemies hanging from those trees. Before their death I shall forgive them all the wrongs they did me in their lifetime. One must forgive one's enemies – but not before they have been hanged.'

Heinrich Heine

PROLOGUE

Not all of them were marked with blood. His body lay on cold marble, the stone proof against red lines dripping down the benches. Those who walked away looked back at least once, hardly able to believe that the tyrant would not rise. Caesar had fought, but they had been too many, too determined.

They could not see his face. In his last moments, the leader of Rome had yanked at the loose folds of his toga, pulling the cloth over his head as they gripped and stabbed at him. Its whiteness was marked with mouths. His bowels had opened as he slumped and fell to one side. The smell of it rose into the air in the theatre. There was no dignity for the broken thing they had made.

More than twenty men were spattered with the violence, some of them still panting in great heaving breaths. Around them were twice as many again, those who had not wielded blades but had stood and watched and not moved to save Caesar. Those who had taken part were still stunned at the

1

violence and the feel of warm blood on their skins. Many had served terms with the army. They had seen death before, but in foreign lands and exotic cities. Not in Rome, not here.

Marcus Brutus touched his blade to both palms, leaving a red smear. Decimus Junius saw him do it and, after a moment of awe, he marked his own hands with fresh blood. Almost with reverence, the rest copied the action. Brutus had told them they would not walk with guilt. He had told them they had saved a nation from a tyrant. Behind him, they took the first steps towards a thick bar of light leading to the outside.

Brutus breathed deeply as he reached the sun, pausing on the threshold and letting the warmth seep into him. He was dressed as a soldier, the only man there in armour and with a gladius on his hip. In his late fifties, his bare brown legs were still strong, still rooted in the earth. There were tears in his eyes and he felt as if shadows of age and betrayal had been lifted, scars scrubbed away from his skin, so that he was made new.

He heard the men in robes gather at his back. Cassius stepped to his side, touching him lightly on the shoulder in comfort or support. Brutus did not look at him. His eyes were raised to the sun.

'We can honour him now,' he said, almost to himself. 'We can heap glory on his memory until he is crushed beneath it all.'

Cassius heard and sighed, the sound like a burr to Brutus' mood.

'The Senate will be waiting for the news, my friend,' Cassius murmured. 'Let us leave the old world behind in this place.'

Brutus looked at him and the wiry senator almost recoiled from what he saw in those eyes. The moment held and none of those behind made a sound. Though they had killed, it was only then that they began to fear the city all around them. They had been swept up like leaves in a gale, casting aside reason to follow stronger men. The reality was drifting through the air, Rome remade in motes of golden dust. Without another word, Brutus walked out into the sun and they followed him.

The roads were busy at first, the trades and wares of thousands on display on every spare ledge or half blocking the stone road. A wave of silence came out of Pompey's theatre, vanishing behind the senators, but staying with them as they turned towards the forum. The hawkers and servants and citizens of Rome froze at the sight of almost sixty men in white togas, led by one in armour whose right hand drifted to his sword hilt as he strode out.

Rome had seen processions before, by the thousand, but there was no joy in those who walked up the Capitoline hill. Whispers and nudges pointed out the red smears on their hands, the splashes of still-bright blood on their robes. Strangers shook their heads in fear and stayed well back, as if the group carried danger or disease.

Brutus strode eastwards and upward. He felt a strange anticipation, the first true emotion since he had pressed iron into his greatest friend and felt the shudder that told him he had reached the heart. He ached to lay eyes on the forum and the senate house, the stone centre of the vast Republic. He had to struggle not to quicken his step, to maintain the slow pace that was both their dignity and their protection. They would not run from what they had done. Their survival depended on showing no guilt, no fear. He would enter the forum as a liberator.

At the top of the Capitoline, Brutus paused. He could see the open space of the forum, ringed with temples. The senate house gleamed white, unsullied, the guards at its doors tiny figures in the distance. The sun was growing hot and he could feel sweat trickle inside his ornate chestplate. The senators at his back moved slowly up, not understanding why they had stopped. The line around him widened, but their authority had

3

been spent that morning and not one of them, not even Cassius or Suetonius, dared to move down the hill without Brutus leading the way.

'We are *Liberatores*,' Brutus said suddenly. 'There are many in that place who will welcome what we have done. There are hundreds more who will breathe in relief when they hear that the tyrant is dead and Rome is safe, the Republic is safe. There will be a vote for amnesty and it will pass. All this has been decided. Until then, remember your dignity, your honour. There is no shame in what we have done.'

Around him, they stood a little taller, many of them raising bloody hands that had been clenched and hidden at their sides.

Brutus looked to Cassius once more and this time his expression was mild.

'I have played my part, Senator. You must do the rest. Carry the small men with you and place every step with care, or we will be hunted down.'

Cassius nodded, smiling wryly.

'I have the votes, General. It is all arranged. We will walk in free and we will be honoured.'

Brutus looked hard at the senator who carried all their futures in his hands. Cassius was a man of bone and hard flesh, with no weakness evident in him.

'Then lead us in, Senator. I will be at your back.'

Cassius' mouth firmed at the suspicion of a threat, but he raised his head and strode down into the heart of Rome.

As they approached the senate house, Brutus and Cassius could hear raised voices, a dim roar of undisciplined sound. The great bronze doors were open, and a voice cried out above the rest. The noise dropped away into silence.

Brutus trembled as he touched the steps, knowing that the few hours left before noon would be among the most important of his life. They had the blood of Caesar on their hands. A wrong word or rash act and their own would be spilled before the sun set. He looked over to Cassius and was reassured once more by the man's confidence. There were no doubts in the senator. He had worked long and hard for this day.

Two legionaries came to attention as Brutus and Cassius ascended. The soldiers were out of their depth and they hesitated when the senator raised his bloody right hand, making sure they saw it before he inclined the palm to include Brutus.

'General Brutus is my guest,' Cassius said, his mind already on the crowd inside.

'He'll have to leave the gladius here, sir,' the soldier said.

Something in the way Brutus looked at him made him drop his hand to his own hilt, but Cassius chuckled.

'Oh, hand it over, Brutus. Don't embarrass the man.'

With ill grace, Brutus untied the scabbard rather than pull a bare blade and frighten the soldier. He gave up his sword and strode to catch Cassius, suddenly angry, though he could not have said exactly why. Julius had never been stopped at the door of that building. It was irritating to be reminded of his lack of status at the very moment of his triumph. In the senate house, Brutus was no more than an officer of Rome, a senior man without civil rank. Well, that could be put right. Now Caesar was dead, all the failures and setbacks of his life could be put right.

More than four hundred men had crowded into the senate house that morning, their bodies warming the air, so that there was a noticeable difference inside, despite the open doors. Brutus looked for faces he recognised. He knew most of them, after many years of standing at Julius' side, but one new face arrested his sweep. Bibilus. Years before, the man had stood with Caesar as consul, but something had happened between them and Bibilus had never appeared in the Senate again. His sudden return spoke volumes about the shift in power – and about how many already knew. Brutus saw Bibilus had aged terribly in the years of isolation. He had grown even fatter, with dark and swollen pouches under his eyes and a web of broken blood vessels on his cheeks. His jowls were scraped raw as if he had shaved for the first time in months. The man's gaze was fever-bright and Brutus wondered if he had been drinking, already celebrating the death of an old enemy.

It did not look as if Cassius' news would cause much shock in that chamber. Too many of the senators had smug and knowing expressions, exchanging glances and nodding to each other like virgins with a secret. Brutus despised them all, hated them for their effete manners and their pompous sense of their own worth. He had seen Egypt, Spain and Gaul. He had fought for the Republic, murdered for it, while they sat and talked the days away and understood nothing of the men who bled for them in the field.

Cassius approached the rostrum. Once it had been an arte-fact of Roman power, carved from the prow of a warship of Carthage. That one had been burned in riots and, like so much else in the building, it was now just a lesser copy of what it had once been. Brutus raised his eyes to the man standing behind it and grew still. He realised he had been the subject of cold scrutiny since he'd entered the chamber.

Mark Antony's latest consular year was not yet over. Before the events of that morning, he had been little more than a figurehead for Caesar, but that had changed. The Republic had been restored and Mark Antony held the reins. He dominated the room and Brutus had to admit he looked the part. Tall and muscular, Mark Antony had the features and strong nose of old Roman bloodlines. None of the Liberatores had known how he would jump when they planned their assassination. One of their number, Gaius Trebonius, had been given the task of distracting the consul. Brutus saw the young senator on the seats nearby, looking so pleased with himself that it made Brutus' stomach twist.

Mark Antony stared over the seated heads at him and Brutus sensed his knowledge and his shock. The consul had been told, or had heard the news as whispers went around the chamber. Caesar was dead. The tyrant was dead. They all knew, Brutus was suddenly certain. Yet the words still had to be spoken.

Cassius took his position at the base of the rostrum, standing a head lower than the consul looming over him. As Brutus watched, Cassius raised his right arm and touched the wood like a talisman. Into the silence, Cassius spoke.

'On this day, the Ides of March, Rome was set free from an oppressor,' he said. 'Let the news fly from here to all nations. Caesar is dead and the Republic is restored. Let the shades of our fathers rejoice. Let the city rejoice. Caesar is dead and Rome is free.'

The words brought forth a wave of sound as the senators cheered, striving to outdo the men around them with sheer volume. They were red-faced as they roared and stamped, making the stones tremble. Mark Antony stood with his head bowed, the muscles in his jaw standing out like tumours.

Brutus thought suddenly of the Egyptian queen in the fine Roman house Caesar had given her. Cleopatra would not yet know what had happened to the father of her son. He imagined her panic when she heard. He did not doubt she would pack her jewels and get out of Rome as fast as good horses could run. The thought made him smile for the first time that morning. So many things would be made new in the months to come. Caesar had been like a weight on the city, pressing them all down. Now they would spring up, stronger and better than they had been before. Brutus could feel it in the air. This was his time at last.

The Senate had almost forgotten how things used to be. Brutus could see the little men revise their opinions of their own power. They had been mere servants. In a morning, in a raw-throated bellow, they had become men again. He had given them that. Brutus lowered his head in thought, but when he heard Mark Antony begin to speak, he looked up, suspicion flaring.

'Senators, be still,' Mark Antony said. 'There is much to be done today, now that we have this news.'

Brutus frowned. The man was a famous supporter of Caesar. His time was *over*. The best he could do was leave the chamber with dignity and take his own life.

'There are legions in the Campus Martius waiting for Caesar to lead them against Parthia,' Mark Antony went on, oblivious to Brutus' irritation. 'They must be brought to heel, before they get the news. They were loyal to Caesar. They must be approached with care, or we will see them mutiny. Only the authority of the Senate stands between us all and anarchy in this city. Senators, *be still*.' The last words were a command, deeper and louder in order to silence the last of the excited chatter.

At the door Brutus shook his head in sour amusement. Mark Antony was not a fool, but he overreached himself. Perhaps he thought he could be part of the new era, despite fawning on Caesar for so many years. It was more politics, but Brutus knew the senators were still numb, still feeling their way in the new world that had been thrust upon them. The consul might even save himself, though he would have to choose each step with care. There were old grudges to be settled yet and Antony would bear the brunt of many of them. Even so, for that morning at least, he was still consul.

'There must be a formal vote before a single one of us leaves,' Mark Antony continued, his strong voice rolling across the chamber. 'If we grant amnesty to the murderers of Caesar, it will choke a rebellion before it begins. The citizens and the legions will see that we have restored justice and law, where it was once trodden down by a single man. I call that vote.'

Brutus froze, a worm of unease itching in his head. Cassius

stood at the rostrum with his mouth slightly open. He should have been the one to call a vote for amnesty. It was all arranged and the Liberatores knew they would win. To have Caesar's favourite pre-empt them with that vital step made Brutus want to bellow out in accusation. The words bubbled up in him, clear in his mind. Caesar had given Rome to Antony when he left the city to attack his enemies. Antony had been his puppet consul, the mask that let him hide tyranny beneath the old forms. What *right* did that man have to speak as if he now led the new Republic? Brutus took a half-step forward, but Mark Antony's voice continued to echo over them.

'I ask only this: that in death, Caesar be given his dignity. He was first in Rome. The legions and the people will expect to see him honoured. Will the men who brought him down deny him that? There should be no suspicion of shame, no secret burial. Let us treat the divine Julius with respect, now that he is gone from the world. Now that he is gone from Rome.'

In frustration, Cassius stepped up to the raised dais, so that he stood at Mark Antony's side. Even then, the consul was a powerful figure beside his slight frame. Before he could speak, Mark Antony leaned close to him and murmured.

'You have your victory, Cassius. This is not the time for small men and small vengeance. The legions will expect a funeral in the forum.'

Cassius remained still, thinking. At last, he nodded. Brutus stayed where he was, his right fist clenched over the empty space on his hip.

'I thank Consul Mark Antony for his clear thinking,' Cassius said. 'And I concur. There must be order first, before law, before peace. Let this vote take place and then we will be free to manage the common citizens, with their petty emotions. We will honour Caesar in death.'

The senators looked to Cassius, and Brutus nodded fiercely at the way he had taken control. There were legal officers whose

9

task it was to announce votes and debates in that place, but even as they rose from their seats around the rostrum, Cassius spoke again, ignoring their presence. He would not allow a delay on that morning, nor another to speak until he was done. Brutus began to relax.

'Those in favour of complete amnesty to be granted to the liberators of Rome, rise and be counted.'

Brutus saw the sweating bulk of Bibilus leap to his feet with the energy of a younger man. The rest followed a bare moment later. Those who were already standing, like Mark Antony, raised their right hands. There was a beat of silence and Cassius nodded, tension flowing out of him.

'Dissenters?'

The assembly sat down as one and not a single man rose. Somehow, it hurt Brutus to see. Half of them owed Caesar their lives and fortunes. Their families had been tied to his, their rise to his. He had picked them one by one over the years, men he wanted to honour in his wake. Yet they would not stand for him, even in death. Brutus found himself obscurely disappointed, for all he understood it. They were survivors, who could read the wind as well as anyone. Yet Caesar deserved better from Rome, on that day of all others.

Brutus shook his head in confusion, aware again of the blood on his hands as it dried and cracked. There was a fountain not far off in the forum and he wanted to be clean. As Cassius congratulated the Senate, Brutus slipped out into the sunshine. He collected his sword from the guards and walked stiffly down the steps and across the open ground.

There was already a crowd around the fountain, men and women of the city in colourful robes. Brutus felt their eyes on him as he approached, but he did not look at them. He knew the news would be on the wing already. They had not tried to hide it.

He rubbed his hands together in the freezing water, brought

by aqueduct from distant mountains, drawn through narrowing lead pipes until it rushed out clear and sweet in the forum. Someone gasped as they saw the red stain that spread into the water from his skin, but he ignored them.

'Is it true?' a woman asked suddenly.

Brutus looked up, then rubbed his wet hands over his face, feeling the rough stubble. Her stola robe was fine, revealing a bare tanned shoulder, her elegance accented by hair piled and caught in silver pins. She was beautiful, kohl-eyed like a courtesan. He wondered how many others across the city were asking the same question at that moment.

'Is what true?' he asked.

'That divine Caesar is dead, that he has been killed? Do you know?' Her dark eyes were rimmed with tears as she stared at the man washing blood from his hands.

Brutus remembered the blow he had struck a few hours and a lifetime before.

'I don't know anything,' he said, turning away.

His gaze drifted to the Capitoline hill, as if he could see through it to the vast building of Pompey's theatre. Was the body still there, lying on the stone seats? They had left no orders for Caesar to be tended in death. For an instant, Brutus felt his eyes sting at the thought of Julius alone and forgotten. They had been friends for a long, long time.

PART ONE

CHAPTER ONE

Octavian winced as he felt the heat of the rocks burning through his thin sandals. Though Rome claimed to have finally brought civilisation to Greece, he could see little sign of it in the hill villages. Away from the coast, the people were either suspicious of strangers or openly hostile. Even a simple request to use a well was met with frowns and doors shut in their faces. All the while, the sun beat down, reddening their necks. Octavian remembered how he had smiled when the local praetor said there were places in Greece where a young Roman had about as much chance of survival as a tax gatherer. It had been an exaggeration, but not by much.

He stopped to wipe sweat from his face. The land itself was wild, with canyons that seemed to drop for ever. Octavian took a deep breath, suddenly certain he'd be walking out. Nothing would give the local boys more pleasure than seeing three footsore Romans searching for stolen mounts.

Octavian stayed alert as he climbed, looking for some sign

of the group of ragged men they followed. The trail had been easy at first, until it split and split again. Octavian didn't know if the bandits knew they would be pursued or had just taken different routes home, vanishing into the cauldron of mountains as their ancestors had done for thousands of years. He felt an itch and craned his neck to see as far as he could. It was too easy to imagine a bowman leaning over the lip of some crag and attacking before they even knew he was there.

'Call out if you see anything,' he said.

Maecenas snorted, waving a hand at bare rocks. 'I'm not a tracker,' he replied. 'For all I know, they could have passed through here with a herd of goats just an hour ago. Why don't we go back to the main group and take up the search from there? This is not how I expected to spend my leave. I imagined more wine and less . . . climbing.' He grunted as they reached a great step in the rocks.

There was no sign of a path and each man heaved himself up, their sandals skidding and scrambling as they went. The sun was fierce above and the sky was an aching blue. All three were sweating heavily and the single flask of water was already empty.

'At least the men from the town know these hills,' Maecenas went on. 'They know where to search.'

Octavian didn't have the breath to respond. The slope grew steeper and steeper until he had to use his hands to steady each step, then really climb. He was panting lightly as he reached the top of a crag and stared, judging the best route down the other side. The maze of grey rocks stretched into the distance, empty of life beyond the lizards that skittered away with every step.

'You'd have me stand by and watch, doing nothing to help them?' Octavian said suddenly. 'A rape and a murder, Maecenas. You saw her body. What honour would there be in letting a few farmers chase them down while we stand

16

and watch, confirming everything they say about idle Romans? *Come* on.'

He jerked his head at a route that would take them to the floor of the canyon and began climbing down. At least the shadowed clefts were cooler, until they climbed back into the burning sun once more.

'Why should I care what Greek peasants say?' Maecenas muttered, though he pitched his voice too low to be heard. Maecenas was of such ancient lineage that he refused to claim descent from the twins who suckled at a she-wolf and went on to found Rome. *His* people, he said, had owned the wolf. When they'd first met, he'd assumed Octavian had known Caesar, so a mere Roman noble could not impress him. Over time, he'd realised Octavian took Maecenas at the value he set for himself. It was slightly galling to have to live up to his own sense of superiority. Maecenas felt that Octavian had rather missed the point of noble families. It wasn't who you were – it was who your ancestors had been that mattered. Yet somehow that simple faith was something he could not shatter in his friend. Octavian had known poverty, with his father dying early. If he thought a true Roman noble would be brave and honourable, Maecenas didn't want to disappoint him.

Maecenas sighed at the thought. They wore simple tunics and darker leggings. Any clothing was too hot for climbing in the noon sun, but the leggings were terrible, already dark with perspiration. He was convinced he'd rubbed himself raw under them. He could smell his own sweat as he climbed and skidded down, wrinkling his nose in distaste. The scabbard of his sword caught in a crevice and Maecenas swore as he freed it. His expression darkened as he heard Agrippa laugh behind him.

'I am glad to provide some amusement for you, Agrippa,' he snapped. 'The pleasures of this day are now complete.'

Agrippa gave a tight smile without replying as he came level and then went past, using his great strength and size to take enormous steps down the crag. The fleet centurion was a head taller than his companions and the constant labour on board Roman galleys had only increased the power in his arms and legs. He made the climb look easy and was still breathing lightly by the time he reached the bottom. Octavian was a few steps behind and the pair waited for Maecenas as he clambered down after them.

'You realise we'll have to go back up that hill again when we turn round?' Maecenas said as he jumped the last few feet.

Octavian groaned. 'I don't want to argue with you, Maecenas. It would be easier if you just accepted we are doing this.'

'Without complaining,' Agrippa added. His deep voice echoed back from the stone all around them and Maecenas looked sourly at them both.

'There are a thousand different paths through these cursed rocks,' Maecenas said. 'I should think the bandits are far away from here by now, sipping cool drinks while we die of thirst.'

Gleefully, Agrippa pointed at the dusty ground and Maecenas looked down, seeing the footprints of many men.

'Oh,' he said. He drew his sword in a smooth motion, as if he expected an immediate attack. 'Probably local herders, though.'

'Perhaps,' Octavian replied, 'but we're the only ones following this path, so I would like to be sure.' He too drew his gladius, shorter than Maecenas' duellist's blade by a hand's breadth, but well oiled, so that it slid free with barely a whisper. He could feel the heat of the blade.

Agrippa freed his own sword and together the three men walked silently into the canyon ahead, placing their steps with caution. Without planning it, Octavian took the lead, with Agrippa's bulk on his right shoulder and Maecenas on his left. Ever since they had become friends, Octavian had led the group as if there were no alternative. It was the kind of natural confidence Maecenas appreciated and recognised. Old families had to start somewhere, even when they began with a Caesar. He smiled at the thought, though the expression froze as they came round a spire of rock and saw men waiting for them in the shadows. Octavian walked on without a jerk, keeping his sword lowered. Three more steps brought him into the gloom of the chasm, with rock walls stretching up above their heads. He came to a halt, looking coldly at the men in his way.

There was another path out on the other side and Maecenas noticed laden mules waiting patiently. The men they faced did not seem surprised or afraid, perhaps because there were eight of them, staring with bright-eyed interest at the three young Romans. The biggest of the men raised a sword from another age, a great length of iron that was more like a cleaver than anything else. He sported a black beard that reached right down to his chest and Maecenas could see the bulge of heavy muscles under a ragged jerkin as he moved. The man grinned at them, revealing missing teeth.

'You are a very long way from your friends,' the man said in Greek.

Maecenas knew the language, though Octavian and Agrippa spoke not a word. Neither of them looked round with so many blades being pointed in their direction, but Maecenas could feel their expectation.

'Must I translate?' he said, dredging up the words from his memory. 'I know the high speech, but your peasant accent is so thick, I can hardly understand you. It is like the grunting of a dying mule. Speak slowly and clearly, as if you were apologising to your master.'

The man looked at him in surprise, anger darkening his face. He was aware that the death of Romans would make him a wanted man, but the mountains had hidden bodies before and would again. He tilted his head slightly, weighing his choices.

'We want the one who raped and strangled the woman,' Maecenas said. 'Hand him over to us and go back to your short and pointless lives.'

The leader of the bandits growled deep in his throat and took a step forward.

'What are you saying to him?' Octavian asked without taking his eyes off the man.

'I am praising his fine beard,' Maecenas replied. 'I have never seen one like it.'

'Maecenas!' Octavian snapped. 'It has to be them. Just find out if he knows the one we came to find.'

'Well, beard? Do you know the one we want?' Maecenas went on, switching languages.

'*I* am the one you want, Roman,' he replied. 'But if you have come here alone, you have made a mistake.'

The bandit looked up the rocks to the blue sky, searching for any hint of a moving shadow that would reveal an ambush or a trap. He grunted, satisfied, then glanced at his sharp-eyed companions. One of them was dark and thin, his face dominated by a great blade of a nose. In response, the man shrugged, raising a dagger with unmistakable intent.

Octavian stepped forward without warning of any kind. With a vicious flick, he brought his sword across so that it cut the throat of the closest man to him. The man dropped his dagger to hold his neck with both hands, suddenly choking as he fell to his knees.

The leader of the bandits froze, then gave a great bellow of rage with the rest of his men. He raised his sword for a crushing blow, but Agrippa jumped in, gripping the sword arm with his left hand and stabbing his short blade up between the man's ribs. The leader collapsed like a punctured wineskin, falling onto his back with an echoing crash.

For a heartbeat, the bandits hesitated, shocked by the explosion of violence and death. Octavian had not stopped moving. He killed another gaping bandit with a backhand stroke against his throat, chopping into flesh. He'd set his feet well and brought the whole of his strength into the blow, so that it almost decapitated the man. The gladius was made for such work and the weight felt good in his hand.

The rest might have run then, if their way hadn't been blocked by their own mules. Forced to stand, they fought with vicious intensity for desperate moments as the three Romans lunged and darted among them. All three had been trained from a young age. They were professional soldiers and the bandits were more used to frightening villagers who would not dare to raise a blade against them. They fought hard but uselessly, seeing their blades knocked away and then unable to stop the return blows cutting them. The small canyon was filled with grunting and gasping as the bandits were cut down in short, chopping blows. None of the Romans were armoured, but they stood close to one another, protecting their left sides as the swords rose and fell, with warm blood slipping off the warmer steel.

It was over in a dozen heartbeats and Octavian, Agrippa and Maecenas were alone and panting. Octavian and Agrippa were both bleeding from gashes on their arms, but they were unaware of the wounds, still grim-eyed with the violence.

'We'll take the heads back,' Octavian said. 'The woman's husband will want to see them.'

'All of them?' Maecenas said. 'One is enough, surely?'

Octavian looked at his friend, then reached out and gripped his shoulder.

'You've done well,' he said. 'Thank you. But we can make a sack from their clothing. I want that village to know that Romans killed these men. They will remember – and I suspect they will break out the casks of their best wine and slaughter a couple of goats or pigs as well. You might even find a willing girl. Just take the heads.'

Maecenas grimaced. He'd spent his childhood with servants to attend to every whim, yet somehow Octavian had him working and sweating like a house slave. If his old tutors could see him, they would be standing in slack-jawed amazement.

'The daughters have moustaches as thick as their fathers', he replied. 'Perhaps when it's fully dark, but not before.'

With a scowl, he began the grisly work of cutting heads. Agrippa joined him, bringing his sword down in great hacking blows to break through bone.

Octavian knelt next to the body of the bandit leader, looking down into the glazed eyes for a moment. He nodded to himself, playing over the movements of the fight in his head and only then noticing the gash on his arm that was still bleeding heavily. At twenty years old, it was not the first time he'd been cut. It was just one more scar to add to the rest. He began to chop the head free, using the oily beard to hold it steady.

The horses were still there when they came back, parched and staggering, with their tongues swelling in their mouths. It was sunset by the time the three Romans reached the village, with two sopping red sacks that dribbled their contents with every step. The local men had returned angry and empty-handed, but the mood changed when Octavian opened the sacks onto the road, sending heads tumbling into the dust. The woman's husband embraced and kissed him with tears in his eyes, breaking off only to dash the heads against the wall of his house, then crushing Octavian to him once more. There was no need to translate as they left the man and his children to their mourning.

The other villagers brought food and drinks from cool cellars, setting up rough tables in the evening air so that they could feast the young men. As Octavian had imagined, he and his friends could hardly move for good meat and a clear drink that tasted of aniseed. They drank with no thought for the morning, matching the local men cup for cup until the village swam and blurred before their eyes. Very few of the villagers could speak Roman, but it didn't seem to matter.

Through a drunken haze, Octavian became aware that Maecenas was repeating a question to him. He listened blearily, then gave a laugh, which turned into a curse at his own clumsiness as he spilled his cup.

'You don't believe that,' he told Maecenas. 'They call it the eternal city for a reason. There will be Romans here for a thousand years, longer. Or do you think some other nation will rise up and be our masters?' He watched his cup being refilled with beady concentration.

'Athens, Sparta, Thebes . . .' Maecenas replied, counting on his fingers. 'Names of gold, Octavian. No doubt the men of those cities thought the same. When Alexander was wasting his life in battles abroad, do you think he would have believed Romans would one day rule their lands from coast to coast? He would have laughed like a donkey, much as you are doing.' Maecenas smiled as he spoke, enjoying making his friend splutter into his cup with each outrageous comment.

'*Wasting* his life?' Octavian said when he had recovered from coughing. 'You are seriously suggesting Alexander the Great could have spent his years more fruitfully? I will not rise to it. I will be a stern and noble Roman, too . . .' He paused. The drink had muddled his thoughts. 'Too stern and noble to listen to you.'

'Alexander had the greedy fingers of a merchant,' Maecenas said. 'Always busy, busy, and what did it get him? All those years of fighting, but if he had known he would die young in a foreign land, don't you think he would rather have spent it in the sun? If he were here, you could ask him. I think he would choose fine wine and beautiful women over his endless battles. But you have not answered my question, Octavian. Greece ruled the world, so why should Rome be any different? In a thousand years, some other nation will rule, after us.' He paused to wave away a plate of sliced meat and smile at two old ladies, knowing they could not understand what he was saying.

Octavian shook his head. With exaggerated care, he put his cup down and counted on his fingers as Maecenas had done.

'One, because we cannot be beaten in war. Two . . . because we are the envy of every people ruled by petty kings. They want to become us, not overthrow those they envy. Three . . . I cannot think of three. My argument rests on two.'

'Two is not enough!' Maecenas replied. 'I might have been confounded with three, but two! The Greeks were the greatest fighting men in the world once.' He gestured as if throwing a pinch of dust into the air. '*That* for their greatness, all gone. *That* for the Spartans, who terrified an army of Persians with just a few hundred. The other nations will learn from us, copy our methods and tactics. I admit I cannot imagine our soldiers losing to filthy tribes, no matter what tricks they steal, but it could happen. The other point, though – they want what we have? Yes, and we wanted the culture of the Greeks. But we did not come quietly like gentlemen and ask for it. No, Octavian! We took it and then we copied their gods and built our temples and pretended it was all our own idea. One day, someone will do the same to us and we will not know how it happened. There are your two points, in ashes under my sandals.' He raised a foot and pointed to the ground. 'Can you see them? Can you see your arguments?'

There was a grunt from another bench, where Agrippa was lying stretched out.

'The ape awakes!' Maecenas said cheerfully. 'Has our salty friend something to add? What news from the fleet?'

Agrippa was built on a different scale from the villagers, making the bench groan and flex under his bulk. As he shifted, he overbalanced and caught himself with a muscular arm pressed against the ground. With a sigh, he sat up and glared at Maecenas, leaning forward to rest his elbows on his bare knees.

'I could not sleep with you two clucking.'

'Your snoring calls you a liar, though I would not,' Maecenas replied, accepting another full cup.

Agrippa rubbed his face with his hands, scratching the curls of black beard he had grown over the previous weeks.

'So I will say only this,' Agrippa went on, stifling a yawn, 'before I find a better and a quieter place to sleep. There will be no empire to follow us because we have wealth enough to withstand any new tribe or nation. We pay for men by the hundred thousand, swords and spears by the million across all our lands. Who could stand against us without the full might of Caesar falling on his neck?'

'It is always about money with you, isn't it, Agrippa?' Maecenas replied, his eyes bright with amusement. He enjoyed needling the bigger man and they both knew it. 'You still think like a merchant's son. I am not surprised, of course. It is in your blood and you cannot help it, but while Rome is full of merchants, it is the noble classes who will decide her future, her destiny.'

Agrippa snorted. The evening had grown cold and he rubbed his bare arms

'According to you, a noble man would spend his day in the sun, with wine and beautiful women,' Agrippa said.

'You *were* listening! I don't know how you do it, snoring all the while. It is a rare talent.'

Agrippa smiled, showing very white teeth against his black beard.

'Be thankful for my blood, Maecenas. Men like my father built Rome and made her strong. Men like you rode pretty horses and gave impressive speeches, just as Aristotle and Socrates once held court in the agora.'

'I sometimes forget you have been educated, Agrippa. Something about you says illiterate peasant whenever I look at you.'

'And something about you says that you enjoy the company of men more than most.'

Octavian groaned at the bickering. His head was swimming and he had lost all track of time.

'Peace, you two. I think we've eaten and drunk an entire winter's store for these people. Apologise and join me in another jug.'

Maecenas raised his eyebrows. 'Still awake? Remember that you owe me a gold aureus if you fall asleep or vomit before me. I am feeling very fresh.'

Octavian held his gaze for a moment, waiting until Maecenas gave way with a grunt.

'Very well, Octavian. I apologise for suggesting Agrippa's skull would find its best use as a battering ram.'

'You did not say that,' Octavian replied.

'I was thinking it,' Maecenas said.

'And you, Agrippa? Will you be as noble?'

'I struggle to reach his level, Octavian, but as you ask, I apologise for saying he would not earn as much as he thinks, renting himself out by the hour.'

Maecenas began to laugh, but then his face grew pale and he turned aside to empty his stomach. One of the old women muttered something he did not catch.

'That is an aureus you owe me,' Octavian told Maecenas with satisfaction. His friend only groaned.

CHAPTER TWO

As the sun rose the following morning, Maecenas was silent and in pain, though he forced himself out of his bed to join Agrippa in the courtyard. The Greek house they had rented for the period of leave was small, though it came with a house slave to look after them. With one eye closed against the sun, Maecenas squinted at the other man, watching him limber up.

'Where is Octavian?' he asked. 'Still sleeping?'

'Here,' Octavian said, coming out. His hair was slick with cold water and he looked pale and ill, but he raised a hand in greeting to his two friends. 'I don't even remember coming back. Gods, my head is cracked, I'm sure of it. Did I fall?'

'Into a jug, perhaps. Otherwise, no,' Agrippa replied cheerfully. Of the three, he seemed best able to shrug off vast quantities of alcohol and he enjoyed watching the other two suffer.

'What plans for our last days of leave, Octavian?' Maecenas asked. 'I'm sure you are tempted to spend them educating the local children, or perhaps helping the farmers in their fields. However, I heard of a private boxing match this evening. I'm waiting for an address still, but it should be worth watching.'

Octavian shook his head.

'The last one turned into a riot, which is no surprise as they almost always do. The same goes for the cockfights. And don't mock; you know I was right. Those men needed killing.'

Maecenas looked away rather than argue.

'We have two more days of leave, gentlemen,' Agrippa said. 'It might be a better idea to spend those days running and training. I don't want to go back to my ship with the wind of an old man.'

'You see, that is just a lack of imagination, Agrippa,' Maecenas said. 'First of all, you are already an old man . . .'

'Three years older than you, at twenty-two, but go on,' Agrippa interrupted.

'. . . and you carry too much weight on your bones, like a bullock. Those of us who have not wasted years lifting heavy weights do not lose fitness so easily. We are racehorses, you see, if the metaphor is not immediately clear.'

'Shall we test your speed against my strength?' Agrippa asked, smiling unpleasantly.

Maecenas eyed the heavy training sword Agrippa was swishing through the air.

'You battered me near senseless last time, which was not sporting. In a real duel, I would cut you up, my friend, but these wooden swords filled with lead? They are clubs for peasants and you swing yours with abandon. The idea is not appealing.' His closed eye opened and he squinted against the sunlight. 'Still, I have been giving it some thought, since your last instruction.'

'I meant you to learn a lesson, so I am pleased,' Agrippa replied.

There was a growing tension on the sandy yard. Maecenas did

not enjoy being bested in anything and Octavian knew it had rankled with him to be knocked around like a child. For one of Agrippa's bulk and strength, the wooden swords could be almost ignored, allowing him to land a punch or a blow that sent Maecenas reeling. He opened his mouth to distract them, but Maecenas had spotted a rack of throwing spears along a wall, long Roman weapons with iron tips and a wooden shaft. His face lit up.

'A different weapon might allow me to demonstrate a few points to you, perhaps,' Maecenas said.

Agrippa snorted. 'So I should let you have three feet of reach over me?' His eyes glinted, though whether it was anger or amusement, it was impossible to tell.

'If you are afraid, I will understand,' Maecenas said. 'No? Excellent.' He walked to the rack and removed one of the long weapons, feeling the heft of it.

Agrippa brought his wooden sword up across his body. He wore only leggings, sandals and a loose tunic and did not enjoy Maecenas gesturing with a throwing spear near him.

'Come, Maecenas,' Octavian said uncomfortably. 'We will find something good to do today.'

'I have already found something good to do,' Maecenas replied. He closed the distance quickly, jerking his arm back to make Agrippa flinch. The big man shook his head.

'Are you sure? That is a weapon for soldiers, not noblemen.'

'It will do, I think,' Maecenas replied. As he spoke, he jabbed the point at Agrippa's broad chest, then back and again at his groin. 'Oh yes, it will do very well indeed. Defend yourself, ape.'

Agrippa watched Maecenas closely, reading his footwork and stance as well as his eyes. They had sparred many times before and both men knew the other's style. Octavian found himself a bench and sat down, knowing from experience that he would not be able to drag them away until they'd finished. Though

29

they were friends, both men were used to winning and could not resist challenging each other. Octavian settled himself.

At first, Agrippa merely stepped back from the jabbing point that struck out at him. He frowned as it came close to his eyes, but slid away from it, raising his training gladius to block. Maecenas was enjoying having the big man on the defensive and began to show off a little, his feet quick on the sandy ground.

The end, when it came, was so sudden that Octavian almost missed it. Maecenas lunged fast and hard enough to score a wound. Agrippa blocked with the edge of his sword, then turned from the hip and smacked his left forearm into the spear. It snapped cleanly and Maecenas gaped at it. Agrippa laid his sword along Maecenas' throat and grunted a laugh.

'A victory,' Agrippa said.

Without a word, Maecenas pushed the wooden sword away and reached down, picking up the broken half of his spear. It had been sawn almost through, the cut hidden with brown wax. His eyes widened and he strode back to the row of spears. He cursed as he examined the rest, snapping them one by one over his thigh. Agrippa began to laugh at his thunderous expression.

'You did this?' Maecenas demanded. 'How long did it take you to prepare every spear? What sort of a man goes to such lengths? Gods, how did you even know I would choose one of them? You are a madman, Agrippa.'

'I am a strategist, is what I am,' Agrippa said, wiping tears from his right eye. 'Oh, your face. I wish you could have seen it.'

'This is not honourable behaviour,' Maecenas muttered. To his irritation, Agrippa just laughed again.

'I would rather be a peasant and win than be noble and lose. It is as simple as that, my friend.'

Octavian had risen to see the broken spears. With care, he kept any sign of amusement from his face, knowing that

Maecenas would already be insufferable all day and he could only make it worse.

'I heard there will be fresh oranges in the market this morning, packed in ice the whole way. Cold juice would help my head, I think. Can you shake hands and be friends for the day? It would please me.'

'I am willing,' Agrippa said. He held out his spade of a right hand. Maecenas allowed his to be enveloped.

The house slave came trotting into the yard as the two men shook with mock earnestness. Fidolus had always worked hard not to intrude on the guests and Octavian did not know him well, beyond finding him courteous and quiet.

'Master, there is a messenger at the gate. He says he has letters from Rome for you.'

Octavian groaned. 'I can feel them calling me back. Caesar is wondering where his favourite relative has gone, no doubt.'

Maecenas and Agrippa were looking at him, their expressions innocent. Octavian waved a hand.

'He will wait a while longer. It's been a year since we had the last leave, after all. Make the messenger comfortable, Fidolus. I am going to the market to buy fresh oranges.'

'Yes, master,' Fidolus replied.

The three young Romans did not return to the villa until just before sunset. They came in noisily, laughing and brash with three Greek women they had picked up. Maecenas had been the one to approach them in a jeweller's, recommending pieces that would suit their colouring.

Octavian envied his friend's talent – it was not one he had himself, despite the masterclass of watching Maecenas. There didn't seem to be much magic to it. Maecenas had complimented the women outrageously, bantering back and forth as he made them try on various pieces. The shopkeeper had watched with patient indulgence, hoping for a sale. As far as Octavian could see, the young women had known from the outset what Maecenas was after, but his breezy confidence made a joke of it.

Octavian squeezed the slim waist of the woman he had brought home, trying hard to remember her name. He had a nasty suspicion that it was not 'Lita' and he was waiting for one of her friends to use her name again so he would not spoil the moment.

As they reached the gate to the house, Maecenas suddenly pressed his companion against the white-painted stone and kissed her, his hands wandering. She wore a new gold pendant at her throat, his gift. Each of the girls wore the same piece, bought with almost all the money they had pooled for the last few days of leave.

Agrippa had not been quite as lucky as the other two. It would have been extraordinary for all three women to be attractive and the one who clung to his arm was fairly heavily built herself, with a dark moustache along her upper lip. Nonetheless, Agrippa seemed pleased. It had been a while since they'd brought women back, and in a drought he could not afford to have high standards. Agrippa nuzzled at her bare shoulder with his beard, making her laugh while they waited for the gate to open.

It took only moments for the house slave Fidolus to come running and unbar the entrance. He looked flushed and his hands slipped on the bar as he heaved it up.

'Master, thank the gods! You must see the messenger.'

Octavian stiffened in irritation. He had a beautiful Greek girl pressing her warmth into his side and the last thing he wanted was to think of Rome and the army.

'Please, master,' Fidolus said. He was almost shaking in the grip of some strong emotion and Octavian felt a stab of worry.

'Is it my mother?' he said.

Fidolus shook his head. 'Please, he is waiting for you.'

Octavian stepped away from the woman on his arm.

'Take me to him,' he ordered.

Fidolus breathed in relief and Octavian followed him into the house at a fast walk, trying hard not to run.

Maecenas and Agrippa shared a glance, both men suspecting they would not be enjoying the evening in the way they had planned.

'That does not sound good,' Agrippa said. 'Ladies, there is a bathing room here that has few equals. I suspect my friend Maecenas and I must attend our friend for a few hours, but if you are willing to wait . . .' He saw their expressions. 'No?' He sighed. 'Very well then. I will have Fidolus escort you back to the city.'

Maecenas shook his head. 'Whatever it is, it will wait for a little while longer, I'm sure,' he said, his eyes wide as he tried to dissuade Agrippa. The woman on his arm seemed equally reluctant and Agrippa grew flushed with sudden anger.

'Do what you want, then. I will find out what is going on.'

He strode into the house, leaving the gate open. Maecenas raised his eyebrows.

'I wonder if all three of you would consider teaching a young Roman more about Greece?'

Agrippa's woman gasped, turning on her heel without a word. After twenty paces, she turned and called to her friends. They looked at each other and for a moment Maecenas thought his luck was in. Some silent communication passed between them.

'Sorry, Maecenas, another time, perhaps.'

He watched wistfully as they swayed away, young and lithe and taking three gold pendants with them. He let out a sharp curse, then went inside, anger and frustration in every step.

Octavian reached the main hall almost at a run, his nervousness growing by the moment at the blank shock he could see in the house slave. He skidded to a halt when the messenger rose to greet him, holding out a package without a word.

Octavian broke his mother's wax seal and read quickly. He took a deep breath, then another, feeling prickles rise on his neck and down his bare legs. He shook his head and took a step to sit down on a bench, reading the lines over and over.

'Master,' Fidolus began. The messenger leaned close as if he was trying to read the words.

'Get out, both of you. Fetch my friends and then get out,' he replied.

'I was told to wait for a reply,' the messenger said sourly.

Octavian surged out of the seat and grabbed the messenger by the front of his tunic, shoving him in the direction of the door.

'Get *out!*'

In the courtyard, Agrippa and Maecenas both heard the shout. They drew swords and ran to their friend, passing the red-faced messenger as they entered the house.

Fidolus had lit the oil lamps and Octavian paced through twin pools of light. Maecenas was a study in calm, though his face was still pale. Agrippa tapped blunt fingers on his knee, the only sign of an inner agitation.

'I *have* to go back,' Octavian said. His voice was hoarse from talking, but he burned with a brittle energy. As he strode up and down the room, his right hand clenched and opened as if he was imagining striking at his enemies. 'I need information. Isn't that what you always say, Agrippa? That knowledge is everything? I need to go to Rome. I have friends there.'

'Not any more,' Maecenas said. Octavian came to a stop and spun to face him. Maecenas looked away, embarrassed at the raw grief he saw in his friend. 'Your protector is dead, Octavian. Has it occurred to you that you will also be in danger if you show your face in Rome? He treated you as his heir and these "Liberatores" will not want anyone who could lay claim to his possessions.'

'He *has* an heir: Ptolemy Caesar,' Octavian snapped. 'The Egyptian queen will keep that boy safe. I . . .' He broke off to curse. 'I have to go back! It cannot go unanswered. There must be a trial. There must be punishment. They are *murderers*, in daylight, killing the leader of Rome and pretending they have saved the Republic. I have to speak for him. I have to speak for Caesar before they cover up the truth with lies and flattery. I know how they work, Maecenas. They will hold a lavish funeral and they will rub ashes into their skin and weep for the great man. In a month or less, they will move on to new plots, new ways to raise themselves, never seeing how petty, how venal they are, in comparison to him.'

He resumed his stiff pacing, pounding out each step on the tiled floor. He was consumed with rage, so intense that he could barely speak or breathe. Maecenas waved a hand, deferring to Agrippa as the big man cleared his throat. He spoke as calmly as he could, aware that Octavian was on the edge of violence or perhaps tears and had been for hours. The young man was exhausted, but his body jerked on, unable to stop or rest.

'Your mother's letter said they had been given amnesty, Octavian. The law has been passed. There can be no revenge against them now, not without turning the entire Senate against you. How long would you survive that?'

'As long as I choose, Agrippa. Let me tell you something of Caesar. I have seen him capture a pharaoh from his own palace in Alexandria. I have been at his side when he challenged armies and governments and no one dared raise a hand or speak a word against him. The Senate have as much power as we choose to allow them; do you understand? Allow them nothing and they have *nothing*. What they call power is no more than shadows. Julius understood that. They pass their pompous laws and the common people bow their heads and everyone declares it is real . . . but *it is not!*'

He shook his head, lurching and staggering slightly, so that his shoulder bumped against the wall. As the other two shared a worried glance, Octavian rested there, cooling his forehead against the plaster.

'Are you ill, Octavian? You need to sleep.'

Agrippa stood up, unsure whether he should approach. He had known madmen in his life and Octavian was at the ragged edge, driven to it by soaring emotions. His friend needed rest and Agrippa considered mixing a draught of opium for him. Dawn had come and they were all exhausted. Octavian showed no sign of relaxing from the rage that knotted and twisted his muscles. Even as he stood there, his legs and arms twitched in spasms underneath the skin.

'Octavian?' Agrippa asked again. There was no reply and he turned to Maecenas, raising his hands helplessly.

Maecenas approached Octavian like the horseman he was. There was something about the twitching muscles that reminded him of an unbroken colt and he made unconscious soothing noises, clicking and murmuring in his throat as he laid a hand on Octavian's shoulder. The skin under the cloth felt burning hot, and at the touch Octavian went suddenly limp, sliding along the wall in collapse. Maecenas leaped forward to catch him, but the unexpected weight was too much and he barely managed to guide his friend to lie along the edge of the room. To Maecenas' horror, a dark patch grew at Octavian's groin, the bitter smell of urine filling the close air.

'What's wrong with him?' Agrippa asked, sinking into a crouch.

'He's breathing at least,' Maecenas said. 'I don't know. His eyes are moving, but I don't think he is awake. Have you seen anything like this before?'

'Not in him. I knew a centurion once with a falling sickness. I remember he lost his bladder.'

'What happened to him?' Maecenas asked without looking up.

Agrippa winced in memory. 'Killed himself. He had no authority with his men after that. You know how they can be.'

'Yes, I know,' Maecenas replied. 'Perhaps it is just this once, though. No one needs to hear of it. We can clean him up, and when he wakes, it will be forgotten. The mind is a strange thing. He will believe whatever we tell him.'

'Unless he knows about the weakness already,' Agrippa said.

Both of them jumped up at the sound of footsteps. The house slave, Fidolus, was returning.

Maecenas was first to speak.

'He mustn't see this. I'll distract Fidolus, give him something to do. You take care of Octavian.'

Agrippa scowled at the thought of removing urine-soaked clothing. Yet Maecenas was already moving and his protest remained unspoken. With a sigh, Agrippa lifted Octavian in his arms.

'Come on. Time for a wash and clean clothes.'

The bathing room in the house was small and the water would be cold without Fidolus to heat it, but it would do. As he carried the limp body, Agrippa shook his head at swirling thoughts. Caesar was dead and only the gods knew what would happen to his friend.

CHAPTER THREE

In shadow, Mark Antony pressed his thumbs against his eyes, struggling with weariness. In his twenties, he'd thought nothing of staying awake for a night and then working through the next day. In Gaul, he'd marched through darkness and fought all morning, alongside ten thousand legionaries doing the same thing. He knew that all things pass, that time takes everything from a man. Yet somehow he had assumed his endurance was a part of him, like his wits or his height, only to find it had seeped away like water from a cracked jug.

The forum was filled with citizens and soldiers, come to honour Caesar for the last time. Rich and poor were forced to mingle and there were constant shouts of irritation and outrage as more and more pressed in from the roads around. A woman cried out somewhere for her lost child and Mark Antony sighed, wishing Julius could have been there to stand with him and watch, just watch, as Rome swirled and coalesced around the body of a god.

There could never be enough space for all those who wanted to see. The sun was a hammer on bare heads as they struggled for the best view. The heat had been building steadily from the first moments of dawn, when Caesar had been laid out and forty centurions of the Tenth legion had taken position around him. The body rested on a golden bier, the focus and the centre of the world for that day.

Mark Antony raised his head with an effort of will. He had not slept through two nights and he sweated ceaselessly. Thirst was already unpleasant, but he dared not drink and be forced to leave the forum to empty his bladder. He would have to sip a cup of wine to speak to the crowd, and a slave stood at his shoulder with a cup and cloth. Mark Antony was ready and he knew he would not fail on that day. He did not look at the face of his friend. He had stared too long already as the corpse was washed, the wounds counted and drawn in charcoal and ink by learned doctors for the Senate. It was just a gashed thing now, empty. It was not the man who had cowed the Senate, who had seen kings and pharaohs kneel. Swaying slightly in a wave of dizziness, Mark Antony closed his right hand tightly on the scrolls, making the vellum crackle and crease. He should have stolen a few hours of sleep, he knew. He must not faint or fall, or show any sign of the grief and rage that threatened to ruin him.

He could not see the Liberatores, though he knew they were all there. Twenty-three men had plunged knives into his friend, many of them after life had fled, as if they were joining a ritual. Mark Antony's eyes grew cold, his back straightening as he thought of them. He had wasted hours wishing he could have been there, that he could have known what was going to happen, but all that was dust. He could not change the past, not a moment of it. When he wanted to cry out against them, to summon soldiers and have them torn and broken, he had been forced to smile and treat them as great men of Rome. It brought acid into his mouth to think of it. They would be watching, waiting for the days of funeral rites to end, waiting for the citizens to settle down in their grief, so they could enjoy the new posts and powers their knives had won. Mark Antony clenched his jaw at the thought. He had worn a mask from the moment the first whispers reached his ears. Caesar was dead and yapping dogs sat in the Senate. Keeping his disgust hidden had been the hardest task of his life. Yet it had been worth proposing the vote for amnesty. He had drawn their teeth with that simple act and it had not been hard to have his remaining friends support his right to give the funeral oration. The Liberatores had smirked to themselves at the idea, secure in their victory and their new status.

'Cloth and cup,' Mark Antony snapped suddenly.

The slave moved, wiping sweat from his master's face as Mark Antony took the goblet and sipped to clear his throat. It was time to speak to Rome. He stood straight, allowing the slave to adjust the folds of his toga. One shoulder remained bare and he could feel sweat grow cold in the armpit. He walked out of shadow into the sun and passed through the line of centurions glaring out at the crowd. In just four steps, he was on the platform with Julius for the last time.

The crowd saw the consul and stillness spread out from that one point in all directions. They did not want to miss a word and the sudden silence was almost unnerving. Mark Antony looked at the grand buildings and temples all around. Every window was full of dark heads and he wondered again where Brutus and Cassius were. They would not miss the moment of their triumph, he was certain. He raised his voice to a bellow and began.

'Citizens of Rome! I am but one man, a consul of our city. Yet I do not speak with one voice when I talk of Caesar. I speak with the tongue of every citizen. I speak today for our coun-trymen, our people. The Senate decreed honours for Caesar and when I tell all his names, you will hear not my voice but your own.'

He turned slightly on the rostrum to look at the body of his friend. The silence was perfect and unbroken across the forum of Rome. Caesar's wounds had been covered in a white toga and undertunic, sewn so that it hid the gashes. There was no more blood in him and Mark Antony knew the toga concealed wounds that had grown pale and stiff during the days of handling and preparation. Only the band of green laurel leaves around Caesar's head was a thing of life.

'He was Gaius Julius Caesar, son of Gaius Julius and Aurelia, descendant of the Julii, from Aeneas of Troy, a son of Venus. He was Consul and he was Imperator of Rome. He was Father to his Country. The old month of Quintilis itself was renamed for him. More than all of those, he was granted the right to divine worship. These names and titles show how we honoured Caesar. Our august Senate decreed that his body be inviolate, on pain of death. That anyone with him would have the same immunity. By the laws of Rome, the body of Caesar was sacrosanct. He could not be touched. The temple of his flesh could not be injured, by all the authority of our laws.'

He paused, listening to a murmur of anger that rumbled through the vast crowd.

'He did not tear these titles by force from the hands of the Senate, from our hands. He did not even ask for them, but they were granted to him in a flood, in thanks for his service to Rome. Today you honour him again by your presence. You are witnesses to Roman honour.'

One of the centurions shifted uncomfortably by his feet and Mark Antony glanced down, then up again, meeting the eyes of hundreds as he looked across the heaving crowd. There was anger and shame there and Mark Antony nodded to himself, taking a deep breath to continue.

'By our laws, by our Roman honour, we gave oath to protect

Caesar and Caesar's person with all our strength. We gave oath that those who failed to defend him would be forever accursed.'

The crowd groaned louder as they understood and Mark Antony raised his voice to a roar.

'O Jupiter and all the gods, forgive us our failure! Grant mercy for what we have failed to do. Forgive us *all* our broken oaths.'

He stepped away from the rostrum, standing over the body that lay before them. For a moment, his gaze flickered towards the senate house. The steps there were filled with white-robed figures, standing and watching. No one had a better view of the funeral oration and he wondered if they were enjoying their position as much as they'd expected. Many in the crowd turned hostile eyes on those gathered figures.

'Caesar loved Rome. And Rome loved her favourite son, but would not save him. There will be no vengeance for his death, for all the laws and empty promises that could not hold back the knives. A law is but the wish of men, written and given a power that it does not own in itself.'

He paused to let them think and was rewarded with a surge of movement in the crowd, a sign of hearts beating faster, of blood rushing from the outer limbs. He had them all waiting for his words. Another centurion glared up in silent warning, trying to catch his eye. Mark Antony ignored him.

'In *your* name, our august Senate has granted amnesty to those who call themselves "Liberatores". In *your* name, a vote, a law held good by your honour. That too is sacrosanct, inviolate.'

The crowd made a sound like a low growl and Mark Antony hesitated. He was as exposed as the soldiers around the platform. If he drove them too far in guilt and anger, he could be swallowed up in the mob. He rode a knife edge, having seen before what the people of Rome could do in rage. Once again, he looked to the senators and saw their number had dwindled as they read the crowd; as they read the wind. He smiled wearily, gathering

mockery of a man which stood before them, supported by Oppius.

'Let me show you, citizens of Rome. Let me show you what your word is worth!'

Mark Antony stepped forward and drew a grey iron blade from his sash. He wrenched the purple robe that clothed the mannequin, baring the chest and the line of the throat. The crowd gasped, unable to look away. Many of them made the horn sign of protection with their shaking hands.

'Tillius Cimber held Caesar, while Suetonius Prandus struck the first blow . . . *here!*' Mark Antony said.

He pressed his left hand against the shoulder of the effigy and shoved his knife into the wax under the moulded collarbone, so that even old soldiers in the crowd winced. The senators on the steps stood rooted and Suetonius himself was there, his mouth sagging open.

'Publius Servilius Casca sliced this wound across the first,' Mark Antony went on. With a savage movement, he sawed at cloth and wax with his blade. He was already panting, his voice a bass roar that echoed from the buildings all around. 'His brother, Gaius Casca, stepped in then as Caesar fought! He thrust his dagger . . . *here.*'

Over by the senate house, the Casca brothers looked at each other in horror. Without a word, both men turned away, hurrying to get out of the forum.

Sweating, Mark Antony pulled back the sleeves of the toga, so that the mannequin's right arm was revealed. 'Lucius Pella made a cut here, a long gash.' With a jerk of his blade, Mark Antony sliced the wax and the crowd moaned. 'Caesar *still* fought! He was left-handed, and he raised his bloody right arm to hold them off. Decimus Junius slashed at him then, cutting the muscle so that the arm fell limp. Caesar called for help on the stone benches of Pompey's theatre. He called for vengeance, but he was alone with these men . . . and they would not stop.'

The crowd surged forward, driven almost to madness by what they were seeing. There was no logic in it, simply a growing, seething mass of rage. Just a few senators still stood by the senate house and Mark Antony saw Cassius turn to go.

'Gaius Cassius Longinus stabbed the Father of Rome then, shoving his thin arms into a gap between the others.' With a grunt, Mark Antony punched the blade into the wax side through the toga, leaving the cloth torn as the knife came out. 'The blood poured, drenching Caesar's toga, but still he fought! He was a soldier of Rome and his spirit was strong as they struck and *struck* at him!' He punctuated his words with blows, tearing ribbons from the ruined toga.

He broke off, gasping and shaking his head.

'Then he saw a chance to live.'

His voice had dropped and the crowd pushed even closer, driven and wild, but hanging on every word. Mark Antony looked across them all, but his eyes were seeing another day, another scene. He had listened to every detail of it from a dozen sources and it was as real to him as if he had witnessed it himself.

'He saw Marcus Brutus step onto the floor of the theatre. The man who had fought at his side for half their lives. The man who had betrayed him once and joined an enemy of Rome. The man Julius Caesar had forgiven when anyone else would have had him butchered and his limbs scattered. Caesar saw his greatest friend and for a moment, for a heartbeat, in the midst of those stabbing, shouting men, he must have thought he was saved. He must have thought he would live.'

Tears came to his eyes then. Mark Antony brushed them away with his sleeve, feeling his exhaustion like a great weight. It was almost over.

'He saw that Brutus carried a blade like all the rest. His heart broke and the fight went out of him at last.'

Centurion Oppius was standing stunned, barely holding the

figure of wax. He flinched as Mark Antony reached over and yanked a fold of the purple toga over the figure's head, so that the face was covered.

'Caesar would not look at them after that. He sat as Brutus approached and they continued to stab and tear at his flesh.'

He held his dark blade poised over the heart and many in the crowd were weeping, men and women together as they waited in agony for the last blow. The moaning sound had grown so that it was almost a wail of pain.

'Perhaps he did not feel the final blade; we cannot *know*.'

Mark Antony was a powerful man and he punched the blade up where the ribs would have been, sinking it to the hilt and cutting a new hole in the ragged cloth. He left the blade there, for all to see.

'Set it down, Oppius,' he said, panting. 'They have seen all I wanted them to see.'

Every pair of eyes in the crowd moved to follow the torn figure as it was laid down on the platform. The common people of Rome visited no theatres with the noble classes. What they had witnessed had been one of the most powerful scenes of their lives. A sigh went around the forum, a long breath of pain and release.

Mark Antony gathered slow-moving thoughts. He had pushed the crowd and ridden them, but he had judged it well. They would go from this place in sombre mood, talking amongst themselves. They would not forget his friend, and the Liberatores would be followed by scorn all their lives.

'To think,' he said, his voice gentle, 'Caesar saved the lives of many of the men who were there, in Pompey's theatre, on the Ides of March. Many of them owed their fortunes and their positions to him. Yet they brought him down. He made himself first in Rome, first in the world, and it did not save him.'

His head came up when a voice yelled out in the crowd.

'*Why should they live?*'

Mark Antony opened his mouth to reply, but a dozen other voices answered, shouting angry curses at the murderers of Caesar. He held up his hands for calm, but the lone voice had been a spark on dry wood and the noise spread and grew until there were hundreds and hundreds pointing to the senate house and roaring out their rage.

'Friends, Romans, countrymen!' Mark Antony bellowed, but even his great voice was swallowed. Those further back pushed forward mindlessly and the centurions were battered by fists and heaving bodies.

'That's it,' one of the centurions growled, shoving back with all his strength to give himself room to draw a gladius. 'Time to get away. On me, lads. Surround the consul and stay calm.'

Yet the crowd were not rushing the consul's platform. They surged towards the senate house and the now empty steps.

'Wait! They will hear me yet. Let me speak!' Mark Antony shouted, shoving past a centurion trying to guide him down the steps.

A stone soared from somewhere further back, hammering a dent in an ornate chestplate and sending a senior man staggering. The crowd were levering up the cobblestones of the forum. The centurion who had taken the impact was on his back, gasping for breath as his companions cut the leather ties that bound him into his armour.

'Too late for that, Consul,' Oppius snapped. 'I just hope this is what you wanted. Now move, sir. Or will you stand and see us all killed?'

More of the black stones flew. Mark Antony could see movements in the crowd, swirling and shoving like patterns in water. There were thousands of angry men in that forum and many of the weaker ones would be trampled to death before their anger gave out. He swore under his breath.

'My feelings exactly, sir,' Oppius said grimly. 'But it's done now.'

'I can't leave the body,' Mark Antony said desperately. He

48

ducked as another stone came past him and he saw how quickly the chaos was spreading. There was no holding them back now and he felt a sudden fear that he would be swept away.

'Very well. Get me clear.'

He could smell smoke on the air and he shivered. The gods alone knew what he had unleashed, but he remembered the riots of years before and the flashing memories were ugly. As he was borne away in a tight mass of soldiers, he looked back at the body of Julius, abandoned and alone, as men clambered up to the platform bearing knives and stones.

The bitter smell of wet ash was heavy in the air across Rome. Mark Antony wore a clean toga as he waited in the outer hall of the House of Virgins behind the temple of Vesta. Even so, he thought he could smell burnt wood in the cloth, hanging on him like a mist. The air of the city carried the taint and marked everything passing through it.

Suddenly impatient, he jumped up from a marble bench and began to pace. Two of the temple women were watching him idly, so secure in their status that they betrayed no tension even in the presence of a consul of Rome. The virgins could not be touched, on pain of death. They devoted their lives to worship, though there had long been rumours that they came out on the festival of Bona Dea and used aphrodisiac drugs and wine to toy with men before killing them. Mark Antony glowered at the pair, but they only smiled and spoke to each other in low tones, ignoring the man of power.

The high priestess of Vesta had judged his patience to a fine degree by the time she finally came out to him. Mark Antony had been on the point of leaving, or summoning soldiers, or anything else that would allow him to act rather than wait like a supplicant. He had sat for a time once more, staring into space and the horrors of the previous day and night.

49

The woman who approached was a stranger to him. Mark Antony rose and bowed only briefly, trying to control his irritation. She was tall and wore a Greek shift that left her legs and one shoulder bare. Her hair was a shining mass of dark red, curling across her throat. His gaze followed the path of the locks, pausing on what looked like a tiny splash of blood on the white cloth. He shuddered, wondering what horrible rite she had been finishing while he waited.

There were still bodies in the forum and his anger simmered, but he needed the goodwill of the priestess. He made himself smile as she spoke.

'Consul, this is a rare pleasure. I am Quintina Fabia. I hear your men are working hard to bring order back to the streets. Such a terrible business.'

Her voice was low and educated and he reassessed his first impression. He had already known the woman was one of the Fabii, a noble family that could call on the allegiance of a dozen senators in any year. Quintina was used to authority and he let the anger seep out of him.

'I hope there has been no trouble here?' Mark Antony asked.

'We have guards and other ways of protecting ourselves, Consul. Even rioters know not to trouble this temple. What man would risk a curse from the virgin goddess, to see his manhood fall limp and useless for ever?'

She smiled, but he could still smell wet ash in the air and he was not in the mood for pleasantries. It was annoying enough that he had been forced to come himself, with so much else to do. Yet his messengers had been turned away without a word.

'I have come to take charge of Caesar's will. I believe it is lodged here. If you will have it brought to me, I can get back to my work. The sun is almost setting and each night is worse.'

Quintina shook her head, a delicate frown appearing between dark brown eyes.

'Consul, I would do everything in my power to help you, but not that. The last testaments of men are my charge. I cannot give them up.'

Mark Antony struggled again with rising temper.

'Well, Caesar *is* dead, woman! His body was burned in the forum along with the senate house, so we can be reasonably sure of that! When will you release his will, if not today, to me? The whole city is waiting for it to be read.'

His anger washed over her with no noticeable effect. She smiled slightly at his harsh tone, looking back over her shoulder at the two women lounging on a nearby bench. Mark Antony was seized by a sudden desire to grab her and shake her out of her lethargy. Half the forum had been destroyed. The Senate were forced to meet in Pompey's theatre while the seat of government lay in rubble and ashes, and still he was being treated like a servant! His big hands clenched and unclenched.

'Consul, do you know why this temple was founded?' she asked softly.

Mark Antony shook his head, his eyebrows raising in disbelief. Could she not understand what he needed?

'It was raised to house the Palladium, the statue of Athena that was once the heart of Troy. The goddess guided her likeness to Rome and we have been its guardians for centuries, do you understand? In that time, we have seen riots and unrest. We have seen the walls of Rome herself threatened. We have watched the army of Spartacus march past and seen Horatius go out to hold the bridge with just two men against an army.'

'I don't . . . What has this to do with the will of Caesar?'

'It means that time passes slowly within these walls, Consul. Our traditions go back to the founding of the city and I will not change them because of a few dead rioters and a *consul who thinks he can give orders here!*'

Her voice had hardened and grown louder as she spoke and

Mark Antony raised his hands, trying to placate the suddenly angry woman before him.

'Very well, you have your traditions. Nonetheless, I must have the will. Have it brought to me.'

'No, Consul.' She held up a hand herself to forestall his protest. 'But it will be read aloud in the forum on the last day of the month. You will hear it then.'

'But . . .' He hesitated under her stare and took a deep breath. 'As you say then,' he said through a clenched jaw. 'I am disappointed you saw no value in gaining the support of a consul.'

'Oh, they come and go, Mark Antony,' she replied. 'We remain.'

CHAPTER FOUR

Octavian woke in the late morning, feeling as if he had drunk bad red wine. His head pounded and his clenching stomach made him weak, so he had to lean against a wall and gather his strength as Fidolus brought out his horse. He wanted to vomit to clear his head, but there was nothing to bring up and he had to struggle not to heave dryly, making his head swell and hammer with the effort. He knew he needed a run to force blood back into his limbs, to force *out* the shame that made him burn. As the house slave went back inside for the saddle, Octavian pounded his thigh with a closed fist, harder and harder until he could see flashing lights whenever he closed his eyes. His weak flesh! He had been so careful after the first time, telling himself that he had caught some infection in a scratch, or some illness from the sour air in Egypt. His own men had found him insensible then, but they had assumed he'd drunk himself unconscious and saw nothing too odd in that, with Caesar feting the Egyptian queen along the Nile.

He could feel a bruise begin to swell the muscle of his leg. Octavian wanted to shout out his anger. To be let down by his own body! Julius had taught him it was just a tool, like any other, to be trained and brought to heel like a dog or a horse. Yet now his two friends had seen him while he was . . . absent. He muttered a prayer to the goddess Carna that his bladder had not released this second time. Not in front of them.

'Please,' he whispered to the deity of health. 'Cast it out of me, whatever it is.'

He had woken clean and in rough blankets, but his memory ceased with the scroll from Rome. He could not take in the new reality. His mentor, his protector, had been killed in the city, his life ripped from him where he should have been safest. It was impossible.

Fidolus passed the reins into his hands, looking worriedly at the young man who stood shaking in the morning sun.

'Are you well, master? I can fetch a doctor from the town if you are ill.'

'Too much drink, Fidolus,' Octavian replied.

The slave nodded, smiling in sympathy.

'It doesn't last long, master. The morning air will clear your head and Atreus is feeling his strength today. He will run to the horizon if you let him.'

'Thank you. Are my friends awake?' Octavian watched closely for a sign that the slave knew something about his collapse, but the expression remained innocent.

'I heard someone moving about. Shall I call for them to join you?'

Octavian mounted, landing heavily and making the mount snort and skitter across the yard. Fidolus began to move to take the reins but Octavian waved him off.

'Not now. I'll see them when I come back.'

He dug in his heels and the horse lunged forward, clearly happy to be out of its stall with the prospect of a run. Octavian saw movement in the doorway of the house and heard Agrippa's deep voice hail him. He didn't turn. The clatter of hooves on stone was loud and he could not face the man, not yet.

Horse and rider surged into a canter through the gate. Agrippa came skidding into the yard behind him, still rubbing sleep from his eyes. He stared after Octavian for a while, then yawned.

Maecenas came out, still wearing the long shift he slept in.

'You let him go alone?' he said.

Agrippa grinned at seeing the Roman noble so tousled, his oiled hair sticking out at all angles.

'Let him work up a sweat,' he said. 'If he's ill, he needs it. The gods alone know what he's going to do now.'

Maecenas noticed Fidolus, who had stayed back with his head down.

'Get my horse ready, Fidolus – and the carthorse that suffers under my friend here.'

The slave hurried back into the stable block, greeted with whinnies of excitement from the two horses in the gloom. The Romans exchanged a glance.

'I think I fell asleep about an hour ago,' Maecenas said, rubbing his face with his hands. 'Have you thought what you're going to do now?'

Agrippa cleared his throat uncomfortably.

'Unlike you, I am a serving officer, Maecenas. I do not have the freedom to make decisions. I will return to the fleet.'

'If you had bothered to use that fascinating mind you hide so well, you'd have realised the fleet at Brundisium no longer has a purpose. Caesar is dead, Agrippa! Your campaign won't go ahead without him. Gods, the legions of Rome are there – who will lead them now? If you go back, you'll be floating without orders for months while the Senate ignore you all. Believe me, I know those men. They will squabble and argue like children, snatching scraps of power and authority now that

Caesar's shadow has gone. It could be years before the legions move again, and you know it. They were loyal to Caesar, not the senators who murdered him.'

'Octavian said there is an amnesty,' Agrippa murmured uneasily.

Maecenas laughed, a bitter sound.

'And if they passed a law saying we should all marry our sisters, would it happen? Honestly, I have grown to admire the discipline of the army, but there are times when the entire board is reset, Agrippa! This is one of them. If you can't see that, perhaps you should go and sit with thousands of sailors, writing your reports and watching the water grow sour as you wait for permission to take on fresh food.'

'Well, what are *you* going to do?' Agrippa demanded angrily. 'Retire to your estate and watch it all play out? I don't have a patrician family to protect me. If I don't go back, my name will be marked "Run" and someone somewhere will sign an order to have me hunted down. I sometimes think you have lived too well to understand other men. We do not all have your protection!'

Agrippa's face had grown flushed as he spoke and Maecenas nodded thoughtfully. He sensed it was not the time to anger him further, though Agrippa's indignation always made him want to smile.

'You are correct,' he said, gentling his voice deliberately. 'I am related to enough of the great men not to fear any one of them. But I am not wrong. If you go back to Brundisium, you'll be picking worms out of your food before you see order restored. Trust me on that at least.'

Agrippa began his reply and Maecenas knew it would be something typically decent and honourable. The man had risen through the ranks by merit and occasionally it showed. Maecenas spoke to head him off before he could vow to follow his oath, or some other foolishness.

'The old order is dead with Caesar, Agrippa. You talk of my position – very well! Let me use it to shelter you, at least for a few months. I will write letters of permission to have you kept from your duties. It will keep the stripes off your back and your rank intact while we see this through! Think about it, big man. Octavian needs you. At least you have your fleet, your rank. What does he have now that Caesar is gone? For all we know, there are men riding here to finish the job they started in Rome . . .' He broke off, his eyes widening.

'Fidolus! Come out here, you Greek shit-pot! Move!'

The slave was already returning with both mounts. Maecenas slapped his hands off the reins and leapt on, wincing as the cold leather met his testicles.

'Sword! Bring me a weapon. Run!'

Agrippa mounted as Fidolus raced across the yard and into the house. It was true that his horse was far stockier in build than those of the others. It was tall and powerful and shone black in the morning sun. As it took his weight, the animal blew air from its lips and pranced sideways. Agrippa patted its neck absently, thinking through what Maecenas had been saying.

'I swear by Mars, there had *better* be some assassins riding around here,' Maecenas snapped, turning his mount. 'I'll be black and blue after half a mile.'

A fresh clatter of hooves sounded outside the grounds, getting louder with every moment. Octavian rode back through the gate, his face pale. He looked surprised to see his friends mounted and Fidolus rushing out with swords clasped awkwardly in his arms.

Octavian's stare snagged on Maecenas, whose shift had ridden up so that his bare buttocks were revealed.

'What are you doing?' he said.

Maecenas tried to stare back haughtily, but he couldn't summon his dignity in such a position.

'Don't you know all young Romans ride like this now? Perhaps it has not spread to the provinces yet.'

Octavian shook his head, his expression bleak.

'I came back to tell you both to pack up your belongings. We need to get to Brundisium.'

Agrippa's head jerked up at the word, but it was Maecenas who spoke first.

'I was just explaining to the keen sailor why that is the last place we would want to go, at least until the city settles down. It will be chaos out there, Octavian. Believe me, every Roman family is doubling their guards right now, ready for civil war.'

'You're right,' Octavian said. 'The legions are at Brundisium as well.'

'So tell me why that isn't the last place in the world we should visit,' Maecenas said.

He saw Octavian's gaze turn inward, his eyes shadowed as he lowered his head. There was silence in the yard for a moment before he spoke again.

'Because those men were loyal to Caesar – to *my* family. If there is anyone left who wants to see revenge for his murder, they will be in that camp by the sea. That's where I must go.'

'You realise there could also be men there who would think nothing of killing you?' Maecenas asked softly.

Octavian's gaze flickered to him.

'I have to start somewhere. I can't let them wipe their hands clean and just go on with their lives. I *knew* him, Maecenas. He was . . . a better man than the snapping dogs in Rome, every one of them. He would want me to walk into their houses and show them the mercy they showed him.'

Agrippa nodded, rubbing a hand through his beard.

'He's right,' he said. 'We have to get back to Brundisium. Out here, we're too far away to know anything.'

Maecenas looked from man to man and for once there was no wry humour in his expression.

58

'Three men?' he said. 'Against the legions of Rome?'

'No, not against them, *with* them,' Octavian replied. 'I know those men, Maecenas. I have served with hundreds, no, thousands of them. They will remember me. I know them better than the greyheads of the Senate, at least.'

'I see. That is . . . a relief,' Maecenas said.

He looked to Agrippa for some sign that he wasn't going along with this madness, but Agrippa was watching Octavian with a fierce intensity. The young man who dropped lightly from his horse and strode across the yard had impressed him from the first time they met, two years before. It was not just that Octavian was a blood relative of Caesar, or had seen the great cities of the east. The young Roman was a man who saw through the febrile twitching of merchants, nobles and soldiers to what really mattered. Agrippa remembered watching him hold court at a party, speaking so well and fluently that even the drunks were listening to him. Octavian had offered them pride in what they could bring to the world, but Agrippa had heard the other strand woven into the words – the cost and burden that they *must* shoulder to represent the city. He'd listened in awe to concepts and thoughts that had never intruded upon his father's endless quest for more wealth.

One of the drunkest nobles had laughed at Octavian. With a quick jerk, Agrippa had tossed the man over the balcony. He grinned as he remembered the amused shock on Octavian's face as half the crowd rushed past them both. It had been enough to begin a friendship neither man had been looking for. They'd drunk and talked until dawn and Agrippa thanked his gods he'd chosen to go out that night at his father's urging. He'd found no new deals to make, nor rich daughters to court, but the following morning he'd gone to the docks and joined his first legion galley. His father hadn't spoken to him since that day.

Sweat patches stood out on Octavian's tunic and his horse was already lathered in strings of spit. Yet his orders were clear and precise to Fidolus as they walked back into the house to pack.

'You did not mention the sickness that struck him last night,' Agrippa observed in a low voice. Maecenas glanced at him.

'It didn't happen. Or if it did, he'll be the one to bring it up.'

Maecenas dismounted and flicked his reins over a post before walking inside to dress. Agrippa watched him go and, when he was finally alone, allowed a smile to spread across his face. He liked them both, a constant wonder for a man who did not make friends easily. For all his studied cynicism, Maecenas had been willing to ride out with his buttocks in the wind the moment he thought Octavian was in danger.

Agrippa took a deep breath of Greek air, deliberately filling his lungs and releasing it slowly. He was a man who valued Roman order, the stability and predictable nature of military life. His childhood had taken him to a dozen different cities, watching his father close a thousand deals. The fleet had saved him from that boredom and given him a home where he felt he was part of something that mattered at last. The talk of chaos worried him more deeply than he would ever say. He hoped Maecenas was wrong, but he knew enough to fear that his noble friend had told the future well. The divine Julius was gone and a thousand lesser men would be rushing to fill the gap he had left. Agrippa knew he might see the Republic torn to pieces as men like his father struggled for advantage. He dismounted and rolled his heavy shoulders, feeling his neck creak. At a time like that, a man should choose his friends with care, or be swept away.

He could hear Maecenas yelling orders inside the house and Agrippa grinned to himself as he tossed the reins over the holding post and followed. At least he would be swept towards Brundisium.

*   *   *

Brutus looked out over a city lit by speckles of fire. The flickering yellow and orange resembled a disease ruining healthy skin, spreading too fast to control. The window brought a warm breeze into the little room, but it was no comfort. The house was in the perfume district, a mile east of the forum. Three floors up from the ground, Brutus could still smell the destruction of the previous days. The odour of rich oils mingled unpleasantly with wet ash and he wanted a bath to rid himself of the scent. He was sick of smoke and the roars of distant clashes. As soon as darkness fell to hide the seething masses, they came out again, in greater and greater numbers. Those with guards had barricaded themselves to starve in their homes. The poor suffered worst, of course. They always did, easier prey to the raptores and gangs than those who could fight back.

Somewhere close by, Brutus could hear the tramp of marching soldiers, a sound as familiar to him as anything in the world. The legions in the Campus Martius had not mutinied, at least so far. The Senate had drafted rushed orders to bring them in, a thousand men at a time. Two separate legions had spread through the city, hard-pressed even so as the mobs gave ground step by bloody step. Brutus rubbed a spot on his forearm where a thrown tile had caught him a glancing blow earlier that day. He had been protected by a century of men, but as they escorted him to his house on the Quirinal hill, the roofs nearby had filled with rioters and a rain of stones and tiles had come arcing over. Had they been waiting for him, or was it just that nowhere was safe?

He clenched his fist at the memory. Even a century could be overwhelmed in the narrow streets. The Senate had reports of soldiers hemmed in on all sides, battered from above, and even one atrocity where oil pots had been thrown and set alight, burning men alive.

With tiles and stones shattering all around, he'd given the order to take a side street. They'd marched away from the location, intending to double back quickly on parallel streets to kick in doors and trap their assailants. He recalled the hooting jeers of lookouts above their heads, watching every step. The roofs had been empty by the time his men reached them, just a litter of broken tiles and scrawled messages. He'd given up on reaching his house and gone back to the safe area around the forum, where thousands of legionaries patrolled.

'I think it's getting worse, even with the new men in from the Campus,' Cassius said, dragging Brutus back to the present. Like him, the senator was staring out over the city.

'They can't go on much longer,' Brutus said, waving his hand in irritation.

The third man in the room stood to refill his cup with rich red wine. The two at the window turned at the sound and Lucius Pella raised his white eyebrows in silent question. Cassius shook his head, but Brutus nodded, so Pella filled a second cup.

'They are drunk on more than wine,' Pella said. 'If we could have saved the senate house, I think it would be over already, but . . .' He shook his head in disgust. A stone building should not have fallen just because wooden benches burned inside. Yet as the fire reached its height, one of the walls had cracked from top to bottom. The great roof had come crashing down, collapsing with such speed that it actually extinguished the fires within.

'What would you have me do, Lucius?' Cassius asked. 'I have brought in legions. I have secured the permission of the Senate to kill those who ignore the curfew. Yet it goes on – no, it spreads! We have lost whole districts of the city to these cattle with their clubs and iron bars. A million citizens and slaves cannot be stopped by a few thousand soldiers.'

'Mark Antony walked to his house today, with just a few men,' Brutus said suddenly. 'Did you hear that? He is their champion, after his speech appealing to the mob. They don't touch him, while my name is howled like a wolf pack. And yours, Cassius – and yours, Pella!' He crossed the room and downed his wine in three long gulps.

'I have to hide like a wanted criminal in my own city, while the consul acts the *peacemaker*. By the gods, it makes me want . . .' He broke off, impotent in his anger.

'It will pass, Brutus. You said it yourself. It has to run its course, but when they are starving, they will quieten.'

'Will they? The gangs emptied the grain stores on the first evening. There were no guards to stop them then, were there? No, they were all in the forum, fighting fires. You know the Casca brothers have already left?'

'I know,' Cassius said. 'They came to me and I had them escorted out. They have an estate a few hundred miles to the south. They'll wait it out there.'

Brutus watched the senator closely.

'Almost all the men who bloodied their hands with us have run with their tails between their legs. You know Decimus Junius is still writing letters to be read in the forum? Someone should tell him his messengers are beaten to death.' He paused, sick with anger. 'You are still here, though. Why is that, Cassius? Why haven't you run yet to your vineyards?'

The senator smiled mirthlessly.

'For the same reason as you, my friend. And Pella here. We are the "Liberatores", are we not? If we *all* seek safety away from the city, who knows what will happen when we are gone? Should I give Mark Antony the power he wants? He will have Rome in the palm of his hand as soon as the crowds stop murdering and burning. I should be here for that. And so should you.'

'Did he plan this, do you think?' Pella asked, refilling his cup. 'He inflamed the commoners with his cursed mannequin. He must have known what could happen.'

Cassius thought for a moment.

63

'A year ago, I would not have believed it of him. I was sure then that Mark Antony was not a subtle man. When he proposed the vote for amnesty, I thought . . . I thought he was recognising the new reality. Even now, I don't think he saw the flames that would follow his funeral oration. Yet he is not such a fool that he won't take advantage when the opportunity is handed to him. He is a danger to us all, gentlemen.'

Pella shrugged, the flush of wine staining his cheeks.

'Have him killed, then. What does one more body matter now? The streets are filled with them and disease will follow like night and day, be sure of it. When the plagues come, Rome will be hollowed out from within.'

His shaking hand made the cup clink against the jug and Brutus saw for the first time how terrified the man was.

'Well, not me!' Pella said, slurring slightly as he raised his cup in a mock toast to the other two. 'I did not kill Caesar to die at the hands of bakers and tanners, or coughing out my lungs in some vile sickness of the dead. That is not what you promised me, Cassius! Hiding in the dark like thieves and murderers. You said we would be honoured!'

'Be *calm*, Pella,' Cassius snapped, unmoved. 'Remember your dignity. You should not leave your wits at the bottom of a jug, not tonight. If you want to get out of the city, I will arrange it. At dawn, if you wish.'

'And my wife? My children? My slaves? I will not leave them to be torn apart.'

Cassius showed a glint of his anger then, his voice cold.

'You sound frightened, Pella. Of course they can travel with you. This is *Rome* and we are both senators. Most of the unrest is in the western half. Do not make it sound worse than it is. In a dozen days at most, there will be order again. I will send for . . .'

'You said three days at the beginning,' Pella interrupted, too dulled by wine to see the deadly stillness of Cassius.

'Go home now, Pella. Ready your family and gather your possessions. You will be spared any further attack on your dignity.'

Pella blinked at him, his mind wandering.

'Go home?' he said. 'The streets are not safe. I thought you said it was too dangerous to leave after dark.'

'Nonetheless, you have made your point. Walk with your head held high and if someone stops you in the road, tell him you are a senator. I am sure they will let you pass.'

Pella shook his head nervously.

'Cassius, I'm sorry. I should not have said such things. It was the wine. I would prefer to stay here with you, at least until dawn. I can . . .'

He broke off as Cassius crossed to the door that led out to stairs and the street. As it opened, the constant noise of shouts and crashes in the background grew louder.

'Go home,' Cassius said. He wore a dagger on his belt and he deliberately dropped a hand to the hilt.

Pella stared open-mouthed. He looked to Brutus but saw no pity there.

'Please, Cassius . . .'

'Get . . . *out!*' Cassius snapped.

Pella's shoulders drooped and he did not look at either man as he left. Cassius tried hard not to slam the door after him.

'Do you think he will get through?' Brutus asked, turning back to the open window.

'It is in the hands of the gods,' Cassius said irritably. 'I could not bear his babbling weakness any longer.'

Brutus would have replied, but in the distance he saw a new bloom of fire spreading. He cursed under his breath and Cassius came to stand by him.

'That's the Quirinal, isn't it?' Cassius asked. He knew Brutus had property on that hill and his voice was dismayed on his behalf.

'I think so. They never touch Caesar's properties, did you know that?' He rubbed the back of his neck, unutterably weary. 'It's hard to tell distances in the dark. I'll know in the morning, if I can find enough men to walk with me.' He spoke through gritted teeth at the thought of the people of Rome pawing his possessions. 'We need those legions from Brundisium, Cassius! Another thirty thousand men could cut through these mobs. We need to smash them, to show enough force that it stops their mouths.'

'If I could have brought them, I would have. Caesar's officers won't answer the messages of the Senate. When this is over, I will have them decimated, or their eagles struck down and made into cups for the poor, but for now, I cannot *make* them move.'

Somewhere in the streets near the house, a man screamed long and loud. Both of them started at the sound, then deliberately ignored it.

'I could go to them,' Brutus said after a time.

Cassius laughed in surprise. 'To Brundisium? You'd be slaughtered as soon as they heard your name. You think *I* am unpopular, Brutus? Your name is the one the mobs chant loudest when they are calling for Caesar's vengeance.'

Brutus blew air out, frustrated to the point of shaking.

'Perhaps it *is* time to leave, then. To have your Senate make me governor of some city far from here. I have not seen the rewards you promised me, not yet . . .' He caught himself, unwilling to beg from the hand of Cassius. Yet Brutus had no civil post and no wealth of his own. His private funds were already dwindling and he wondered if a nobleman like Cassius even understood his predicament. 'Caesar would be laughing if he could see us hiding from his people.'

Cassius stared into the night. The fires on the Quirinal had spread at breathtaking speed. In the distance, hundreds of burning houses lit the darkness, like red cracks in the earth.

There would be blackened bodies by the thousand in the morning and Pella was right, disease would follow, rising from the dead flesh and entering the lungs of healthy men. He made a sound in his throat and Brutus looked to him, trying to read his expression.

'There are legions in Asia Minor,' Cassius said at last. 'I have considered going out to them as the representative of the Senate. Our eastern lands must be protected from the chaos here. Perhaps a year or two in Syria would allow us to put these bloody days behind.'

Brutus considered, but shook his head. He remembered the heat and strange passions of Egypt and had no desire to return to that part of the world.

'Not Syria, not for me at least. I have never visited Athens, though I knew Greece well when I was young.'

Cassius waved a hand.

'Propraetor then. It is done. I will have your command and passes drawn up, ready for use. By the gods, though, I could wish it had not turned out like this! I have not brought down one tyrant only to see Mark Antony take his place. The man is a greased snake for slipperiness.'

'While we stay, the riots go on,' Brutus replied, his voice hard. 'They *hunt* for me, whoreson gangs of filthy slaves, kicking down doors looking for *me*.'

'It will pass. I remember the last riots. The senate house was burned then, but the madness faded eventually.'

'The leaders died, Cassius, that was why those riots came to an end. I had to move twice yesterday, just to be sure they could not box me in.' He made a growling sound, at the end of his patience. 'I would be happier if Mark Antony had fallen on the first day. Yet he walks where he pleases, with no more than a few guards. They do not hunt him, not the noble friend of Caesar!'

There was a crash from outside and both men jerked round,

staring at the door as if it would burst open and bring the ugly mobs of Rome surging into the room. A woman screamed nearby, the sound suddenly choking off.

'We underestimated him, it seems, or at least his ability to survive,' Cassius replied, speaking more to break the silence than from thought. 'I too would be happier if Mark Antony was another tragic casualty of the riots, but he is too careful – and right now, too well loved. I know a few men, but they are as likely to tell him of a plot as carry it through.'

Brutus snorted. More crashes and screams sounded from the street, though he thought they were moving on.

'Draw up the orders then,' he said wearily. 'I can spend a year or two governing Athens. When the sting is drawn from Rome, I will see her again.'

Cassius pressed a hand to his shoulder.

'Depend on it, my friend. We have come too far together to see it all lost now.'

CHAPTER FIVE

Brundisium had never been as busy. It was like an overturned beehive, with soldiers and citizens scurrying everywhere and no sign of the languor of Rome. In the port city, everyone hurried, moving supplies for the fleet and legions: wooden casks of water, iron nails, ropes, sailcloth, salted meat and a thousand other essential goods. Despite being allowed to pass by the outer fleet, it was almost noon before the ship had its turn through the massive gates across the inner harbour, winched open each morning by teams of sweating slaves.

As the merchant vessel reached the quay, the sailors threw ropes to dockers, who heaved them in the last few feet and tied them to great iron stanchions set in the stone. A wide wooden bridge was lifted up and over, forming a path from the ship to the quayside. Octavian and Agrippa were the first to step off as Maecenas settled the fee with the captain and remained to oversee the unloading of the horses. A dozen workers and two empty carts trundled over to carry crates and chests from the ship, men who had bought the right to that section of the docks and charged high fees for the privilege. By the time the horses were led out, even Maecenas was complaining about the venal nature of the port, which seemed designed to take every last coin he had.

'There isn't a room or a stable free for thirty miles or more,' he reported when he joined them. 'According to the dockers, six legions are encamped and the officers have taken every tavern in the city. That makes it easier to find one who might know you, Octavian, but it will take time to find lodgings. Give me half a day.'

Octavian nodded uneasily. His plan to get an audience with the senior officer in Brundisium had seemed a lot simpler before he'd seen the chaos of the city. Its population had quadrupled with soldiers and he needed Maecenas more than ever. His friend had already employed runners to carry messages for him, sending them sprinting off into the maze of streets away from the port. Octavian didn't doubt he'd find somewhere to store their belongings before the sun set.

'What is your business in Brundisium?' a voice said behind him. 'You can't leave that lot here, you know, blocking the docks. Tell your captain to cast off. There are two more ships waiting already.'

Octavian turned to see a bald man in optio's armour, short and powerful with a sword on his hip and two robed clerks in his wake.

'We are arranging porters, sir. Right now, I need to know the name of the commander in Brundisium and to arrange a meeting with him.'

The officer smiled wryly, running a hand over the polished dome of his head and flicking away sweat.

'I can think of at least seven men who might answer your description. But you won't get to see them, not without a few weeks of waiting. Unless you are a senator, perhaps. Are you a senator? You look a bit young for that.' He smiled at his own humour.

Octavian took a deep breath, already irritated. At Caesar's side, he had never been questioned. He looked at the man's amused expression and realised he could not bluster or threaten his way past. He could not even give his true name while there was a chance he was being hunted.

'I . . . carry messages for the senior officer in the city.'

'And yet you don't have his name?' the optio replied. 'Forgive me for doubting a young gentlemen such as yourself . . .' He saw Octavian's frustration and shrugged, his expression not without kindness. 'Look, lad. Just get your goods off my dock, all right? I don't care where, as long as I don't have to see it. Understand? I can put you in touch with a man who has a warehouse not far from here, if you want.'

'I need to see a general,' Octavian went on doggedly. 'Or a tribune.'

The optio just stared at him and Octavian raised his eyes in frustration.

'Maecenas?' he said.

'Here,' Maecenas replied. He dug in his pouch and removed two sesterces. With the smoothness of long practice, the optio accepted the coins without looking at them, rubbing them together as he made them disappear.

'I can't arrange a meeting with a legate, lad. They've shut themselves away for these last few days, ever since the news from Rome.'

He paused, but the expressions of the three young men showed they already knew.

'You might try the tavern on fifth street, though.' He glanced at the sun. 'Tribune Liburnius eats there most days around noon. You could still catch him, but I warn you, he won't enjoy being interrupted.'

'Fat, is he?' Maecenas said lightly. 'A big eater?'

The optio shot him a look and shook his head.

'I meant that he is an important man who does not suffer

71

fools.' He took Octavian by the arm and moved him a step to one side. 'I wouldn't let that one anywhere near him; just a bit of advice. Liburnius isn't known for his patience.'

'I understand, sir. Thank you,' Octavian said through clenched teeth.

'A pleasure. Now clear your belongings off my docks, or I'll have them dropped into the sea.'

There were three taverns on fifth street and the first two wasted another hour. Agrippa, Octavian and Maecenas rode with porters, the laden cart and a dozen street urchins following them, hoping for a coin. When the owner of the third tavern saw the large group heading towards his establishment, he flicked a cloth over his shoulder and came out to the street with his hands held wide and his large head already wagging from side to side.

'No rooms here, sorry,' he said. 'Try the Gull in Major, three streets over. I heard they still have space.'

'I don't need a room,' Octavian snapped. He dismounted and threw his reins to Agrippa. 'I am looking for Tribune Liburnius. Is he here?'

The man stuck out his chin at the tone from a man half his age.

'Can't say, sir. We're full, though.'

He turned to go back in and Octavian lost his temper. Reaching out, he shoved the man back against the wall, leaning in close to him. The tavern-keeper's face went red, but then he felt the coldness of a knife at his throat and stayed still.

'I've been here for just one morning and I am already getting tired of this city,' Octavian growled into his ear. 'The tribune will want to see me. Is he in your place or not?'

'If I shout, his guards will kill you,' the man said.

Behind Octavian, Agrippa dismounted, dropping his hand to

the gladius he wore. He was as weary as Octavian and he could smell hot food wafting from the tavern kitchen.

'Shout then,' Agrippa said. 'See what you get.'

The tavern-keeper's eyes rose slowly to take in the massive centurion. The resistance went out of him.

'All right, there's no need for that. But I can't disturb the tribune. I need the custom.'

Octavian stepped away, sheathing his knife. He wrestled a gold ring from his hand. Given to him by Caesar himself, it bore the seal of the Julii family.

'Show him this. He will see me.'

The tavern-keeper took the ring, rubbing his neck where the knife had touched. He looked at the angry young men facing him and decided not to say anything else, disappearing back into the gloom.

They waited for a long time, thirsty and hungry. The porters who accompanied them put down their burdens and sat on the cart or the sturdier chests, folding their arms and talking amongst themselves. They didn't mind holding the horses and wasting the day if it meant more pay at the end.

The street grew busier around them as the life of Brundisium went on with no sign of a lull. Two messengers from the morning managed to find their way back to the listless group, accepting coins from Maecenas as they brought news of a friend with an empty house in the wealthy eastern half of the city.

'I'm going in,' Octavian said at last. 'If only to get my ring back. By the gods, I never thought it would be this hard just to speak to someone in authority.'

Agrippa and Maecenas exchanged a quick glance. In their own way, both had more experience of the world than their friend. Agrippa's father had taken him to the houses of many powerful men, showing him how to bribe and work his way round layers of staff. Maecenas was the opposite, a man who employed such men on his estates.

73

'I'll go with you,' Agrippa said, rolling his head on his shoulders. 'Maecenas can stay to watch the horses.'

In truth, neither of them wanted Maecenas anywhere near a Roman tribune. A man of his rank could order them killed at the slightest insult to his dignity. Maecenas shrugged and they went in, squinting as the light changed.

The tavern-keeper was back behind his bar. He did not speak to them and his expression was something just short of a sneer. Octavian strode up to him, but Agrippa touched him on the shoulder, inclining his head towards a table across the room, far from the dust and heat of the main door.

Two men sat there in togas dyed dark blue, almost black. They were eating from a plate of cold meats and boiled vegetables, leaning over the table with their elbows on the wood and talking earnestly. A matched pair of guards in full legionary armour stood facing the room, just far enough away to give the men the illusion of privacy, if not the reality.

Octavian took heart from the colours of mourning they wore. If they were men who showed they grieved for Caesar, perhaps he could trust them. Yet they had not returned his ring, so he was wary as he approached.

One of the men at the table had a tribune's cloak draped over his chair. The man looked fit and tanned, his head almost bald with just a band of white hair by his ears. He wore no breastplate, just a tunic that left his arms bare and revealed white chest hairs below the open collar. Octavian took all this in before one of the guards raised a flat palm casually to stop him. The two men at the table continued their conversation without looking up.

'I need to speak to Tribune Liburnius,' Octavian said.

'No you don't,' the legionary said, deliberately keeping his voice low as if every word could not be overheard by the men at the table. 'You need to stop bothering your betters. Apply to the barracks of the Fourth Ferrata legion. Someone will hear you there. Off you go now.'

Octavian stood very still, simmering anger clear in every line of him. The guard was unimpressed, though he glanced at Agrippa, whose size made him worthy of a quick assessment. Even so, the legionary just smiled slightly and shook his head.

'Where are the barracks?' Octavian said at last. He knew his name would get him an audience, but it could equally get him arrested.

'Three miles west of town, or thereabouts,' the legionary replied. 'Ask anyone on the way. You'll find it.'

The soldier took no obvious pleasure in turning them away. He was just doing as he had been told and keeping strangers from bothering the tribune. No doubt there were many who sought to reach the man with some plea or other. Octavian controlled his temper with an effort. His plans were baulked at every turn, but getting himself killed in a seedy tavern would accomplish nothing.

'I'll have my ring then and be on my way,' he said.

The legionary did not answer and Octavian repeated his words. The conversation at the table had ceased and both men were chewing food in silence, clearly waiting for him to go. Octavian clenched his fists and both guards looked straight at him. The one who had spoken shook his head again slowly, warning him off.

'I'll be back in a moment,' Octavian said curtly. He turned and stalked to where the tavern-keeper was watching with a greasy look of nervousness. Agrippa went with him, cracking his knuckles as he stood at Octavian's side.

'Did you hand over the ring I gave you?' Octavian demanded of the tavern-keeper. The man's expression was unpleasant as he wiped cups and put them back in a neat row on the bar. He glanced to where the tribune sat with his guards and decided he was safe enough.

'What ring?' he replied.

Octavian snapped his left arm out and cupped the back of the tavern-keeper's head. The man stiffened against it, holding himself neatly in place as Octavian punched him in the nose with his right hand. The man went over backwards in a crash of breaking cups.

One of the tribune's guards cursed across the room, but Octavian was around the bar and on the fallen tavern-keeper before they could move. The man's hands flailed at him, knocking his head up with a lucky blow before Octavian landed two more solid punches. The burly man slumped then and Octavian searched the pockets of his apron, rewarded with the feel of a small lump. He drew out the ring just as the guards came storming over with swords drawn. One of them placed a palm against Agrippa's chest, with a blade raised to strike at throat height. Agrippa could only hold up empty hands as he backed away. At a word from the tribune, they were both dead.

The other guard reached over and wrapped an arm around Octavian's neck, heaving backwards with all his strength. With a strangled shout, Octavian was yanked over the bar and they fell back together.

Octavian struggled wildly as the arm around his throat tightened, but his air was cut off and his face began to grow purple. He clung on to the ring as his vision began to flash and fade, never hearing the dry voice of the tribune as he strolled over to them.

'Let him go, Gracchus,' Tribune Liburnius said, wiping his mouth with a square of fine linen.

The guard released Octavian, pausing just long enough to punch him hard in the kidneys before standing up and smoothing himself down. On the floor, Octavian groaned in pain, but he held up his hand with the ring pinched between two fingers. The tribune ignored it.

'Twenty lashes for brawling in public, I think,' he said. 'Another twenty for disturbing my lunch. Do the honours, would you, Gracchus? There is a whipping post in the street you can use.'

'It would be a *pleasure*, sir,' the guard said, panting from his exertions. As he laid hands on Octavian again, the young man came to his feet, so far gone in fury that he could hardly think.

'My ring is stolen from me and you call this Roman justice?' he demanded. 'Should I let some fat taverner steal a gift from Caesar himself?'

'Show me the ring,' the tribune said, a frown line appearing on his forehead.

'No, I don't think so,' Octavian said. Agrippa gaped at him, but he was practically shaking with rage. 'You are not the man I want to see; I know that now. I will take the lashes.'

Tribune Liburnius sighed.

'Oh, save me from young cockerels. Gracchus? If you wouldn't mind.'

Octavian felt his arm gripped and his fingers forced open. The ring was tossed through the air and the tribune caught it easily, peering closely at it in the gloom. His eyebrows raised as he studied the seal marked in the gold.

'Just a month ago, this would have gained you entry almost anywhere, young man. But now it only raises questions. Who are you and how did you come to have this in your possession?'

Octavian tensed his jaw defiantly and it was Agrippa who decided enough was enough.

'His name is Gaius Octavian Thurinus, a relative of Caesar. He speaks the truth.'

The tribune digested the information with a thoughtful expression.

'I believe I have heard that name. And you?'

'Marcus Vipsanius Agrippa, sir. Centurion Captain of the fleet, sir.'

'I see. Well, gentlemen, a ring from Caesar has won you a place at my table, at least for an hour. Have you eaten?'

Agrippa shook his head, dumbfounded at the sudden change in manner.

'I'll order for you when the tavern-keeper wakes up. Gracchus? Throw a bucket of slops on him . . . and spend a moment or two teaching him that stealing has consequences, if you wouldn't mind. I'll need to find a new inn tomorrow.'

'Yes, sir,' the legionary responded. He had recovered his dignity and looked with satisfaction on the unconscious figure sprawled beneath the bar.

'Come, gentlemen,' the tribune said, gesturing back to his table and his still-seated companion. 'You have my attention. I hope you don't regret it.'

Tribune Liburnius placed the ring on the table before them as Octavian and Agrippa pulled up chairs. He did not introduce his companion and Octavian wondered if he was a client or perhaps a spy for the tribune. The man met his eyes briefly, revealing a flash of interest and intelligence before looking away.

The tribune looked up at the sound of a bucket clattering to the ground and a stifled cry from behind the bar.

'I'm sure the wine will be here in a moment or two,' he said. He reached out and held the ring once more, turning it in his hands. 'This is a dangerous little thing these days. I wonder if you realise that?'

'I'm beginning to,' Octavian said, touching a hand to a swelling lump by his right eye.

'Hah! Not thieves. There is far more danger in those who are struggling even now to keep a grip on the mother city. We're out of it here in Brundisium. If I have my way, we will remain so until order is re-established. Yet Greece is further still, so perhaps this is all news to you.'

Octavian blinked. 'How did you know I came from Greece?'

To his surprise, Liburnius chuckled, clearly delighted.

'By the gods, you really *are* young! Honestly, it makes me nostalgic for my own youth. You truly think you can come into this port, throwing silver coins around and demanding to speak to senior men, without it being reported? I dare say every rumour-monger in the city has your description by now, though perhaps not your name, not yet.'

Octavian flicked a glance at the tribune's silent companion and the man sensed it, smiling slightly without looking up.

'Your presence is an interesting problem for me, Octavian. I could have you sent in chains to Rome, of course, for some senator to dispose of as he sees fit, but that would gain me just a favour, or a few gold coins, hardly worth my trouble.'

'You have no loyalty then?' Octavian demanded. 'The Fourth Ferrata was formed by Caesar. You must have known him.'

Tribune Liburnius looked at him, biting the inside of his lower lip in thought.

'I knew him, yes. I cannot say we were friends. Men like Caesar have few friends, I think, only followers.' Liburnius drummed his fingers on the table as he considered, his eyes never leaving Octavian.

The drinks arrived, brought by the tavern-keeper. The man was a bedraggled mess, his face swollen and one eye half shut. There was a piece of green vegetable in his hair. He did not look at Octavian or the tribune as he placed a jug and cups carefully and departed, limping. The legionary, Gracchus, took up his position once more, facing out.

'And yet . . .' Liburnius said softly. 'The will of Caesar has not been read. He had a boy with the Egyptian queen, but they say he loved you also like a son. Who knows what Caesar's gift might mean to you, when we hear? It could be that you are the horse to back, at least for now. Perhaps we can come to some arrangement, something that benefits us both.'

The fingers drummed again and the tribune's companion poured for all of them. Octavian and Agrippa exchanged glances, but there was nothing to do but remain silent.

'I think . . . yes. I could have documents drawn up. A tenth of whatever you inherit, against my time and funds getting you to Rome and my support securing whatever you are owed. And leaving you alive and unflogged, of course. Shall we shake hands on it? You will need that ring to seal the agreement, so you may have it back.'

Octavian gaped at him. After a moment's hesitation, he reached out and snatched up the ring, working it onto his finger.

'It was never yours to return,' he said. 'A tenth! I would have to be insane to agree to such a bargain, especially before I know how much is at stake. My answer is no. I have funds enough to find my own way. I have friends enough to stand against the men who killed him.'

'I see,' Liburnius said, wryly amused at the young man's anger. Drops of wine had spilled on the ancient table and he drew circles with them on the wood as he thought. He shook his head and Octavian gripped the edge of the table, ready to shove it over and run.

'I don't think you understand how perilous Rome has become, Octavian. How do you think the Liberatores will react if you enter the city? If you charge into the senate house, demanding and blustering, as if you had a right to be heard? I give you half a day at most, before you are found with your throat cut, perhaps not even that long. The men of power will not want some relative of Caesar inflaming the mob. They will not want a claimant on his wealth that would otherwise find its way into their hands. Are you going to tip this table over, by the way? Do you think I am blind or a fool? My guards would cut you down before you could stand up.' He shook his head ruefully at the rashness of the young. 'Mine is the best offer you will receive today. At least with me, you will live long enough to hear the will read.'

Octavian removed his hands from the table, sitting with his thoughts racing. The tribune was a real threat and he realised he could not get out of the tavern without losing something. He wondered what Julius would have done in his place. Tribune Liburnius watched him closely, a smile lifting the corners of his thin mouth.

'I will not sign away my inheritance, or any part of it,' Octavian said. Liburnius tutted to himself and raised his eyes to the guards to give an order. Octavian went on quickly, 'But I was there when Caesar and Cleopatra bargained with the Egyptian court. I can offer more than gold in exchange for your support. You can be useful to me, I will not deny it. It is why I sought you out in the first place.'

'Go on,' Liburnius said. His eyes were cold, but the smile still remained.

'I saw Caesar give favours that men valued far more than coins. I can do that. I will put his ring to an agreement that offers you a single favour, whatever you wish, at any point in my life.'

Liburnius blinked and then gave a great bark of laughter, slapping the table with his palm. When he settled, he wiped a tear from his eye, still chuckling.

'You are a joy to me, lad. I cannot fault you for the enter-tainment. It was looking to be such a dull day as well. You know, I have a son about your age. I wish he had a pair like yours, I really do. Instead, he reads Greek philosophy to me; can you imagine? It is all I can do not to vomit.'

Liburnius leaned forward on the table, all sign of humour vanishing.

'But you are not Caesar. As things stand in Rome, I would

not lay a silver coin on you surviving a year. What you have offered me is almost certainly worthless. As I say, I applaud your courage, but let us end this game.'

Octavian leaned forward as well, his voice clear and low.

'I am not Caesar, but he *did* love me as a son and the blood of his family runs in me. Take what I have offered and one day, when your fortunes have changed for the worse, or those of your son, perhaps then my promise will be the most valuable thing you own.'

Liburnius made a fig hand quickly to avert even the suggestion of an evil fate in store for him. He shoved his thumb between the first and second fingers of his right hand and pointed it at Octavian. After a pause, he unclenched his hand and let it fall to the table.

'With that promise and ten thousand in gold, I will have ten thousand in gold,' he muttered.

Octavian shrugged. 'I cannot promise what I don't have,' he said.

'That is why I asked you for a tenth, boy. You cannot lose by such an arrangement.'

Octavian knew he should have agreed, but something stubborn in him still refused. He folded his arms.

'I have said all there is to say. Accept my favour and one day it could save your life. If you remember Caesar, consider how he would want you to act.' Octavian looked up at the ceiling of the tavern. 'He died at the hands of men who now live well. If he can see us now, will he see you treat me with honour or disdain?'

He waited for an answer and Liburnius drummed his fingers on the wood, the only sound in the tavern. For an instant, his eyes flickered upward, as if he too was imagining Julius watching.

'I can't decide if you don't understand . . . or you just don't care to preserve your life,' he said. 'I have met a few like you in my time, young officers mostly, with no sense of their own mortality. Some rose, but most of them are long dead, victims of their own overconfidence. Do you understand what I am saying to you?'

'I do. Gamble on me, Tribune. I will not be brought down easily.'

Liburnius blew air from his lips in a wet sound.

'To be brought down, you have first to rise.' He made a decision. 'Very well. Gracchus? Fetch me a parchment, reed and ink. I will have this poor bargain sealed in front of witnesses.'

Octavian knew better than to speak again. He worked hard to hide the triumph that seared through him.

'When that is done, I will secure your passage to Rome. The will is to be read in eight days, which gives you time to spare to get there, on good horses. I trust you will not object to Gracchus travelling with you to keep you safe? There are bandits on the road and I would like to be among the first to hear what Caesar left to his city and his clients.'

Octavian nodded. He watched Liburnius dip the hollow reed with a sharpened tip and write with a sure hand. The tavern-keeper brought a lit candle and the tribune melted wax, dripping a fat glob of it onto the dry parchment, so that oil spread beneath. Octavian pressed his ring into the soft surface and the two guards added a scrawled 'X' where Liburnius had written their names. It was done.

Liburnius sat back, relaxing.

'More wine, I think, Gracchus. You know, lad, when you are my age, if you should be lucky enough to live that long, when colour and taste and even ambition have lost the brightness you think is so natural, I hope you will meet a young cockerel just like you are now – so you can see what I see. I hope you will remember me then. It is a bitter-sweet thing, believe me, but you will not understand until that day.'

A new jug arrived and Liburnius poured the cups full to brimming.

'Drink with me, lad. Drink to Rome and glorious foolishness.'

Without looking away, Octavian raised his cup, draining it in quick swallows.

CHAPTER SIX

The first light of the sun showed over the Esquiline and Viminal hills, gilding the roofs around the forum and reaching across to the Palatine on the far side. The round temple of Vesta there gleamed with the rest, coming alive after the darkness. Neither that ancient building nor the much larger House of Virgins behind had been touched by the fires raging through the city. Their own sacred flame still burned in the hearth of the temple and the bands of rioters had steered clear of the wrath of the goddess, making the fig hand or the horned hand to ward off her curse and moving on.

Mark Antony knew he cut a fine figure as he walked across the forum. As well as six lictors, carrying the traditional axes and bound rods for scourging, two centurions accompanied him, their armour shining and long dark cloaks sweeping against their ankles. The consul of Rome had come to hear the will of Caesar and if the senate house was blackened rubble, at least in his own person Mark Antony still represented the authority of the state. He could feel eyes on him as the crowd gathered, but there was no sense of danger, not that day. He was certain many of those crowding in had been involved in the riots, perhaps just hours before, but the dawn sun was cool and there was almost a sense of truce. The whole city wanted to hear the last words of Caesar to his people.

Mark Antony reached a spot in front of the circular temple, so that he could see the eternal flame flickering along the walls inside. His men took up positions around him, feeling no threat in the quiet crowd. Mark Antony looked for the remaining Liberatores and could not see them. He had spies reporting to him each day and he knew many of them had already left, to save their skins.

He kept his expression stern, though their absence was yet another sign that he had gained most from the slaughters and riots. If powerful men like Brutus and Cassius no longer dared to show their faces, how could they ever hope to regain their authority in Rome? It was a subtle victory. No doubt they had men in the crowd to report back every word, but their absence spoke volumes and he would not be the only one to remark on it. A month before, he could not have dreamed of anything like this day. Caesar had been alive then and the world had been set in ruts of stone, unable to do more than go forward on the path. The Liberatores had changed all that with their knives, but it was Mark Antony whose fortunes were on the rise. *He* triumphed, step by step, as they failed.

Taller than most, Mark Antony was able to look over the heads of the crowd. The forum was not full, by any means. Heat-scorched stones lay empty behind him, but at least three thousand men and women were there and still they walked out of every side road and down every hill, dark streams of citizens and slaves coming to the heart of Rome. There was order of a sort in most of the city; he had seen to that. The gates were open again and fresh produce flowed in, commanding ridiculous prices. There was a queue outside every baker and butcher as they worked through the night to make loaves and slice meat. There was not enough for all and he had been forced to set patrols at key points to stop fights breaking out. Starvation and disease were the enemies now, the violent energy of the rioters fading almost as quickly as it had sprung up. No one knew how many bodies had been dumped in the Tiber to tumble away to the sea.

His gaze snagged on a group of four men on his right, all armed and obviously together as they talked in low voices. Two of them looked vaguely familiar to the consul, slim figures against the massive shoulders of the man next to them, yet Mark Antony could not bring the names to mind. Hundreds in the crowd would have been clients to Caesar, men who owed their estates and rise to him and had accepted a small stipend each month for their support. The number of them was said to have been in the thousands. Rich and poor, they would all want to know if their patron had remembered them in his will.

Mark Antony continued to crane his neck around, peering particularly at anyone with their head covered. He recognised senators among those, many of them travelling with guards provided from the legions or mercenaries hired for the day. Still, the crowd grew with the sunlight, until the coolness of dawn faded and he could smell sweat and spiced food in the warming air. The spring sky was clear and the city would become unpleasantly hot by noon. He eased his weight from one foot to the other, waiting impatiently for the priestess to show herself.

The crowd stilled as they heard singing coming from the House of Virgins, straining to catch the first glimpse of the Vestal virgins. Mark Antony suppressed a smile as he saw them, more aware than most of the power of pageantry in the city.

They bore small cymbals on their fingers and wrists and clashed them together with every step so that the discordant sound rose above their voices. He watched as the procession formed in front of the temple and the song built to a climax followed by total silence. Disappointingly, the young women revealed almost nothing in their stola dresses and long palla robes that concealed their legs. The priestess had shown more flesh when he visited her before and he had to smile at the adolescent part of him. Each one had been chosen for physical perfection, but they had vowed thirty years of celibacy before they could leave the temple. Looking at some of the faces, Mark Antony could not help thinking it was a shocking waste.

He waited through a ritual of thanks to Minerva and Vesta, only sighing as the sun rose and the heat built. After what seemed an age, they brought a wooden platform from the temple, draping it with dark red cloth. Quintina Fabia stepped up to it and her eyes met those of Mark Antony, perhaps recalling that he too had stood and spoken to Rome not long before. The effects could still be seen around them. He saw cold amusement in her eyes, but he was interested only in the carved cedar box brought out from the temple. It was both locked and sealed, so that two of the women had to strike the binding with hammers before they could open the lid. From inside, they raised a square block of wax tablets, wrapped around in strips of lead and then marked in a great disc of wax sealed by Caesar himself. Mark Antony shuddered at the thought of his friend's hand being the last to touch it before that day.

They handed the block up to the priestess and she used a knife to cut away the wax, showing everyone there that it remained untouched. With care, she bent back the lead strips and passed them down. What remained were five wooden tablets with a thin sheen of wax on their surfaces. Mark Antony could not see the words inscribed there, but he inched forward with everyone else, suddenly desperate to know what Caesar had written.

Untouched by the impatience of the crowd, Quintina Fabia handed four of the tablets back to her companions and read the first to herself, nodding slightly at the end. When she had finished, she looked up at the massed crowd.

"'For the honour of Rome, hear the will of Gaius Julius Caesar,'" she began. She paused and Mark Antony groaned quietly at the theatrical impulse.

'Come on,' he muttered.

She glanced over to him as if she had heard before continuing to read.

"'Gaius Octavian is my heir. I acknowledge him as blood of my blood and, by these words, I claim and adopt him as my son.'"

The crowd murmured and Mark Antony saw the small group of four stiffen almost as one, looking at each other in shock and wonderment. The simple words were typical of the man who had written them, without ornament or fanciful rhetoric. Yet Caesar had written and lodged the will before his return from Egypt, perhaps even before he had left Rome to fight Pompey in Greece. He had not known then that the Egyptian queen would bear him an heir. Mark Antony breathed slowly as he thought it through. It would have been better to have some foreign whelp as the main inheritor, one who could never come to Rome and contest for what was legally his. The consul had met Octavian a few years before, but he had been little more than a boy and Mark Antony could not even recall his face. He looked up as the priestess continued.

"'All that I have is his, beyond the sums and properties I allocate here. Of those, the first is the garden estate by the river Tiber. That is my first gift to the people of Rome, in perpetuity, that they may take their ease there as public land.'"

As the crowd muttered in wonderment, she handed down the tablet and took up two more. Her eyebrows rose as she read silently before speaking the words.

"'As well as a place to walk in the sun, I give each citizen of Rome three hundred sesterces from my estate, to be spent as they see fit. They were my champions in life. I cannot do less for them in death.'"

This time, the reaction from the crowd was a roar of excitement. Three hundred silver coins was a huge sum, enough to feed a family for months. Mark Antony rubbed his forehead as he tried to work out the total. The last census had recorded almost a million inhabitants of the city, though only half of those would be citizens. Wryly, he acknowledged that the riots would have reduced the number, yet still they swarmed like ants and they would all demand their money from the treasure houses controlled by the Senate. Caesar could not have known, but that simple bequest was a blow against the Liberatores. They would not be able to walk the streets without the shout of 'Murderers!' going up, not after this. He closed his eyes briefly in memory of his friend. Even in death, Julius had struck back at his enemies.

Quintina Fabia continued, listing the individual sums left to clients. Many shouted for quiet so they could hear, but the chattering went on even so, all around them. They would have to apply to the temple to read the tablets in private if they wanted to hear those details, Mark Antony thought. Remembering his own meeting with the priestess, he wished them luck.

She worked her way through to the last of the five tablets, allocating gold and land to members of his family and all those who had supported Caesar. Mark Antony heard his name and bellowed for those around him to be silent. His voice succeeded in crushing the noise of the crowd where others had failed.

"'. . . to whom I give fifty thousand aurei. I give an equal sum to Marcus Brutus. They were, and are, my friends.'"

Mark Antony felt the gaze of the crowd on him. He could not hide his shock at hearing Brutus given the same amount. Mark Antony had lavished gold on the lifestyle of a consul and his own clients. Although the legacy was generous, it would barely cover his debts. He shook his head, aware of the awe in those who looked on him and yet bitter. Fifty thousand was not so much for the man who had roused the crowd on Caesar's behalf. It was certainly far more than Brutus deserved.

"'The rest is the property of Gaius Octavian, adopted as my son, into the house of Julii. I leave Rome in your hands.'"

Quintina Fabia stopped speaking and handed the last tablet down to her waiting followers. Mark Antony was astonished to see the gleam of tears in her eyes. There had been no grand words, just the business of recording Caesar's legacies and responsibilities. It was, in fact, the will of a man who did not truly believe he was going to die. He felt his own eyes prickle at the thought. If Julius had lodged the will with the temple before leaving Rome, it was the year he had made Mark Antony governor of the city, trusting him completely. It was a window to the past, to a different Rome.

As the priestess stepped down, Mark Antony turned away, his men moving smoothly with him so that the crowd was forced to part. They did not understand why he looked so angry. Behind him, a clear voice rang out. As Mark Antony heard, he stopped and turned to listen, his men facing outwards to counter any threat.

Octavian remembered Mark Antony very well. The consul had changed little over the intervening years, whereas Octavian had gone from a boy to a young man. As the consul arrived at first light, Maecenas had marked his presence first. Agrippa used the breadth of his shoulders to come between them,

91

relying on the crowd to hide Octavian. It was their second day in the city, after a ride of three hundred miles from Brundisium. They had been forced to change horses many times, almost always losing quality in the mounts. Maecenas had arranged for their own horses to be stabled at the first stopping place, but at that point none of them knew if they would be going back to the coast.

The legionary, Gracchus, had not been a pleasant companion on that journey. Knowing he was at best tolerated, he barely spoke, but he remained doggedly in their company as they rode and planned, dropping exhausted into rough beds at the closest inn they could find as the sun set. He had his own funds from the tribune and more than once had slept in the stables to eke out his coins while Maecenas ordered the best rooms.

Octavian was not sure the fast run had been worth it. He'd come into Rome two days before the will was to be read, but the world of peace and order he had known had been torn apart. According to a friend of Maecenas who'd offered them his home, it had been even worse before and was beginning to settle down, but great sections of the city had been reduced to blackened beams and grubby citizens picking through the rubble for anything valuable. Tens of thousands were starving, roving the streets in gangs in search of food. More than once he and his friends had to draw swords just to cross neighbourhoods that had become feral even in daylight. The city looked as if it had been in a war and Octavian could hardly reconcile the reality with his memories. In a way, it suited the grief he felt for Julius, a fitting landscape for such a loss.

'Here she is at last,' Agrippa said under his breath.

Octavian snapped back from his reverie as the priestess of Vesta came out. He had been searching the crowd for the faces of men he knew. If Brutus had been there, he did not know what he would have done, but there was no sign of the man he wanted to see dead above all others. Two days in Rome had been enough to hear the details of the assassination and he burned with new energy at the thought of those Liberatores who sought to profit from murdering a good man. In the silence of his own thoughts, in the shadow of the temple of Vesta, he swore oaths of vengeance. The state of the city was the crop they had sown, the result of their greed and jealousy. He had not known what strength could come from hate, not before seeing Rome again.

As the priestess unbound the will of Caesar from its box and lead straps, Octavian continued to glance back at the crowd. He recognised some faces he thought might be senators, but in cloaks and mantles against the morning cold, he could not be certain. He had been away too long.

Agrippa nudged him to pay attention as the priestess scanned the first tablet, a line appearing on her forehead. When she looked up, she seemed to stare straight at Octavian. He waited, his heart thumping painfully in his chest and his mouth drying, so that he ran his tongue around the inside to free his lips.

"'For the honour of Rome, hear the will of Gaius Julius Caesar,'" she began.

Octavian clenched his fists, hardly able to stand the tension. He felt Gracchus look over at him, the man's expression unreadable.

"'Gaius Octavian is my heir. I acknowledge him as blood of my blood and, by these words, I claim and adopt him as my son.'"

Octavian felt a great shudder run through him and he would have staggered if Agrippa hadn't put out an arm. His hearing vanished in the pounding of his pulse and when he felt an itch on his face, he scrubbed at it, leaving a red welt on his skin. It was too much to take in and he hardly heard the lines that followed, watching the priestess of Vesta hand down the tablets as she read them out. At one point, the men and women in the crowd cheered raucously and Octavian could not understand why. He was numb with emotion, overwhelmed at the hand of Caesar reaching out from death to touch him.

The face of Gracchus was the picture of sourness as he considered the fortune his patron could have had, with a tenth of Caesar's wealth. It was almost a legend, how much gold the leader of Rome had brought back from his conquests, at one point flooding so much of it into the city that it devalued the currency by almost a third. Octavian was the heir to all of it and Gracchus decided on the instant to be a more amenable companion. He would never again stand in the presence of such wealth, he was certain. Reaching out, he was about to clap Octavian on the back, but Maecenas caught the wrist and just smiled at him.

'Let's not make a show, not here,' Maecenas said in a low voice. 'We are unknown to the crowd and that is the way it should stay until we have had a little time to think about all this.'

Gracchus forced a sickly grin and nodded, jerking back his arm from a grip of surprising strength. He had not seen Maecenas spar or train in their rush from the coast and he never noticed the short blade in the noble's other hand as he let go, or the fact that Agrippa was behind him, ready to hammer him into the ground at the first sign of aggression.

The list of clients and individual bequests seemed to take an age. Octavian glowered in disgust when he heard the name of Brutus and the huge sum of gold left to him. There was no mention of Cleopatra and the son that she had borne. All Maecenas' friends knew was that she had left Rome after the assassination, presumably to go home to Egypt.

'"The rest is the property of Gaius Octavian, adopted as my son, into the house of Julii. I leave Rome in your hands."'

Octavian felt his eyes sting. It was too easy to imagine Julius sitting in some quiet room, writing the words in wax, with the future laid out before him. Octavian began to wish he was alive for the thousandth time since hearing the news, then wrestled himself free of the thought as it formed. There was no going back, no wishing away of the new Rome.

The priestess handed down the last tablet and saw it placed with reverence back into the chest. One of her acolytes put out a hand and she stepped down, her part finished. Octavian looked around him as the crowd exhaled held breaths and began to talk. He saw Mark Antony nod to his men and begin to move.

'Time to go, I think,' Maecenas said softly by his ear. 'We can use the house of Brucellus this evening. It is untouched by the riots and he promises to provide a fine meal for us. There is a lot to discuss.'

Octavian felt his friend's hand on his shoulder, gently pushing him away from the temple of Vesta. He resisted, suddenly sick of being made to walk in secrecy in his own city.

'Priestess!' he shouted, without warning.

Maecenas stiffened at his side.

'What are you doing?' he hissed. 'Half the Senate have spies here! Let me get you away first and then we can decide what to do.'

Octavian shook his head.

'Priestess!' he called again.

Quintina Fabia paused in the act of accepting a mantle of rich cloth from one of her followers. She looked around, finding him from the reaction of the crowd as they stared.

'I am Gaius Octavian, named as heir in the will you have just read,' he said clearly.

Maecenas groaned, keeping his dagger ready in case one of the crowd attacked them. None of them knew their enemies in the city, not yet.

'What do you want of me?' she said. It was rumoured that she had been an actress in her youth. Whether that was true or not, she had a performer's instinct, ignoring the offered cloak and stepping back onto the low platform.

'I wish to record a change of name with you, as the keeper of records.'

The priestess cocked her head slightly as she thought. The young man she faced in the crowd had just been given incredible wealth, if he could live long enough to lay hands on it. She glanced over to where Mark Antony watched the scene playing out between them. Her first instinct had been to tell Octavian to wait for an audience, but under that sulphurous gaze, the corner of her mouth quirked.

'What name would suit the heir to Rome?' she said.

'Only one,' Octavian replied. 'Gaius Julius Caesar, that I may honour the man whose name I will bear.'

Quintina Fabia smiled wider at that, delighted at the bravado of the young Roman. His friends stood in shock around him, while she wanted to applaud.

'You will need two witnesses of good standing to swear to your identity,' she said, after a moment's hesitation. 'Come and see me at noon, in the House of Virgins.' She paused again, watching Mark Antony from under her lashes. The consul was standing like a stunned ox.

'Welcome home, Octavian,' she said.

He nodded, mute. Away on his right, the consul began to stride off and Octavian turned to follow him.

'Consul!' he shouted.

Maecenas put a hand on his arm. 'Don't do anything rash, Octavian,' he murmured. 'Let him go.'

Octavian brushed off the hand and kept going.

'He was Caesar's friend,' he said. 'He will hear me.'

'Agrippa!' Maecenas called.

'Here.'

The big man was already moving, pushing through the packed crowd after Octavian. With a curse, the legionary Gracchus followed in their wake.

As Mark Antony watched the priestess talk with the young man, he shook his head, feeling sweat break out on his skin. It was too much to take in. The Senate had summoned him for a meeting at noon and he wanted to bathe first, so that he could face them fresh and clean. He turned away, his lictors and centurions all around him. He heard his title called across the forum but ignored it. He had barely gone twenty paces before the bristling awareness of his men made his temper rise. The group of four were pushing closer as he reached the edge of the crowd.

'Consul!' Octavian called again.

Mark Antony hunched his shoulders. His lictors were tense at being approached from behind and the two centurions had drifted back to put themselves between the groups. With a raised hand, Mark Antony halted them all. He could not be seen to scurry away, as if he had something to hide.

'What do you *want*?' he snapped.

Before him he saw a young man with grey eyes and dark blond hair bound at his neck. He supposed Octavian was in his early twenties, but he looked younger, with a smooth face and no sign of a beard. Somehow the sight of the young man served only to irritate Mark Antony further. He wanted nothing to do with some distant relative of Caesar intruding on him with his demands.

Octavian drew to a sudden stop at the harsh tone, the smile dying on his lips. As the consul watched, Octavian straightened subtly, his eyes hardening.

'Octavian . . .' Agrippa muttered warningly at his side. The lictors with the consul were not just an affectation of power.

With a word from Mark Antony, they would unstrap their axes and rods, driving anyone guilty of insult from the forum or killing them on the spot.

'I thought I would greet an old friend,' Octavian said. 'Perhaps I was mistaken.'

The reply seemed to rock Mark Antony. He closed his eyes for a moment, summoning his dignity.

'I am in error, Octavian. I have not congratulated you on your adoption.'

'Thank you,' Octavian said. 'I am pleased to see you thriving in such sad times. That is why I came to you. The will must be formally affirmed in Senate. I need a Lex Curiata. Will you propose it for me today?'

Mark Antony smiled tightly, shaking his head.

'You may have noticed the city is only now recovering from riots. There is more than enough business to occupy the Senate until the end of the month. Perhaps then I will ask for time for your request.'

Octavian stood very still, aware of the lictors watching him.

'It is just a formality. I thought that, for Caesar's memory, you might move a little faster.'

'I see. Well, I will do what I can,' Mark Antony replied carelessly. He turned and walked away quickly.

Octavian would have spoken again, but both Agrippa and Maecenas laid hands on him, holding him still.

'Don't say another word!' Agrippa said. 'Gods, you will get us all killed if you can't rule your mouth. You've made your request; now let him go.'

Maecenas was a study in concentration as he watched the consul depart the forum. He looked over at Gracchus, standing uncomfortably as if he were not sure of his place in the small group.

'I believe your part in this is at an end, Gracchus,' Maecenas said. 'I think it is time for you to report back to your master in Brundisium, is it not?'

Gracchus glowered at him.

'That's not for you to decide,' he said. 'Liburnius told me to keep your friend safe. I can send a message back along the road.'

Maecenas dropped his hand from Octavian's shoulder and stepped right up to the legionary.

'How can I put this, so you will understand?' he said. 'I would like to talk to my friend before he gets himself killed. I do not want your ears flapping while I do. You know we will be at the House of Virgins at noon – you heard the priestess yourself. So why don't you walk over there and wait for us?'

Gracchus stared back impassively, too old a hand to be intimidated. Without another word, he stalked off, his sandals clacking on the stones of the forum. Maecenas relaxed slightly. He raised his hands and moved his two friends into a clear spot. The crowd had thinned to avoid the consul's party of lictors, so it was not hard to find a place where they could not be overheard.

'By all the gods, Octavian! If the consul had thought it through, he could have had your inheritance in exchange for a single order. His lictors would have cut you down and Agrippa and me as well!'

'I thought he would help,' Octavian said stubbornly. 'So much has changed. I can barely take it all in.'

'Well, put your head in a fountain or something,' Maecenas snapped. 'You need to be sharp now.'

Both Agrippa and Octavian looked at him in surprise. He shook his head slowly.

'Have you any idea of the importance of that will to you, to those in power?'

Octavian shrugged. 'I know the sums are great, but until I can lay hands on them, I . . .'

'I'm not talking about the gold, Octavian! Though you are

now the richest man in the richest city of the world. I'm talking about the clients! Do you understand now?'

'Honestly, no,' Octavian said.

Agrippa looked similarly mystified and Maecenas took a deep breath. He had grown up in a world where such things were common knowledge, but he saw that neither of his friends truly appreciated Caesar's gift.

'Jupiter save me from common men,' he said. 'Noble houses secure their power with clients, families in their pay. You must know that much.'

'Of course,' Octavian said. 'But . . .'

'Caesar had *thousands* of them. He was famous for it. And they are all yours now, Octavian. His adoption of you gave you more than just a house name. You can call on the service of half of Rome, half of the legions of Rome if you want to. For all we know, Tribune Liburnius is now sworn to your service and Gracchus with him.'

Octavian furrowed his brow.

'I can't inherit them like a jewel or a house.'

'The adoption says you can,' Maecenas insisted. 'Oh, there will be a few malcontents who fall away – there are always honourless bastards. But you are the son of the divine Julius, Octavian. Have you realised? The oaths of service they swore will pass to you.'

'But I don't even know who they are!' Octavian said. 'What good does this talk of thousands do me? I have the clothes I am wearing and a horse somewhere back on the road to Brundisium. Until the Senate pass the Lex Curiata, it is all in the breeze anyway.'

Maecenas did not reply immediately. He looked across the forum to where the old senate house lay broken and burned, the worst of many scars they had seen in the city over the previous two days.

'There will be lists somewhere, but they *don't know* you have nothing, Octavian. From now on, you must play the game, for your life – and for the destruction of your enemies. Taking his name was brilliant. You want to see these Liberatores brought down? Then walk as the heir to a god and the richest man in Rome. Walk as one who can call down the wrath of Mars with a snap of his fingers.' He thought for a moment. 'It was a mistake asking for help from the consul. You may already have enough loyalty in the Senate to force a vote through without him.'

Octavian stared. 'I can walk any way I choose, but it will not bring me the gold I need, nor the clients.'

'You have a meeting at the House of Virgins in a couple of hours,' Maecenas said. 'Octavian, your favour is a token any man in Rome would want, from this day onwards. You do not need to seek them out. They will come to *you*.'

CHAPTER SEVEN

Octavian felt refreshed as he approached the House of Virgins. For a few coins, he, Agrippa and Maecenas had found a service-able bath-house and eaten at a roadside vendor. It was true he wore a second-hand toga loaned to him by one of Maecenas' friends, but he felt more confident. In the steam, with the bath-house slaves told to wait outside, they had made their plans. As the sun reached its height, he walked to the temple with confidence, striding past Gracchus and the guards outside as if he had every right to ignore them. They did not challenge him and in a few steps the three men were out of the heat and in cool rooms dedicated to worship. Perhaps older men would not have stared quite so openly, but the Vestals were renowned for their beauty as well as their innocence, a combination that interested even so jaded an appetite as that of Maecenas.

Quintina Fabia appeared from a stone doorway to welcome them. She had changed out of the morning's formal robes into a fine cotton stola that revealed her figure rather than keeping it hidden.

She approached Octavian with light steps, taking his hands in hers and kissing his cheek.

'I grieve for you and with you,' she said. 'I only wish Caesar's ashes could have been gathered for a tomb, but the riots were terrible. For a time, no one dared to go out. I am so sorry.'

Octavian blinked. He had not been expecting sympathy and it threatened to reach the part of him where sorrow was still raw.

'Thank you,' he said. 'I think you are the first person in the city to say that to me.'

'You must forgive the men in power, at least for that. They have had their hands full with the unrest. Honestly, you have no idea how bad it was for a time.'

'What of these "Liberatores"? Where are they hiding?' Octavian said.

'A few like Lucius Pella were killed by the mobs. The rest read the wind quickly enough after that and scattered to their estates and provinces. You will not find them here, not this year, though they have their supporters in the Senate still. In time, I do not doubt they will creep back to Rome, hiding their faces.' She shrugged, gripping his hands tightly. 'I am glad of it. They tried to remove the shame from what they did, but the citizens would not allow it. In all the chaos, there was at least that.'

'Shall we go through, Quintina?' Maecenas said.

She looked over at him.

'I see you are still around, Maecenas. How long has it been?'

'A few years, I suppose. You look well.'

'I am well enough. Shall I take your greetings to your mother, or will you visit her yourself?'

'You know each other?' Octavian said.

'I should do. Quintina Fabia is my aunt,' Maecenas replied without embarrassment. 'Not a favourite aunt or anything; just, you know, an aunt.'

'And he is far from my favourite nephew, lazy as he is,' she replied, though she smiled as she said it. 'But who is this fine and silent man?'

'Agrippa?' Maecenas said. 'The smell of fish should have warned you, Quin. He's a sailor, a rough and simple man, but loyal, like a good dog.'

Agrippa ignored Maecenas as his own hands were gripped in turn and he found himself flushing under the scrutiny.

'Maecenas thinks he is amusing, Agrippa,' she said. 'I have given up apologising for him.'

'There is no need,' he said. 'He is just nervous. It has been . . . an interesting morning.'

She cocked her head slightly.

'I am glad to see he has such friends,' she said. 'His mother despairs at the low company he usually keeps. Will you be the witnesses to the document of identity?'

Maecenas nodded, with a glare at Agrippa.

'Good, then come through.'

They followed her into the maze of rooms and halls beyond the main entrance. The House of Virgins was many times larger than the round temple that faced the forum. Young women scurried past in simple white shifts, often carrying sheaves of parchments or bound scrolls.

Quintina saw their interest and smiled.

'You assumed they would spend their days in prayer? My girls are part of the beating heart of Rome, gentlemen. Believe me when I say they know more about the laws of the city than the most august orators in the courts or the Senate. When their time in the temple is up, they have no difficulty finding good husbands, with households to run.'

'I never doubted it,' Maecenas said. He stumbled as he

tried to watch one long-legged young woman who had just passed them. Quintina saw the interest.

'Though, of course, until then they are children of the goddess. If their purity is, shall we say, removed, they are buried alive – and the man is impaled before the crowds.'

'A harsh punishment,' Maecenas said wistfully.

'But necessary. Men can be wolves, nephew.'

'Shocking, truly shocking.'

They reached a door of polished oak and the priestess led them in. On a large table lay piles of wax tablets and cut parchment pieces, along with ink and reed pens and all the paraphernalia of a business. Quintina seated herself behind the desk, leaving them standing.

'This is a simple matter. I have prepared the document to be signed in front of your witnesses. I will add my name and then, Octavian, you will be Gaius Julius Caesar.' She shuddered slightly as she said the name. 'I had not thought to hear it again so soon. It is a name of honour. I hope you bear it well.'

'I will,' Octavian said. He read the single page, then each man signed his name with the reed pen Quintina handed to them.

The priestess touched a lump of wax to the small flame of an oil lamp. She wore no rings, but used an iron stick imprinted with the seal of Vesta. Octavian repeated her action with Caesar's seal and she looked at the imprinted image with fond sadness.

'He was loved, you know. If you are half the man he was, you will make his shade proud.'

She picked up a tiny bell and rang it, waiting as the door opened and a woman of delicate beauty came in and took it from her hands. As the woman passed Maecenas, she made a slight sound and stared angrily back at him. He looked innocent.

'It is done, then. I hope you understand I could not allow

the argentarii to enter the house. It is unusual enough to have the three of you in these rooms. They are waiting for you in the garden on the far side. The gate there leads out to the Palatine.'

'Argentarii?' Octavian asked.

Quintina looked taken aback.

'The moneylenders. They have been applying to me all morning to see you. What did you expect?'

'I don't need a loan . . .' Octavian began.

Maecenas snorted. 'From this morning, you have the richest line of credit in Rome,' he said. 'So unless you intend to live on my funds, you do.'

Quintina shook her head.

'I don't think you understand,' she said. 'They are not here to offer credit. Caesar had deposits with the three largest societies of argentarii. I think they are here to ask what you want to do with the gold.'

Mark Antony felt a twinge of satisfaction at the sight of the senators facing him. Having been forced to use the theatre of Pompey for their meetings while the senate house was being rebuilt, they found that the sheer scale of the new building subtly undermined their authority. Their numbers had filled every space in the old building, but in the theatre they were surrounded by empty seats by the thousand, diminishing them in comparison. As consul, Mark Antony faced them on the stage, and there too the design favoured him. His voice boomed out as the architects had intended, while theirs sounded reedy and thin whenever they rose to speak.

The senators avoided one area of the theatre in particular. The stones had been scrubbed clean, so that it was hard to be certain of the exact place, but no one sat where Caesar had been killed.

Before the formal session, Mark Antony had waited patiently with the senators while scribes droned through a formal list of appointments, appeals and points of law that had been brought to their attention. He had been deep in conversation when his ear caught names he knew and he broke off to listen. Cassius had arranged a post for himself in Syria and Brutus had Athens. With Decimus Junius already in the north, many more had been given posts as far away as Jerusalem and Spain or Gaul, content to wait out the troubles in Rome until they could return safely. Mark Antony only wished they had all gone. Suetonius was still there, balding badly, with a sheen of thin hair brushed over the dome of his head. He was the last of the Liberatores to remain and was always in the presence of Bibilus, chief among his supporters and cronies. They made a tight group with Hirtius and Pansa, the senators already marked to succeed Mark Antony at the end of his consular year. Mark Antony could feel their dislike when they looked at him, but he did not let it ruffle his calm.

The first formal discussion concerned Caesar's will, particularly the bequests that were to be administered by the Senate. Those few who had not already heard were shocked to whispers by the sums involved. More than a hundred million sesterces would be given out to the people of Rome, a vast undertaking that would require identification of individuals by family and hundreds of trusted men to give out the silver. Mark Antony showed nothing of his inner turmoil as he waited through tedious speeches from men like Bibilus, demanding that the Senate delay the payments. Of course they would not want Caesar's generosity to be the talk of every street, as if that bird hadn't already flown.

'Senators,' Mark Antony said at last, allowing his voice to boom over their heads and silence Suetonius even as he began to speak. 'The citizens of Rome know very well what they have been given. In this one thing, we can only step back and allow it to go ahead. We have barely recovered from riots, gentlemen. Would you see them return? Caesar had funds in every major temple and fully six parts in ten of the Senate store of coins has his name marked against it. Let no man call us thieves when our popularity is already at such a low ebb. His bequests must be honoured and quickly.'

Suetonius rose again, his continually flushed face showing spite.

'Such funds would be better spent rebuilding the city. Why should they be given silver when they have done ten times as much damage over the previous month? I propose we hold back the funds until such time as the city has been restored – and the old senate house must be first among those projects. Should there be no consequences for the damage they have done to our city? Let them see their precious few coins going on something worthwhile. Let them see also that we are not afraid to offend their delicate sensibilities, or we will forever live in fear of the mob.'

Hundreds of voices grumbled loud agreement and Mark Antony felt his throat tighten with irritation. He wondered if Cassius was behind the mean-spirited point. Disbursing the funds would go a long way towards repairing their status in the city and yet other senators were jumping up to support Suetonius, their voices sounding tinny and harsh in the open space.

To Mark Antony's disgust, the vote to delay the payments passed by a huge majority and the Senate sat back on the benches, smug with the exercise of their authority. Mark Antony stepped aside temporarily while one of the Senate staff read a series of letters from legion officials in Gaul. He was fuming at the setback, more for what it revealed about his standing in the Senate than anything else. The men who ruled Rome had not missed his special treatment during the riots, it seemed. Now that he was aware of it, he could see the open animosity in many more than just those who were creatures of the Liberatores. He rubbed his chin, hiding his indignation. On one hand, the Senate were stretching their muscles, and on the other, he had a young fool naming himself Caesar, heir to half the gold in Rome. It was infuriating.

As the Senate meeting continued, Mark Antony made a decision in his private thoughts. The discussion had moved on to the legions at Brundisium, with the Senate calling for a vote of censure. Hundreds of eyes stared his way while they waited for the consul to continue with the formal structures. Mark Antony returned to the rostrum, seeing his salvation.

'Senators, we have heard calls for the legions in Brundisium to be punished,' he began. If he had judged them right, he could force them to go in the direction he wanted. 'In normal times, I would agree, but these are *far* from normal times. Those legion commanders were Caesar's men, almost without exception. That name is still a talisman for the citizens. You have said we should not fear them and I accept that, but should we poke and prod at their pride until they are forced to react in anger? Can the Senate stand another blow to the esteem in which we are held? I think not. Like so many others, the Brundisium legions were lost without strong leadership from Rome. However, that is in the past. Order has been restored and it ill behoves us to seek petty revenge. Some of you have talked blithely of having the legions decimated, but have you considered how Rome will react to such news? One man in ten, beaten to death by his fellows, and for what? For staying where they were while Rome was in chaos. It would be a thankless task for any man to give that order.'

His heart leapt as he saw the bulk of Bibilus come to his feet to speak. Suetonius was up as well. Mark Antony took a deep breath, knowing his own future was in play. He acknowledged Bibilus first, taking a seat while the other man spoke.

'I am astonished and sickened to hear the authority of the

Senate discussed in such a fashion,' Bibilus began. His cronies and supporters made noises of assent, spurring him on. 'We are discussing legions under lawful authority who refused orders at a time of national crisis – and the consul would have us forgive them without punishment? It is unconscionable. Instead, I suggest to this house that only one of consular authority can take the will of the Senate and see it carried out. I recommend that Consul Mark Antony travel to that city and decimate each of the six legions there. The public death of a few thousand common soldiers will make the point for us far better than any rhetoric or noble speeches. It will be a mark that legions will remember in the future when mutiny rears its head once more. "Remember Brundisium" they will say, and it will die still-born before it has even begun.'

There were cheers then and Bibilus patted the air for quiet.

'Not many of us here have been quite as fortunate as the consul in the recent riots. Unlike the leader of this house, we have lost property and slaves to fire and looting. Perhaps if he had suffered with us, he would have a better understanding of the stakes involved!'

A great roar of appreciation echoed around the theatre. Mark Antony kept his face a mask. It was true his properties had remained untouched in the riots while those of other senators had been deliberately targeted. He had been a friend of Caesar, his name whispered as the one who had delivered the oration, who had inspired the crowds to revenge for the assassination. The Senate were still seen as the men who had brought Caesar down and that rankled with them.

As Bibilus sat, Mark Antony rose, judging the moment was right and preferring not to let the poisonous Suetonius speak as well.

'I am a servant of Rome, as Senator Bibilus knows full well. If it is the will of this house that I carry your orders to Brundisium, I will do so. However, let my objections be made part of the record. Such an action achieves nothing but revenge at a time when we must be unified. I call the matter to a vote.'

The voting was over in a matter of moments, with a triumphant jeer ringing out through the theatre. Bibilus sat back with his friends patting him on the back. They had shown what they thought of Caesar's favourite.

Mark Antony continued to play his part, hiding his satisfaction. He waited through a few minor speeches and discussions, hardly contributing, until the senators were ready to depart. He endured Bibilus' insolent triumph as the man levered his bulk up to leave, surrounded by his favourites. Mark Antony shook his head slightly. Julius had never spoken of what passed between those two men, but Mark Antony had made a few enquiries of his own. Caesar had taken a group of child slaves from the ex-consul's house, passing them to families without children. Bibilus had replaced them with adults and never bought a child since that day. The truth was there to be read and Mark Antony wondered if Bibilus had resumed his old cruelties now that Caesar was gone. He made a private vow to have the man watched. He had been ruined once and could be again.

As Mark Antony came out into the open air, the Campus Martius stretched into the distance, the great training field of the city. It was almost hidden from view by the loyal legions camped there and he felt a pang of doubt. If he succeeded in taking control of the army at Brundisium, it would be a challenge to the new authority of the Senate. The legions before him on the Campus might be ordered to march against him. As his lictors gathered, he firmed his jaw. He had come too far, risen too far, to sink back into the mass of men claiming to rule Rome. He had Caesar's example to follow. Men like Bibilus and Suetonius would not be able to stop him. For the first time in years, Mark Antony thought he understood Julius a little better. He felt alive with the challenge and the tasks ahead. To rule Rome, he needed the legions at Brundisium. With them at his command, he would be immune from anything the Senate could do. That prize was surely worth the risk.

CHAPTER EIGHT

Evening was coming on in smooth shades of grey by the time Octavian reached the street on the Aventine hill where the consul had his main property. He yawned, suppressing tiredness. From the moment at dawn when he had heard his legacy from Caesar, he had hardly stopped moving. He'd visited three different homes in the city, complete with slaves and staff, all of whom were now his. It was dizzying. He had come into Rome with nothing, but it was somehow fitting that Caesar's will had been the agent of his change in fortune. Alive, Caesar had been unpredictable, given to ignoring laws and rules as he saw the fastest way to achieve his objectives. Octavian had learned from him. If he hesitated, those who might oppose him would have time to gather their strength.

It was strange to see the consul's property pristine and untouched. On the streets nearby, Octavian had passed through great swathes of rubble and ash, seeing views of the seven hills that had not existed for a century or more. There were already builders and sweating workmen in those places, paid by the wealthy owners. The vistas created by destruction would not last long. Yet Mark Antony's homes remained, his reward for firing the emotions of the city.

'Maecenas and I both think this is a terrible idea,' Agrippa said, as they strode up the hill.

Gracchus was with the three men, in the main because he had made himself useful all day. His motive for sudden loyalty was obvious and Maecenas baited him at every opportunity, but another sword was undeniably useful and Octavian had not sent him away.

Octavian did not reply and the four of them reached the massive oak door set into the wall that ran alongside the cobbled street. There was a small iron grille and Agrippa bent down to peer through it, raising his eyebrows at the courtyard within. It was chaotic, with more than a dozen slaves running to and fro, loading a carriage and bringing draught horses into position.

'It seems we have chosen a busy time for the consul,' he said. 'There is no need to do this, Octavian.'

'I say there is. And you will have to get used to the new name. I have the right to it, by blood and adoption.'

Agrippa shrugged.

'I will try to remember, Julius. Gods, it doesn't sit well to call you that.'

'It will get easier. Use makes master, my friend.'

In the courtyard, one of the scurrying slaves had noticed the big man peering in and approached them, making waving motions with his hands.

'Whatever you want, the consul is not available,' he said. 'If it is official business, see your senator.'

'Tell him Caesar is here,' Octavian said. 'I think he will come out for me.'

The slave's eyes widened.

'Yes, sir. I will let him know.' The man trotted away, looking back over his shoulder every few paces until he had disappeared into the main house.

'There's nothing to be gained here; you do know that?' Maecenas said. 'Even your excited new dog knows it, don't you, Gracchus?' Gracchus merely glared at him, saying nothing. 'At best, you will anger a powerful man.'

Mark Antony came out into the courtyard, looking harassed and flushed. He gave orders as he went and more men and women scurried around him, staggering under chests and bales tied with leather.

The consul made a gesture to a man they had not yet seen, presumably guarding the door on the inside. They heard the rattle of iron as a bar was lifted and bolts drawn. It opened smoothly and Mark Antony stopped a pace within his property, regarding them with impatience in every feature. His gaze took in the fact that they were armed and his mouth firmed.

'What is so important that you must trouble me in my home? Do you think the name of Caesar has such power still?'

'It brought you out,' Octavian replied.

Mark Antony waited a beat. Following the letter of the Senate's orders, he could have gone to Brundisium with just a few servants. The reality was that he was moving his household, including his wife and children. He did not know when he would return and his mind was on the labyrinthine politics of the Senate, not the young man who called himself Caesar.

'It must have escaped your notice that I am busy. See me when I return to Rome.'

'Consul, men speak of you as one who was Caesar's friend. I have read the text of your oration and it was . . . noble, no matter what came next. Yet the terms of his will have not been ratified in Senate and will not be, without your support. What of the legacy to the people of Rome?'

'I'm sorry. The Senate have already voted. They will pay the legacy only when the damage to the city is restored. I will

115

be away from Rome for a time, on orders from the Senate. There is nothing more I can do.'

Octavian stared at him, hardly able to believe what he was hearing. 'I came to you in peace, because I thought you, of all men, would support me.'

'What you thought is no concern of mine,' Mark Antony snapped. He turned to the unseen figure on his right. 'Close the door now.'

It began to creak shut and Octavian put out a hand to the wood.

'Consul! I will have justice, with you or not. I will see Caesar's assassins brought down, no matter what they call themselves or where they hide! Will you stand with them, against the honour of your friend?'

He heard Mark Antony snort in disgust as he walked away and the pressure on the door increased as the man inside threw his weight against it. It slammed shut in his face. Octavian hammered on it, enraged.

'Consul! Choose a side! If you stand with them, I will . . .'

'By the *gods*, grab hold of him, would you?' Maecenas said.

He and Agrippa took Octavian by the shoulders and pulled him away from pounding on the consul's door.

'That may have been the worst idea you ever had,' Maecenas said grimly as they walked Octavian down the hill. 'Why not shout out all your plans to the Senate, perhaps?'

Octavian shook him off, walking in stiff rage and looking back at the consul's door as if he could force it open with anger alone.

'He had to be told. If he has the sense to see it, I am his natural ally. If he wasn't such a blind fool.'

'Did you think he would welcome you with open arms?' Maecenas said. 'He is a consul of Rome!'

'And I am Caesar's son and heir. That is the key to all locks, with or without Mark Antony.'

116

Maecenas looked away, unsettled by his friend's intensity.

'It's late,' Agrippa said. 'What do you say to going back to the house on the Esquiline?'

Octavian smothered a yawn at the very thought of sleep. The house was one of five he had inherited that morning, the deeds presented to him by the argentarii.

'Without a law passed in Senate, I am not yet the official heir to Caesar,' he said. A thought struck him, so that he stopped, bringing the small group to a halt. 'But thousands heard the priestess read the will. That was enough for the argentarii. What does it matter if the law isn't passed? The people know.'

'The people have no power,' Agrippa said. 'No matter how they riot, they are still helpless.'

'That is true,' Octavian replied. 'But there were soldiers there as well. The legions in the Campus know that I am Caesar. And they *do* have power, enough for anything.'

By the time night fell, the consul and his retinue were barely three miles out of Rome, trundling along the flat roads east. Mark Antony had called a brief halt at the walls of the city, dismounting to burn a brazier of incense to Janus. The god of beginnings and gates was a suitable patron for everything he hoped to achieve.

Over a hundred men and women travelled with him. His wife Fulvia was at the heart of it, with their two sons, Antyllus and Paulus, and her daughter Claudia from her first marriage. Around them, dozens of scribes, guards and slaves marched or rode. The reins of his horse were tied to a flat-sided carriage where his wife lounged on cushions, shaded from the vulgar gaze. He could hear his boys bickering through the wooden walls, still annoyed that he had refused their demands to ride ahead with him. Only Fulvia knew all his plans and she was far from a prattler. He jumped down to the road and strode along, stretching his legs for the ride ahead.

The legions at Brundisium had been loyal to Julius, loyal enough to refuse the orders of a Senate they saw as tainted by the Liberatores. That was the revelation that had come to him while Bibilus spoke in spite. Mark Antony had not planned to be the champion of those who had loved Caesar, but he could take the role. The legions of Brundisium would surely follow him if he asked in Caesar's name.

As he walked alongside the carriage, the face of Octavian came to mind and Mark Antony grunted in exasperation. The young man was no more than a distraction, at a time when he could not afford to be distracted. Six legions waited at the coast, no doubt in fear of the Senate's anger. They had not yet mutinied, at least not formally. If he found the words to call them, they would be his to command. It was exactly the sort of grand stroke Julius would have attempted and the thought warmed him.

With the energy of a younger man, Mark Antony put his foot on the step and leapt up onto the carriage, clambering in through the narrow door to where his wife and children were eating. Fulvia and her daughter were playing a game with a long string wound about their fingers. They were in mid-laughter as he appeared among them, the sound cut short. Mark Antony nodded to his two sons and stepdaughter, ruffling the hair of Antyllus as he stepped over him.

In her thirties, Fulvia had broadened across the hips and waist, though her skin and black hair were still lustrous. Claudia moved to give him space and Fulvia held out her arms to her husband. The consul almost fell into them in the low space, landing with a gasp on the bench as his feet tangled in cloth. Paulus yelped and Claudia smacked his leg, making the younger boy glare. Mark Antony leaned close to Fulvia, speaking into her ear.

118

'I think I have waited my whole life for a chance like this,' he said, smiling.

She kissed him on the neck, looking up at him in adoration.

'The omens are good, husband. My soothsayer was amazed at the signs this morning.'

Mark Antony's high spirits dampened slightly, but he nodded, pleased that she was happy. If he had learned one thing from the years at Caesar's side, it was that omens and entrails were not as important as quick wits and strength.

'I'm going ahead. You'll see me in Brundisium and I hope with more than just a few guards at my back.'

She winked at him, smiling even as their sons demanded to know what he meant. Mark Antony cuffed their heads affectionately, kissed Claudia and Fulvia goodbye, then opened the door and vaulted down to the road, leaving his wife to deal with the endless questions.

In just moments, he had gained the saddle of his gelding and untied the reins. His personal guards were mounted and ready, keen to be off. On a Roman road, they had no fear of bad ground in the moonlight. They would be twenty miles clear by dawn.

The rising sun brought pale light through the blown-glass windows high in the walls. Maecenas sat back, enjoying the sense of utter relaxation that came from a private bath-house. Steam filled his lungs with every breath and he could barely see his companions.

Caesar's town house had been in a state of half-life when they entered it, with most of the furniture covered in great sheets of dusty, brown cloth. In just a few hours, the staff had lit the fires and the floors were already warm enough to walk on in bare feet. In the presence of a new owner, they had scavenged fresh fruit from one of the markets and begun to prepare a cold meal. Maecenas thought idly that he was sitting where

119

Caesar himself had sat. Where Caesar *still* sat, he corrected himself with a smile, looking through the mist at Octavian. Dripping with sweat and steam, his friend stared into some private vision, his muscles as tight as ropes in his arms and shoulders. Looking at him, Maecenas remembered his friend collapsing, sightless and pale. He did not want to see that again.

'Are you ready yet for the cold bath or the massage?' he said. 'It will relax you.'

At least Gracchus was not present. Maecenas had given him the task of bringing life back to the house. The legionary was still working hard to remain and Octavian had not objected. Despite his misgivings, it was almost pleasant to deal with one whose greed for gold made him transparent.

'Agrippa?' Maecenas asked again. 'What about you?'

'Not yet,' Agrippa rumbled, his voice echoing oddly in the steam.

'Oct . . . Caesar?' Maecenas said, catching himself.

Octavian opened his eyes, smiling tiredly.

'Thank you. I must get used to the new name. But we are private here and I do not want to be overheard. Stay.'

Maecenas shrugged slightly, letting the warm air flow out of his lungs and then sucking in a deep breath.

'I hope today will not be as busy as yesterday, that's all I am saying,' Maecenas said. 'I seem to have gone from a relaxed holiday with friends to the most unpleasant levels of excitement. I have suffered through sea voyages and galloping horses, as well as arguments and threats from sad little men like that tribune. I think perhaps we should relax here for a few days. That would be a tonic for us all. At least I slept well enough. Caesar kept a fine house; I'll give him that.'

'I don't have time to waste,' Octavian said suddenly. 'The murderers of Caesar have gone to ground and it is my task to dig them out and kill them with a spade. If you were in my place, you would do the same.'

120

'Well, I *am* in your place, or at least in the same bath-house. I am not certain of that at all,' Maecenas replied. He scratched his testicles as he spoke, then leaned back against the cooler tiles, enjoying the heat. Of the three of them, he sat closest to the simmering copper trough that thickened the steam in the room, delighting in the weakness that deep warmth brings.

'I need information, Maecenas. You say I have thousands of clients sworn to support me, but I don't know who they are. I must have all Caesar's properties searched and catalogued and his informers contacted, to see if they will continue their work for me. I imagine I need to pay the stipend for thousands more, so I will need educated men by the hundred to arrange such things.'

Maecenas smirked. 'I can tell that you have not grown up with servants. You do not manage so many yourself, or you would end up doing nothing else. There will be estate managers on the staff; give the job to them. The sun is barely up, but they'll have what you need by noon, just to please the new master. Give them the chance to run themselves ragged for you. They love it, believe me. It gives their lives purpose and frees the noble owner from tedious details.'

Agrippa rubbed a hand down his face, gasping in the heat.

'Listening to you is always an education, Maecenas,' he said wryly. 'How your slaves must love you, to have their lives given meaning in such a way.'

'They do,' Maecenas replied complacently. 'I am like the rising sun to them, the first name they think as they wake and the last before they sleep. When Caesar here allows us a few days of relaxation, I will show you my estate in the hills near Mantua. It will take your breath away, for sheer beauty.'

'I look forward to it,' Agrippa replied. 'For now, though, I have had enough of sipping my breath. I'm for the cold and the massage table.'

'Wait just a little longer, my friend,' Octavian said as Maecenas began to stand up. 'Wait and tell me if I have thought it through well enough.' Both men settled back and he went on. 'The Senate are seasoned with Liberatores, or at least their supporters. The rest have fled, but we can depend on the Senate to protect them even so, if only to secure their own interests. That much we have learned. They cannot support me, and Mark Antony is my natural ally, if he would but realise it. Still, wherever they've sent him, he is away from the city for the present, removed from the board. Those who are left are my enemies almost to a man.'

'I don't see how that is cause for celebration,' Maecenas said. 'They are the ones who make the laws, in case you had forgotten.'

'But they enforce them with the legions,' Octavian said. 'Legions that Caesar gathered in the Campus for a campaign. Legions that were either formed by him or sworn to him. As I see it, I can claim that loyalty, just as I can with his clients.'

Maecenas sat straight, his languor vanishing.

'That is what you meant last night? The legions have spent the last month walking the streets of the city, killing rioters and enforcing a curfew. They are the Senate's men now, no matter what Caesar intended for them. You cannot seriously be thinking they will mutiny for you.'

'Why not?' Octavian said angrily. 'With Mark Antony out of the city, they are ruled by the same toothless traitors who granted amnesty to Caesar's murderers. No one has answered for that, not yet. I have seen their loyalty, Maecenas. I have seen it in Gaul and in Egypt. They will not have forgotten him. And I am his son, a Caesar.'

Maecenas stood up and opened the door to the outer rooms. A fire crackled in the grate and two male slaves came over immediately to do his bidding. With a sharp gesture, Maecenas sent them outside, so that he could not be overheard. The steam had grown too thick and his senses swam just as he needed to be sharp. In the colder air, he drew deep breaths.

'Join me in the plunge pool, Caesar. It will clear your head before you commit us to a course which can only see us all crucified for treachery.'

Octavian glared at him but rose with Agrippa and crossed the room to where a deep pool sat dark and undisturbed. The water was near freezing, but Maecenas stepped down into it without hesitation, his skin prickling in goosebumps as it tightened. Agrippa joined him with a hiss of breath and Octavian slid over the edge, bending his knees so that the chill water reached his neck. When he spoke again, his teeth chattered so much that he could barely be understood.

'You think I should live in the sun, M-Maecenas? As you said Alexander would choose, if he could see his whole life laid out before him? I d-did not believe it then and I don't now. I cannot rest until the Liberatores are all dead. Do you understand? I will risk your life and mine a thousand times until that is true. Life *is* risk! I feel the shade of Caesar watching me and who else will bring him justice? Not Mark Antony. It falls to me and I will not waste a single day.'

The cold bit to the heart of him and his arms were almost too numb to heave himself out and sit on the stone edge. Agrippa was just a moment behind, while Maecenas remained, his brown arms and legs in sharp contrast to the pale skin of the rest of his body. The cold had numbed him, but his heart raced even so.

'All right,' he said, putting out an arm. 'Pull me up.' Agrippa gripped his hand and lifted him out. 'I do not desert my friends just because they have decided to infuriate the Senate and the legions of Rome.'

CHAPTER NINE

The group that mounted horses outside Caesar's town house on the Esquiline was considerably larger than the four weary men who had entered the night before. Octavian had followed Maecenas' advice and given orders to the most senior slaves to act as factors for him. They were visibly determined to do well for the new master. Bringing in legion-trained mounts from one of the other properties was just the first of a thousand tasks. A dozen other men had gone out from the house on errands to all the holdings of Caesar, including the garden estate on the Tiber, as it had not yet been passed to the people of Rome. What records and accounts existed would be found and made ready.

Maecenas had insisted Gracchus also bathe before accompanying them. The soldier was still damp-haired and flushed from his hurried wash, but they all felt better for being clean. It was as if they could put the mistakes and trials of the past behind them, scraped away like the black muck that came off with the brass strigils and oil.

Turning west down the hill, the wary group drew the attention of a few street boys. Octavian assumed they were after stray coins, but there were no outstretched hands and they kept their distance. He wondered if they had been sent by someone to keep an eye on his progress, the cheapest spies Rome had to offer. Yet every street they crossed added more to the crowd and the newcomers were not mere urchins. Men and women pointed him out in hushed tones, their eyes swivelling in interest as friends hissed the name of Octavian or, more often, Caesar. They too walked with him, until there were dozens then hundreds in the wake of the horses, all heading to the Campus Martius.

Octavian sat his mount stiff-backed, in a set of armour that had been fitted to him by the house staff. Maecenas was resplendent in armour and cloak, though as far as Octavian knew, he held no formal rank. For himself, he had considered a toga, but unlike Maecenas, he had commanded Roman soldiers, and the officer's cloak sent a signal to those who watched for such things.

As they came to an open market square, the busy crowd fell silent and again he could hear the name of Caesar like a breeze through them. His group swelled again, doubling and redoubling in size until it felt as if he led a procession through the heart of the city. By the time he reached the foot of the Capitoline, he was surrounded by hundreds of men and women, all craning for a glimpse of the single man at the centre. His new name was called and shouted from groups and always the numbers swelled. Octavian kept his gaze stern as he walked the horses onward.

'Don't look now,' Maecenas said, bringing his horse in close, 'but I think we're being followed.'

Octavian gave a snort, the break of tension almost reducing him to undignified laughter. He went on up the Capitoline hill and did not pause when the horses reached the crest. Pompey's theatre lay below on the other side, a vast building three times the size of the old senate house in pale stone. There were no flags flying on the roof as the crowd streamed down the hill. The Senate were not in session that day, though Octavian did not doubt they would have heard of his progress across the city. He smiled grimly to himself. Let them hear, he thought. Let them wonder.

At a crossroads, Agrippa nudged him at the sight of Roman legionaries standing guard. Those men looked on in sheer astonishment at the undisciplined rabble coming out of the city. Octavian could see the soldiers arguing as he passed and he did not look back to see if they had joined the rest. They would find out soon enough what he intended.

Beyond Pompey's theatre, the vast space of the Campus Martius opened up, though it was far from empty. For centuries, it had been the place where Romans exercised and came to vote, but the field of war was also the muster spot for legions about to march. Those who had gathered at Julius Caesar's orders for the campaign against Parthia had been there for much longer than they had planned or expected and the marks were everywhere, from toilet pits and trenches to thousands of oiled leather tents and even small buildings dotted around the plain. Octavian led his column towards the centre of them.

The Seventh Victrix and Eighth Gemina legions were in a twin camp laid out to specifications created long before by Caesar's uncle, the consul Marius. Nothing had changed in almost half a century and Octavian felt a wave of nostalgia as he reached the outer boundary. Only respect for the ancient Roman plain had prevented the legions from raising a great barrier of earth as set down in the regulations. Instead, the camp was marked with massive wicker baskets, tall as a man and filled with stone and earth, a symbolic structure rather than a true obstacle.

As he approached the line, Octavian glanced back and blinked in surprise as he saw how many had come from the city. At least a thousand walked with him, their faces bright as if they were on a public holiday. He shook his head in silent amazement, then took heart from it. This was the power of the name he had been given. It was also a reminder that they supported Caesar rather than the Senate that had killed him.

The afternoon sun was hot on his back as he halted. Two legionaries stood at the entrance to the encampment, staring forward without looking at the man facing them. Octavian sat his mount patiently, patting the animal on its broad neck. He had seen soldiers entering the camp ahead of him, racing to carry the news. He was content to wait for the officers to come to him, accepting the advantage it gave him as his due.

As if echoing his thoughts, Maecenas leaned in close to speak in a low voice.

'No doubts now, my friend. Show them a little noble arrogance.'

Octavian nodded stiffly.

Four horsemen came trotting through the camp, visible over the boundary from some way off as they moved down the wide avenue. From the distance of a few hundred paces, Octavian could see that two were cloaked, wearing ornate armour in silver, with markings of brass that spread down onto layered leather tiles over their bare thighs. Their companions wore simple togas, with a large purple stripe running along the edge.

Agrippa looked at Octavian in satisfaction. It had not been that long ago that they had struggled to get a meeting with a single military tribune in Brundisium. Yet here were two legates and two military tribunes, riding out to meet a man who had not even asked for them.

'It seems the name of Caesar still has currency,' Agrippa murmured.

Octavian did not reply, his expression set in stern lines.

The Roman officers reined in facing the crowd from the

city, fixing their collective gaze on Octavian. The citizens fell silent and tension grew in the still air. It was a matter of delicacy, as the man with the lower rank should greet the other, but no one knew for certain what rank Octavian held. After an uncomfortable pause, the senior legate cleared his throat.

'How should I address you?' he asked.

Octavian looked him over, seeing a man in his late forties with grey temples and a world-weary air. The legate's face was lined and weathered by a dozen campaigns, but his eyes were bright with interest, almost youthful.

'Why, address me as Gaius Julius Caesar,' Octavian replied, as if puzzled. 'Son of the man who formed your legion and commanded your utter loyalty. You are Legate Marcus Flavius Silva of the Seventh Victrix. My father spoke well of you.'

The older man rested his hands on the pommel of his saddle, staring.

'I am honoured to hear that, Caesar,' he said. 'My companion legate . . .'

'. . . is Titus Paulinius of the Eighth Gemina,' Octavian interrupted. 'We have met before, in Gaul.'

'It's him,' the other legate muttered. The tribunes might have introduced themselves then, but Flavius Silva nodded and spoke first.

'In honour of Caesar, you are welcome in the camp. Might I enquire what business has brought such a crowd from Rome? I have had nervous reports for the last hour. The riots are not yet forgotten here, not by my legion.'

He looked with distaste at the crowd behind Octavian, but they only stared back, unafraid and fascinated. Octavian chewed the inside of his lip for a moment. He suspected the legates would be easier to handle if every move and word was not witnessed. He had not planned on having such an audience.

He turned his horse on a tight rein and addressed the crowd.

'Go to your homes now,' he ordered. 'You will know when I have remade Rome. It will be all around you.'

Legate Silva gaped at his words, exchanging a worried glance with his colleagues. Octavian continued to glare at the crowd, waiting. At the back, more than one child was held aloft to see the new Caesar, but the rest were already turning. They were not sure what they had witnessed, but the lure had been inescapable and they were not displeased. Octavian watched them go, shaking his head in wonderment.

'They just wanted to see me,' he said, under his breath.

Agrippa clapped him on the shoulder, his voice a low rumble.

'Of course they did. They loved Caesar. Remember that when you are dealing with the Senate.'

When Octavian looked back, it was to see the legion officers watching him closely.

'Well?' he said, remembering Maecenas' words on Roman arrogance. 'Lead me in, gentlemen. I have a great deal to do.'

The two legates and their tribunes turned their horses into the camp, with Octavian, Agrippa and Maecenas riding together on the wide road. Gracchus brought up the rear, praying to his household god that he would not be killed that day. He had hardly been able to believe the presence of four such senior men coming out to meet Octavian. He decided to send another message to Tribune Liburnius back at the port as soon as he had a moment to himself.

The command tent of the Seventh Victrix legion was as large as a single-floored house in some respects, supported by wooden beams and a lattice above their heads that would withstand even a gale. The horses were taken by experienced grooms and led away to be watered and fed. Octavian entered to find a long table laid with thick vellum maps piled at one end. Legate Silva saw his glance.

'Routes and plans for Parthia, months of work,' he explained. 'All wasted now, of course. I have not offered my condolences, Caesar. I can hardly tell you the grief felt among the men for your loss. The riots went some way to keeping our minds off the assassination, but it is still keen, still sharp.'

As one, they drew up chairs and took places around the table. Octavian inclined his head in thanks.

'You broach the very matter that brought me here,' he said.

A legionary chose that moment to bring in wine and water on a tray. Octavian waited for the drinks to be served and raised his cup.

'To Caesar, then,' he said. The legion men were already echoing the toast as he added, 'And to revenge on his killers.'

Flavius Silva sputtered into his wine cup, almost choking. He was red-faced by the time he could breathe clearly again.

'You don't waste words, do you?' he said, still coughing into his fist. 'Is that your purpose in coming here? Caesar, I . . .'

'You have failed in your duty, your sworn oath,' Octavian snapped. He hammered his fist on the table with a crash. '*Both* of you! The Father of Rome is murdered in daylight, while you drink wine on the Campus and *what*? What happens? Do his loyal soldiers enter Rome and demand the trial and execution of his killers? Do you march on the senate house? No, *none* of these things. The Senate declare an amnesty for murdering filth and you accept it meekly, reduced to keeping order in the city while those who *do* care for justice and honour take to the streets! How sickening, that those without power must do what you will not – and then see you draw swords on them, serving the very masters responsible for the crime! You asked me why I came here, Legate Silva? It was to call you to account for your failures!'

The legionary with the wine jugs had fled. Both legates and tribunes were leaning away from the table as Octavian rose from his seat and harangued them. They reacted as if his words were the lashes of a whip, staring down at the table in horrified humiliation.

'How *dare* you sit there while the dogs who killed your master, your *friend*, still sit in the Senate and congratulate each other on their success? Caesar trusted you, legates. He knew that you would stand for him when all the world was against him. Where is that honour now? Where is that trust?'

'The Senate . . .' Titus Paulinius began.

Octavian rounded on him, leaning over the table in his fury.

'The Senate did *not* command your legions until you meekly handed them over. You are Caesar's right hand, not the servants of those old men. You have forgotten yourselves.'

Legate Flavius Silva stood slowly, his face ashen.

'Perhaps,' he said. 'I cannot speak for Titus, but when we had the news, I did not know what to do. The world changed in a day and the senators were quick to send new orders. Perhaps I should not have accepted them.' He took a deep, slow breath. 'It does not matter now. With your permission, I will see to my affairs.'

Octavian froze, struck by the precise phrasing Flavius Silva had used. It was too late to take back what he had said and he thought furiously as the legate waited for permission to leave. Octavian had accused him of vast and irretrievable dishonour. He knew with sudden clarity that Flavius Silva would take his own life, the only choice Octavian had left him.

He had depended on a show of Roman arrogance to bring him to this point. He could not retreat from it. He firmed his mouth, resting his fists on the table.

'Sit *down*, Legate,' he said. 'Your responsibilities cannot be so easily evaded. You will live, so that you can put right every stain on the honour of the Seventh Victrix.'

Outside the tent, he could hear the sound of marching men. The two legates were instantly aware of it, as a ship's captain might notice a change of course almost before it had begun.

Flavius Silva lost some of the wintry look in his eyes, dragged back by Octavian's scorn and the noise of his men moving. He resumed his seat, though his gaze flickered to the great flap of the door and the dust-speckled light that shone into the darker tent.

'I am at your command, Caesar,' he said. The words brought colour back to his pale cheeks and Octavian allowed himself to relax a fraction.

'Yes, you are,' he replied. 'And I need you, Flavius Silva. I need men like you – and you, Titus. Men who remember Caesar the Imperator and everything he achieved. The Senate will not shelter murderers from us. We will root them out, one by one.'

The noise beyond the tent had grown and Octavian frowned at the interruption, just when he needed to weigh every word. He gestured to the door without looking.

'Maecenas, see what is going on, would you?'

His friend rose and Octavian was unaware of the look of awe in his eyes. Maecenas nodded slowly and walked to the door. He was gone only a few moments.

'Caesar, you should see this,' he said.

Octavian looked up at the formal use of the new name, raising his eyebrows. Maecenas would not waste his time at such a moment, not after what he had just witnessed. Of all of them, he knew the knife edge Octavian walked with every word and step. Octavian glanced back at Flavius Silva, but he looked blank, still in shock from his reprieve.

'Very well,' Octavian replied. He went to the door and the legates rose behind him.

As he threw back the leather flap, Octavian stood still. The tent was surrounded by legionaries in lorica armour. They bore shields and swords and the standard-bearers of the Seventh Victrix had taken position on either side of the command tent, so that Octavian looked up at fluttering standards and a legion eagle. Once more he was reminded of the legacy of his family.

Marius had made the eagle the symbol of Roman might, from Egypt to Gaul, replacing a host of banners with just one. It gleamed in the sun.

Octavian forced a semblance of calm. He had survived meeting the legates, but the reality was that he was powerless. The sight of the ranks stretching into the distance on all sides made his heart sink. He raised his head, suddenly stubborn, and glared round at them. They would not see him afraid, no matter what happened. He owed Caesar that much.

They saw him come out, a young man in armour with hair almost gold in the sunlight. They saw him look up at the eagle standard of the Seventh Victrix and they began to cheer him and thump their fists against their shields in a crashing thunder that rolled across the Campus Martius as far as the city beyond. It spread from the first ranks to those so far behind they could not even make out Caesar, come to inspect his legion.

Octavian struggled to keep his astonishment hidden. He saw Legate Flavius Silva come out, with Titus Paulinius close behind. Maecenas, Agrippa and Gracchus stepped to the side so that they could see what he saw. The sound built and built until it was a physical force, making the air shake and thumping in Octavian's ears.

'We have not forgotten Caesar,' Flavius Silva shouted at his side. 'Give us the chance to prove to you we have honour still. We will not let you down again, I swear it.'

Octavian looked to Titus Paulinius and was astonished to see the brightness of tears in the other man's eyes. Paulinius nodded, saluting.

'The Eighth Gemina is yours to command, Caesar,' he said above the thunder.

Octavian raised his hands for quiet. It took a long time, spreading out from the point where he stood until even those a hundred ranks back grew quiet. In the delay, he had found words.

'Yesterday, I believed Roman honour was dead, lost in the murder of a good man. But I see I was wrong, that it survives here, in you. Be still now. Let me tell you the days to come. I am Gaius Julius Caesar, I am the *divi filius* – son of a god of Rome. I am the man who will show the Senate they are not above the law, that the law rests in the *least* of those among you. That you are the lifeblood of the city and that you will stand against all enemies of the state – in foreign lands and *within*. Let yesterday be forgotten. Let that be your new oath today.'

The hammering clamour began again as they heard and understood. Spears jabbed into the air as his words were shouted into a thousand ears down the ranks.

'Prepare them to march, legates. Today, we will occupy the forum. When we stand in the heart of the city as its guardians, we will wipe out the stain of what went before.'

He looked towards the walls of Rome. He could see Pompey's theatre there and he inclined his head to the memory of Caesar, hoping the old man could see him just this once. There too lay the Senate, and he showed his teeth at the thought of those arrogant noblemen waiting for him. He had found his path. He would *show* them arrogance and power.

The two legates gave the order and the machinery of the legion began to act, commands echoing across the camp as each layer of officers took charge of actions as familiar to them as breathing. The legionaries jogged to collect their kit for a march, laughing and talking among themselves as they went.

Legate Paulinius cleared his throat and Octavian looked at him.

'Yes?'

'Caesar, we were wondering what you wanted done with the war chest. The men have not been paid for a month and there has been no word from the Senate about using the funds.'

Octavian stood very still as the older man shifted from foot to foot, waiting for an answer. Julius Caesar had been preparing to leave Rome for years. Octavian had not even considered the gold and silver he would have gathered for the campaign.

'Show me,' Octavian said at last.

The legates led his small group across the camp to a heavily guarded tent. The legionaries there had not deserted their posts to see him and Octavian could see their pleasure. He smiled at them as he ducked inside.

There was more than just one chest. The centre of the tent was stacked with boxes of wood and iron, all locked. Flavius Silva produced a key, matched by another in the hands of Paulinius. Together, they opened a chest and heaved back the lid. Octavian nodded, as if the shining mass of gold and silver coins was no more than he had expected. In theory, the funds belonged to the Senate, but if they had not asked for them to be returned by then, there was a chance they did not even know of their existence.

'How much is there?' Octavian asked.

Flavius Silva did not have to check the amounts. Being in charge of such a sum in the chaos Rome had endured must have ruined his sleep for a month.

'Forty million, in all.'

'That is . . . good,' Octavian said. He exchanged a brief glance with Agrippa, who was glassy-eyed at the sum. 'Very well. Give the men what they are owed . . . and a bonus of six months' pay. You are familiar with the bequest made by Caesar to the people of Rome?'

'Of course. Half the city is still talking about it.'

'I will ask for the funds from the Senate when we are in the forum. If they refuse, I will pay it from these chests and my own funds.'

Flavius Silva smiled as he closed the chest and locked it once more. Simply having such a fortune in his possession had gnawed at him like a broken tooth he could not leave alone. He felt a weight lift at being able to pass the responsibility to another.

'With your permission, sir, I will see to the camp.'

'But not your affairs, Legate.'

The older man flushed.

'No, Caesar. Not my affairs. Not today.'

PART TWO

CHAPTER TEN

Mark Antony arrived at Brundisium after sunset, seeing the gleam of thousands of lamps and watchfires against the black horizon. He had known the numbers of men waiting there. Caesar had discussed the plans with him the previous winter, as they prepared the campaign against Parthia. The horsemen of that eastern empire had been a thorn in Roman skin for many years and Caesar had not forgotten the old enemy. There were debts to be paid, but that massive undertaking had been ruined by assassins' blades, like so much else.

That forewarning had not prepared Mark Antony for the reality of six full legions of veterans camped around the city – and the navigation lamps of the fleet like fireflies on the dark sea. As the consul and his guards reached the outskirts of one Roman camp, they were challenged by alert legionaries. His consular ring allowed him to pass, though he was stopped and questioned again and again as they crossed the territory of the different legions. Any hope of travelling incognito was lost, so that by the time the sun rose, the entire city had been told the consul was coming and the wrath of the Senate was finally at hand. They had waited for a long time to know what would follow the chaos in Rome and the usual bustle of the city scraped to a halt in the face of potential disaster.

Mark Antony found lodgings in the town by the simple expedient of ordering every other patron out of their rooms. Some of them were senior officers in the legions, but not a word was raised in complaint and they hurried back to the main camps as fast and as unobtrusively as possible.

The consul ate a silent breakfast of porridge sweetened with honey and some fresh melon and slices of orange. Mark Antony had ridden hard for three nights and was weary enough to call for a tisane of heated wine and herbs to restore him. The tavern-keeper was nervously obsequious as he brought the tall cups, bowing and retreating at the same time. The consul had the power to order thousands of men dead by the end of the day and the people of Brundisium whispered of nothing else as he finished his food and sat back.

On impulse, Mark Antony rose and walked out to the seafront, taking a path to the rocky crags that overlooked the deep waters. He took pleasure in the sharp air, away from the smell of too many people crammed into too small a space. It cleared his head to stare out across the sea.

The sight of the fleet and the rising sun improved his spirits, a floating symbol of Roman power. He only wished he had somewhere to send them, but his objectives lay with the soldiers of the legions. For the time being, he was the Senate in transit, their plenipotentiary, with all their authority lodged in him. He made a mental note to tell his wife Fulvia how it felt when she arrived.

As he walked back into the streets, Mark Antony spotted two of his men dogtrotting along the road towards him. They drew up and saluted.

'Where are the legates?' he demanded.

'They have gathered in the main square to wait for you, sir.'

'Very well,' he said, striding on. 'Lead the way, I haven't been here for years.'

He could hear the noise and voices filtering back through the side roads long before he reached the central square. It was the Roman forum in miniature, with too many soldiers in it for comfort. The consul had an unpleasant memory of the last crowd he'd addressed.

A shout went up when he was spotted and centurions with vine sticks cleared a path for him, shoving men back with curses and oaths so that the consul could walk forward. Mark Antony did not have to feign a grim countenance. He had expected to find soldiers terrified of senatorial justice. Instead, he saw only anger as he walked through them. Any commander knew he occasionally had to be deaf when he walked through his men, but this was more than cheerful mockery from the safety of a crowd. The legions heaved and struggled against their officers and the insults were obscene.

It was customary for a consul to be greeted with cheers and applause as he stepped up to a platform to address a legion. Mark Antony left his guards at the base, but as he climbed the steps, the noise fell away, leaving only the six legates clapping him on. In such a packed space, it was a pitiful sound, followed quickly by hard laughter. The legates were sweating as he stood at the oak rostrum. Mark Antony had a fine voice and he drew himself up to make it echo back from the buildings around the square.

'I am consul of Rome, the Senate-in-transit. In my person the authority of Rome resides, that I may judge others for their offences against the state.'

The laughter and calls died away. He let the silence stretch, choosing how he would proceed. He had intended to show mercy and so win them to his side, but somehow they had been turned against him.

'What of *your* offences?' a voice yelled suddenly from somewhere in the crowd. 'What of Caesar?'

Mark Antony gripped the rostrum with his big hands, leaning forward. He realised they saw him only as a representative of the Senate. He was lucky they had not rushed the platform where he stood.

'You talk of Caesar?' he snapped. 'I am the man who gave his funeral oration, who stood with his body as it was consumed in fire. I was his friend. When Rome called on me, I did not hesitate. I followed the lawful path. None of you can say the same.'

He was about to continue, but more and more voices shouted out angrily against him, individual complaints lost in the raucous bawling. When it did not die down, he saw some of them were actually leaving, walking off in all directions from the square as if he could say nothing they wanted to hear. He turned in frustration to the legates at his back.

'Bring out the troublemakers, gentlemen. I will make an example of them to the rest.'

The closest legate blanched.

'Consul, we have the men ready, as you ordered, but the legions know that you proposed the Senate amnesty. If I give that command, they could tear us apart.'

Mark Antony's chest swelled as he took a step towards the man, looming over him.

'I am weary of being told the dangers of crowds. Is this a mob? No, I see Roman legionaries, who *will* remember their discipline.' He spoke more for the benefit of those listening than the legate himself. 'Take pride in that discipline. I tell you, it is all you have left.'

The legate gave the order and a line of bound men were brought out from a nearby building. Centurions forced their way through the packed crowd, dragging the men into position so that they faced the rest. In any legion, there were always a few offenders who fell asleep on watch, or raped local women, or stole from their tent-mates. Optios and centurions kicked and cuffed the chosen hundred to their knees.

Mark Antony could feel the rage sweeping through the rest. As the grumbling roar swelled, the legate appealed to him once again, keeping his voice low.

'Consul, if they mutiny now, we are all dead. Let me dismiss them.'

'Step *away* from me,' Mark Antony said in disgust. 'Whoever you are, resign your commission and return to Rome. I have no place for cowards.'

He stepped back to the rostrum and his voice was a harsh roar.

'Rome has moved on while you sat here and mourned the death of a great man,' he bellowed. 'Has grief stolen your honour? Has it torn away your ranks and traditions? Remember you are men of Rome, no, soldiers of Rome. Men of *iron* will, who know the value of life and death. Men who can go on, even in the face of disaster.'

He looked down at the miserable legionaries on their knees. It had not been hard for them to guess their fate when they were rounded up and left in darkness to await the consul's punishment. Many of them struggled against their ropes, but if they tried to stand, they were kicked back down by the watchful centurions.

'It was mutiny when you refused orders,' Mark Antony told them all. 'Mutiny must be washed in blood. You have known that, from the first moments the orders came from Rome. This is the stone that began to fall that day. Centurions! Carry out your duty.'

With grim faces, the centurions removed hatchets from their packs, smacking the blunt ends into their palms over the heads of the kneeling soldiers. In swift, cracking blows, they broke skulls, raising their arms high again and again, then moving on to the next.

Spatters of blood and brains were flung up with the raised weapons, reaching the faces of the closest ranks. The legionaries there began to growl and their officers roared at them. They stood, with chests heaving and expressions feral, repelled yet fascinated as the men died.

As the last body was released to spill the pale contents of its skull onto the ground, Mark Antony breathed hard, facing them again. Slowly the dipped heads came up. The gazes were still hostile, but no longer filled with his imminent destruction. They had held. Most of them realised the worst was past.

'And the stone has fallen. There is an end,' Mark Antony said. 'Now I will tell you something of Caesar.' If he had promised them gold, he could not have achieved a more perfect silence as the noise fell away.

'It is true that there has been no vengeance for the Ides of March. I called the amnesty myself, knowing that if I did, his killers would see no danger from me. I wanted to speak to the people of Rome and not have myself exiled or slaughtered in turn as a friend of Caesar. That is the nest of snakes that politics has become in Rome.'

They were no longer drifting away at the edges. Instead, they were pressing back in, thirsty for news from a man who had been present. Brundisium was far away from Rome, Mark Antony reminded himself. At best, they would have only third-hand gossip about what had gone on there. No doubt the Senate had its spies to report his words, but by the time they did, he would have moved again. He had made his choice when he left Rome with his wife and children. There was no taking it back.

'Some of those responsible have fled the country already. Men like Cassius and Brutus are beyond our reach, at least for now. Yet one of the men who murdered Caesar on the steps of Pompey's theatre is still in Italy, in the north. Decimus Junius believes he has moved far enough from Rome to be safe from any vengeance.'

He paused, watching the expressions change as they began to believe in him.

'I see the men of six legions before me. Decimus Junius has a region near the Alps with barely a few thousand soldiers to keep the peace. Is he safe from us? No, he is not.' He showed his teeth as his voice grew in strength. 'You called for vengeance for Caesar. I am here to *give* it to you.'

They responded with cheering as wild as their anger had been only moments before. Mark Antony stood back, satisfied. The Senate had intended him to lose face in decimating the legions. Instead, for the lives of a hundred criminals, he had won them to him. He smiled at the thought of Bibilus and Suetonius hearing the news.

He turned to the legates, his expression changing to a frown at the sight of the man he had ordered to resign, still present and pale as wax.

'What legion do you lead?' Mark Antony demanded.

'Fourth Ferrata, sir.' For an instant, desperate hope of a reprieve shone in the legate's eyes.

'And who is your second in command?'

The man's expression was sickly with fear, his career in ruins.

'Tribune Liburnius, Consul.'

'Tell him to see me, that I may judge his fitness for command.'

The legate chewed his lip, summoning his dignity.

'I believe that is a Senate appointment, sir,' he said.

'And I have told you. Today, I am the Senate, with all their powers to appoint or dismiss. Now leave. If I see you again, I will have you killed.'

The man could only stand back and salute with a shaking right hand before walking away. Mark Antony transferred his attention to the other legates.

145

'All of you, with me. We have a campaign to plan.' A thought stopped him as he was on the steps down to the square. 'Where is the war chest for Parthia?'

'In Rome, sir. We had it here, but Caesar gave orders for it to be sent to the Campus Martius and Seventh Victrix.'

Mark Antony closed his eyes for a moment. The riches of Caesar had been within his grasp and he had let them slip. The gods gave him legions and then took away his ability to pay them in the same breath.

'Never mind. Come, gentlemen, walk with me.'

Agrippa rubbed weariness and sweat from his eyes. He had found a spot to take the weight off his feet, against a pile of oat bags under a temporary wooden shelter. He needed just a few moments, then he would go on, he told himself. Octavian was like a winter gale blowing through the Campus Martius. Before his arrival, the legions had been adrift. To an observer, they might have seemed the same as before, with guards exchanging watchwords, and food lines and the forges of smiths working all hours to keep the legion in a high state of readiness. Agrippa tried to stifle a yawn and his jaw cracked painfully.

He had once seen a sailor struck on the head with a falling mast in a storm. The rain had washed the blood away and the man continued to work, fastening down sails and tying off loose ropes while the wind howled. Some hours later, when the storm had passed, the sailor was walking back from the prow when he gave a great cry and fell unconscious to the deck. He had never woken and they had put his body over the side a day later. In a similar way, the legions had been stunned by the death of Caesar. They had continued with their duty but had been just as glassy-eyed and mute as the sailor. Octavian's arrival had changed all that, Agrippa thought. He had given

146

them a purpose once more. Agrippa saw it in the cheerful greetings of strangers as they recognised him as one of Caesar's friends. He saw it in the bustle that revealed what had gone before as listlessness and despair.

He smiled at the sight of Maecenas jogging through the camp with two horses on long leads behind him. The Roman noble was flushed and sweating and they exchanged an amused look of mutual suffering as they passed.

'Resting those heavy bones, are we?' Maecenas called over his shoulder.

Agrippa chuckled, though he did not move from the spot. He had never appreciated his choice of a naval life as much as he did then. A centurion captain was master of his vessel and he rarely had to walk far or move the mountains of supplies and equipment that these men took everywhere with them. There had been no news of fresh orders for the fleet. Maecenas had been right about that. Yet he too had been swept up in Octavian's progress, dragged along despite his misgivings. There had hardly been time to reflect on what they had achieved before Octavian was off again, driven by some source of manic energy Agrippa could only envy.

Even a fleet officer like Agrippa had to admit to being slightly impressed at the way the legion formed up to march. The routines and lines of command were so deeply entrenched that they could go from apparent chaos to shining ranks of sword and shield in no time at all. Yet this was more than a sudden rush to battle formations. Octavian had given orders for the entire camp to be packed up, and as the morning progressed, the soldiers finished their tasks and stood in silence, facing the city. Agrippa looked into the distance, his eyesight sharp for detail after years of peering at horizons. Like Maecenas, he had been staggered at Octavian's ambitions. It felt like madness and treachery to consider a march into the centre of the city in the teeth of the will of the Senate. He shook his head, smiling wryly to himself. Yet he did not follow Octavian. He followed Caesar. If Caesar sent his men into Hades, they would follow without hesitation.

Agrippa moved when a dozen workmen came to shift the sacks onto carts. The Campus was bare as far as he could see in all directions: toilets filled in and raked, wooden buildings taken down beam by beam and packed. He walked to the front, where a legion servant waited patiently with a helmet and horse.

Maecenas and Octavian were already there, with the constant shadow of Gracchus watching everything with bright eyes. Legates Silva and Paulinius were splendid in the sunshine, their armour burnished to a fine glow. They looked almost younger since the first moments he had seen them. Agrippa mounted up, ignoring the protest from his sore muscles.

As the sun reached its highest point, noon-bells began to sound across the city, rung in temples and markets and work-shops to mark the change of shift. Agrippa looked back at ten thousand legionaries and another four thousand camp followers in their wake. They shone, the greatest fighting men of the greatest nation. It was not often that he recognised a moment as important in his life. As a rule, the decisions that mattered could only be understood months or even years later. Yet for once he knew. He took slow breaths as he savoured the sight of so many. The name of Caesar would not have been enough on its own. Octavian had found the words to call them. Agrippa pulled down his helmet and tied the leather strap under his chin.

Octavian looked left and right at Agrippa and Maecenas, his eyes bright with humour and possibility.

'Will you ride with me, gentlemen?' he said.

'Why not, Caesar?' Maecenas said. He shook his head in wonder. 'I would not miss a moment.'

Octavian smiled. 'Give the signal to march, Legate Silva. Let us remind the Senate they are not the only force in Rome.'

Horns blared across the Campus Martius and behind them the Seventh Victrix and Eighth Gemina legions began to march in step towards the city.

CHAPTER ELEVEN

The gates of Rome were open to the legions as they came in from the Campus Martius. Beyond the shadow of the walls, citizens were gathering, the news spreading across the city far faster than men could march. The name of Caesar flew before them and the people came out in droves to see the heir to Rome and the world.

At first, Octavian and the legates rode with stiff backs and hands tight on the reins, but they were greeted with cheering and the crowds only grew with each street. There had been many processions before in the city. Marius had demanded a Triumph from the Senate of his day and Julius Caesar had enjoyed no fewer than four of them, celebrating his victories and scattering coins as he went.

For those with eyes to see, the citizens were thinner than they had been before the riots. Much of the city still lay in ruins or charred beams, but they had pride even so and they roared their appreciation. Octavian felt their excitement like a jug of wine in his blood, raising him. All that was missing was the slave at his shoulder to whisper 'Remember thou art mortal.'

All the previous Triumphs had ended in the great forum and the crowds seemed to understand that, running ahead of the legions so that the roads grew more and more choked. Citizens and slaves began to chant the name of Caesar, and Octavian felt his face redden, overwhelmed. On his horse, he and his friends were at the level of the lowest windows overhanging the street and he saw women and men leaning out as far as they could, just a few feet from his head.

At three separate street corners, other men shouted furious insults and were shouted down in turn by those around them. One of the agitators fell senseless after a crack round the head from a middle-aged tradesman. The legions moved on towards the heart and Octavian knew he would never forget the experience. The Senate may have turned on his family, but the people themselves showed their adoration without shame.

They came over the Capitoline hill, walking the same route the assassins had taken. Octavian clenched his jaw at the thought of those who called themselves Liberatores holding out their red hands in pride. Of all things, that brought him fastest to rage. Murder was an old thing for the Republic, but masking the crime in dignity and honour was not. He hated the Liberatores for that, as much as for their jealousy and greed.

He did not doubt the Senate were sending feverish messages to their houses, calling each other in for the emergency. Octavian smiled bitterly at the thought. Without the might of the legions, they were just a few hundred ageing men. He had revealed that, throwing back the curtain that concealed how weak they truly were. He hoped all those who had voted for amnesty could hear the noise of the crowd as they welcomed Caesar. He hoped the sound chilled them.

Even the vast open space of the forum could not hold two legions at full strength. The first few thousand marched right across, allowing the rest to enter the heart of Rome. Legates Silva and Paulinius began to send runners back down the column, ordering their men out in all directions rather than have the crush increase. Every temple would house a few hundred. Every noble mansion would be the billet for as many men as it could take. When those were full, the legions would make their camps in the streets themselves, closing all the roads leading to the forum. Cooking fires would be lit in stone gutters for the first time and the centre of Rome would be theirs.

It took time to halt and organise the column, with both the legates and their officers working hard. The clot of men at the centre spread out in every direction, legionaries walking in and sitting down wherever there was space. They closed off the forum, allowing the crowds to filter out as the day wore on. Only the House of Virgins was untouched, as Octavian had ordered. Apart from the debt he owed to Quintina Fabia, the presence of legionaries among those young women could only result in disgrace or tragedy. He began to appreciate the difficulties Caesar had faced with any large movement of soldiers, but the legion structure was designed to respond to the commands of one man and he did not have to think of everything, only to trust that his officers would work hard and well for him.

The evening light was still soft as horns called across the forum, across the heads of thousands of men. They could not raise tents on the stones, even if there had been room. They would sleep out in the sun and rain, to sweat and freeze in turn. Those same soldiers had cheered him on the Campus and they did not complain at being led by a Caesar into Rome.

The site of the old senate house had been cleared of rubble, ready to be rebuilt. Its foundations lay exposed, rough brick and stone still heat-scorched and dark yellow against the grey cobbles. It made a sort of sense to have the legates construct a rough building there, their legionaries hammering in spikes to bind the beams, then heaving great leather sheets over to form a roof. Before it was fully dark, the shelter was snug and proof against rain, with couches, tables and low beds laid out inside like any command post on campaign. As if to make them prove their competence, dark clouds came in as the sun set. A light drizzle dampened the holiday atmosphere of the legions as they cooked a meal and found whatever shelter they could.

Octavian stood looking out on the darkening forum, with one shoulder resting against an oak beam, much marked and holed from previous use. Around him, legionaries moved with lamps and oil, refilling and trimming wicks so that the legates would have light. He had gambled everything on this one action and for that night at least he was the power in Rome. All he had to do was keep it.

He yawned, pressing a hand to his mouth.

'You should eat, sir,' Gracchus said. The legionary held a wooden plate covered in strips of various meats, sliced thin. Octavian smiled wearily.

'I will, in a while.' On impulse, he decided to speak again, addressing a problem he had ignored for days. 'I am surprised to see you still here, Gracchus. Is it not time for you to return to Tribune Liburnius?'

The legionary just stared dully at him.

'Are you even on my side?' Octavian continued. 'How can I tell? It wasn't so long ago that you were thinking of flogging me in the street for disturbing your tribune.'

Gracchus looked away, his face shadowed against the warm light from the lamps.

'You were not Caesar then, sir,' he said uncomfortably.

'Send him home to Brundisium,' Maecenas called from

behind them. His friend was already seated with Agrippa and the two legates, enjoying a spread of cold food and warm wine.

'You are not a client of mine, Gracchus, nor your family. I have seen the lists now. You owe me nothing, so why do you stay?' Octavian sighed. 'Is it the thought of gold?'

The legionary considered for a moment.

'Mainly, yes,' he said.

His honesty surprised Octavian into laughing.

'You've never been poor, sir, or you would not laugh,' Gracchus said, his mouth a thin line.

'Oh, you're wrong, Gracchus, and I'm not laughing at you. I have been poor – and starving. My father died when I was very young and if it hadn't been for Caesar, I suppose I could very well be standing where you are now.' He became serious, studying the man who had almost strangled him in a tavern.

'Gracchus, I need men around me who are loyal, who will take the risks with me and not think of the rewards. I am not playing a game. I will see these Liberatores destroyed and I don't care if I have to spend all Caesar's fortunes to do it. I will throw away the years of my youth for the chance to break those men. Yet if gold is your only ambition, you can be bought by my enemies.'

Gracchus looked at his feet, frustration making him grim. In truth, it was not just the thought of gold that kept him there. He had lived with these men for some of the most extraordinary days of his life.

'I am not a man who speaks well,' he said slowly. 'You cannot trust me, I know that. But I've lived with the fear of senators, no . . . I'm not making it clear. You are taking them on. It's not just about coins . . .' He waved a hand, almost dropping the plate. 'I'd like to stay. I'll earn your trust in time, I promise.'

The rest of them were quiet at the table, hardly bothering to pretend they were not all listening. Octavian leaned away from the beam, intending to invite Gracchus to join them for the meal. As he moved, he felt the weight of a pouch at his waist. On impulse, he untied the leather thongs that bound it to his belt and held it up.

'Put the plate down and hold out your hands, Gracchus,' he said.

The legionary went to the table and returned.

'Hold them out, go on,' Octavian prompted.

He emptied the pouch into Gracchus' hands, a stream of heavy gold coins. The legionary's eyes widened at the sight of a small fortune.

'Twenty . . . two, twenty-three aurei, Gracchus. Each one worth around a hundred silver sesterces. What is that? Five or six years' pay for your rank? At least that much, I should think.'

'I don't understand, sir,' Gracchus said warily. He could hardly drag his eyes away from the yellow coins, but when he did, Octavian was still watching him.

'You can take that and go now, if you want, without censure. You have finished your work for me and for Tribune Liburnius. It's yours.'

'But . . .' Gracchus shook his head in confusion.

'Or you can give it back to me and remain.' Octavian gripped his shoulder suddenly, passing by the legionary and moving to the table. 'It's your choice, Gracchus, but I must know, one way or the other. You are either with me to the death, or you are not.'

Octavian sat down and deliberately ignored the dumbfounded soldier standing with his hands full of gold. He called for the wine jug and Agrippa passed it to him. Maecenas was smiling wryly as they shared the food, each man at the table trying not to look over their shoulders at the figure in the lamplight.

'What do you think the senators are doing tonight?' Octavian asked the others as he ate.

Flavius Silva was relieved to be able to reply and spoke quickly through a mouthful of roasted pork.

'They will bluster at first, I have no doubt,' he said, chewing. 'I have dealt with many of the senators over the last month and they will not react well to this challenge. I might advise you to ignore whatever they say for a day or two until they have had time to consider their position, with two legions camped in the centre of Rome.'

'Whatever they threaten, they have no way of enforcing it,' Octavian replied, taking a deep gulp of wine and wincing slightly.

Flavius Silva saw his reaction and chuckled. 'Not so good, I agree. I will find some Falernian tomorrow.'

'I've never tasted it,' Octavian said.

Maecenas tutted to himself. 'This is horse piss in comparison, believe me,' he said cheerfully. 'I have a few amphorae of it at my estate, laid down three years ago. It should be ready to drink this year, or perhaps next. You'll see when you come.'

'Leaving aside the qualities of the wine for a moment,' Agrippa said, 'the Senate will ask you what you want, eventually. What *do* you want from them?'

'The Lex Curiata, first of all,' Octavian said. 'I need the law passed so that no one can ever say I am not the legitimate heir to Caesar. In normal times, it is just a formality, but they must still vote and lodge the record. They must also honour the will with Caesar's funds, or I will pay the legacies myself and shame them. After that, I want only a reversal of the amnesty they granted.' He grinned suddenly. 'That small thing.'

'They will not agree to making criminals of the Liberatores,' Maecenas muttered into his wine cup. When he felt the eyes of the table on him, he looked up. 'Men like Cassius have too much support still.'

'You know these men,' Octavian said. 'What would you do?'

'I would march the centurions in there and whip the Senate out of Rome,' Maecenas said. 'You have caught them for a brief moment without power, but there *are* other legions, Caesar. You can't stop the senators sending messages out of the city and then their supporters will march. How many men are passing information to you now? The Senate have their own clients and I would imagine there is someone on the road to Brundisium as we speak. If Mark Antony moves quickly, he could have legions here in just a few days.' He looked around the table. 'Well, you did ask. Either you follow this through to the end and seize your moment, or we will shortly be defending this city from Roman soldiers.'

'I won't remove the Senate,' Octavian said, frowning. 'Even Julius Caesar kept them on, with all his influence and power. The people won't welcome us so readily if we set about dismantling the Republic in front of them. If I make myself a dictator, it will force them together to act against me.'

'You should consider it even so,' Maecenas said. 'Take command of the legions one by one as they come in. You have the name and the right to do it.' He refilled their cups and almost as one they all drank the sour wine. Maecenas saw the two legates exchange a worried glance and spoke again.

'The Senate will know they only have to hold on for a few weeks before you are faced with loyal legions at the walls. If you don't execute some of them, they will be deciding your fate before the end of the month. You said you wanted to see the Liberatores brought down? It may not be possible to lay hands on them within the law, not when the Senate have made those laws. Perhaps you could demand the least of them to be turned over into your custody. Hold a trial for them in the forum and let the Senate see that you understand dignity and tradition.'

'There's only Gaius Trebonius and Suetonius left in Rome, I think,' Octavian said slowly. 'Trebonius did not even wield a blade with the rest. I could take them both by force. But that will not bring me the others, especially those who have been given powerful posts. It will not bring me Cassius or Brutus.

All I need is a renunciation of the amnesty and then they can *all* be brought to trial.'

Maecenas shook his head. 'Then you must be willing to cut a few throats, or at least threaten to do so without bluffing.'

Octavian brought his knuckles up to his eyes, pressing out the weariness.

'I will find a way, when I have slept.'

He rose from the table, stifling another yawn that spread quickly around the table. Almost as an afterthought, Octavian looked towards the doorway where he had left Gracchus. It was empty. The lamplight lit only the gentle drizzle coming down through the air of the forum.

Pompey's theatre was at its best at night. The huge semicircles of stone seats were lit by hundreds of lamps swinging high above. Servants had climbed ladders to reach the larger bowls of oil that flickered above the stage itself, creating conflicting shadows that moved in gold and black.

In the absence of Mark Antony, four men stood to face the others and direct the debate. Bibilus and Suetonius had the least right to do so, though Bibilus had been a consul years before. Senators Hirtius and Pansa were not due to take up their consular posts until the new year, but the emergency required the most senior men to put aside differences and they had the attention of the Senate that night. All four had discovered that the position facing the benches gave their voices a new power and resonance and they relished being able to quell discussion with just a sharp word.

'Consul Mark Antony is not the issue,' Hirtius said for the second time. 'Fast messengers are on their way to him and there is nothing more we can do until he has returned. There is no point debating whether he will be successful in punishing the mutinous behaviour at Brundisium. If he has sense, he will have them marching without delay and leave their decimation as a condition of their success in relieving us here.'

Several senators stood up and Hirtius picked a man that he knew would at least add something useful instead of raging pointlessly about factors they could not influence.

'Senator Calvus has the floor,' Hirtius said, gesturing to him. The others sat down on the curving benches, though many of them talked among themselves.

'Thank you,' Senator Calvus said, staring grimly at two men talking close to him until they broke off in embarrassment. 'I wished only to remind the Senate that Ostia is closer than the legions at Brundisium. Are there forces there which can be brought in?'

It was Bibilus who cleared his throat to reply. Senator Hirtius nodded to him out of courtesy.

'In normal times there would be at least a full legion at Ostia. Until two months ago, that legion was the Eighth Gemina, one of the two currently infesting the forum. Caesar's campaign against Parthia brought in legions from as far away as Macedonia, ready to join the fleet. Ostia has no more than a few hundred soldiers and administrators at the port, perhaps as many again in retired men. It is not enough to scrape these invaders out of the city, even if we could be certain they would remain loyal to us.'

Angry voices answered him and Bibilus wiped sweat from his brow. He had not sat a single day in the Senate until Caesar's death and he was still not accustomed to the sheer noise and energy of the debates.

Senator Calvus had remained on his feet and Bibilus gave way to him, sitting down with a thump on a heavy bench dragged to the front for that purpose.

'The question of loyalty lies at the heart of the problem facing us tonight,' Calvus said. 'Our main hopes rest with the legions of Brundisium. Yet the consul has gone not to forgive them, but to exact punishment. If he has not suppressed their treachery, we have no other way to bring them back to Rome. It is possible that this adopted son of Caesar knows full well that there will be no help coming from the east. His tactic has all the marks of a wild gamble, unless he knows the Brundisium legions will not come.' The noise around him had risen and he spoke louder. 'Please, gentlemen, point out the flaws in what I have said, if they are clearer to you than to me.'

Three more senators rose immediately to reply and Calvus ignored them rather than be forced to sit through the interruptions.

'It is my feeling that it would be unwise to rest all our hopes on consul Mark Antony. I propose we send messages to legions in Gaul to come south. Decimus Junius has a few thousand men close by the Alps . . .'

From the stage, Suetonius broke in, speaking easily over Calvus.

'They would take weeks to get to Rome. However this is resolved, Senator, it will be over long before they could arrive. Is there nothing closer? Given months, we could bring in legions from half the world, but who knows what will have happened by then?'

'Thank you, Senator Suetonius,' Hirtius said, his voice cold enough for Suetonius to glance at him and subside. 'Senator Calvus has raised a valid point. Though there are no other legions within a day's march of the city, there are two in Sicily, two more in Sardinia that could be ordered home by ship. If the Senate agree, I will send riders to Ostia to bring them in. In two or three weeks at most, there can be four legions here at full strength.'

A rumble of agreement echoed around the theatre and the vote was passed quickly and without dissent. Senator Hirtius summoned a runner while the debate went on and pressed his ring to orders that would be carried west. When he was finished, he listened for a time and then addressed them all.

'It is almost dawn, senators. I suggest you return to your homes and guards to get some sleep. We will meet again . . . at noon? Noon it is. No doubt by then we will have heard more from this new Caesar.'

CHAPTER TWELVE

Mark Antony was in a foul mood as his legions marched north, snapping at anyone foolish enough to address him. The Via Appia was a wonder: six paces wide and well drained for hundreds of miles. Only on such a smooth surface could the legions make twenty to thirty miles a day, the legionaries counting off each milestone as they reached it. The problem was that he had not intended to go anywhere near Rome. One dusty and exhausted messenger from the Senate had changed all his plans.

Mark Antony stared into the distance, as if he could see the Senate waiting for his triumphant return. He *felt* them there, like a nest of spiders twitching threads that ran under his feet. He shook his head free of the image, still struggling with sheer disbelief. Octavian had to be insane to have attempted such a rash move! What was the boy thinking? The anger he had caused was there to be read in the Senate orders. Bibilus, Hirtius and Pansa had sealed it with the Senate symbol, the visible sign of their authority over all legions. Mark Antony was ordered back with all speed and one purpose – to destroy the upstart in the forum.

The men ahead began to cheer and Mark Antony dug in his heels and trotted forward to see what had pleased them. The road had been rising gently for most of the morning, cutting through chalk hills in great clefts that represented years of labour. He knew before he saw it, catching a hint of salt on the cool breeze. The Mare Tyrrhenum came into sight at the head of the column, a dark blue vastness on his left shoulder. It meant Rome was no more than a hundred miles further along the road and he would have to decide soon where to rest the men and let the camp followers catch up.

The cheering rippled oddly down the lines of marching men, as each century caught the same view and hollered out for good luck, proud of the pace they had set. Mark Antony drew his mount aside for a time, watching them pass and nodding with stern satisfaction to anyone who sought out his gaze. He had not told them yet that they were going home.

Mark Antony thought in frowning silence, weighing the problems before him. Two full legions had broken their oaths and mutinied for a boy who called himself Caesar. If the name had that sort of effect, he could not trust that the Senate would be able to contain him. All Mark Antony's instincts told him to strike north, to continue with his original plans against Decimus Junius. The legions of Brundisium had refused to answer orders once already. They'd come close to cutting Mark Antony to pieces when they thought he was one of those who had sanctioned Caesar's murder. What would they do when they discovered he had been ordered to attack the man's heir? Gods, it was impossible! The far north under Decimus Junius was ripe for plucking and he had the forces to do it. Yet he dared not leave Octavian with two legions answering to him. The real Caesar had achieved much with fewer men.

He looked back down the marching ranks, taking solace from the sight of thirty thousand soldiers. If they kept discipline, he knew he could force Octavian to surrender. Let the Senate worry about what to do with him after that, he thought. While men like Bibilus debated his fate, there would be no one watching Mark Antony. He could still take the legions north.

The walls of Rome were not as high as many of the buildings they contained. Even at night, looking inward, the dark masses of tenement blocks rose above the three men standing on the stone walkway above a gate. The poorest families lived as high as six or even seven storeys up, without running water and in the unhappy knowledge that they could not possibly escape a fire. To Octavian, the gleam of oil lamps at their open windows seemed like low stars in the distance, too high to be part of the city at his feet.

Agrippa and Maecenas leaned against the inner part of the wall. The city itself had not been threatened since the slave army of Spartacus, but the defences were still maintained, with an entire network of support buildings and access steps. In more normal times, it would be one of the duties of city guards to walk the walls, more often to remove gangs of children or pairs of young lovers than because of any threat to the city. Yet such mundane tasks had been ignored since the legions occupied the forum and the entire city waited in fear for the tension to break. The three friends were alone, with the empty walkway stretching in both directions. Even so, they kept their voices low, constantly aware that the Senate would love to overhear what they planned.

'You don't need to worry about Silva and Paulinius,' Agrippa said. 'They won't change their loyalties again, no matter what the senators promise or threaten. It would cost them too much – the gods alone know what sort of punishment the Senate would impose. Execution of the senior ranks at the very least. Their lives are bound up with ours, as things stand.'

Octavian looked at him, nodding. The moon was approaching full and the stars were bright enough to wash the city in pale light. He felt exposed on the wall, but he had to admit it was more private than anywhere else. Idly, he kicked a small stone off the sandy surface, watching it vanish into the darkness below.

'I'm not worried about their loyalty. What worries me is what we are going to do when the consul comes back from Brundisium with six legions.'

Agrippa looked away, reluctant to say what he had been thinking during the days of negotiation with the Senate. There had been a sense of progress before that afternoon, when the messenger to Mark Antony made it back to Rome. In just an hour, the Senate had regained some of their wavering confidence and the news of returning legions had spread across an already fearful city. Agrippa kicked irritably at a loose stone. The meeting on the wall was not to discuss how to turn the negotiations into a triumph, but how to prevent destruction and dishonour.

Maecenas cleared his throat, leaning back against the wall as he regarded both men.

'So, gentlemen, we are in a difficult spot. Tell me if I have it wrong, won't you? If we do nothing, we have the Senate's legions just a few days' march away. We don't have enough men to hold the walls, not for long. If we use the time left to execute Gaius Trebonius, Suetonius, perhaps Bibilus and a few others, we will only anger the consul further and make him even less willing to keep us alive. You will not abandon the legions here and run for the hills . . .?'

'No,' Octavian muttered.

Maecenas blew out air, disappointed.

'Then I think we are going to be killed in a few days and

165

our heads put on this wall as a warning to others. At least, well, at least there is a view.'

'There has to be a way out of this!' Octavian said. 'If I could make those whoreson senators grant me just *one* concession, I could withdraw the legions in something that would not be utter defeat.'

'As soon as they understood you weren't going to have them dragged out and slaughtered, they knew they had won,' Maecenas went on. 'There is still time for that, at least. You'll get your concession – your Lex Curiata, say – then we can withdraw to somewhere Mark Antony won't feel stung into attacking. Remaining in the forum is the problem. He has to respond to that!'

Octavian shook his head without reply. They had discussed it many times, but it was a line he would not cross. In his desperation, he had considered a few judicious murders, but such an action would destroy how he was seen in the city. If he ever faced the Liberatores in the field, it would be very different, but his entire position rested on him being a champion for the old Republic and the rule of law. Even Caesar had kept the Senate benches filled and refused to call himself a king. Octavian hawked phlegm into his throat and spat out his irritation. The amnesty could be overturned, he was certain, but he had not yet found the lever he needed to do it.

'You haven't tried bribery yet,' Agrippa said, making them both turn towards him. In the moonlight, he shrugged. 'What? You said you'd listen to anything.'

'They think they have only to wait to see us crumple and fail,' Octavian said, bitterness flooding his voice. 'There's nothing I can offer them that they won't think they can have anyway when I am dead.'

Maecenas moved off the wall, looking up at the bright moon. After a time, he nodded.

'Then we're done. You can't stay for a pointless gesture that

166

will see us all killed and two legions destroyed. All you can do is march the men out of Rome and put this down to experience. It's a loss, but you'll learn from it if you survive.'

Octavian opened his mouth, but despair stole away any words. He could not shake the feeling that Caesar would see a way through. It was partly an echo of that man that had pushed him into occupying the forum in the first place, but since that day, nothing had worked out the way he'd hoped.

Agrippa saw the desolation in his friend and spoke, his deep voice rumbling.

'You know, Caesar lost his first battle in the civil war. He was captured not too far from this gate and held for torture. He lost everything, his uncle, his position, his wealth, *everything*. It is not the end to fail and move on, is it? As long as you are alive, you can begin again.'

'I have two legions in the centre of Rome and for the next few days, no one is close enough to stop me,' Octavian snapped suddenly. 'There must be some choices left. There *must* be!'

'Only the ones you won't consider,' Maecenas replied. 'At least let me send a century to take Suetonius. I could do it tonight, Octavian, while the pompous little shit is asleep. What does it matter now to talk of trials and formal execution? You don't have the power for such things, not today. But you can do that much.'

Octavian looked south, to where the Via Appia stretched into the distance. It would not be too long before the consul's legions came marching up that wide road. He could see them in his mind's eye, bringing an end to all his hopes.

'No,' he said, his fists clenched. 'I've told you. *They* are the ones who plotted and moved in secret. They are the murderers. If I am not the defender of the Republic, if I show so little respect for the law that I can butcher a senator in his house, I have no standing at all, no call on the people of Rome.' He made a bitter decision, weighed down by impossible choices. 'Get the legions ready to march. We have a few days still. Perhaps I can wring something from those theatre fools by then.'

CHAPTER THIRTEEN

On the Via Appia, entire villages had sprung up to service and care for travellers. All along its length, it was possible to purchase anything from glass, jewellery and woven cloth, to hot food and even horses.

The Brundisium legions marched past all the usual stopping places, pushed to their best possible pace by the strange urgency that had obsessed Mark Antony. On a good road, they could manage thirty miles if the need was great, though he began to lose men to sprains and exhaustion. For once, those with obviously bloody feet or swollen knees and ankles were not punished further. One or two lucky members of their century remained to watch over groups of ten or a dozen at whichever roadhouse was closest. With Rome almost in sight, they would catch up quickly, or lose skin off their backs.

Mark Antony gave the order to halt the column only when he was certain they were in range of the city for the following day. On grain-fed mounts, he and the legates were relatively fresh compared to the marching men, but still he ached.

With the sun setting, he dismounted in the courtyard of an inn that looked as if it had been there from the time the first stones were laid for the road. Servants, or perhaps the children of the owner, ran to take his horse and accepted the coins he tossed to them. He went inside, ducking his head under a low lintel and seeking out the table where the legates would be eating.

They stood watchfully as he approached. With Rome in range, he knew he had to tell them why he had been pushing so hard. It would leave only the morning for the men to hear and digest the news. With just a little luck, they'd be in the forum before they had a chance to consider rebelling against their new orders.

'Where is Liburnius?' Mark Antony asked. 'I'd have thought he'd be the first one here.'

No one answered, though they looked at each other or at the serving girl bringing jugs of fish sauce to the table.

'Well?' Mark Antony demanded. He pulled out a chair for himself.

'The Fourth Ferrata has not halted, sir,' Legate Buccio said. 'I . . . we assumed it was on your orders.'

Mark Antony's hand dropped from the back of the chair.

'What do you mean "has not halted"? I gave no such order. Send a rider out and get him back.'

'Yes, sir,' Buccio replied.

He left to pass on the errand to some unlucky soldier and Mark Antony settled, allowing the others to sit down. He poured pungent fish sauce onto his plate, smelling it with satisfaction before reaching for bread to dip into it. As he took his first mouthful, he became aware that the remaining men were still stiff and uncomfortable in his presence. He smothered a sigh.

Buccio returned, his glance flickering around the other men

of his rank. Mark Antony looked up as the legate took his seat and poured his own sauce. The man was an ancient compared to some, with deep wrinkles like the lines of a map in his neck and shaven head. His brown eyes were unaccountably worried as they met those of the consul.

'I've sent the runner, sir.'

'I believe you were going to discuss the . . . difficulties we've been having, Buccio,' one of the other legates said, toying with his food and not looking up.

Buccio glared at the speaker, but Mark Antony was looking at him by then and he nodded, making the best of it.

'I have had some . . . comments, Consul. I have trusted men in my legion, men who know I will not hold them responsible if they pass on the gossip of the barracks.'

Mark Antony's mouth firmed.

'The men have given their oaths, Legate. To spy on them after that undermines their honour and yours. You will cease the practice immediately.'

Buccio nodded hurriedly.

'Very well, sir. But what I have learned is serious enough for me to bring it to you, no matter the source.'

Mark Antony stared at him, chewing slowly.

'Go on,' he said. 'I will be the judge of that.'

'They have heard about the new Caesar, Consul. Not just my men, by any means. Legate Liburnius was saying the same thing to me only yesterday. Can you confirm it, sir?'

Mark Antony stiffened, the sinews standing out on his neck. He should have guessed the legionaries would have heard the news. They marched together all day and the slightest rumour spread like a rash. He cursed under his breath. He should have burned the Senate orders, but it was too late for that. Folding his hands in front of him, Mark Antony tried to conceal his irritation.

'Whatever Octavian calls himself now,' he said, 'I will deal

171

with him when I return to the city. If that is all you have heard . . .'

'I wish it was, Consul.' Buccio took a deep breath, steeling himself for the reaction. 'They are saying they will not fight against Caesar.'

The hush that followed was unbroken as every man there suddenly found his food fascinating.

'You are talking about mutiny, Legate Buccio,' Mark Antony said grimly. 'Are you saying your men have not yet learned that particular lesson?'

'I . . . I'm sorry, sir. I thought it was something you should hear.'

'And you were correct in that, though I cannot help doubt your ability to lead if this is how you deal with it. Internal legion matters should be kept internal, Buccio! I would have thought nothing of a few floggings in the morning. A commander does not have to hear everything that goes on; you know that! Why bring idle gossip to my attention?'

'Consul, I . . . I could handle a few fools rousing the others, but I understand that half the men are saying they will not fight, not against Caesar. Not in Rome, sir.'

Mark Antony leaned back. He waited while steaming chickens were brought to the table and torn apart by the hungry men.

'You are all senior officers,' he said when the serving staff had moved away to give them privacy. 'I will say this to you. Rome gives your soldiers everything: a salary, status, a sense of brotherhood. But they endure the discipline because they are men of Rome.'

He waved a hand in frustration, trying to find words that would make it clear to the mystified faces around the table. Before he could go on, another of them cleared his throat to speak. Mark Antony rubbed the back of his neck in irritation. Legate Saturnius had not impressed him in their deliberations to that point. The man had no shame when it came to seeking his favour.

172

'You have something to add?' he said.

'Yes, sir,' Saturnius replied, leaning forward onto the table. 'More often than not they come from impure lines, sir. I believe that is the problem. How can we expect the sons of prostitutes and merchants to understand our beliefs? They are prey to every new fashion, every wild speaker in the Republic. A few years ago, I had to have an agitator strangled because he was copying out the words of some Greek politician. The very few who could read were whispering his dangerous ideas to the ones that couldn't. That one man was very nearly the rot that broke a legion!'

Saturnius looked to Mark Antony for approval, but found him gazing stonily back. Oblivious, Saturnius wiped his mouth of grease and went on.

'The common soldiers are like unruly children, and in the same way, they must be disciplined.' He began to sense the others were not with him and looked around the table. 'It is all they understand, as the consul said.'

There was a moment of silence as some of the other men cringed internally. Saturnius looked from face to face in confusion.

'Is that not so?' he said, growing red.

'It does you no credit to say so,' Mark Antony replied, 'or to put words in my mouth that I have not said. I do not know where you have served, Saturnius, but I have seen those sons of prostitutes and merchants risk their lives to save me, when my life could be measured in heartbeats. I said they were men of Rome. The *least* of them is worth something.'

Saturnius rubbed his face with both hands to make himself more alert. His voice took on a wheedling tone as he replied.

'I thought, sir, after the executions in Brundisium, that you shared the same outlook. I apologise if that is not the case.'

Mark Antony glowered.

'In Brundisium, they understood that punishment *must* come.

173

Do you think it gave me pleasure to order a hundred criminals to their deaths? I was within my rights to order the *decimation* of every legion – the deaths of three thousand men, Saturnius. What I did was a gesture of strength – a demonstration that I would not be cowed by their anger. For those with the wit to see, I saved more than I killed. More importantly, I brought the rest into the fold. I gave them back their dignity and honour.'

He turned from Saturnius, ending the conversation as he addressed Buccio once more.

'This Octavian claims a name that rings out to our men. It is not surprising, when Julius Caesar himself created many of the legions represented at this table. Of course they are saying they will not fight against his adopted son! It would be a surprise if they did not.'

He paused, knowing he had to have these men on his side.

'There are limits to our authority, limits to what we can make the men do. The legions can be pushed only so far – beyond that, they must be led. I have seen it, gentlemen. I have seen Caesar himself talk to mutinous legions, risking his own life.' He glanced back at Saturnius, his expression scornful. 'If you treat them as children or wild dogs, they will eventually turn on you. Discipline is the core of what we do, but they are not Greeks or painted Gauls. They are Roman men, who understand something of the Republic, even if they do not always have the words to say it. Well, you must give them the words they need, Buccio, Saturnius. You must remind them that Caesar may be gone but the Republic can still be revived. I will not allow some blond boy to pretend to the authority of my friend, no matter what an old will said about his adoption. There is *no* new Caesar. Tell them that.'

Buccio had grown thoughtful as the consul spoke, his hands splayed firmly on the table before him, to hide his tension. He had, if anything, understated the position. Some of his most senior officers had dared to come to him and the consul did not seem to understand the seriousness of the situation. Yet with Mark Antony watching him, he could only nod and attack his food in bitter silence.

Mark Antony sat through another two courses before anyone said another word beyond the most strained comments on the food. He was content to spend the time thinking about the Senate and what they would demand from him when he returned. He hoped Octavian would surrender, rather than force him to test his men further. He could not ignore the warnings of the legates, for all he was angry at Buccio for handling things so badly. If 'Caesar' could be captured quickly, it would end all the talk Buccio had discovered.

The evening had grown late by the time the meal came to an end. Mark Antony was heavy with weariness, desiring nothing more than a room with a fire to sleep. As he rose from the table, his action copied instantly by the legates, they all heard the clatter of hooves on the stone yard outside. The messenger Buccio had sent entered the tavern and went straight to the consul's table.

'Report then,' Mark Antony said. 'Have they halted? I am beginning to think I was too quick to promote Liburnius.'

'They have not halted, sir,' the messenger said nervously. 'I rode to the front rank and tried to approach the legate, but three of his officers drew swords as soon as they saw me. As I rode away, they shouted to tell you . . .'

His voice died away as he realised the enormity of repeating an insult to a consul in the company of legates. Mark Antony had the same sense of foreboding and raised a hand.

'Just give me the idea,' he said.

'They are not coming back, sir. They are going to fight for Caesar.'

Mark Antony swore loudly, cursing the name of Liburnius. His gaze fell on Buccio, who was standing in sick awareness that he had become the target of a consul's wrath.

'Get back to your legions. If Liburnius can march through the night, so can we. I'll run him down, I swear it. Go!'

Mark Antony crushed a yawn as it began, furious with himself and his men. If the legions had been rebellious before, a night muttering to each other about the consul would not improve things. As he called for the horses to be resaddled, Mark Antony decided Octavian had to be killed. The young man had chosen a name that made him too dangerous to be left alive.

The exterior of Pompey's theatre was as impressive as its long-dead sponsor had intended. Though Gnaeus Pompey had died in Egypt years before, his name was preserved in the sheer grandeur of the building that dominated the once pristine grass of the Campus. Not even Caesar could have paid for solid marble, but the walls were sheathed in the milky stone, lightly veined and glittering slightly in the sunshine. Limestone paving had been laid all around the main building, ending at the great pillars that held up the portico, itself carved in white marble.

The Senate had come out to Octavian as he approached. They were dressed in white and purple-trimmed togas to a man and they made an impressive sight, standing in a group and waiting for him. They had rejected all his demands and their confidence had grown.

Octavian had chosen to wear armour, knowing he would be seen in contrast to the civil powers. He rode down the Capitoline hill with three centuries of men, one of them composed entirely of centurions. Together, they represented his claim to authority in the city and if the senators were in clean colours, at least his men shone.

As the sound of his mount's hooves changed to a clatter on stone, Octavian swept his gaze across the crowd of senators. He could see Bibilus, with Suetonius at his side as always. They had both known Caesar, Suetonius in particular. The passing years had been kind to neither of them, almost as if their cruelty was written in sagging flesh. Octavian could not help compare himself with those old men and he straightened his back at the thought. He brought his centuries right up to them, not needing to give new orders. They spread out in perfect ranks against the hundreds in togas, standing still so that there was no sound at all beyond the calls of birds floating high above their heads. Not one of the senators would speak first, he was certain. Octavian and Maecenas had discussed the protocol and he smiled at them all.

'I have summoned you here to announce that I will pay the legacies of Caesar myself, beginning with the three hundred sesterces to each citizen of Rome.' He was pleased at the angry mutter that went through them at his choice of words. 'I assume you will waive the right to your part of it. Are senators not citizens? Yet if you wish, I will have your share sent to your homes in the city.'

He hoped they would register the subtle threat before he went on with his main demand. He knew where they lived. The implications would surely not be lost on most of them.

Bibilus stepped forward through the crowd facing Octavian. The man's bulk was well-disguised in the folds of his toga. He stood with his right hand gathering up the folds of cloth, his fleshy features already bright with perspiration.

'Once more, then. We will not bargain or negotiate while legions camp in the sacred forum, Octavian. If you have nothing new to add, I suggest you return to the city and wait for justice to descend on you.'

Octavian controlled a spasm of anger. To have such a man speak to him of justice was calculated to enrage, so he showed them nothing.

'You have refused every demand, senators,' he said, making his voice ring across them all, 'certain that I would not draw swords on the representatives of the city of my birth. What I asked was just, but you continued to protect murderers. That is at an end. I see Senator Suetonius there among you. I will take him today, for trial in the forum. Step aside and let him walk out to me. I have shown my respect for the law by my patience, though I have legions at my back. You need not fear that he will receive anything but justice at my hand. But he *will* receive justice at my hand.'

As he had ordered the night before, ten of his most senior centurions stepped forward from the ranks, moving towards Suetonius before the senators had time to react. At the first steps, Bibilus shouted out.

'We are immune! You may not lay hands on a member of this august Senate. The gods themselves will curse whichever of you defies their will.'

With those few words, a ripple of anger spread through the gathered senators and they stepped out, holding up their hands against the armoured soldiers. With sheer numbers, they blocked a path to Suetonius as he cowered at the centre of four hundred men.

One of the centurions looked back at Octavian, unsure what to do, while the others pressed on. The senators had not dared to draw the daggers they all carried. Yet they clustered and shifted, standing in a clot of men that could not be breached without violence. Octavian seethed, knowing that he could give a single order and they would fall back in bloody rags. Maecenas had predicted they would refuse, but Octavian had not expected to see any kind of courage from those men, certainly not to withstand the terror of hardened legionaries coming at them.

'Stand down, centurions,' he ordered, furious with them all as well as himself.

The line of legionaries disengaged, leaving red-faced senators in their wake, their togas in crumpled disarray. Octavian could only glare at them, his hand twitching to draw the sword that lay at his hip. He held his honour like iron bands around him, but he could hardly bear the poisonous triumph he saw on the faces of Bibilus and Suetonius.

Silence spread again, broken only by panting men. One of the centurions turned to Octavian and, in doing so, saw movement on the Capitoline hill. A rider was coming down to the Campus at a gallop. Octavian turned to see what had arrested the man's attention and his heart sank. They had been dreading the news for days and there was only one thing that would send a rider charging out to him that morning. The senators still waited for him to speak and when he did, his voice was low and cold.

'As I bear the name of Caesar, I will not shed more blood onto these stones. Yet my patience has its limits, gentlemen. I tell you solemnly – do *not* depend on it again.'

It was not enough to wipe the smirk from Bibilus' face, but Octavian knew he was out of time. Sick with rage, he turned his horse and trotted out to meet the rider. His centurions formed up and marched with him, leaving the senators behind.

Octavian reined in as he reached the young extraordinarii soldier, breathing hard from his ride through the city. The man saluted and Octavian stared back at Rome. He did not know when he would see it again.

'Legions sighted, sir. On the Via Appia.'

Octavian nodded and thanked him.

'Go back and tell Legate Silva to bring the men out at their best pace. I am finished here. I will await them on the Campus.'

It was not long before the first marching ranks appeared over the brow of the Capitoline. They came out of the city without any of the cheering or fanfare that had announced their arrival. They marched in sombre mood, knowing that Mark Antony was approaching Rome with three times as many men.

Maecenas and Agrippa reached him first. Maecenas nodded to him, glancing over to where the Senate still stood watching.

'They refused?' he asked, though he had already guessed.

Octavian nodded. 'I should have killed them,' he said.

Maecenas looked at his friend and shook his head.

'You are a better man than I am. It will be remembered that you did not, with legions at your back. They will not be able to accuse you of running wild, at least. That counts for something.'

Octavian looked past him at the gleaming ranks of men marching away from Rome. If all else failed, he had agreed with the legates to head north along the Via Cassia.

'Does it?' he said bitterly.

'Probably not,' Maecenas replied with a grin. Agrippa snorted, though both men were pleased to see Octavian smile in response. 'But it might. You still have two legions and we'll be far enough away in Arretium. I have a small house there and it's pleasant enough.'

'Did you recommend a winter at Arretium because you have a *home* there?' Agrippa asked in disbelief.

Maecenas cleared his throat and looked away.

'Not . . . entirely. It is not as grand as my estate in Mantua, you know. But Arretium is a quiet town and off the main routes.'

Octavian shook his head, his friend's irrepressible nature cheering him. He had gambled and lost, but Maecenas seemed untroubled. Octavian grinned suddenly, letting his mood lighten.

'Come on then,' he said. 'The Senate are watching. Let's ride with a little dignity.'

He dug in his heels, despair and anger tearing into wisps on the breeze.

CHAPTER FOURTEEN

Exhausted, the Fourth Ferrata called a halt in sight of the walls of Rome, with Legate Liburnius sending riders ahead to take his urgent messages. Before the murder of Caesar, the idea of mutiny of any kind would have been unthinkable. Liburnius rubbed his horse's ears as he reflected on the previous months. He had been a leading voice when they decided to ignore the original Senate summons. It was difficult to express the sense of chaos that had ripped through the legions at Brundisium. Many of them had fought at Caesar's side in Greece and Egypt and Gaul, and there were few who could not remember seeing the Father of Rome or hearing him speak over the years. Some even recalled words he had said to them individually with great pride. They were bound by oaths that were as much a part of them as their armour and traditions, but an unspoken loyalty ran even deeper. They were Caesar's men. To be called to the command of the senators who had murdered him had not been an order they could obey.

Liburnius bit the inside of his lip as he looked at the city ahead, surprised at the strength of his pleasure in simply coming home. He had not seen Rome for years and yet somehow he found himself returning at the head of a freshly mutinous legion, no doubt with an enraged consul coming up fast behind. After his promotion to legate, it was not exactly how he had seen his career going and he smiled wryly at the thought. Yet when he looked for doubts, there were none. His men did not know about the favour he carried in his packs, or even the fact that he had met the new Caesar. They knew only the name and the adoption, the mark of family that linked Octavian to the very man who had formed them. It was enough.

When Liburnius had told them his decision to head north and join Caesar's rebellion, they had been too cautious to cheer, but their delight had been obvious. He shook his head, amused at himself. In all his years as tribune, he had not known one hundredth part of the popularity he had gained then. It was frankly surprising how much he appreciated it, a man who had always assumed he was above seeking the adoration of those under his command. Liburnius knew he was no lion of Rome, like Marius, Sulla or Caesar himself. He had been content with his rank and that the men obeyed out of simple discipline. The murder of Caesar had rocked his foundations as much as any of them, altering the way he saw the world.

He breathed in relief as he saw the first of his messengers come galloping back to his position. Mark Antony could not be too far behind. The last thing Liburnius wanted was to be caught against the walls of the city before he could even join Octavian. His men were footsore and weary, but they had pushed on all night, making the best pace possible and not daring to leave any man behind. Whether the decision to mutiny was right or wrong, there was no going back from that point and they all knew it.

The extraordinarii rider was flushed and sweating. His horse skidded on damp stones as he pulled up, making the animal's haunches bunch with a heave on the reins.

'Caesar's legions have left the city, sir, heading north.'

'Shit!' Liburnius said in disbelief. 'How long ago? What forces remain in the city?' He fired more questions at the hapless rider, who could only hold his hands up.

'I don't know, sir. I asked a temple priest. As soon as I heard the news, I swung round and came back.'

Liburnius felt his mood crumble into bitterness. He would not be entering Rome that day, not alone. The consul and five other legions would be hammering up the road at him while he sat there.

'Well, which road did they take?' he snapped.

The young rider only shook his head, but he turned the mount on the spot.

'I'll find out, sir.'

He galloped back the way he came and Liburnius could see worry and fear on the faces of all those who had heard, the news spreading fast through the ranks of waiting men.

'Why would Caesar have waited for us?' he asked them. 'He didn't know we were coming to join him. Centurions! Take the Fourth Ferrata around the city walls to the Campus Martius. We have a chase on our hands.'

To his satisfaction, the closest men grinned, setting off in matched step despite their exhaustion.

Mark Antony drew up angrily, his personal guard holding a tight formation around him. He could smell his own sweat and his face was rough with stubble. He was in no mood to be challenged by Legate Buccio that morning.

'Why have you countermanded my orders and called a halt?' he demanded. 'You can rest when we reach the city.'

Four legions continued to march doggedly down the last miles of the Via Appia, while Buccio's legion stood with their heads down in ranks, looking shattered. They had marched all night, passing another twenty-two of the milestones after the thirty they had managed the day before.

The legate saluted properly, though his eyes were red with exhaustion.

'I did try to warn you, sir. I did not want to go sneaking off in the night.' He took a deep breath. 'My legion will not go further with you, sir.'

Mark Antony gaped at him, unable to understand at first what the legate was saying so calmly. When he took it in, the consul's jaw firmed and he dropped his hand to the sword hilt sticking up by his right thigh.

'I have four legions I can call back, Legate Buccio. Obey my orders or I will see you strung up.'

'I regret, Consul, that I cannot obey that order,' Buccio replied. To Mark Antony's shock, the man smiled as he went on. 'The Ninth Macedonia will not take arms against a Caesar.'

Mark Antony became aware that their conversation was being closely watched by Buccio's men. As his gaze drifted over them, he saw they were standing like dogs on a rope, ready to lunge forward. Their fingers moved on the hafts of spears and they did not look away. He could not order his guards to take Buccio into custody. The barely checked aggression of the legionaries made clear what would happen if he tried.

Mark Antony leaned down from his saddle, dropping his voice so that it would not carry to the waiting men.

'No matter how this turns out, Buccio, no matter what happens at the city, there is no force in Rome that does not punish mutiny and treason. You will not be trusted again. The Ninth Macedonia will be struck from the Senate rolls and disbanded, whether by me or by the Senate themselves. Will you have your men become brigands, homeless traitors unable

184

to sleep anywhere without the fear of attack? Think about that before you go too far along the path and I can no longer save you from your own foolishness.'

The words struck Buccio like blows, but his mouth tightened to a pale line.

'They and I are of one mind, Consul. They can be pushed only so far and then they must be led, just as you told me.'

Mark Antony glared to have his own words repeated to him.

'Then I hope we meet again,' he said, 'in better times.'

The consul turned his horse and jerked his head for the guards to follow him. He had lost two legions and he could read the wind well enough. He clenched his jaw as he rode after the ones he still had left.

By the time Buccio's legion marched up the Via Appia, some hours later, Mark Antony had left the road to head north, taking a wide line around the city. The legate halted briefly at the signs of their passing, a great swathe of trampled and muddy grass showing the tracks of twenty thousand men disappearing into the distance. Buccio nodded to himself, then summoned his own extraordinarii rider.

'Ride ahead, to Caesar. Let him know the Ninth Macedonia are with him. Tell him Consul Mark Antony no longer comes to Rome. And if you see Legate Liburnius, tell him he owes me a drink.'

As the rider galloped off on the stone road, Buccio's tribune came up. Patroclus was a young noble, barely twenty years of age, and from one of the better families in Rome. He watched the rider dwindling into the distance.

'I hope Caesar appreciates what we've risked in his name,' Patroclus said. The man had a pink lump with a white head on his eyelid that had swelled his eye almost closed. He scratched irritably at it as he spoke.

'You can have that steamed out in Rome, Patroclus,' Buccio said.

'I am not worried about my eye, sir, just the rest of me. My mother will collapse when she hears I've mutinied.'

'You have mutinied *for* Caesar,' Buccio said softly. 'You have placed your faith in *him*, for the man and his adopted son, over the Senate that murdered him. That is not the same thing at all.'

The atmosphere in Pompey's theatre was sulphurous, filled with panicky anger as groups of opposing senators tried to shout over each other. The fragile truce that had existed while Octavian and the legions remained in the forum had cracked apart the moment they marched north. Without properly appointed consuls to keep order, the debates had deteriorated quickly and Bibilus had been challenged as speaker by a powerful group of senators that morning. Forced to give up his position, he sat back on the marble benches with Suetonius and his clique of supporters, watching and waiting for a weakness.

Hirtius and Pansa stood before the other senators. Every passing day brought their consular year closer and together they had bluffed that position into something like authority. It was Hirtius who picked speakers as it pleased him. He waited through the latest round of recrimination and argument before deciding to speak once again.

'Senators, this clamour has no place here! We have all the facts we need to make a decision, brought in by men risking their lives. It is enough! Rome lies vulnerable until the legions from Ostia arrive. They have landed safely, but will we waste the day in pointless argument? Senators, be silent!'

Under his furious glare, they quietened in patches and then as a whole. It was the third meeting in as many days and the news had only worsened with each one. Every man there was aware of the ugly mood in the city. Without legions to keep order, crimes against citizens and property had risen tenfold and there were few present who did not have some story of theft or rape or murder to recount. They were frustrated and angry, but the lack of a clear path through only added to the chaos. Outside the theatre, almost a thousand mercenary guards waited for their employers to come out. Only in their presence could the senators return to their homes and even then crowds gathered quickly to shout and jeer and violence was constantly in the air. In all its centuries, Rome had never felt as close to a complete breakdown of order as it did then and Hirtius saw fear as much as anger in the ranks of robed men. It did not trouble him particularly. In such an atmosphere, he considered he might win far greater authority and advantages than any other year.

'I have reports from a dozen men observing the movement of legions around this city,' Hirtius said loudly. 'I'm sure you can confirm it all from your own clients and informers. The situation is perilous, no doubt, but not beyond salvage, not if we act quickly.' He waited through a sudden tirade by one of the more elderly senators, staring the man down until he subsided and took his seat once more.

'Thank you for your courtesy, Senator,' Hirtius said with as much acid as he could manage. 'But the facts are simple enough. Mark Antony has taken four legions north. I had to waste a man who had been my client for a dozen years to bring me his destination. We know the consul's intention to attack a loyal member of this Senate: Decimus Junius.'

Cries went up from the senators and Hirtius shouted over them.

'Yes, Mark Antony flouts our authority! There is no point going over the same ground. Our *response* is the issue, not the crimes of the consul. Decimus Junius has no more than three thousand legionaries assigned as staff and guards for the region.

He *will* fall and we will have another small king established there to scorn all we do. However, gentlemen, it may not come to that. I have discussed it with Senator Pansa and we have a potential solution.'

For the first time that morning, the men on the benches were properly silent and Hirtius smiled tightly. He was a stern man, with many years as tribune and legate of legions behind him.

'I ask only that you hear me out before you begin baying once more. You do yourselves no service with this howling and gnashing of teeth.'

There was some muttering at being lectured in such a way, but he ignored it.

'Four fresh legions are gathering at Ostia, drawn from Sicily and Sardinia. They will be here in two days. Apart from those, there is only one army of sufficient strength in range of the consul. There is only one other force capable of heading off the attack on Decimus Junius.' He paused, expecting some sort of protest as they realised his drift, but to his surprise it did not come. The senators were truly afraid and for once they were listening.

'Octavian, or Caesar as I suppose we must call him now, has four legions at full strength. Both the Fourth Ferrata and Ninth Macedonia have followed him north. We do not yet know his destination. With the four from Ostia coming here, those are all the legions on the mainland, senators. The question we must ask is how best to use them to sanction our rogue consul.'

He paused again, catching the eye of Senator Pansa at his side, who nodded.

'I remind you that this new Caesar refrained from violence against this Senate when he had every opportunity to do so. It is my feeling that we have not lost the argument with him, if we were to grant at least some of his requests.' He saw

Suetonius and Bibilus rise to their feet and talked over them as they began to reply. 'I have *not* forgotten his illegal occupation, senators, only that he carried it out without bloodshed or loss of *honestas* – integrity. Even so, I would not turn to him if he did not command the only force capable of taking on Mark Antony!

'The choices come down to one, senators. Give me your authority. Confirm Senator Pansa and myself as consuls ahead of time. We will take four legions to Caesar and assume command of a unified army capable of bringing Mark Antony to heel. The consul has mutinied and must be stripped of his rank. Who else but consuls have the right to take the field against him – and the authority of the Senate to do it?'

Bibilus had been caught in mid-argument by the suggestion and he sat down to think it through. It was not lost on him that removing Hirtius and Pansa from the Senate would leave very few capable of challenging his own position. A thousand men from the legions at Ostia would be enough to keep Rome quiet for a little while longer. He began to think he could vote for such a course.

Suetonius felt the sudden space at his shoulder as Bibilus sat, but he did not resume his own seat.

'What concessions will you give Octavian in exchange for his service?' he called, then repeated himself even louder as the men around him told him to be quiet.

'I do not intend to renounce the amnesty, Suetonius,' Hirtius said dryly. 'You don't need to worry on that point.' A chuckle went around the benches and Suetonius flushed as Hirtius continued. 'This young Caesar has asked for a Lex Curiata, which we can grant. It is nothing more than his right and such a gesture costs us nothing. In addition, we will also win over good Romans who depend on that vote to take control of their own properties. I have entreaties from them every day. Finally, I propose to offer him the rank of propraetor, to welcome him

189

back into society, where we can make use of him. He has no formal rank at present and I do not think his change of name will take him much further.'

Suetonius sat down, apparently satisfied. Hirtius breathed in relief. It was beginning to look as if he might get his way. The thought of a campaign against Mark Antony worried him not at all, not with the forces that would be at his disposal. He looked over the benches to where Bibilus was watching him. Hirtius smiled at the man's obvious satisfaction. Men like Bibilus thought they ruled the city, but they could never lead a legion, or appreciate anything beyond their own sense of importance. When he returned with Pansa as consuls, he would deal with Bibilus as Caesar had once dealt with him. Hirtius smiled openly at the thought, nodding to the fat senator as if to an equal.

For once, no one rose to oppose or add to the debate. Hirtius waited, but when they remained in their seats, he cleared his throat.

'If there is no dissent, I will call for a vote to bring our consular year in early and take our legions to command Caesar in the field.'

'What if he refuses, even so?' Suetonius called from the benches.

'Then I will have him killed, though I do not think it will come to that. For all his faults, this new Caesar is a practical man. He will see his best chance lies with us.'

The vote passed quickly and with very few opposed. It would have to be confirmed by the citizens of Rome, but if the new consuls returned victorious, it would be a formality. Hirtius turned to Pansa and raised his eyebrows.

'It seems you and I are in for a long ride, Consul.'

Pansa grinned at the new title. Just the thought of getting away from the endless bickering of the Senate brought contentment. The prospect was invigorating. Pansa scrubbed a hand through the white bristle of his hair, wondering whether his armour would need polishing when he had it brought out of storage.

CHAPTER FIFTEEN

Arretium was a military town, barely a hundred miles north of Rome. Whatever Maecenas' reasons for recommending it, it had the benefit of being within swift range of the capital, while far enough away to give the Senate the sense that they were not immediately threatened.

The Fabii property Maecenas owned was indeed a delight, a low complex of buildings and gardens that stretched up a hill on various levels, each host to a bewildering display of imported fruit trees and statues in white stone. It felt like a place to rest and enjoy the end of summer, with the struggle safely behind them. A banqueting hall led out onto the gardens and Maecenas had agreed to host the legates of four legions in rooms on the estate. Twenty thousand legionaries had descended on the town itself and doubled its population, so that prices went up and those who could not afford rooms camped in fields.

Legates Silva and Paulinius had welcomed Liburnius and Buccio like old friends. In fact, the four men had met before on campaigns, but they could all take comfort in knowing they had not risked the wrath of the Senate alone.

Octavian said a brief prayer to Ceres as he sat at the table, thanking the goddess for producing the meal that lay before them. Maecenas had produced the Falernian and Octavian had to admit it was superior to the sour wine Silva had served before.

'So are you going to tell us?' Maecenas asked, pulling a cooked goose apart with his fingers. He saw Octavian frown. 'There are no surprises with twenty thousand men camped all around the town, Caesar. A messenger from Rome cannot be kept secret. Are we to be branded traitors, then? Have they sent a demand for our heads?'

'I would know how to react to that,' Octavian replied.

He looked around the table at the six men who had risked everything for him. Agrippa was watching every change of expression on his face, as if trying to read his thoughts. Liburnius kept his gaze on the food, still very aware of the change in their respective statuses since their last meeting. Yet he too had done what mattered and marched men north to follow Caesar. Octavian had welcomed the newly promoted legate with only a dry comment on the rising value of the favour he still carried. Presumably, Gracchus would catch up with him eventually, though Octavian was amused at the thought of the dour legionary still searching for his lost commander.

From his tunic, Octavian withdrew a scroll and unrolled it, ignoring the spots of grease his fingers left on the dry surface.

'I have orders here,' he said, 'orders to report to consuls Hirtius and Pansa and to put myself under their authority.' His eyes scanned the page yet again. 'They are coming north with four legions and it seems I have been made a propraetor, by will of the Senate.'

The men around the table gaped at him in rising excitement. In just a few words, they had gone from standing outside the law to being welcomed back. Liburnius and Buccio looked up together, the same thought striking them both. It was Buccio who managed to speak first.

'If they have appointed consuls before the year is up, it can only mean Mark Antony is out.'

Liburnius nodded as he speared a piece of slow-cooked lamb with his knife and chewed slowly.

'Will you do it?' Agrippa asked for all of them. 'Will you accept Senate authority after all that has happened? Can you even trust them, Caesar? For all we know, this is some ruse to get close enough to attack.'

Octavian waved a hand, almost overturning his cup of wine and then gripping it to keep it steady.

'How many legions could they have summoned at such short notice? Even if it is a trap, they would just smash themselves against our men. I am inclined to believe them, gentlemen, but that does not solve my problem, does it? Why would they make such an offer? Why would they even want my legions, if not to punish Mark Antony? Yet he should be fighting *with* me, not against me! He goes north to attack Decimus Junius, one of those who wielded knives on the Ides of March. Should I join the Senate and prevent him achieving exactly what I would like to see happen? By the gods, how can I join my enemies, to fight against my only ally?'

As he spoke, the sense of excitement drained from the men at the table. For just an instant, they had seen a way through the fear and chaos of their position, but Octavian's anger snuffed out their hopes.

'So you will not join the new consuls, Caesar?' Legate Silva said.

'No, I'll join them. I'll even march north against Mark Antony with them.' Octavian hesitated, considering how much he could tell them. He had already made his decision. 'Why would I resist marching north? Mark Antony is right – Decimus Junius is away from Rome, but still in reach. I would be following the same path before too long. Let these new consuls think whatever they like. Let them believe whatever they like. They are bringing me reinforcements.'

Maecenas rubbed his forehead, feeling the tension that would lead to a headache. To avert it, he drank a full cup of the Falernian, smacking his lips.

'The men around this table came to follow Caesar,' he said. 'Heir to the divine Julius. Will you now tell them they must also accept orders from the Senate? From the very senators who voted an amnesty for his killers? They've mutinied before for less.'

His words prompted a furious response from Buccio and Paulinius, both men shouting over the other at the insult to their honour. Maecenas looked at them, his own anger simmering.

'So we march to attack Mark Antony, to save that whore's whelp Decimus Junius?' Maecenas continued. 'Have you all gone deaf, or can you hear me say that?'

Octavian glared at his friend, rising from the table and leaning on his knuckles. His eyes were cold as he stared and Maecenas had to look away as the silence swelled and became uncomfortable.

'Ever since I came back from Greece,' Octavian said, 'my path has been strewn with rocks. I have suffered through fools and greedy men.' His gaze fell on Liburnius then, who suddenly looked away. 'I have had my rightful demands scorned by fat senators. I have seen plans turned on their head and ruined in front of my eyes – and yet, despite *all* that, I find myself here, with four legions sworn to me alone and another four on the way. Would you have me tell you all my plans, Maecenas? For friendship, I will, though it will make the task a thousand times harder. So I ask you this. Put aside the demands of friendship and act, for *once*, as an officer under my command.

I will accept the rank of propraetor and if any man asks how I can put myself under Senate authority, tell that man that Caesar does not share his plans with every soldier under *his* command!'

Maecenas opened his mouth to reply, but Agrippa shoved his wooden trencher across the table, butting him in the chest.

'Enough, Maecenas. You heard what he said.'

Maecenas nodded, rubbing his temples where an ache still throbbed.

'I have no choice,' Octavian said to them all, 'but to be the very model of Roman humility and discipline. I will accept the command of Hirtius and Pansa because it suits my aims.' His voice was hard as he went on. 'I will have to show these new consuls more than just words and promises. We should expect to be sent first into battle, or any other situation where our loyalty can be tested. They are not fools, gentlemen. If we are to survive the coming year, we have to be sharper and faster than the consuls of Rome.'

Hirtius and Pansa rode on well-groomed geldings in the third rank of their new legions. Both men were in fine form as they trotted along the wide stone route of the Via Cassia. Hirtius looked back over his shoulder at the trudging ranks, reliving old memories and seeing no flaw in the men he had been given. Their very solidity was a balm after the raving chaos they left behind. There were no arguments on the road, no riots. He and Pansa were of one mind, delighted that Mark Antony's mistakes had raised them to the highest post in Rome six months early. It was clear to both of them that the man should have been quietly executed on the Ides of March, but there was no point in regrets. If Caesar had lived, Hirtius and Pansa both knew they would have become puppet consuls for the Father of Rome, able to act only at his bidding. Instead, they were free and in command of legions. There were worse fates.

'Do you really think he will fall in line?' Pansa asked suddenly. Hirtius did not have to ask whom he meant. The subject had come up at some point every day out of Rome.

'It is a perfect solution, Pansa, as I've said. Octavian is just a youth. He reached too far and had his fingers burned. All he wants now is to salvage a little dignity.' He patted his saddlebag, where the Senate orders rested in their pouch. 'Making him propraetor gives him recognition, though you will notice it makes him governor in name, but without a place to govern. What a gift, that is worth so much and yet costs us nothing!' Hirtius smiled modestly, hoping his colleague would remember who had suggested it.

'He is too young, Pansa, and much too inexperienced to rule Rome. The ridiculous fiasco at the forum showed that. I suspect he will fall on our necks with gratitude, but if he doesn't, we have both the rank and the men to enforce the Senate will. His men are not fanatics, remember, for all their talk of a new Caesar. They did not offer to fight to the death when they thought Mark Antony was returning to Rome. Not them! Instead, they charged away in the opposite direction. Legionaries are practical men, Pansa – and so am I.'

Arretium had grown up on the Via Cassia, a town made prosperous by the ease with which trade goods could reach it and travel from it to other regions. Neither Hirtius nor Pansa knew the area well, but their extraordinarii riders kept a wide ring around them as they went north, reporting back in a chain so that they were informed of all that lay ahead. Before the sun reached the western hills on their flank, their riders came back accompanied by strangers, seeking out the consuls and reporting with all the formality they might require. Hirtius accepted the messages of welcome and safe passage as if they had been expected all along, though he could not resist a smug glance at his co-consul.

'It is too early to stop for the night,' Hirtius said in an aside to his colleague. 'I would rather take the legions into Arretium and make sure the Senate orders have been properly . . . understood.'

Pansa nodded immediately, already cheerful at the thought of a return to civilisation. Hirtius seemed to thrive on sleeping out, but at sixty years of age, Pansa's bones ached each morning.

The legions had not stopped for their consuls to receive messages. They marched on without expression as the orders came down the line. It mattered little to them whether they slept in tents by the road or in tents by a Roman town. At the end of the day, they were the same tents.

Manoeuvring such large numbers required a fair level of skill and both consuls were happy to leave the deployment to their subordinates. As they came within a mile of the walled town, a dozen extraordinarii and three of Octavian's tribunes came out to help them organise the halt without adding to the problems of the legions already in the vicinity. The best places were all taken, of course, but Hirtius and Pansa cared nothing for that. They accepted the invitation to meet Caesar in a fine provincial home outside the walls. Both men rode in with their lictors and personal guards, so that they made an impressive group. They had been offered a truce to approach and Hirtius did not expect treachery, but he still had enough men to fight his way out if necessary. In any case, his new rank demanded such a following and he enjoyed the sight of stern lictors watching for the slightest insult to his person.

The estate was small compared with those around Rome, but Hirtius approved of the taste and wealth that had gone into its creation. The main house was reached through open gates and a wide courtyard, where servants scurried to take their horses. Hirtius looked to the pillared entrance and saw Octavian waiting there. He stood with no sign of tension and Hirtius realised with prickling irritation that the young man was handsome, with broad shoulders and long hair tied into a club at his neck. It was the first time they had ever met, but there was no mistaking the confidence in the grey eyes watching the consuls.

Hirtius and Pansa walked up the steps together. The evening was soft and warm and the air smelled of cut hay. Hirtius took a deep breath of it, feeling some of his tension ease.

'This is a splendid house, Caesar,' Hirtius said. 'Is it yours?'

'It belongs to a friend, Consul,' Octavian said. 'You will meet him tonight and you can tell him then, though he is already too proud. You are welcome here. I give you my oath and my protection while you remain in Arretium. There are rooms for your lictors and followers if you wish. If you'll follow me inside, I have had food laid out for you.'

Pansa stepped forward immediately at the thought of a meal. Hirtius looked askance at his companion but walked in behind, sending the waiting lictors away with a flick of his fingers. There were times when a man had to trust his host and constant suspicion insulted them both. He reminded himself that Octavian could have slaughtered the Senate but had not.

The legates had gathered in the banqueting hall to greet the consuls from Rome. When Hirtius and Pansa entered, all the men rose, including Maecenas and Agrippa. They stood like soldiers in the presence of senior officers and Hirtius nodded to them, accepting Octavian's invitation to sit at their table. He and Pansa had been placed together at the head and he wasted no time in taking his seat. As nobody had been sure when the consuls would arrive, the meal was cold, but it was still much better than they had eaten on the road north.

'Sit, sit, gentlemen,' Hirtius said. 'Your manners do you

credit, but we have much to discuss.' He hesitated at the sight of Pansa already heaping thin slices of cured ham onto his plate, but the other consul was oblivious.

A slave approached with a jug of wine and Hirtius noticed the delicate glass vessels on the table. He raised his eyebrows slightly, aware that he was being treated as an honoured guest. He sipped the wine and his eyebrows went further up.

'Excellent,' he pronounced. 'I prefer the table to couches. It feels . . . delightfully barbaric. I take it, then, you have received the missive from the Senate?'

'Yes, Consul,' Octavian replied. 'I can tell you it was something of a relief to be offered formal rank.'

Consul Pansa nodded, smacking his lips and draining his cup of wine.

'I imagine it was, Caesar. Whatever our differences in the past, I'm sure the news of a true mutiny, by no less a name than Mark Antony, was as shocking to you as it was to the senators.'

'As you say, Consul,' Octavian replied, inclining his head to Pansa in agreement as the man began to work his way through a plate of melon slices sprinkled with ginger.

Hirtius spent a moment cleaning a fingernail with one of the others. He would have preferred outright command, of course, but Pansa was theoretically his equal and not easily dismissed. Either way, the young rebel seemed to bear no animosity towards his guests. Hirtius nodded stiffly, choosing dignity over rubbing Octavian's face in his failures. He cleared his throat as Pansa dug in to the main dishes, spearing the carcasses of some small birds fried in olive oil.

'Very well, then. To the task at hand. Mark Antony is perhaps a week on the march ahead of us. We know his path and his destination. We know his strengths very well – I believe some of you were with him in Brundisium?' Buccio and Liburnius nodded uncomfortably. 'Then you may have some insight worth hearing. I will send men to record your thoughts, though I doubt there is anything new to say. I have known Mark Antony for many years. He is an impressive speaker, but if you remember, Caesar did not trust him with many men in Gaul. He is more suited to governing a city. I do not expect his four legions to cause us too much difficulty.' Hirtius looked around the table as he spoke, drawing them all into his confidence.

'Do we know what forces Decimus Junius has at his disposal?' Flavius Silva asked.

Hirtius smiled at his contribution, sensing they were trying hard to work in the new structure his presence had created.

'The region by the Alps is hardly bristling with soldiers. There are a dozen legions in Gaul, but up in the north, no more than a few thousand men. It is not an impossible obstacle for Mark Antony, if we were not here to oppose him. However, I think he will be unpleasantly surprised to see eight legions and new consuls to bring him to justice.'

Hirtius leaned forward, tapping a single knuckle on the table as if he did not already have their full attention.

'My orders are simple enough, gentlemen. For a short time, you have all found yourself outside the law. This is your chance to wipe the slate clean. From this moment, this is a lawful assembly, under command of the Roman Senate.' He paused, but when there was no reply from the men at the table, he nodded, satisfied. 'We will march at dawn and make the best speed possible north. When we are in range of Mark Antony, we will engage and either force an immediate surrender or destroy his legions with superior numbers. I would prefer him to be brought back to Rome for trial and execution, but I will not complain if he fails to survive the fighting. Is all that understood?'

The men around the table nodded and Hirtius glanced at Octavian.

'I hope it is as clear that Decimus Junius is our ally. His life is under the protection of Senate authority and he will not be touched. Those are my terms.'

'I understand, Consul,' Octavian said. 'Though you have not said what part I will play in this. I accept my rank of propraetor, but it is a civil position. My legions will expect to see me command.' His grey eyes glinted dangerously and Hirtius raised his palms, fending off the objection.

'I am here to bring you back into the Roman fold. It would not serve to reduce a Caesar to the ranks. However, you will appreciate the perils of a split command. Pansa and I will give joint orders to the eight legions. You will be praefectus of two legions in the vanguard. You will march under our orders, in good formation, until you have met the enemy.' His voice hardened subtly then. 'You will give no orders of your own, not against Mark Antony. Your men have a history of independent thinking and I cannot afford to indulge their taste for it.'

Being first into the line of battle was an honourable position, but Octavian could not help the suspicion that the older man would be happy to see him fall. Even so, it was as much as he had hoped. There had never been a chance that the consuls would leave him in charge of half the army they commanded.

'Very well,' Octavian said. 'And after the battle is won?'

Hirtius laughed. He had not yet touched his food, but he sipped his wine again, sucking it over his tongue with a hissing sound.

'I appreciate your confidence, Caesar! Very well, *when* the battle is won, we will have order restored. Pansa and I will return to Rome, of course, with the legions. I do not doubt you will be honoured in some way by the Senate. They will give you your Lex Curiata, and if you are a man of sense, you will stand for election as senator in the new year. I imagine you will have a long and successful career. Between you and me, I would enjoy seeing a little younger blood in the Senate.'

Octavian smiled tightly in response, forcing himself to eat a few mouthfuls. The consul was working to be charming, but Octavian could see the hardness in him, the personification of Roman authority. He reminded himself that the consuls had denied him everything when they thought he was powerless. Four legions had bought him a place at the table, but they were not true allies.

'I will consider it, Consul . . .' he said. Octavian saw Hirtius frown and decided he was offering too little resistance and making the man suspicious. 'Although you will appreciate how difficult it is for me to imagine sitting at peace with men like the Liberatores.'

'Ah, I understand your reluctance, Caesar. The name says it all. Yet we are practical men, are we not? I would not waste my youth railing against enemies beyond my reach.'

Hirtius sensed the sentiment was not echoed in the cold-eyed young man across from him. The meeting had gone better than he had hoped and he struggled to find something else to smooth over the moment of ill-feeling.

'If I have learned anything, Caesar, it is that nothing is certain in politics. Enemies become friends and vice versa, over time. Those who sit around this table are proof enough of that. However, it is also true that men rise and fall. Who knows where we shall find ourselves in a few years? It may be that when enough time has passed, once powerful men will find their stars have set and others are on the rise.'

He snapped his mouth shut then, rather than make promises he could not possibly keep. He had intended to raise a little hope in the young Roman. Hirtius had lived long enough to know that a brief and careless mention of promotion would keep some men working for years without reward. Yet words were just wind until they were written down and sealed. He was pleased to see Octavian's expression ease and Hirtius raised a cup of the Falernian in a toast, the gesture quickly copied around the table.

CHAPTER SIXTEEN

Mark Antony shivered in a wind which came straight from the mountains looming over him. The cloak that had seemed so thick in the south felt threadbare, no matter how he wrapped and folded it. He could see his own breath and the ground itself was covered in a constant dusting of frost. Even his horse was shod with leather on each hoof to protect its feet.

From first light, he had set men to constructing catapults and scorpion bows, assembling the massive weapons of wood and iron from the train of carts he had brought with him. The cold made injuries unavoidable and he already had two men with crushed fingers being tended by healers.

His sons, Antyllus and Paulus, were in the thick of it, of course, tolerated by the legionaries as they ran and carried tools and nails, hardly feeling the cold at all. Mark Antony had been tempted to have Fulvia and Claudia round them up before they got themselves hurt, but the instinct had been forgotten in the face of a thousand other tasks. They had made good time on the coastal road north, arriving a week after him and with his wife exhausted and irritable. It would suit her to have them run free for a day.

Decimus Junius had not been idle, despite the shock he must have felt at seeing four legions marching into the fields around his fortresses. Mark Antony had surrounded and disarmed two thousand legionaries three days before, forcing the remainder of Junius' forces to abandon them and run. The captured men were under guard at the permanent camp of Taurinorum, huddled in misery, though warmer than he was.

Mark Antony was not yet certain where Decimus Junius had placed himself in the chain of forts, but some guiding hand had withdrawn most of the remaining soldiers into the largest one, a massive wooden structure that squatted over the entrance to the pass. There were two other strongholds further away, but they could be broken or starved at leisure. Beyond the pass and the main fort lay Gaul, with all its wealth and vast green land. It seemed almost a dream while icy air bit at his exposed skin, but Mark Antony wanted at least one route to Gaul open and unopposed.

He did not intend to cross the mountains, not that year. Decimus Junius had been given a rich plum here in the north for his part in the assassination. Away from the peculiar climate of the mountains, it was rich land, producing vast quantities of grain and meat for Roman cities. If Mark Antony could secure it for himself, he would have both wealth and power over the Senate, no matter how they raged at him. In just a few years, when his sons had grown, he would have restored his position. He let the thought cheer him as the wind increased and his face went completely numb. One of his Brundisium legates was standing by for orders, the man's nose and cheeks pink with cold.

'Send a demand for surrender to the fort,' Mark Antony said. 'At least we might confirm if Decimus Junius is inside. If they don't respond, wait for my signal and then smash the thing down around his ears.'

The legate saluted and hurried back to the waiting catapult teams, pleased to be moving. Mark Antony turned his horse, viewing the waiting legions with a stern eye. They were ready to rush in once the gates were broken and he found no fault with them. There had been no hint of disloyalty facing this particular enemy. He recalled that Caesar had once warned him never to give an order the legions would not obey. There was insight there, but he did not enjoy it. He knew there would be times when he sent his men against enemies they did not approve of and he could not risk them failing, as Buccio and Liburnius had failed. As the wind moaned past him from the mountains, Mark Antony licked his chapped lips and wondered how he could restore their discipline to unthinking obedience.

No formal response came from the fortress, not that he had really expected one. Mark Antony waited as the pale sun moved behind clouds in the sky. By then the chill had numbed him so deeply that he could not feel his hands or feet.

'Enough of this,' he said to a cornicen, his teeth chattering. 'Blow two short notes.'

The sound rang out and the response came quickly. Small rocks launched from torsion weapons, driven by twisted ropes of horsehair three times the thickness of a man's leg. Mark Antony could hear the teams roar as they beat the larger cata- pult to the first shot, but when it launched, the echoing thump of the beam silenced them. Twenty thousand men watched the huge stone fly on a shallow arc, soaring towards the fortress gates. With no resistance from within, they had been able to take their time placing the weapons. All the shots flew true, hitting the central gate one after the other. There was an explo- sion of splinters and dust and Mark Antony knew from the cheering that a gap had appeared in the defences. He squinted through the biting wind, his vision far better over distance than it was reading messages. The torsion weapons were wound once again by the teams, the only ones warm that morning on the plain. The catapult too began to come up, drawn peg by peg against the massive strength of the beam itself and great iron spars that bent like a bow. Mark Antony gripped his cloak tighter around his throat, twitching the folds of red cloth with his free hand so it covered his thighs and part of the horse's flank. The animal snorted at the contact and he patted it, waiting.

He sensed movement out of the corner of his eye even as the heavy machines punched rocks into the air once more. His men shouted in excitement, but his own pleasure turned to bitter worry as he saw one of his riders come galloping across the white plain. Mark Antony had them out in two rings, ten and twenty miles from his position. He was not surprised to see the man panting after such a ride.

'Legions sighted, Consul,' the rider said.

'You know how to report!' Mark Antony snapped.

The young rider looked stricken, but he collected himself quickly.

'Discens Petronius reporting, Consul!'

'Report,' Mark Antony went on, glowering at him.

'Legions sighted, Consul, marching north. A large force, with auxiliaries and extraordinarii.'

Mark Antony tapped his fingers on the saddle horn, considering his choices.

'Very well, Discens Petronius,' he said. 'Return to your position.'

He watched the young man ride away, his mind whirling like the frost the wind kept flinging against his skin. It could only be Octavian. All the plans Mark Antony had made were collapsing into dust. He could not hold the north for a single winter, not against a force at least equal to his own. That was if his men would fight at all, once they learned who they faced.

He paused for a moment, reflecting. His hand came up and patted his chest, where a crumpled letter lay in a pocket. He'd read it many times, in disbelief and dread. With a muttered curse, he realised his choices had narrowed to just one. No matter what else happened, he *had* to open the pass to Gaul. He looked up, his eyes as cold as the mountains as he stared at the fortress in his way.

Mark Antony raised his arm and dropped it, the signal for which his legions had been waiting. They surged forward, heading to the broken gates past catapult teams who lounged on their weapons, their work done.

As they poured in, he heard the first clashes and screams echoing back from the hills above. He looked to his left, though the wind made him narrow his eyes to slits. Somewhere out there, a young Roman held Mark Antony's future in his hands. He looked across the fort, to where the pass wandered up through the mountains before disappearing into the whiteness above.

'Mars protect me,' he murmured. Every instinct told him that fleeing would see him destroyed. Gnaeus Pompey had run the length of the world, but Caesar still caught him. Mark Antony knew he could send the auxiliaries and camp followers through the pass and win them time to get clear. At least his wife and children would be safe for a while longer.

'*Julius* protect me,' he whispered into the wind. 'If you can see me now, old friend, I could use a little help.'

Octavian seethed as he rode, matching the pace of the legions. With so many men around him, he could not speak to Agrippa or Maecenas, but simply had to carry out the orders he had been given. Hirtius had placed him on the left wing, in the first of two lines of four legions. Legates Silva and Liburnius rode with him, the fairest choice he could make, while Buccio and

Paulinius held station in the second line. Yet the formation ignored their superior numbers. The consuls had made the sort of Roman hammer that had failed so spectacularly against Hannibal three hundred years before. Octavian looked right to where the consuls rode in splendid cloaks and armour in the third rank. He could see them as distant spots of white and red, their lictors mounted to keep up with them. It was also the sort of deep formation that showed little trust in the men they commanded, which would hardly be lost on veteran legions. Those in the front ranks would feel their colleagues breathing down their necks the whole way, with everything that implied.

Octavian made a tunnel with his hands to focus his vision far away, an old scout trick. Through the moving circle he could see the mountains and Mark Antony's legions like busy ants at their foot. They were forming lines as well, though less deep, so they could command a wider stretch of ground. Octavian glanced at the cornicen, but he could not give orders. Hirtius and Pansa were in command and the consuls had made themselves very clear. Octavian's formal rank of praefectus was just an empty honour, at least for that battle. Octavian clenched his teeth until they ached.

The legions tramped on and as the sun reached the noon point, they were less than a mile from the ranks waiting for them. Octavian could see the remains of a fort across the pass, reduced to broken beams and rubble by thousands of willing hands. He had studied the maps Hirtius and Pansa carried and he knew the pass led through to southern Gaul, where the summer was still warm. When he was close enough to make out individual figures, he spotted a trail of carts winding into the mountains, away from the plain. Once more, he looked right to where Hirtius and Pansa sat in their ornate armour. It was possible they wanted Mark Antony to keep an escape route open, but if so, they had not shared it with their subordinates.

For the first time in his life, Octavian understood the terrifying reality of facing standing legions on a flat plain. Mark Antony had been given time to assemble his scorpion bows, weapons the size of carts that could send an iron bolt right through half a dozen legionaries. Octavian had made his plans, but they took him only so far. A single spear-thrust could put an end to all his hopes.

The temperature of the air had dropped in the wind coming off the hills and he shivered as he rode with his rank. All around him, legionaries were readying the heavy spears that would land the first blow. They would not draw swords until the first three waves had been heaved into the air, but unstrapping the wooden shafts with their iron tips brought that moment closer. The pace increased unconsciously and the centurions had to bellow to hold them steady. They strained forward as they marched and still Octavian could give no orders. He leaned in his saddle, wanting the clash to come rather than suffer any longer through a tension that built with every step.

Maecenas unsheathed a spatha sword on his left, longer than the usual gladius so he could cut down from the height of a horse. The Roman noble wore a breastplate that was perfectly smooth and polished to a high gleam. When Agrippa had mocked him for the way it caught the sun, Maecenas had only smiled. The gorgeous filigree and decoration favoured by senior officers made it easier for a sword tip to snag and then punch through. Agrippa had found himself a set of lorica armour, so that he clanked as he rode. They stayed close to Octavian and both men understood their role in the fighting to come. They knew Hirtius had hamstrung him, forcing him to accept the man's consular authority. They would protect him, above all else.

Octavian looked for Mark Antony in the lines across the plain but could not see him. The man would be back in the third rank on his right wing, just as Hirtius and Pansa had chosen.

It meant Octavian would be riding straight at his position. He did not yet know what he would do if he saw Mark Antony hard-pressed. Plans and stratagems swirled in his mind, but too much depended on the actions of others and Mark Antony in particular. The man *had* to trust him.

Octavian clenched his fists on the hilt of his own spatha sword, taking comfort from the weight and swinging it lightly through the air to warm his shoulder. He felt strong as he tied the reins to the high saddle pommel and drew up a long shield from where it bumped along behind his leg. From four hundred and forty paces, he would guide his horse with his knees alone.

At three hundred paces or less, the legions with Mark Antony remained still. By then, both sides could read the symbols held high by signifers next to the Roman eagles. Octavian wondered how they would react to the sight of the Fourth Ferrata coming at them, men they had known well in Brundisium. How many of them would realise they were facing Caesar in battle? With legions bearing down on them, Mark Antony's men had no choice but to fight. On his own, he might have halted and let them see, perhaps even sent a messenger across to demand their surrender.

Octavian looked right to see if the consuls were reacting in any way, but no new orders came down the line. He bit his lip, feeling his bladder grow tight. Mark Antony did not want his men to rush ahead of the opening to the pass. He had positioned them with a clear line of retreat. That was useful information and if Octavian had been free, he knew he would have detached a thousand to threaten a block across the pass, forcing Mark Antony to respond. Yet the consuls only came on, closing the gap step by step.

At a hundred paces, horns sounded on both sides and the scorpion bows lurched on their stands, their bolts snapping out too fast for the eye to see. They ripped into the lines of legionaries, punching down files of men who never knew what

212

had killed them. The only response was to move in fast before the teams could reload. Octavian kicked his horse into a trot to match the sudden lurch in pace. As well as Maecenas and Agrippa, a diamond formation of heavily armoured men jogged with him, their task to protect the senior officer at the heart. His horse would mark him as a target from the first moments, but like the legates and tribunes of the eight legions, he needed the height to see. The legionaries in the ranks jogged smoothly, holding heavy spears low and ready for the first cast along a line that stretched for more than a mile.

When it came, Octavian had to struggle not to flinch. On both sides, thousands of men let out an explosive grunt as they heaved the spears up and immediately passed another from left hand to right. There were few among them who could guide the path, but they counted on speed and force over accuracy to smash an opponent's charge even as it began. Some fell on the scorpion teams, spearing them and then plunging into the ground so that the helpless, screaming men were held upright as they died.

Octavian raised his shield, staring as the air before him seemed to fill with whirring black stripes. The desire to crouch low in the saddle and hide behind his shield was almost unbearable, but he knew his men would despise him if he did. He had to stay upright and keep watching to fend off the spears and protect his horse. The animal's chest was partially covered by a bronze plate but was still vulnerable. If the fighting reached his rank, standing men could choose their spot to thrust from below.

All along the lines, legionaries raised their shields against the storm of wood and iron. The rushing hiss became a thumping clatter, with men yelling in shock and pain on both sides.

Octavian knocked a spear aside as it came down almost from above. It spun crazily as he deflected it, tripping a marching legionary, who looked up with a curse. Octavian could not

213

respond as he threw himself forward to smack the shield into another spear coming down at his horse's neck. That too fell away and by then the second wave was in the air.

For a long time, the spears seemed to come only at him. Octavian was sweating as he battered and swung at them. One passed between his shield and his bare calf, striking the man behind him, who fell to his knees unseen. All the time, they marched forward and both sides drew swords at the same moment, when the third spear had been sent. They were men who took satisfaction in their tools and the armies met at a run, using the shields like a ram and thrusting swords forward with savage strength.

Octavian rushed in with the others, unable to stop even if he had wanted to. The first two ranks on both sides were veterans. They protected the man on their left with their shields, while jabbing swords out at anything they could see. Octavian saw two of those guarding him go down, their bodies shuddering as blades punched through their armour. More of his diamond rotated up to the front, but he found himself pressed forward into the enemy. His horse snorted and tossed its head, panicky as it kicked out.

The ranks facing him were vulnerable to horsemen. Their shields could not be raised high without leaving them open to attack from below. When they shoved forward to reach him, Octavian swung instantly, feeling the shock up his arm as he cut through the softer metal of a helmet. The sight of a mounted officer drove the enemy soldiers to press in eagerly. As they were spotted, Octavian, Maecenas and Agrippa became the targets for those further back who had yet to throw their spears.

Octavian roared, forcing out his fear as spears came buzzing towards him. He had to split his attention between those trying to hack at his horse's legs and the ones further back who were still striving to hit an officer with anything they could throw. The men at the front of his diamond had fallen again, trying to protect him, and the crush was too great to allow the others to move up ahead. For a time, Octavian fought in the front rank. Maecenas and Agrippa worked well on either side, killing the men who went low with swift cuts and using their shields to protect each other when spears came soaring in.

Octavian heard his horse scream and the animal lurched. He felt a hot stripe across his face and he cried out as his horse fell into the gloom between his friends' mounts. Both sides saw him go down and his own men bellowed in anger, pressing forward in a rush. Sickened, Octavian wiped warm blood from his eyes. He could hear his horse screaming behind him for a moment, then the sound was cut off as someone killed it to stop the wild kicking.

Maecenas and Agrippa moved on with him as he staggered up, so that he walked at the level of their knees. The rush had forced a hole in the enemy line, though new, fresh soldiers were coming in fast to support the breach. A legionary with no helmet and bloody teeth opened his eyes wide as he saw who faced him. For an instant, Octavian thought he was holding up his sword to surrender rather than attack, but then Agrippa swung at the man from above, slicing an ear free and hacking into the joint between head and shoulder. The soldier fell to his knees and Octavian kicked him in the chest to knock him backwards before walking over the body. Through the horses, he could see milling men fighting and shouting in a red-faced combination of terror and rage.

He wiped blood from his face, wondering where his shield had gone. The horses on either side made a strange corridor, where enemies could come only one at a time. His arms felt leaden already, his hearing half gone with the constant crashing on all sides. Gods, he could not see Mark Antony! The men behind still roared and pushed, so that he was buffeted forward and the two horsemen cursed. He heard Maecenas yell, either in fury or pain, he could not tell which. The light seemed too

215

bright and Octavian found himself wet with sweat. He began to fear he would collapse, his heart racing so hard that it made him dizzy. His foot turned on a body and he staggered into Agrippa's mount, feeling the heat from the horse's skin. The men behind would not stop if he fell. They did not like walking over the fallen, as many of them could still stab in their last breaths. Each rank would be likely to plunge a sword into him until he was just a bloody, ragged thing, lost somewhere on the field of battle.

'Agrippa! Pull me up, you big sod. I have to see!' he shouted.

His friend heard and reached down with his shield strapped to his forearm. Octavian scrambled up behind him, hiding his relief. He had come close to panic on the ground and yet his heart was settling and the light had dimmed enough for him to make out the forces he faced.

The sun had moved. Somehow, his moments down by the snorting, stamping horses and men had taken longer than he had thought. He shook his head to clear it. The lines he faced had thinned to no more than four ranks deep, while the main force battered the right wing. In that first glimpse, Octavian had a sense that the ranks ahead were only holding, jamming their shields into the earth and linking them in an unbroken wall.

'Slow advance! Slow there!' Octavian ordered.

Gods, Hirtius could hardly object to marching orders. The command was echoed by centurions and optios back down the line, so that the press from behind eased. Still the first two ranks clashed, stabbing and cursing as they jammed their own shields into the churned mud and fought on around them.

Octavian caught sight of Mark Antony on his horse, shouting and pointing to send in different units and shore up the lines. Octavian knew he had to support the right flank. He formed the order in his head to have two or three cohorts cut across to protect the consuls, but he did not give it. A moment passed, then another, as his own advance slowed and came to a stop. The lines of linked shields ahead presented a solid obstacle, but he knew he could flank them. He had entire legions at his command to swing out and cut in from the sides, enveloping the soldiers of Mark Antony. He kept his mouth shut.

Maecenas looked over to him, a brief glance away from the danger of spears and sudden thrusts. Mark Antony was risking everything to attack the right wing of eight legions. It was an insane gamble and it meant his entire force could be turned on the other side, rolled up until he was surrounded. His destruction lay in a few orders, but Octavian only stared and waited.

'Caesar?' Maecenas shouted. 'We can flank them here!'

Octavian tensed his jaw.

'Send to consul Hirtius for new orders,' he snapped.

Maecenas stared, but he turned quickly, whistling to a runner then leaning low in the saddle to give quick instructions. The man hared off between the ranks.

Octavian leaned past Agrippa's shoulder to observe the locked battle ahead. The plain was open to his left and, even without orders, his legion had begun to swell past the fighting front, driven by the press from behind. Octavian nodded, making his decision. He could not let Mark Antony win the day.

'Seventh Victrix! Seventh Victrix!' he roared suddenly. 'Cohorts One to Four saw left and flank! Double speed! Flank!'

Men who had wondered at his silence cheered raucously. Their cramped ranks eased as two thousand men marched left and out of the main press, widening their line and coming around the heaving battle at the front.

The effect could be felt immediately as Octavian's men jogged in, striking the exposed sides of soldiers still pressing forward. Octavian felt the block waver ahead of him as his cohorts slaughtered enemy legionaries behind the fighting front, driving them into their own ranks so they could not maintain the line of shields. He grunted in satisfaction as his men began to march forward once more, going faster.

Octavian almost killed the runner who touched him on the leg. He jerked his sword down and held the blow just in time. He cursed the unfortunate messenger for his foolishness.

'What orders?'

'Consul Hirtius has been killed, Praefectus. Consul Pansa is badly injured and is being withdrawn to the rear. You have command.'

Over the noise of thousands of men, Octavian could not be sure he had heard correctly.

'What?'

The messenger repeated himself, shouting the words. Many of the soldiers around them heard, raising their heads.

Octavian looked up sharply. He could end it all. He had the men and the position to swing round and destroy Mark Antony's legions. For an instant, he considered it, but the man had dealt fairly with him. Mark Antony had trusted him and he was not an enemy.

'Sound the disengage!' Octavian roared at the closest cornicens. They began to blow the single long note, the sound echoing down the lines. He waited, nodding as his horns were matched on the other side by the order to withdraw.

A space appeared between the two armies, though dying men fell into it. It widened, leaving a red line on the grassy plain. Hundreds of voices bellowed orders in Mark Antony's legions as they too backed away, panting and desperate, unable to believe they would not be rushed.

'Dismount, Agrippa. I need to be seen now,' Octavian said.

His friend swung his leg up over the horse's head and dropped to the ground, landing easily.

'Form and dress ranks! Square formation!' Octavian ordered, making his voice ring across the lines of his men. His men.

Without Hirtius and Pansa, he was in sole command and Mark Antony's battered forces looked small in comparison. He watched as eight legions completed the disengage, putting a hundred clear paces between the opposing ranks. By then, four of the legates had ridden across to him, their faces flushed and angry.

Octavian was pleased to see that none of his own generals had thought to question the order he had given. He turned to face the group as the closest man spoke.

'Caesar, the enemy are in disarray. We have them!' the man said.

Octavian looked at him coldly, seeing the legate's barely hidden outrage.

'These are legions of Rome, Legate' Octavian said. 'My orders are to form squares in close formation. They will be allowed to march clear. Repeat your orders.'

The legate gaped at him, but he dipped his head.

'Form square. Close formation. They will be allowed to retreat, Praefectus,' he said.

'Well done. Now, return to your legions and await further orders.'

The four legates were not used to being dismissed in such a way, but Octavian had given the clearest of commands. Stiffly formal, they could only salute and ride away, taking different paths to their own positions.

Octavian turned back, watching Mark Antony's legions withdraw to the broken fortress and the pass that led into Gaul. He saw the man himself ride along the marching lines and then stop, looking back to where Octavian sat on Agrippa's horse. For a long moment, they regarded each other in silence, then Mark Antony turned his mount and moved on.

Mark Antony was no longer cold. The previous hour had been one of the worst of his life and he could still hardly believe he was being allowed to leave the battlefield. His legions were in a state of shock, unable to understand what they had witnessed. They *knew* they had lost the battle. It made no sense for an overwhelming force simply to watch them march clear. They knew by then that they had faced Caesar in battle and the talk was that he had showed them mercy.

As Mark Antony rode down the line, he reined in and stared back at the eight legions that had come north, still mostly intact. He could not see the bodies of the dead. They had not moved more than half a mile since the first barrage of spears and bolts and the corpses were hidden by the standing ranks. Mark Antony looked for Octavian among the mounted men. There was one in particular who might have been him, but he could not be certain. The letter crackled under his breastplate and Mark Antony almost reached for it and read it again, though he had done so a hundred times before. It was a simple message, brought to him by an extraordinarii rider three days before.

If we meet in battle, the consuls will stand on the right. If they fall, the battle is over, on my honour. Keep the messenger.

It was sealed with a symbol Mark Antony knew well. He had not wanted to gamble with the lives of his men. Until he had seen the size of the army come to face him, he had intended to ignore the message. His heart had been in his mouth for the entire attack, spending the lives of loyal soldiers in a wild surge against the right wing, without defence or a second plan. Yet it had worked. His veterans had overwhelmed legionaries, lictors and guards, smashing through the first two ranks with massive numbers brought to bear on a single point. Mark Antony had lost hundreds of men in that single attack. It should have been suicide and he had not been able to shake the sense that Octavian had manoeuvred him to his own destruction. Yet when the consuls fell, the battle came to a shuddering halt.

His men re-formed in squares, moving steadily towards the broken fort and the pass that led to Gaul and freedom. Mark Antony smiled suddenly as a thought struck him. He was the only consul of Rome once again and it would be weeks before the Senate even heard of the reverse in their fortunes. He had thrown the coin Octavian had given him, but it had come down on the right side.

As his legions began to march up the pass, Mark Antony summoned the closest extraordinarii rider.

'Petronius, isn't it?'

'Yes, Consul,' the young man replied.

'Go back and find . . . Caesar,' Mark Antony said. 'Tell him I am in his debt.'

CHAPTER SEVENTEEN

Octavian felt his head dipping again as tiredness overwhelmed him. It was true that fighting wearied a man more than any other activity, and he was not alone, the yawns going back and forth among the legates who had gathered in the command tent on the plain. The wind still howled outside, but iron braziers gave some semblance of warmth and wine kept the rest of the chill away. The legionaries did not have the luxury of rest, as he had ordered a rampart built around their massive camp before dark. It had gone up quickly, thousands of men making short work of the stony ground with their spades. Even so, Octavian was determined to move the legions south the following day, away from the mountain chill and back to the soft breezes of a northern summer.

The mood among the men was also warm and Octavian smiled to himself as he heard Maecenas laughing at something one of the legates had said. He lay on piled blankets, with more rolled under his head to form a cushion. A platter of cold food was at his elbow and camp servants stood close by to refill his cup whenever it was empty. Octavian ached in every bone and muscle, but it was a good ache and nothing like the threat of collapse he had feared in the battle.

From half-closed eyes, Octavian watched the group of four legates Hirtius and Pansa had brought north. They stood together uncomfortably, though he had told the rest to make them welcome. He had congratulated them on the victory, but there was more to do before they realised they were now a part of his army and not simply on loan from the Senate. He rubbed his eyes, deciding to get up rather than drift off to sleep in the warmth. Their men had fought with Caesar, whether the legates realised the significance of that or not. They were his to command after that day. The continuing power of the name still astounded him, but he had learned to accept its magic. Rome may once have belonged to the Senate and the great orators, but Julius Caesar had made the legions his own.

As he stood, Maecenas and Agrippa cheered him and Octavian grinned at them.

'He rises!' Maecenas said, passing him another cup. 'I was just telling Paulinius here that we could do more with archers. Did you see the arrows fly today? Mark Antony has a unit of Syrian bowmen who made a fine showing.'

Octavian had not seen that particular action and he only shook his head. He realised they were all watching him closely, waiting for him to speak.

'I do not take too much pride in a battle against an army half the size of our own, but it is better than losing, gentlemen. To victory!'

He raised his cup and they drank. He looked over at the new legates and decided to spend the evening in their company, to learn their strengths and weaknesses. He recognised the most senior of them, who had spoken to him at the end of the battle. Justinius did not look as if he had fought that day. His formal toga was fresh from his baggage and the man himself watched and listened politely as if he were at a Senate banquet rather than a field camp.

Octavian was in the process of crossing the low tent to speak to the man when one of the legionary guards entered and saluted.

'Decimus Junius has arrived, sir,' he said to Octavian. 'He is asking to speak to consuls Hirtius and Pansa.'

'No easy task,' Maecenas muttered.

Octavian shot a warning glance at him. Pansa still lingered in the healer tents, his delirium and fever beyond anything they could do for him. Yet Octavian could not be seen to take delight in the way fortune had apparently favoured him.

'Send him in,' he said. His tiredness had vanished at the name and he faced the tent flap with bitter anticipation, wondering what he would do.

The man who entered was a stranger to Octavian. Decimus Junius had a round, fleshy face that gave him a look of youth. Yet he was trim enough in the toga of a Roman senator and he looked sternly around the command tent, finally saluting with stiff formality.

'I am told Consul Hirtius has been killed,' he said. 'Who commands now, that I may lay my complaint before him? Who allowed Mark Antony to escape to Gaul when he was in our grasp?'

Eyes turned to Octavian, who said nothing at first. He savoured the moment while Decimus Junius looked around from face to face, confused by the silence.

'I believe my ranks of propraetor and praefectus entitle me to command,' Octavian said at last. 'Either way, I am Gaius Julius Caesar and this army is mine.'

He spoke as much for the benefit of the new legates as Decimus Junius, but the name was not lost on the man, who went pale and stammered as he tried to continue.

'I . . . Propraetor Caesar . . .' he began, struggling to find words. Decimus Junius took a deep breath and went on, though his eyes were sick with worry. 'Two thousand of my legionaries are still held at the Castra Taurinorum, guarded by some of Mark Antony's men. I seek your permission to free them and rebuild the fortresses. I was fortunate that the consul passed me by as he went for the pass, but my supplies are low. If I am to keep my position here, I must ask for food and materials . . .' He trailed off under Octavian's cold stare.

'Your *position*, Decimus Junius?' Octavian asked. 'It is simple enough. You were one of those who murdered the Father of Rome. As his adopted son, it falls to me to demand justice.'

Decimus Junius paled further, his skin bright with sweat.

'I . . . I was granted amnesty by the Senate of Rome, Propraetor,' he said, his voice shaking.

'An amnesty I revoke,' Octavian said.

'By what authority? The Senate . . .'

'Are not here,' Octavian interrupted. 'I am the commander in the field and you will find my authority is absolute, at least so far as it relates to you. Guard! Place this man under arrest and hold him for trial. You may choose anyone you like to speak for you, Decimus Junius. I suggest you find someone of uncommon skill.'

The guard laid a hand on Decimus Junius' shoulder, causing him to jerk.

'You can't do this!' he shouted. 'I was granted amnesty for bringing down a tyrant. Will you make yourself another? Where is the rule of law in this? I am immune!'

'Not from me,' Octavian said. 'I will convene a court of senior officers for tomorrow morning. Take him away now.'

Decimus Junius slumped, his expression appalled as he was led away. Octavian faced the other men in the tent, focusing on the new legates in particular.

'Will you criticise me for this?' he asked them softly.

Justinius was the only one of the new men who met his gaze. The legate shook his head.

'No, Caesar,' he said.

The sun was barely above the eastern horizon when the trial began. Eight legions were encamped around a single laurel tree, so that the small space was at the centre of a vast host of men. The cold had deepened overnight, though the sky was clear and once again the wind whipped particles of frost against the exposed skin of the men as they waited for the judgement.

Decimus Junius had chosen to defend himself and he spoke for almost an hour while the legions waited and watched. In the end, he ground to a halt and Octavian stood up.

'I have listened to your words, Decimus Junius. I find your arguments empty. There was no amnesty when you were one of Caesar's murderers. That it was applied later is irrelevant. The Senate cannot order the sun to set after it has risen. In giving you some sense that you were absolved of your crime, they stepped beyond the bounds of their authority. As Caesar, I revoke that amnesty in the field and will do so formally when I am next in Rome. You are the first of the Liberatores to receive justice for your crimes. You will be one of many when you meet again across the river.'

Decimus Junius only stared at him, his eyes resigned. He had not doubted the result of the trial for a moment and he raised his head, refusing to show fear.

'I pronounce you guilty of murder and blasphemy against the divine Julius,' Octavian said. 'The sentence is death. Hang him.'

Octavian watched without expression as two legionaries took hold of Decimus Junius, leading him over to the tree. They threw a rope over a branch and tied a loop around his neck while he stood, his chest heaving. Decimus Junius swore at them then, cursing them by all the gods. Octavian nodded to the legionaries, who joined together to pull the rope.

Decimus Junius' voice was strangled into silence at the first jerk. One of his hands raised to touch the rope, the fingers scrabbling at the rough line tightening around his throat. As the soldiers continued to heave, he was raised to the tips of his toes and then, with a lurch, he left the ground. His legs kicked out and both hands were at his throat. On instinct, he gripped the rope above his head and pulled himself up. The soldiers exchanged a brief communication and one of them braced himself to take the weight, while the other approached the kicking figure and knocked his arms away.

Decimus Junius jerked and sagged in spasms, his bladder emptying as he choked. It was not a quick death, but the legionaries waited patiently, only having to remove his hands once more before he was still, turning gently in the breeze. When it was over, they heaved on the legs until the neck snapped, then lowered the body down and took back the rope. One of the legionaries used his sword to hack the head from the corpse. It took three blows before it came free and the soldier held it up to the crowd as a prize. They cheered the sight of it, fascinated by the white upturned eyes as it was turned to show all those who crowded close.

Octavian let out a long breath, shuddering in release. He hoped the news would spread to the ears of more powerful men, such as Brutus and Cassius, or the ones who still scrambled in Rome as Suetonius did. They would hear, eventually, and they would consider what it meant for them. He had only begun to collect the debt they owed.

'Legates, attend me,' he ordered.

The eight men came to him, hushed and calm after what they had witnessed. They saw Octavian in spotless armour, his face unlined and youthful energy in every part of him.

'The men have seen my purpose, my intentions,' he said to

them. 'I would have their voices behind me before I move on. I recall that Caesar would sometimes summon a soldiers' assembly when he was in the field, to take the feeling of the men. I will do that here, to know I have their support.'

His gaze fell on the legates who had come north with Hirtius and Pansa and they did not misunderstand. He had demonstrated his authority and they knew better than to refuse.

'Summon all officers, down to tesserarius. I will speak to them and ask what they would have me do.'

The legates saluted without hesitation, walking back to their horses in disciplined silence. As the sun rose, the main body of the legions pulled back from the command tent, while two thousand officers walked in to hear Octavian speak. He waited for them, drinking only a little water and thinking back over the death of Decimus Junius. He had hoped for some feeling of satisfaction, but he had never met the man before and it was not there in him. Even so, he offered up a short prayer to Julius that he would bring the same justice to the rest of the Liberatores, one by one.

When the assembly of officers had gathered, he went out to stand before them.

'You know why I am here now,' he said, making his voice carry. 'If you did not understand before, you know why I let Mark Antony leave the field yesterday. My enemies are those who murdered my father Caesar, divine Imperator of Rome. I have moved rashly before and made decisions I cannot take back. I stand here with you because I remember Caesar and he knew the wisdom of the legions he commanded.' He paused to let the compliment sink in before going on. 'With you, I am the right hand of Rome. I am the sword that will cut out traitors like Decimus Junius. Without you, I am no more than one man and the legacy of my father ends with me.'

'What do you ask of us, Caesar?' someone shouted back at him.

Octavian looked over to the massed officers.

'Talk to each other. Talk to your men. We have eight legions and that is enough for any task. Caesar told me you could be wise, so show me. Let me know what I should do.'

He stepped deliberately away from his position, so that the officers did not feel bound to remain. To his satisfaction, he heard conversations begin among them and after a time he walked to his tent and lay in the gloom, listening to the murmurs and shouts and laughter of the men as they discussed what to do.

Barely three summer hours had passed when Justinius came to find him, the legate staring as if he could see Octavian's heart with eyes alone.

'The men have decided,' Justinius said.

Octavian nodded, walking with him back to the same spot. They had gathered once more to answer him and he saw many were smiling.

'Which of you will speak for the rest?' Octavian called to them.

Hands went up and he picked one at random. A burly centurion rose to his feet.

'Caesar, we are honoured to have been asked.'

A great bellow went up and Octavian had to raise his arms and pat the air for silence.

'There are some who think you should take over from Decimus Junius in the north,' the centurion said.

A few men cheered, but the majority remained silent as he went on.

'The rest – most of us – have considered that Rome has at least one consular post fallen vacant,' he said. They laughed at that and Octavian smiled with them. 'You are too young, it's true. No man can be consul before the age of forty-two in normal times. But exceptions have been made in the past, not least for the divine Caesar himself. We think the presence of eight legions at your back will be enough to persuade the Senate that your age is not a barrier to election as consul.'

They roared to show their support and Octavian laughed aloud. Standing at his side, Maecenas bent close to his ear.

'I'm sure it is just a coincidence that they are suggesting exactly what you wanted to hear,' he murmured, smiling. 'You are getting better at this.'

Octavian looked across at him, his eyes bright. As they quietened to hear his response, he took a deep breath.

'You have spoken and I have heard. Yet if I go south to stand for consul, it will not be as the head of an invading army. I will ask the citizens of Rome for their vote, but I will not take legions into Rome, not again. If the people see fit to make me consul, I will gain the justice that has been denied to me – and to you – for too long. Is it your wish that we return?'

The response was never in doubt, but still Octavian was pleased at the battering roar that came back to him, quickly echoed instinctively by the mass of legionaries further out. They would hear the news in time. They were going home to elect a new Caesar as consul.

In the tents of the healers, Consul Pansa heard the roar and sucked in a molten breath. In his weakness, his tongue slipped back into his throat, the fat length of flesh cutting off his air. Bitter vomit rose, spilling from his open mouth and broken nose as he clawed at his face. He grunted and waved his hands as he strangled, but the soldiers were all outside, listening to their officers cheer Caesar. By the time they returned to tend him, he was dead, his eyes bulging.

The Senate watched each change of expression in the young man before them. He had answered every question and they had been impressed. His lineage was beyond reproach. Only his youth held them back from outright endorsement. Yet he did not look abashed and when he spoke, it was with the fluency of an honest and an older man.

Bibilus couldn't take his eyes off Sextus Pompey. It was as if a Greek athlete stood there for their judgement, slim of shoulder and hip, with the sort of fine musculature that only came from an active life. Bibilus wiped his brow with a square of cloth, moving it down to take the wet shine off his lips. At the end of three hours in the theatre, they were all weary, but the subject of the emergency meeting still looked fresh. More than anything, Pompey's unruffled calm helped to persuade the older members. In years alone, he was far too young for such a serious appointment, but the life he had led gave him a maturity and seriousness of which they could approve.

Suetonius was the last one still prepared to question the youth. When he rose from his bench, Pompey's steady gaze fastened on him, so that he hesitated and forgot what he was about to ask.

'You, um . . . you have described the death of your father in Egypt,' Suetonius began, aware as he spoke of the sighs and grunts of irritation all around him. The rest of the senators wanted to move to a vote and then go home. Suetonius tensed his mouth and ran a hand over the hair he had plastered so carefully across the dome of his head.

'You have also provided details of your brother, murdered by forces of Caesar in Spain. You say your sister yet survives . . . Lavinia. Yet, um . . . most of your experience has been on land, yet you are asking for command of the fleet? Tell this house why we should grant such authority to a young fellow of your age.'

Sextus Pompey looked up and around before he answered. The gesture was not lost on many of the men there and they chuckled as he smiled.

'My father built this theatre, Senator, though I have never seen

231

it before today. I am glad it is being used for more than even he intended. I am also glad his name is not forgotten, despite the best efforts of the Caesarian faction that has proved such a poison in the politics of this city. Is the line of Caesar not a dagger at your throats once again? The markets in the city are full of such chatter, with talk of him occupying even the forum.'

He paused with the natural gift of an orator, letting his audience soak in each point while he planned the next.

'In me, you have more than a father's son, though I do not fear to rest my honour on that of Gnaeus Pompey. I have fought against the armies of Caesar in Spain for almost as long as I can remember. Before that, I saw my father stabbed to death by foreign slaves in Alexandria, just to please Caesar. In my opposition to Octavian, you need never fear for my loyalty. I am perhaps the only man in Rome whose enmity is as set as the path of the stars.'

He paused again, knowing Suetonius would prompt him on the subject of the fleet. As the senator opened his mouth, Sextus Pompey went on.

'I have fought on board ships, Senator. As I said, I have three galleys of my own, each one captured from Caesar's forces and used to attack more. While he led Rome, I could be nothing more than a pirate with my name and my blood, but you have changed that. This new Caesar who undermines the authority of the Senate, who dares to flout the rule of Rome, will always be my enemy. But if the rumours are true . . .' he smiled wryly, certain that he had not misjudged the panicky news flying through the city over the previous few days, 'then he has an army too great to oppose in Roman lands, at least for this year. When he reaches Rome, he will dig himself under the skin and it will take a hot knife to get him out once more.'

Suetonius was nodding at the summary of all his own fears as Pompey went on.

'But he does not have the fleet at Brundisium. Not yet, at

least. It is the last remaining power at your disposal, at your command and in your gift. I ask only that you seal orders putting me in charge of it. I will use it to bring terror and destruction to this new Caesar, in the name of this Senate. At the very least, I will take it out of his grasp. My name tells you I can be trusted, senators, as you sit in my father's house.'

'I am satisfied,' Suetonius said weakly, resuming his seat.

The ballot passed quickly, with no more than a few abstentions and votes against. Sextus Pompey would command the fleet, an authority almost absolute in its lack of oversight and control. Even those who remembered his father knew it was a great risk, but they knew also that Caesar was marching south to Rome and this time he had eight legions with him. They could not let him have the fleet as well, or the entire Roman world would be at his mercy.

CHAPTER EIGHTEEN

The gates of Rome were closed and sealed as the sun rose. The male voting population of the city had come out in darkness to the Campus Martius. Every free citizen was there, arranged in centuries of class and wealth, while the city filled with the odour of tens of thousands of meals being prepared for their return.

In times past, the voting days would have had an air of festival, with street performers and food sellers making more money in a day than they could in a normal month. Yet across the Tiber, eight legions camped, a great sea of shining armour waiting for the result. The sight of such a force within range of Rome dampened the spirits of the citizens considerably.

The representatives of each voting century came to cast their votes in huge baskets, filling them slowly with wooden tokens. Octavian stood close by, wearing a simple white toga. He was aware of the awe in the crowds that milled around him and he smiled at anyone who approached, exchanging a few words and thanking them for their support. There were many of those.

He looked across to where Bibilus stood and sweated, despite a slave fanning him and another holding a sunshade above his head. Years before, Bibilus had stood with Caesar as consul and Octavian knew the memories would be sharp in him that day. He had heard the stories and it was hard not to glance across to the Janiculum hill, where a flag was raised high. While it fluttered, the election continued, but if the men at the peak saw an army approach, it would drop and the entire city would be made ready to defend itself. When Bibilus had stood before, his friend Suetonius had arranged for the flag to fall when the results went against them. Caesar had planned for the treachery and his men had kept the signal high, long enough to make their master consul. Octavian smiled at the thought.

'Forty-two Caesar and Pedius; forty-eight Bibilus and Suetonius!' the diribitores called.

The Senate had used a lot of favours to get so many votes from the first voting centuries. Octavian smiled, unworried. They had less influence with the poorer classes, he knew, while the name of Caesar rang like a bell for all those who had been paid their silver legacy.

'I had hoped for more by now,' Pedius said at his side.

Octavian wondered again if he had made the right choice for his co-consul. Pedius was his senior by thirty years, a man with a deeply seamed face and a narrow chin that came almost to a point. Everything about him looked sharp, but Pedius was a nervous little man who chewed his inner lips when he was worried. It was true that he had once been a client and a friend of Caesar. That friendship had not been enough for Pedius to vote against the amnesty, but he was at least a man who had not sided too openly with the Liberatores. Octavian studied him, seeing Pedius as those who came to vote would and sighing to himself. He had been forced to flatter and bribe Pedius with little subtlety to get him to stand. They both knew it was only to keep Bibilus or Suetonius from the second consular post, but still

Pedius had debated the proposition as if it might have been his destiny. Octavian looked away from the watery-eyed senator, staring out over the vast Campus with a hundred thousand free men moving across it. Once again, he wished Maecenas had wanted the post. Yet Maecenas would hear none of it and only laughed at him when he asked.

'Fifty Caesar and Pedius; fifty-three Bibilus and Suetonius!' the diribitores chanted, bringing a cheer from some of those still waiting to vote. They could not enter the city until the seals were struck from the gates and there was impatience there from some, while others were enjoying a day of enforced leisure away from work and their families.

Octavian clapped Pedius on the back, making him jump.

'The noble centuries have voted now,' he said. 'The merchant classes will support us over Bibilus and Suetonius, I think.'

Pedius moved his mouth as if he were manoeuvring a difficult bit of gristle from his teeth.

'I hope you are correct, Caesar. I do not need to tell you the danger of losing this particular election.'

Octavian looked west to where forty thousand legionaries waited. He had halted them beyond the Tiber and waited a full day before coming to the senate house and announcing his name for consul. He had done everything he could to remove the sting of an armed threat to the city, but still, there they were. Heads in the crowd turned constantly to see them. Octavian did not think Rome would vote against a man holding a knife to its throat, for all his efforts to hide the blade.

Octavian smiled as the voting tokens began to pile up. He could see Bibilus seething as the tally for Caesar and Pedius grew, but the votes kept coming, a trend becoming a flood as the merchant centuries took their chance to show what they thought of the men they perceived as having murdered Caesar. It helped that the count was public, so that each man approaching the baskets with his token knew already that he was part of the general mood.

Octavian saw their satisfaction and many of the voters bowed their heads to him as they dropped the wooden tokens, hundred after hundred of the citizens of Rome, showing him he had their support. It was intoxicating, he realised. He had wanted the consular role for the power and security it would win for him, but the reality was far greater. The people of Rome had been denied a voice and the riots had been put down with savage force. This was their revenge on the Senate, and Octavian savoured every moment of it.

In the early afternoon, a point was reached where the mass of poorer classes could no longer affect the result. The diribitores conferred, then signalled to the legion cornicens to blow. The notes soared across the Campus Martius and beyond the Tiber, the waiting legions roared like the distant ocean.

The noise spread, from those who had voted to the tens of thousands who would not get their chance. They too wanted to show their approval and the sound crashed at Octavian. He sagged, breathing hard and feeling the sweat that made his toga stick to his skin. He had told himself it was never in doubt, but he became aware of a painful tension that held every muscle tight. The flag on the Janiculum hill was lowered under the formal gaze of the citizens and as the horns sounded, the seals of bronze and wax were hammered into pieces and the city gates opened. Women, children and slaves came out by the thousand to join their husbands, brothers and sons and the festival air grew as they heard the news and celebrated in turn.

Octavian had brought only a pair of guards, all he was allowed for the formal voting. They were unable to stop the thousands who came to speak to him, to touch him and clap him on the back. It was too many and he had to start walking before they clustered too deeply around him, or knocked him down in their enthusiasm. The movement brought some relief, but they still cheered and followed as he strode across the field to where six guards held a white bull in a pen built for the sacrifice. Agrippa and Maecenas were there, looking proud. Octavian nodded to them, knowing they understood what he had gone through to stand in that place. The new consuls would take the omens and almost a hundred priests and officials and scribes had gathered there to record the event. More soldiers created a clear space for the ritual and the omen-takers prepared the bellowing animal.

Quintina Fabia was dressed in blinding white, her face painted so well that it was almost a mask of youth. She bowed to Octavian and Pedius as they approached, holding out an iron sickle with a keen edge. Octavian took it and tested the implement on the hairs of his forearm as he looked over at the massive bulk of the bull.

'I do not doubt Julius can see you now,' the high priestess said warmly. 'He would be proud of his son.'

Octavian dipped his head to show his appreciation. The guards drew ropes on the bull, heaving it over to the edge of the enclosure. It had been drugged with a mixture of opium and other herbs in its feed, so that it was dazed and sluggish. The omens would not be good if they had to chase a wounded animal across the Campus. Octavian fought not to smile at the image in his mind. He knew it was just giddiness, after the election, but he was required to be solemn and dignified until it was done.

The chanting began as the omen-takers and soothsayers implored the gods to send a sign and give their blessing to the consular year to come. Octavian stood mute and Quintina finally had to jog his shoulder to tell him it was time.

He approached the tethered bull, close enough to see its lashes and smell the clean scent of its skin. He placed a hand on the top of its head and saw the animal was chewing idly, unaware of what was going to happen. The image reminded him of Pedius and again he had to struggle not to laugh.

With a jerk, he reached under the powerful neck and drew the blade across in one swift slash. Blood spattered like rain onto bronze dishes held below. The animal grunted and did not seem to feel pain at first. The bowls filled and were replaced, passed to the omen-takers, who stared into the red liquid for patterns into the future.

The bull began to moan and struggle, but its lifeblood still poured. It collapsed slowly onto its knees and the dark brown eyes grew wild. It moaned louder and the ropes grew tight as it tried to struggle up. Octavian watched, waiting for it to die and thinking of Decimus Junius. He was woken from his reverie by a shout from one of the haruspices, pointing at the sky with a shaking hand. Octavian looked up with the rest of the crowd and was in time to see a flight of dark birds cross the city in the distance. He smiled, delighted at the sight of vultures in the air. The history of the city said that there had been twelve as Romulus founded Rome. With thousands of citizens, he counted the dark birds in his head, struggling to be certain as they overlapped and dwindled.

'I saw twelve,' Quintina Fabia said loudly and clearly.

Octavian blinked. The birds were passing into the setting sun and he could not be sure. The number was echoed around him and he laughed at last.

'It is a good omen,' he said. He had Caesar's luck, for all he was sure there had been only nine birds. They had gone into the sun, but it was enough. The sighting of twelve would send a message of rebirth to the people of Rome.

When the bull's liver was cut out, the end of it was folded over and Quintina Fabia beamed. She held up the bloody organ, spattering her white robe with red life that ran down her arms. The omen-takers cheered and the scribes wrote down every detail on wax tablets, to be entered into the city records later that evening. The omens were superb and Octavian could only shake his head in pleasure and send a silent prayer of thanks to his mentor and namesake.

The bulk of the crowd had followed the new consuls to watch the sacrifice. As the omens were read and proclaimed across the Campus, Bibilus and his coterie of supporters remained by the voting baskets. Bibilus swept his hand through the polished wooden tokens, letting them fall back one by one. With a sour expression, he looked at Suetonius and Gaius Trebonius.

'I have ordered horses brought for you,' he said, 'and arranged a ship. You will find it at the docks in Ostia. Go with my blessing.'

His tone was grim with dissatisfaction, but he could feel the tide turning as well as anyone. Octavian had won the highest post of the city and the Caesarians were rising with him. Clients in the Senate would no longer withhold their votes. Bibilus thanked his personal gods that the fleet was not in their grasp. There was at least that, slim straw though it was to ease his disgust.

Suetonius looked over the city and around at the Janiculum hill. He remembered a different election and another Caesar, but he had been younger then and more able to withstand the reverses of capricious fate. He shook his head, wiping a hand over the thinning hair that the breeze picked up and flicked over to reveal his baldness.

'I will go to Cassius,' he announced. 'This is just a single day, Bibilus. Sextus Pompey has the fleet in the west. Cassius and Brutus hold the east. Rome will starve without grain by sea and this city will suffer, held on both sides until it is strangled. This vote, this *obscenity* today, is one small failure, nothing more. I will see this place again, I swear it.'

He turned to Gaius Trebonius, the one who had distracted

Mark Antony during the assassination of Caesar. The younger man had been so proud to be named as one of the Liberatores, even though he had not wielded a blade. Now, the legacy of that decision haunted him and he looked ill.

'This is not right,' Trebonius said, his voice shaking. He had never left Rome before and the thought of foreign cities filled him with unease. 'He had Decimus Junius hanged without a proper trial! How does he remain immune while we must run? We removed a tyrant, an enemy of the state. Why do they not see that?'

'Because they are blinded by gold and names and foolish dreams,' Suetonius snapped. 'Believe me, I have seen more of it than I could ever tell you. Good men work in silence and what of their dignity, their honour? It is ignored for those who shout and prance and pander to the unwashed crowds.'

He reached out to grip Trebonius by the shoulder, but the younger man pulled away by instinct, his face flushing. For an instant, Suetonius clawed the empty air, then let his hand fall.

'I have lived with Caesars. I have even killed one,' he said. 'But men like Cassius will not let this rest, believe me. There will be a price in blood and I will be there to see it paid.'

For the first time in many years, the new consuls would not enter the city proper. The senate house was still nothing more than a scorched foundation and Octavian and Pedius walked instead to the open doors of Pompey's theatre. The crowd followed them right to the point where they passed behind a line of soldiers, there to guard the dignity of the Senate.

Octavian paused at the enormous pillars of white marble, looking at the flecks of bull's blood on his hands as the senators streamed in around him. Many congratulated them both as they passed and he acknowledged them, knowing that he should begin the subtle web of alliances that he needed to pass even a simple vote. Yet the omens had given him a momentum that the senators would not resist.

Pedius stayed at his side, his mouth working constantly as if he tried to consume himself from within. He alone seemed to take no joy in the omens or the appointment, though it would place his name in the history of the city. Octavian stifled a grin at the older man's nervousness. He had not chosen Pedius for ideals or a fiery intelligence, far from it. Pedius had been the best choice simply because he was not strong. Octavian had learned from his mistakes, particularly from the disaster of entering the forum with armed legionaries earlier that year. He knew by then that he could not ignore the importance of how he was seen. The people and the Senate would resist a crude grab for power in any form. Even as consul, he would tread warily. Pedius was his shield.

'Consul,' Octavian said to him. The older man started at the title, a tentative smile playing around his chewing mouth. 'I am happy to propose the Lex Curiata myself. It would honour me if you would call the vote to overturn the amnesty.'

Pedius nodded immediately. Octavian had agreed to fund a new home for him in the sea town of Herculaneum, a place where only the richest men of Rome dwelled. Pedius appreciated the delicacy and politeness, but he knew his support had been bought and was nothing more than a formality. Yet he had known divine Caesar and admired him for years. The shame of failing to vote against the original amnesty still stung in him. Though Octavian did not know it, the house by the sea was just froth compared to that.

'It would be a pleasure, Caesar,' he said.

Octavian smiled. Rome was his. In the weeks of preparation, one man had never doubted he would become consul on a wave of public acclaim. Mark Antony had written to him, asking for a meeting in a neutral place where they might plan a campaign against the Liberatores. It would begin today.

PART THREE

CHAPTER NINETEEN

The river Lavinius wandered across the north. Near Mutina, it had formed a dozen small islands in the water, ranging from rocky outcrops with a single tree to patches of dense woodland surrounded by the current and cut off from the world.

Octavian looked across the flowing waters to where Mark Antony waited for him. Neither man trusted the other completely, which made the island a perfect meeting place. On the other bank, two Gaul legions stood patiently in square formation, but they were helpless to intervene if Octavian planned treachery, just as the Seventh Victrix and Ninth Macedonia would not be able to help, if Mark Antony planned to kill him.

Simply reaching that point had been like an elaborate dance, with the two sides exchanging messages and promises as they came together. Both had guaranteed safe passage for the other, but the reality always involved a final gamble. Octavian looked at Agrippa and Maecenas. They had crossed once before to search the island for hidden soldiers or traps of any kind. It was impossible to be too cautious, Octavian thought. He took a deep breath, looking dubiously at the rocking boat.

'I think, if we have missed something, if this does not go well, I would like to go to my death with the certain knowledge that Mark Antony will not be long behind me,' he said. 'Those are my orders. If I am killed, he is not to leave that island alive.'

He judged the distances, seeing that Mark Antony had picked a spot out of reach of legion spear-throwers.

'Bring up the scorpion bows and have the teams aim out over the river,' Octavian said.

His legions had been able to assemble the massive weapons over the previous day and it gave him some relief to watch them dragged up by teams of oxen and aimed at the island. On the far bank, he saw the same thing happening and wondered what it would be like to stand on that small isle and hear the snap of the bows as they sent iron bolts streaking across the water.

'Are you ready?' he asked his friends.

Agrippa answered by clambering down into the boat and checking ropes with a tug. Maecenas shrugged, still staring out at the figures waiting for them.

'You've done all you can. If it's a plot, he won't live through it, I can promise that much.'

'Unless he isn't even there,' Agrippa said as he settled himself. 'The big man with the armour could be just an officer to draw us in to a place he can strike with his own catapults and bows.'

'Always the optimist, Agrippa,' Maecenas said.

Even so, Maecenas climbed into the boat and took a grip on the tall prow, preferring to stand. There were four rowers already in place in the skiff, all veteran swordsmen with weapons at their feet that they could grab at a moment's notice. As one, they looked up at Octavian and he nodded to them.

'Come on,' he said. 'Let's see what he wants.' He climbed in and sat against the wooden rail of the skiff, his gaze already focused on their destination. 'Cast off, or row, or whatever the command is,' he said.

Agrippa looked pained, but the rowers pushed away from the bank and the boat turned into the current. With four oars stroking through the water, it accelerated quickly towards the island. Octavian was surprised to find he was enjoying himself. Agrippa saw his expression change and smiled.

'There is a magic to small boats,' he said. 'But galleys are better still.'

Octavian's smile slipped at the reminder of the massive fleet that had vanished from Brundisium. His co-consul Pedius had pushed through a vote to remove the authority of Sextus Pompey, but that did not bring the ships back.

'When I am finished here,' Octavian said, 'I will need my own fleet.'

'You're *in* your fleet at the moment,' Maecenas replied blithely.

Octavian snorted. 'I have been thinking about that. Sooner or later, I must take Sextus Pompey on. Without control of the seas, we will never be able to take legions against Cassius and Brutus.'

Agrippa rubbed his chin, nodding.

'It will cost fortunes,' he replied. 'Sextus has, what, two hundred galleys? To build even half that number would cost tens of millions of sesterces – and the time to retrain legionaries.'

'What good is a deal with Mark Antony if I can't leave Rome for fear of pirates?' Octavian said. 'I will find the money – and the men. You have a free hand, Agrippa. Build me a fleet.'

When they reached the island, the three passengers climbed out. Without a word, the rowers began to pull on legionary armour that could have drowned them before. Octavian waited impatiently, his fingers rubbing the hilt of his gladius.

Mark Antony himself strolled down to the sandy landing place, watching their preparations with something like amusement. He looked healthy and strong, standing almost as tall as Agrippa and with the trim frame of a soldier despite his years.

'Welcome, Consul,' he said. 'You've come a long way since I held the title you bear now. As I wrote to you, my honour guarantees your safety here. We meet under truce. I would like to introduce you to my companions, so will you walk with me?'

The man Octavian had last seen riding hard for Gaul seemed to have no fear of the armed soldiers with Octavian. He looked as relaxed as any noble Roman enjoying an afternoon on the river. Octavian smiled at his manner, playing along.

'I'll walk with you,' he said. 'We have a great deal to discuss.'

'Now that he's decided to listen,' Maecenas muttered.

The group of six accompanied Mark Antony to where a tent and tables had been laid out on the grass. From that side of the island, Octavian could see the Gaul legions on the opposing bank much more clearly. It was almost certainly no accident that the river was narrower on that side. A dozen scorpion bows and two centuries of archers watched him in turn, ready for the first hint of treachery. Strangely, it pleased Octavian that he too was considered a threat. He did not want to be the only one tying himself into knots with worry.

Mark Antony was in an ebullient mood as host. He saw Octavian looking at the standing legionaries.

'These are difficult days, Caesar, are they not? Lepidus here thought so, when I arrived in Gaul. I give thanks that he saw no conflict in handing over command to a consul of Rome.'

'An ex-consul of Rome,' Octavian said automatically. He saw Mark Antony begin to frown and went on quickly. 'But still a man Julius Caesar called a friend and, I hope, an ally in these times.'

'As you say. I find the more legions I have, the easier it is to find allies,' Mark Antony replied with a booming laugh. 'Lepidus? Let me introduce the new Caesar and the latest consul.'

The man he brought forward with a hand to his shoulder looked awestruck and out of place in that gathering. Octavian did not know Lepidus personally, only that he had been prefect of Gaul and appointed by Caesar after the Imperator's return from the east. Lepidus was not an impressive figure at first glance. He had a slight stoop that made him look like a scholar rather than a senior officer, though his nose had been broken many times and one of his ears had been battered badly in some old conflict. It was little more than a flap of gristle, pink and without the usual curves. His hair was full but completely white. Against them, Octavian felt his youth as a strength rather than a weakness.

'I am honoured to meet you, Caesar,' Lepidus said. His voice was low and firm and gave some sense of the man behind the ageing exterior.

Octavian took his outstretched arm and gripped it.

'As I am honoured to meet you both, gentlemen. As consul of Rome, I suppose I have the most senior rank. Shall we sit?'

He gestured to the long table, deliberately moving towards it rather than letting Mark Antony set the pace. Maecenas and Agrippa came smoothly with him, taking positions at his back as he chose a chair at the head of the table.

Mark Antony looked irritated, but he gave way with good grace and seated himself opposite Octavian, with Lepidus at his side. Four more of their men stood far enough back not to present an obvious threat, though their purpose was clear. Octavian glanced behind him to his rowers, who had taken position automatically, facing the others. They made two clear groups across from each other and the tension was suddenly present once more as Mark Antony rested his arms on the wood.

'Shall I begin?' Mark Antony said. He went on before anyone could reply. 'My proposal is simple. I have fifteen legions at my command in Gaul, with Lepidus. You have eight, Caesar, as well as a consular year to come. You want the forces to bring down the Liberatores and I want rank and power in Rome, rather than as an outsider in Gaul. We should be able to come to an agreement, don't you think?'

Octavian gave silent thanks for Roman bluntness. In that at least, he and Mark Antony shared a similar dislike for the games of the Senate.

'Where does Prefect Lepidus stand in this?' he asked, giving no sign of a reaction.

'Lepidus and I speak as one,' Mark Antony said before the man could reply. 'Rome has known a triumvirate before. I propose that we share power between us, with the aim of breaking the Liberatores in the east. I do not think you can accomplish that without my legions, Caesar.'

Octavian felt his mind whirling. It was a good offer, if he could trust it. With Crassus and Pompey, Caesar himself had created the first triumvirate. He hardly had to mention how badly it had ended for two of them. He looked deeply into Mark Antony's eyes, seeing the tension there. The ex-consul seemed to have a strong position, but there was something bothering him and Octavian searched for the right words to reveal it.

'It would have to be recognised in the Senate, for it to be legal,' he said. 'I can offer that much, at least. I have enough clients there now to win any vote.'

As Mark Antony began to relax, Octavian looked past him to the legions encamped on the river bank.

'Yet it strikes me that I gain very little from this. I am consul, with a Senate who do not dare to cross me. Yes, there are enemies to be faced, but I can raise new legions.'

Mark Antony shook his head. 'I have reports from Syria and Greece that tell me you don't have that kind of time, Caesar. If you wait much longer, Brutus and Cassius will be too strong. What I offer is the strength to break them before they reach that point.'

Octavian thought deeply as both men stared at him, waiting. Consuls were limited in authority, for all the semblance of power they wielded. Like a temporary dictatorship, what Mark

Antony proposed would put him above the law, beyond its reach for crucial years while he built his fleet and his army. Yet he thought he had not yet found the weakness that had brought Mark Antony to negotiate and it nagged at him. He looked again past those at the table, to the legions on the river bank.

'How are you paying your men?' he asked idly.

To his surprise, Mark Antony flushed with something like embarrassment.

'I'm not,' he said, the words dragged out of him. 'Part of our agreement must include funds to pay the legions I command.'

Octavian whistled softly to himself. Fifteen legions amounted to seventy-five thousand men, with perhaps another twenty thousand camp followers. Octavian wondered how long they had gone without silver. Poverty was a harsh mistress and Mark Antony needed him, or at least the funds in Rome and from Caesar's will.

Octavian smiled more warmly at the two men he faced.

'I think I understand the main arguments, gentlemen. But what sort of a fool would I be to accept battle against Cassius and Brutus and lose Gaul for lack of soldiers there?'

Mark Antony dismissed the point with a gesture.

'Gaul has been peaceful for years. Caesar broke the back of their tribes and killed their leaders. There is no High King to follow Vercingetorix, not any more. They have fallen back into a thousand squabbling families and will remain so for generations. Yet I will not take every Roman. I can leave two or three legions to man the forts for a few seasons. If the Gauls rebel, I will hear very quickly. They know what to expect if they do.'

Octavian looked dubiously at the older man, wondering if he overreached himself. The last thing Octavian wanted was a battle on two fronts. Mark Antony played a dangerous game in stripping Gaul, for all it had brought him to the negotiating table.

After a long, tense moment while the others watched him, he nodded.

'Very well, gentlemen. I can see you have had time to consider how such a triumvirate might work. Tell me how you see it and I will consider what is best for Rome.'

Three days of negotiations had left Mark Antony exhausted, while Octavian seemed as fresh as the first moment he had sat at the table. He returned each dawn to the same spot, once the island had been checked for hidden men by Maecenas and Lepidus. There was no treachery and Octavian was filled with a sense that the agreement might actually work. Even so, he argued and discussed every point with great energy, while the two older men wilted.

Octavian offered the passage of a law making their arrangement legitimate. In return, Mark Antony promised him complete control of Sicily, Sardinia and all of Africa, including Egypt. It was a barbed gift, with the fleet of Sextus Pompey controlling the western sea, but Octavian accepted. Mark Antony was to keep Gaul as his personal fiefdom, while Lepidus would gain the region in the north where Decimus Junius had ruled for such a short time. Spain and the rest of Italy would be their joint domain. Octavian arranged for three million sesterces to be sent over the river in boats and had the pleasure of seeing Mark Antony relax and look young for a while, before they lost themselves in the details once more.

On the third day, the agreement was written to be sealed by all three men. Together, they would form 'A Commission of Three for the Ordering of the State', an ugly and unwieldy title that went some way to hide what it really was – a temporary truce between men of power to gain what they truly wanted. Octavian had no false hopes on that score, but Mark Antony had never been his enemy, for all the man's Roman arrogance. His true enemies grew stronger by the day and he needed legions and power to take them on.

The final part of the agreement caused more argument than the rest of it. When Cornelius Sulla had been Dictator of Rome, he had allowed what he called 'proscriptions' – a list of men condemned by the state. To be named on such a list was a sentence of death, as any citizen could carry out the charge, handing over the head of the named man for the reward of part of his estate, while the rest was sold for Senate coffers. It was a dangerous power to wield and Octavian felt the lure of it from the beginning and struggled to resist. The only names he allowed on his behalf were the nineteen remaining men who had taken part in the assassination of Caesar in Pompey's theatre. Lepidus and Mark Antony added their own choices and Octavian swallowed nervously as he read the names of senators he knew well. His colleagues were settling old scores as their price for the agreement.

For another two days, they wrangled over inclusions, vetoing each other's choices for personal reasons and negotiating them back onto the list one by one. In the end, it was done. The proscriptions would create chaos in Rome, but when those men had their estates put up for auction, he would have the funds he needed to build a fleet and fight a war. He shuddered at the thought, reading the list yet again. Brutus and Cassius were the first ones on it. The eastern half of Roman lands were not mentioned anywhere in the agreements. It would have been a fantasy to parcel them out while they were still held by those men. Still, it was a mark, a line drawn. Cassius and Brutus would be declared enemies of the state, where once they had been protected by law and amnesty. It was not a small thing to see them heading the list.

Six days after he had first landed on the tiny island, Octavian was there again. Mark Antony and Lepidus were glowing with their achievement, brought back into the fold by the only man with the power to do it. There was still little trust between them, but they had developed a grudging respect for each other in the days of argument. Mark Antony breathed slowly and calmly as he watched Octavian seal the triumvirate agreement and readied his own ring to add his family's crest.

'Five years is enough to put right the mistakes of the past,' Mark Antony said. 'May the gods smile on us for that long at least.'

'Will you come back with me to Rome now, to see this made law?' Octavian asked him, smiling curiously.

'I would not miss it,' Mark Antony said.

The coast of Sicily was a perfect location for a fleet of raptores. The high hills close to the coast allowed Sextus Pompey to read flag signals, then send out his galleys in quick dashes, the oar-slaves straining until the prows cut white through the sea. He squinted against the glare to read the flags as the sun came up, showing his teeth as he saw the red cloth like a distant drop of blood against the mountain peak. It was almost hidden behind the pall of smoke from the volcano on the massive island, the grumbling monster that shook the earth and caused dead fish to float to the surface, where his delighted men could spear them and find them already cooked. At night, they could sometimes see a dim glow from the peak, as molten rock bubbled and spat.

It was a landscape that suited his hatred and it was a heady thing to have both the authority and the ships to enforce his will. No longer did he have to risk the wrath of the Roman fleet whenever he sent out his crews to attack merchant vessels. The Roman fleet was his to command, with orders on waxed parchment, sealed in a great disc of wax and ribbon. The senior officers could only salute and place themselves under his authority when they saw that seal. From that moment, he had possessed a weapon as powerful as anything wielded by Rome. More so, given his stranglehold on the coast. Grain ships from Africa and Sicily itself no longer sailed to the peninsula. Rome was cut off from half the food and supplies they needed and he could do still more.

Sextus Pompey turned to his new second in command, Vedius. It would perhaps have been more conciliatory to appoint one of the senior legion captains, but Vedius had been with him for years as a pirate and Sextus trusted him. Vedius was in his twenties, but he didn't have the sharp eyes needed to read the flags and he waited to hear the news, almost quivering with excitement. The man had been a tavern wolf when Sextus had found him, making a rough living fighting for coin, most of which he lost in gambling or drink. They had recognised something in each other the first time Sextus had knocked him down, breaking his jaw. Vedius had attacked him three times in the months after that, but each time had been worse and eventually he had given up on revenge and taken an interest in the Roman noble who talked and acted like a commoner. Sextus grinned at the man, who had never known regular food until he joined the galley crews that preyed on Roman shipping. Even a wolf could be tamed with cooked meals, it seemed.

'The red flag is up. There is some brave soul out there, risking his life to get trinkets through to his mistress.'

In the old days, a second flag would have been vital to know the number of ships. One or two made a target, but more than that was too great a risk and his men stayed hidden in the bays and coves along the coast.

Sextus felt his heart beat faster, an old pleasure. He was standing on the deck of a fine Roman galley, with legionaries and slaves ready to send it surging out. In the small bay where he had spent the night, another five galleys were sheltering at anchor, waiting for his orders. He shouted to the signaller, watching as his own flag ran up to the tip of the mast and the rowers were woken from sleep with a whip cracking by their ears. The other galleys reacted with the sort of discipline he had come to love, heaving up anchors from the seabed and readying their oars in just moments. He wanted to laugh aloud as he felt his ship move through the dark water towards the open sea. The others leapt forward, like hunting hawks. His raptores, just half a dozen of the deadly vessels he had been given. The coast sheltered two hundred of the galleys from prying eyes, all waiting on his orders.

The movement brought his sister up from her tiny cabin, introducing a new note of tension into her brother's frame. He did not enjoy the way Vedius looked at her. At eighteen, Sextus was father as well as brother to her and he kept her close rather than leave her among the coarse men in his inland camps.

'No cause for alarm, Lavinia. I am doing the noble work of the Senate, keeping the coast clear. You can stay unless there is fighting. Then I want you safe below, all right?'

Her eyes flashed in irritation, but she nodded. Though she had the same blonde hair as he did, it framed a face that seemed years younger, still very much a child. Sextus looked fondly at her as she tied her hair back and stared out to sea, enjoying the wind and spray. He was very aware that Vedius followed her every movement with his own dull stare.

'Keep watch for enemy ships,' he told Vedius, his voice curt.

The man was ugly, there was no other word for it. Vedius had been so battered about the face that his nose, lips and ears were a mass of scarring and his eyebrows were just thick pink lines from being ripped too many times by iron gloves. Their first fight had begun when Sextus had told him he had a face like a testicle, but without that lucky blow against his open mouth, Sextus knew he could have been killed by the fighter. Still, no one does well once their jaw has been broken and he had introduced Vedius to the reality of swords after that. He would certainly not allow the man to court his sister. For all her youth, she was of noble blood and Sextus would have to find her some wealthy senator or praetor very soon. He saw Lavinia squinting at seabirds on the high ropes and he smiled in affection.

The galleys came out at half-speed, their slave rowers warming up as they moved into the sun. Sextus exulted at the sight of them forming into an arrowhead formation without fresh orders. His original crews had simply rushed upon target ships, lunging at them with raucous cries. The fleet galleys were disciplined and deadly, and as he often did, he raced to the prow to lean out over it and stare into the distance as his ship crashed through the waves.

Two ships lay ahead, mere specks against the glare of the sun. Even as he watched, they spotted his galleys and began to turn back for the mainland. It was already too late. Unless they made it to a proper port, all they could do was run their craft onto a beach and vanish to save their lives. Sextus chuckled as he was sprayed with salt water, holding on with only one arm against the gleaming bronze eye that looked over the waves. That part of the coast offered no sanctuary, only rocky cliffs that would smash the merchants to kindling faster than he could. He bellowed back to the legion officers and the drumbeat grew faster, the great oars dipping in and out of the sea. Their speed increased and the ships around him matched the acceleration smoothly, soaring over the waters as the merchants realised their mistake and tried to tack back out to sea.

Sextus was close enough by then to see the single sail, while the other ship was a galley under full strain, easily outpacing its charge. He was surprised to see the galley turn away and head straight for him, as if its captain thought he had a chance against six. Sextus had expected to chase them up the west coast for thirty miles or so before he could board them.

Vedius appeared at his shoulder.

'He wants a quick end, maybe,' he said.

Sextus nodded, unconvinced. The actions of the galley

captain made no sense at all and he could see the oars dipping and rising like sun-whitened wings as they pushed on towards him.

'Put up flags "one" and "two" and "attack", with the "minor" signal,' he said.

He loved the legion systems and he had mastered them quickly, delighting in the complex orders he could give. Two of his galleys would chase down the merchant while he dealt with this stranger who thought he could race right down his throat. Sextus watched as two of his group veered off, keeping the same speed, as he called for his remaining four ships to ease back to half.

Still the enemy galley came on, unafraid.

'If we hit him from both sides, he'll go down, quick as spitting,' Vedius said, leering at the incoming vessel.

'There are easier ways to commit suicide,' Sextus said, shaking his head. 'He's risked it all to reach us. We have the numbers to take him easily, no matter what he does now.'

The galley coming at them was far from shore and the rowers would be tiring. Even if they turned and ran at their best pace, Sextus knew he could catch and ram them before the galley reached the coast. In the distance, he could see his pair of ships overhauling the hapless trader. Its sails were coming down in surrender and his men would strip the ship of anything useful before setting fires. He turned back to see the plunging oars of the single galley come up out of the water and shorten as the slaves inside pulled the gleaming lengths across themselves. Deprived of speed and over deep water, the galley bobbed like a piece of driftwood in the swell, suddenly helpless.

'Quarter-speed!' Sextus yelled. 'Lavinia, go down now.'

He risked a glance back to her, but she didn't move, holding on to the mast and staring out with her dark eyes, taking it all in. Gods, he sometimes thought the girl was a fool. She seemed to understand nothing about danger. He could not order Vedius to take her below, so he turned back, fuming. There would be words later.

His galley inched closer and closer, until he could make out the faces of men on the heaving deck. He was ready to order backed-oars at the first sign of a trick, but there were no catapults on deck and no sign of archers or spear-throwers.

'Take me in close,' he called to Vedius, who passed on the orders.

The vessels crept together, with the rest of his galleys forming up around them. Sextus was ready for the sudden appearance of archers as he leaned over the prow and yelled to the men waiting on the galley's deck.

'That ship is a fine gift!' he shouted. 'You have my thanks. Surrender now and we'll kill only a few of you.'

There was no reply and he saw a team of slaves manhandling a small boat to the edge, heaving on ropes and pulleys to suspend it over the deck and then pushing it out so that it could be lowered into the water. Two men climbed down the side of the galley past the dripping oar-blades, then took up smaller oars in the boat and began rowing over to him. Sextus raised his eyebrows as he looked back at Vedius.

'This is new,' he said, though he felt a spasm of worry. Caesar had been made consul and it was not beyond possibility that the men in the small boat were bringing orders to relieve him of his authority. Not that it would matter. He had the sealed orders and his captains had not been allowed to read the contents. As far as they were concerned, he had command and could not be relieved unless he allowed it.

Sextus called a full halt and his stomach lurched as the galley swung and bobbed in the waves. He watched as the two men rowed right up to him.

'Who are you then?' he said, hardly having to raise his voice.

'Publius and Gaius Casca,' one of the men replied. He was

gasping, unaccustomed to the hard work of rowing through the swell. 'Free men and Liberatores, in search of sanctuary.'

Sextus considered leaving them to drown for a moment, but at the very least they would have more current news of Rome. He heard Vedius stropping a short dagger at his back and shook his head reluctantly.

'Bring them on board and secure that galley. I know those names. I would like to hear about the assassination from men who were there.'

In the distance, he could see the merchant ship burning. He smiled at the sight of the dark plume rising into the sky like a flag.

'Lavinia! Go below, now!' he snapped suddenly.

'I want to see! And to hear what they have to say!' she replied.

Sextus looked around him. It was not as if the two brothers were a danger.

'Very well, this once,' he said reluctantly. He could refuse her nothing.

Vedius smiled at her, revealing broken teeth and withered gums. She ignored him completely and his expression soured.

CHAPTER TWENTY

The sun was still warm on Agrippa's back, though the seasons had begun to turn and every tree had taken on rich hues of red and gold. He stood on the edge of Lake Avernus, looking out over half a mile of deep water. Where once the lake had supported only a small village on the shore, it had now become an outpost of Rome, with tens of thousands of men working hard from dawn to dusk. On one edge, twelve galley hulls were under construction in immense cradles. Even from the far side, he could see men swarming over the beams and the sound of hammering carried to him in the still air. Three completed ships surged across the surface of the lake, darting around each other as they trained.

'All right, I am impressed,' Maecenas said at his shoulder. 'You've done wonders in just a few months. But I can see one small problem with your plans, Agrippa.'

'There is no problem. Octavian gave me two legions and every carpenter and shipbuilder left in Italy. Two days ago, I signed an order to strip the woodland from a senator's estate and the man did not even dare object. I can build the ships, Maecenas.'

Maecenas stared across the lake, watching as the galleys lunged and feinted at each other.

'I don't doubt it, my friend, though even a few dozen galleys won't be enough to take on the fleet. However . . .'

'With forty galleys, I will take him on,' Agrippa interrupted. 'I've been on these ships for years, Maecenas! I know every inch of them and I can improve them. Walk to the new ones with me. I've had an idea for a weapon that will surprise Sextus Pompey.'

The two men began to walk along the lake's edge. Maecenas could hear the shouted orders to the rowers on the glassy surface. His friend had taken the idea of unlimited funds to heart, so much so that Octavian had sent Maecenas south to see what was costing so many millions each month. From what Maecenas could see, that sum would only increase.

'I have spotted a flaw in your plan, Agrippa,' he said, grinning to himself. 'You have your secret fleet and I can see you are training legionaries to use them. Yet there will be a small difficulty when it comes time to take them out to sea.'

Agrippa glowered at him. 'I am not an idiot, Maecenas. I know the lake has no access to the coast.'

'Some men would consider that a problem for an ocean fleet,' Maecenas observed.

'Yes, I can see it amuses you. But the coast is only a mile away and I chose this lake carefully. I have unlimited numbers of labourers. They will build me a canal to the sea and we will float the ships out.'

Maecenas looked at him in amazement.

'You think it can be done?'

'Why not? The Egyptians built pyramids with thousands of slaves. I have surveyors out preparing the route. One mile,

Maecenas! That is not too far for men who have laid a thousand miles of road.'

The noise of hammering grew as they approached the construction site. Men carrying bags of tools trotted everywhere, pouring with sweat as they worked in the sun. Maecenas whistled softly as he looked up at the closest galley. He had never realised how big they were before. Eleven more in various stages of completion stretched into the distance. He reached up to the oak beams that held the main length of a galley keel. The air smelled of fresh-cut wood and he could see hundreds of carpenters on the ladders and platforms that allowed them to reach any part of the ship's structure. As he watched, a team of eight men held a beam in place, the ends slotting together so that one of their number could use a hammer to knock in a massive wooden peg as wide as his arm.

'What are you paying the men?' he asked.

Agrippa snorted. 'Twice what they could earn anywhere else. The master carpenters are on three times their usual wage. Octavian told me I had a free hand and the most important thing was speed. That does not come cheaply. I can build his fleet, but the costs are high if he wants them quickly.'

Maecenas looked at his friend, seeing the weariness but also the pride. Agrippa had wood shavings in his hair and his cheek was white with sawdust, but his eyes gleamed and he was sun-browned and healthy.

'You are enjoying the work,' Maecenas said, smiling.

Before Agrippa could reply, they both heard a carriage approach, rattling down the road that led the ten miles to Neapolis.

'Who's that?' Agrippa said suspiciously.

'Just a friend. He wanted to see the ships.'

'Maecenas! How can I keep this site secret if you invite your friends to see what I'm doing? How did he even get past the guards on the road?'

Maecenas flushed slightly.

'I gave him a pass. Look, Virgil is a poet and he knows how to keep secrets. I just thought he could write a few verses about this place.'

'You think I have time for poets? Will you be bringing painters and sculptors out here? This is a secret fleet, Maecenas! Send him back. He's already seen too much just by being here. I see he has a driver. Well, I'm keeping him now. I'll put him on the payroll with the others, but no one leaves until spring.'

'I'll take Virgil back myself then,' Maecenas replied.

They both watched the poet step down, staring around him at the massive structures. There was dust in the air and Virgil sneezed explosively, wiping his nose with a square of expensive silk.

'Over here,' Maecenas called to him. His friend saw the two men and waved briefly, walking towards them. 'Look,' Maecenas murmured to Agrippa. 'He really is good, and Octavian likes him. He's already famous in the cities. It will not hurt to be pleasant to such a man. He'll make you immortal.'

'I don't *want* to be immortal,' Agrippa snapped. 'I want to get this fleet built before Sextus Pompey starves the country to death.'

The man who approached was portly and short, his face framed in black curls. As he came close, he sneezed again and moaned softly to himself.

'I swear, Maecenas, I thought the air here would be good for me, but the dust is very unpleasant. You must be Agrippa, the genius shipbuilder. I . . . am Virgil.' He paused, visibly disappointed when Agrippa just stared blankly at him. 'Ah. I see my small fame does not precede me out here. Never mind. Maecenas has told me you have some sort of new design for the galleys?'

'Maecenas!' Agrippa said in disbelief. 'How many more have you told? At this rate I'll have Pompey's fleet waiting for me when I come out.'

Maecenas looked embarrassed, but he held up his hands.

'I told him a few details to catch his interest, that's all. Virgil understands not to say a single word to anyone else, don't you?'

'Of course,' Virgil replied immediately. 'Poets know many secrets. In any case, I suspect I am not long for this world. I grow weaker every day.'

He blew his nose with great energy and Agrippa looked irritably at him.

'Well, I'm keeping your driver,' he said curtly. 'Maecenas will take the horse team back to the city with you.'

Virgil blinked. 'He's exactly as you said, Maecenas. Stern and Roman, but built like a young Hercules. I like him.' He turned to Agrippa. 'So, given that I have already seen your fleet in the making, will I be trusted with a tour?'

'No,' Agrippa replied, barely holding his temper in check. 'I am busy.'

'Caesar said I should look over the detailed plans, Agrippa,' Maecenas said. 'I choose to have Virgil with me to make notes. You have my word he is trustworthy.'

Agrippa raised his eyes in frustration and guided Maecenas a dozen paces further off, too far for Virgil to overhear.

'He does not strike me as a . . . manly sort, Maecenas. I have heard those kinds of men cannot be trusted. They gossip like women.'

'What men do you mean?' Maecenas asked innocently.

Agrippa blushed, looking away.

'You know what I mean. At least tell me he is, you know . . .' his throat seemed to choke him as he forced the words out, '. . . a giver, not a taker.'

'You've lost me now,' Maecenas said, though his eyes gleamed with amusement. Agrippa would not look at him.

'A sword, not a scabbard! Gods, I don't know how you say such things. You *know* what I mean!'

'Yes, I do, ' Maecenas replied, laughing. 'I just wanted to see how you would phrase it. Virgil! My friend here wants to know if you are a sword or a scabbard?'

'What? Oh, a sword, definitely. Good Roman steel, me.'

Agrippa groaned. He glowered at both of them for a long moment, but he was proud of what he had created by the lake and part of him wanted to show them.

'Walk with me then,' he said.

He stalked off immediately and Virgil shared a grin with Maecenas as they followed him. Agrippa reached a ladder and climbed up it, stepping from platform to platform with the ease of practice. Maecenas and Virgil came after him at slower speed, until they were looking down on an unfinished deck. Parts of it were still bare of planking, so that they could see right down to the rowing benches below.

'I tried four corvus bridges rather than the usual one at first. The result is at the bottom of the lake – it made the galleys top-heavy. I'll still adapt a few, as it allows me to pour men on board an enemy ship, but if the waters are choppy, they're just not stable enough. I still have to find a way to make the numbers tell.' He glanced at Maecenas for understanding, but his noble friend just looked bewildered.

'The rowers will not be slaves, not on these ships. Each one will be a swordsman, chosen by competition from Octavian's legions. I'm offering twice the normal pay to anyone who can win his place. In terms of fighting men, we should outnumber any of Sextus Pompey's crews by three to one at least.'

'That is an edge,' Maecenas admitted. 'But Pompey has two hundred galleys at his command. You'll need something more than that.'

'I do have more than that,' Agrippa said sourly, looking at Virgil. 'If I show you this, I want your oath you will die before speaking of it to anyone. It's been hard enough keeping my workers from vanishing back to the city and spilling details to every listening ear.'

'Once more, you have my word, on my honour,' Maecenas said. Virgil repeated the words seriously.

Agrippa nodded and whistled to one of the men working on the deck.

'Bring the catapult up,' he called.

'Catapults are nothing new,' Virgil said a little nervously. 'All the fleet galleys have them.'

'To shoot stones, which miss more often than they hit,' Agrippa growled. 'Accuracy was the problem, so I worked around it. They have nothing like this.'

Under the orders of the carpenter Agrippa had called, six more men brought up spars and ropes from below. As Maecenas and Virgil watched, they began to assemble a machine on the deck, hammering a circular platform into holes in the oak planks, so that it would be steady even in a storm. Onto that, they slotted cast bronze balls with pegs of the metal that fitted into slots cut for them. When another wooden circle was attached, they had a platform six feet across that could rotate easily, even under weight. The rest of the catapult was built on that foundation with the speed of long practice.

'I see a grapnel there . . .' Maecenas began.

'Just watch,' Agrippa said.

The catapult was wound back against bending iron spars, a miniature version of the scorpion bows legions used. Yet there was no cup to hold a heavy stone. A huge iron grapnel with four bent spikes was slotted into place and tied to a mound of coiled rope. The men below looked up for his signal and Agrippa dropped his hand. All three of them jerked as the weapon leapt and the grapnel shot into the air, trailing a snake of rope with a whirring sound. It soared up for a hundred paces before dipping down and striking the soft earth below.

Agrippa looked pleased as he turned to the two men.

'A stone can miss or skip over the deck and drop into the sea. The grapnels will fly right over the enemy ships and catch on the wood. They'll try to cut the ropes, of course, but I have copper wire laced into the cords. There will be three of these on each deck and when they fly, the men will drag the galleys quickly together. The corvus bridges will go down and we'll be on board before they can organise a defence.'

Maecenas and Virgil were nodding, but they did not seem impressed.

'You'll see,' Agrippa said. 'The ships on the lake have the new weapons fitted already. I was going to test them today before you arrived to waste my morning.'

He turned and yelled an order over the lake to the nearest galley as it practised fast manoeuvres. His voice carried easily and the captain acknowledged with a raised hand. The rowers backed oars, bringing the galley into range of the one pursuing it. Maecenas and Virgil both turned in time to see three ropes and grapnels soar out from the deck, right over the other galley, so that they stuck fast and held. Teams of legionaries took hold of spars on a capstan, reeling the ropes back like a fishing line as they shoved against footholds on the wooden deck.

'Now you will see,' Agrippa said.

The ropes had caught the opposing galley at an odd angle. As they grew taut, the opposing crew rushed over to the side where they expected the attack. It unbalanced their ship, which tipped suddenly and violently so that the deck became a slope. More men slid to the lower side, yelling in panic. The oars on one side raised out of the water and on the other the rowers thrashed in panic as the lake came pouring in. Before Agrippa could roar another order, the galley turned right over with a huge crash of water, revealing the shining curve of its hull.

Maecenas swallowed nervously, knowing he had just witnessed the drowning of two hundred men or more. Even those few who could swim would be hard-pressed to escape as the cold waters poured in. Down on the lake, the first galley crew sat still and stunned at what they had done.

He looked at Agrippa and saw his friend caught between horror and delight.

'By the gods, I thought . . .' He shouted for the galley crew to seek out anyone in the water and wiped sweat from his face.

'Did you know that was going to happen?' Virgil asked, his eyes wide in shock.

Agrippa shook his head. 'No,' he said grimly. 'But this was never a game. I will use anything, take any advantage I can get.'

On the lake, the galley was surrounded by hissing bubbles and they could hear the faint cries of drowning men, still trapped with dwindling air in the rowing deck. Against the odds, some of those inside had struggled out. They bobbed up to the surface, thrashing and yelling, trying desperately to stay afloat long enough to be rescued.

'I need another twenty million sesterces to build the canal to the sea,' Agrippa said. 'I will get Caesar the galleys he needs and I will destroy Sextus Pompey, whatever it costs.'

'I'll see it reaches you,' Maecenas said, his usual cheer absent as he watched men drown.

Octavian raised his hand and the other bids stopped instantly.

'Four million sesterces,' he said.

The auctioneer nodded and put aside the sealed ownership papers for him to pick up after the sale was finished. No other bidder would risk the displeasure of a consul and triumvir, though the Suetonius estate was a good one, with river access and a fine house on a hill near to Rome. It adjoined another property Octavian had inherited from Caesar and he could not pass up the chance to increase his holdings. Still, it felt a little odd to bid on properties he had caused to come onto the market. Ten per cent of the final price went to whichever citizen had handed over the proscribed owner and there had been appalling scenes since the lists were published, with mobs breaking down the doors of named men and dragging them out into the street. On more than one occasion, only the head of the man had been used to claim the reward.

The Suetonius estate was unfortunately not one of those. The senator had vanished immediately after the consular elections and Octavian had every spy and client in his employ searching for news of him, as well as the other Liberatores still alive. In his absence, the Suetonius estate had been confiscated and the bulk of the proceeds would go to training and preparing new legions.

'The next lot is a country villa by Neapolis, originally owned by Publius Casca.'

Octavian knew that name, one of two brothers who had managed to elude those hunting them. He had heard a rumour that the Cascas had thrown themselves on the dubious mercy of Sextus Pompey, but he could not be certain. He had no desire to bid on their property at that time, but he waited even so, to see how much silver would be coming into the war coffers.

The bidding began weakly as wealthy men in the room tried to guess whether the consul and triumvir would take it from them at the last moment. Octavian felt their eyes on him and shook his head, turning slightly away. The bidding increased to a rapid tempo then, as the estate in the south was renowned for its vineyards and farmland. There was still money in Rome, Octavian thought. His task was to gather as much of it as he could for a campaign that would need an even greater war chest than the one Caesar had collected for Parthia.

He rubbed his eyes wearily as the price reached four million sesterces and most of the bidders dropped out. Agrippa's secret fleet was proving to be an appalling drain on the state finances, but he could see no other choice but to pour more silver and gold into the ships. Without a fleet, the legions he controlled with Mark Antony were effectively useless. The price of bread had already tripled and though many of the citizens still hoarded much of the silver Caesar had given them, he knew it would not last much longer before they were rioting again, just to eat. Octavian shook his head at the thought.

The bidding came to an end at six million, four hundred thousand. He made a gesture to the auctioneer, who paled when he saw it, thinking it was a late bid. Octavian shook his head again and gestured to the batch of sealed papers that represented the estate he had bought. They would be sent on to one of his city houses, the funds disbursed by one of the hundreds of factors and servants working directly for him. The men in the room relaxed visibly as he left.

The auction house was high on the Quirinal hill and Octavian barely noticed the lictors who fell into step with him as he walked down towards the forum. The new senate house was almost complete and he had agreed to meet his co-consul Pedius at the temple of Vesta to oversee the laying of the final stone. Rome bustled around him as he made his way down the hill and his mouth quirked as he recalled previous times when he could hardly move for cheering crowds. They did not cheer him that day. He shivered as he walked. The air in Rome was growing colder as the year came to an end. In all ways, the new spring seemed very far away.

As he reached the forum, the sense of the energetic city all around him increased. The open space was filled with thousands of men and women on the business of Rome, from the administration of a thousand trading houses, to senators and specialists in law discussing every topic, many of them with crowds listening. Rome had been made and remade on words and ideas before swords and it still felt young, just as he did. The senators were not isolated from the citizens, at least at certain times each month. They walked among the crowds in the forum and listened to requests and appeals from those they represented. Anything from a problem with a neighbour to a murder charge could be brought to them, and as Octavian walked, he saw

Bibilus deep in conversation with a group of wealthy merchants only slightly slimmer than himself. Like Octavian, Bibilus had increased his holdings during the proscription auctions. There was no doubt he had men in the room Octavian had just left, bidding on his behalf for the choicer properties.

Bibilus saw the stern lictors passing by and his cold eyes sought out Octavian walking in the centre of them. Despite his gains, Octavian knew there was no truce there, not from him. It was because of Octavian that Mark Antony had returned to the Senate with more power and fewer restraints than he had enjoyed before. Octavian could feel Bibilus' dislike from a distance and he let it warm him. Bibilus did not call a greeting, preferring to pretend he had not seen him pass by.

Pedius was standing in the entrance to the temple of Vesta, in conversation with Quintina Fabia. Octavian brightened at the sight of the older woman, whose company he enjoyed. He had hardly spoken to her since becoming consul, but she was one of those he had begun to assume were among his supporters, at least for the sake of her nephew Maecenas.

To his surprise, Quintina Fabia came forward to him with open arms.

'Caesar, I hear I should congratulate you,' she said.

Octavian glanced at Pedius, who shrugged. He allowed himself to be embraced with surprising strength.

'On what?' he asked when she released him.

'Your betrothal, of course,' she said.

'Ah. I do not take much joy from the prospect of a twelve-year-old wife, Quintina.'

He had met Mark Antony's daughter only once since returning to Rome and the marriage to come was little more than a bargaining piece in their negotiations. He felt sorry for Claudia, if anything, but marriages were a currency of Rome and a statement of their mutual support. It would not interfere with his current popularity among the noble mistresses of the city. Octavian was slim and young and in power, a powerful cocktail that led to a different partner every night, if he chose. He suspected Quintina knew that very well and was teasing him, so he tried to take it with good grace.

'I have other things on my mind at the moment, Quintina; I apologise.'

'Of course. Young men are always in love,' she replied.

'Perhaps, I cannot say. I dream of new legions, trained and hardened over a winter.'

He looked to Pedius, who seemed embarrassed by the exchange and somewhat flustered by the attentions of the priestess.

'Report, Pedius. I have not come here to talk of love, not today.'

The older man cleared his throat.

'With regret, Lady Fabia, I must leave our conversation to another time.'

'Oh very well, though I know a few Roman widows who would be thrilled to meet a mature man as well, Pedius. They are deeper pools than these young girls Caesar favours. Their rivers have not run dry in the years without a man. In fact, the opposite is true. Think on that while you talk away a fine morning.'

She strolled back into the temple then, leaving the two of them staring after her. Pedius shook his head, caught between the suspicion he was being mocked and genuine interest.

'We've raised six new legions and placed their names on the Senate rolls. At the moment, they are little more than farmers and shop boys. They are training around Arretium, but they have to share swords and shields on a rota.'

'So buy more,' Octavian said.

Pedius blew air out, exasperated.

'I would if I had the gold to do it! Have you any idea what it costs to make equipment for five thousand men, never mind thirty? The swords must come overland from Spain while Sextus blockades the western coast. A thousand miles, Caesar! Instead of a month at sea, it takes four times as long, but until then, they must train with sticks and mismatched weapons more than a century old. Yet wherever I look for funds, I am told Caesar has been there before me and the chests are all empty.'

Octavian hardly needed another reminder that Sextus Pompey was harassing the coasts. With Cassius and Brutus growing stronger all the time in Greece and Macedonia, he was only too aware of the strangling grip cutting the life's blood from the country.

'I have gold coming by land as well, from mines in Spain – and I am working on a solution to the fleet with Sextus Pompey. It is draining the treasury, but I have to be able to protect legions as they cross.'

'I would prefer it if you'd share more of your planning with me,' Pedius said. 'Though the proscriptions have silenced some of your enemies, the main problems persist. We cannot begin a campaign without more legions to keep Rome safe and of course ships to carry them. Until we have those, we are trapped on our own mainland.'

'All right, Consul. There is no point in labouring over our difficulties. I have been in worse positions, believe me.'

To his surprise, Pedius smiled, chewing at the insides of his lips as he looked up.

'Yes you have, haven't you? And you have come through them. The city still looks to you to make everything right, Caesar, as if you can bring cheap grain once more with just a wave of your hand.' He leaned a little closer, so the ever present lictors could not overhear. 'But everything you have won can be taken away, if men like Brutus, Cassius and Sextus Pompey can find another ally in Rome.'

Octavian looked sharply at the older man, watching his moving jaw.

'Are you seeking to warn me? Mark Antony has cast his lot

with me, Pedius. He would not be such a fool as to risk an alliance with men like those.'

'Perhaps,' Pedius replied. 'I hope you are right. Perhaps I am just a suspicious old man, but it is sometimes a good idea to be suspicious. You are very young, Caesar. The future is longer for you than it is for me. It might be an idea to think of those years as you make your choices.'

Octavian considered for a moment. He knew Caesar had been warned many times about assassins and always ignored the threat.

'I will be ready for anything, Pedius. You have my word on it.'

'Good.' Pedius smiled. 'I have come to enjoy being consul with you, young man. I don't want it to come to an end too soon.'

CHAPTER TWENTY-ONE

Brutus smothered his anger, which was more at his own failing stamina than the Greek who danced around him with the training sword. There had been a time when he could have humiliated the younger man with ease, but a large part of his speed had vanished over the years. Only his daily routine of sparring kept his fitness from disappearing completely.

He knew his face and bare chest were red as he heated up. Each breath felt as if it came from an oven and sweat poured off him while his opponent still looked fresh. It was galling and ultimately pointless, but he wished for just a moment of his youth to return so he could batter the Greek into quick submission.

Cleanthes was still wary of the Roman governor who had challenged him to a sparring bout. For all the difference of thirty years in their ages, he had not been able to land a crippling blow, only to stripe the man's arms with the red ink daubed on his wooden blade. Even so, he felt the bout turning in his favour and it did not hurt to have his friends calling their encouragement from the side of the training ground. Athens may have been ruled by Rome, but the crowd were open in their support for the young Greek.

Driven on by their cheering, Cleanthes blocked an attack with his buckler shield and lunged at the Roman's throat. It was a dangerous blow, one of the few that could be fatal with the wooden weapons. Brutus tensed with anger as he knocked it aside, launching a series of strikes that forced Cleanthes back step by step. He had once been very, very good and his form was still impressive, though he was panting and sweat spattered from his wet hair.

Cleanthes hesitated rather than press back. Everything he had learned in the sparring classes had failed to break through the man's guard. Yet he did not want to win by virtue of exhausting his opponent. He faced Brutus squarely and brought his sword back to the scabbard position on his hip. They wore only leggings and there was no strap to hold the weapon, but his intention was clear. Brutus curled his lip, yet he too had been arrogant once. He accepted the threat and stepped in close, watching Cleanthes carefully as he brought his own sword back to his hip, ready for a single strike. It was the sort of thing that appealed to young men, a test of draw speed alone. Brutus watched the eyes of the younger man, relaxing himself completely.

The attack came without warning, a blow that Cleanthes had practised a thousand times in his young life. He made the decision to move and his hand whipped the sword up fast. To his shock, Cleanthes felt a line sear across the side of his throat, leaving a red stain that mingled with his sweat and dripped down his bare chest. Brutus followed it with two more quick strikes, one to the inner thigh, where a man would bleed to death quickly, and another to the Greek's side. It happened in a heartbeat and Brutus grinned unpleasantly at him as he stepped back.

'The second man to move is often faster; did they not teach you that?' Brutus said. 'If he is trained, his reaction is swifter than a planned blow.'

Cleanthes reached up to his throat and the red stain that came away on his fingers. He looked down to see the ink dripping down his right leg. The crowd had fallen silent and he bowed stiffly to the Roman governor.

'I will remember the lesson,' Cleanthes said. 'Once more?'

Heads jerked round at the sound of clapping hands echoing in the training yard. Brutus saw Cassius at the rail, looking fresh and fit. He recognised Suetonius and Gaius Trebonius with him and tensed his jaw. With a quick gesture, Brutus tossed the training sword to Cleanthes, who was forced to catch it.

'Not today,' Brutus called over his shoulder. 'It seems I have guests.'

He walked over to the group of three waiting for him.

'Will you join me in the baths? I need to wash the sweat off.'

Cassius nodded, though Suetonius looked uncomfortable and wiped a hand across his hair. Gaius Trebonius was staring around him with unabashed interest. They followed Brutus to the training house baths and all four men stripped, handing their clothes to slaves to be brushed and steamed clean. Brutus ignored the others, knowing they would wait on him, whatever it was they wanted. He stood stoically as buckets of water were emptied over him, then headed into the hottest steam room to sweat out the dirt from his skin. Surrounded by strangers, Cassius could hardly discuss their plans and as a group the men sat in silence as the steam billowed around them, then followed Brutus through the cold plunge and finally onto the tables, where other slaves worked oil into their skins and scraped them clean with lengths of ivory, wiping black muck onto their waistcloths.

A good hour passed before they were left alone. Some men preferred to doze for a while afterwards, while many more wished to discuss their business in private. The slaves left discreetly, though they would be waiting at the outer door in the hope of a few extra coins when the customers went out to the street.

Suetonius was not aware that his hair had become thin snake tails in the steam and oil, doing nothing to hide his baldness. He lifted his head from the table where he lay and saw the others resting with their eyes closed.

'As pleasant as it is to find a competent Roman house in Athens, there is much to discuss,' he said.

Brutus made a sound close to a groan, but he sat up even so. The others did the same, though Suetonius rested his hands over his sagging paunch and wrinkled thighs. The baths stripped away dignity and he wished for his toga to be returned.

'So what has brought you to me here?' Brutus said. 'I was hoping to catch the orator Thenes when he speaks in the agora.'

'Is he worth hearing?' Cassius asked.

Brutus shrugged, waving a hand.

'You know the Greeks. They see only chaos in the world and offer no solutions. It's all froth and wind, compared to Roman thinkers. At least we are practical. When we see chaos, we stamp on its head.'

'They are an arrogant people, I've always found,' Cassius replied. 'I remember one of them telling me they had invented everything, from gods to sex. I pointed out that Romans took their ideas and improved on them. Ares became Mars, Zeus became Jupiter. And of course, although we could not improve on sex, we are the ones who thought of trying it with women.'

Brutus laughed, clapping him on the shoulder.

'I don't like to interrupt your discussion of philosophy,' Suetonius said, breaking in. 'But we do have more pressing concerns.'

Cassius and Brutus shared an amused glance that Suetonius noticed, his mouth becoming a thin line of disapproval. Gaius

Trebonius just watched them all, not confident enough to join the conversation.

'Tell me, then,' Brutus said with a sigh. He was feeling wonderfully relaxed. 'What or who has brought you out of Syria, Cassius?'

'Who else but Caesar?' Cassius replied. 'You know he has formed a triumvirate?'

'With Mark Antony and some Gaul general named Lepidus, yes. I am not so far from Rome that I don't hear such things.'

'He has taken the power of an emperor to himself!' Suetonius snapped, tired of the mellow tone of the conversation. 'He acts as a dictator, selling our properties and making a mockery of the law. You know about the proscriptions?'

Brutus smiled unpleasantly. 'I'm on the list, I know that much. What of it? I'd do the same in his place.'

'You are not so resigned to another Caesar rising above us all, no matter what you pretend,' Suetonius said waspishly.

Brutus stared coldly at him until he was forced to look away.

'Watch yourself, Suetonius, at least around me. I am governor of Athens, after all. I don't know exactly . . . what *you* are.'

Suetonius gaped at him as Cassius grinned and turned away to hide it.

'I am dispossessed! That's what I am. I am one of the Liberatores! I saved Rome from an insane tyrant who made a mockery of the Republic, who destroyed centuries of civilisation by being too powerful to check or balance. That is who I am, Brutus. Who are you?'

Brutus treated the outburst like noise from a yapping dog, though his smile grew tight. Suetonius waited only a beat before going on, the words flooding out of him after too long held inside.

'Yet despite what I have done for the Republic, my family home is taken from me, my legal amnesty is revoked and my life threatened. Even here in Greece, I am in danger from any Roman who sees a chance to take my head and earn himself a fortune. You think you are immune, Brutus? We have come too far to lose everything because of some bastard relative trying to steal power he has not earned. He will bring us all down unless we stop him.'

'You sound like a frightened old woman, Senator,' Brutus replied. 'Try to remember your dignity.'

'My *dignity*?' Suetonius said, his voice rising.

Brutus turned away from him, leaving him open-mouthed in astonishment.

'I have not been idle, Cassius,' Brutus said. 'I have been working with the legions and councils here, securing their loyalty. I've raised taxes to pay for two more legions, mostly Greco-Roman stock, but fit. They train every day and they are mine alone, sworn to me. Can you say the same?'

Cassius smiled. 'I have seven legions in Syria and four more from Egypt. I can field eleven at full strength, well supplied and equipped. They value the Republic, and without the poison of Caesarians whispering in their ears, they are utterly loyal to those who liberated Rome. I have not wasted my time. You know me better than that.'

Brutus was pleased at the numbers and he inclined his head to acknowledge it before glancing at Suetonius.

'I do,' he said. 'You see, Suetonius, Cassius and I have been working together. We have built an army while you were preening yourself and talking the months away in Rome.'

Naked as Suetonius was, they could all see the mottled flush that spread down from his outraged face to his groin.

'It was I who secured all our futures by handing over the fleet to Sextus Pompey!' Suetonius replied. 'If Bibilus and I hadn't achieved that much, you would be looking at an armed invasion *this* year, Brutus. That is what all my "preening" bought you – the time we need!'

'I'm sure we all agree that was a fine decision,' Cassius said, trying to ease the tension between them. 'Sextus Pompey is young, but his enmity for Caesar's faction is well known. Are you in contact with him?'

'I am,' Brutus said. He saw Suetonius look up and shrugged. 'He has the only fleet in the west and my name is not a disadvantage in that camp, not to him. Of course I am in contact. You know the Casca brothers reached him?'

'No, I didn't,' Cassius replied. 'Good. Though their estates have been sold for the state coffers.'

'All the more motive to keep them on our side,' Brutus said. 'I do not want any surprises at this point. We can use the fleet to land on Roman territory or wait for them here. Yes, Suetonius, I know they will come. Octavian and Mark Antony cannot ignore us while the grain runs out in Rome. They must come. They will cross to land in Greece, just as Julius Caesar did against Pompey. This time, though, I think they will lose half their men when Sextus sends them to the bottom of the sea. Do I have it right, Cassius?'

'It is my hope, yes,' the thin senator replied. 'It is our *best* hope to end it all.'

As they left the bathing complex, Brutus reached inside a pouch to find a few bronze coins for the staff. He paused as he drew out a silver sesterce and flicked it through the air to Cassius. The older man examined it with a frown, then laughed.

'"Saviour of the Republic"? Really, Brutus? It seems, well, a little immodest.'

Brutus smiled wryly, tossing another one to Suetonius, who caught it and peered at the face printed on the metal.

'I could hardly fit your names as well. It is a good likeness, don't you think? As governor, I'm responsible for the Athens mint, so it wasn't much trouble. It does not hurt our cause to remind the citizens *why* we murdered a man in Rome.' He nodded to Suetonius. 'On that we can agree, I hope.'

Cassius had pursed his lips at the word 'murdered', but he handed back the coin with something like satisfaction on his face.

'Indeed. Image is everything. That is something I've learned over the years. The people know very little, just what they are told. I have discovered they will believe almost anything I tell them.'

Brutus grunted and tossed the silver coin to the bath attendant. The slave bowed his head, delighted at the windfall.

'I never denied having personal reasons for my part in it, Cassius. Everything I have done, everything I *achieved*, was as nothing in his shadow. Well, I shone a light into the dark places and cast him *off*. The coins are true in their way. We did save the Republic, unless we lose it now to this boy Octavian.'

'We will not lose,' Cassius said. 'He will come to us, and when he does, he must come by sea.'

'Unless they march round the north of Italy and strike south by land,' Suetonius said grimly. Brutus and Cassius looked at him, but he was long past courting their admiration. 'Well? It is no further than Syria. You cannot simply ignore the threat of a land attack. What is a thousand miles or so to legions?'

'Senator,' Brutus said scornfully, 'if they move so many men that far north, we will be told. We have the fleet, remember? If the Caesarians take their army north, we will be safe in Rome for months before they can make it back. I'd be happy for them to try it! It would solve all our problems at once.'

Suetonius grunted unintelligibly, his face red as they left the bath-house. The Romans stood out in the Greek crowd, if only for their short-cropped hair and military bearing. As he reached the street, Brutus gestured to a group of soldiers waiting for him and they saluted smartly, forming up on all sides.

'I have to say you did well in choosing Athens, Brutus,' Cassius observed, looking around him as they walked. 'This is pleasant, a home away from home. I'm afraid Syria is too hot in summer and much too cold in winter. It is a harsh place, but then the legions there are harder still.'

'How many ships do you have to bring them over?' Brutus asked.

'Ships? None at all. The ones I had I sent to Sextus Pompey. I don't need them, with land all the way from here to Beroea. There are ferry boats to take them across the Bosphorus strait, by Byzantium. You should see that place one day, Brutus, if you do not know the area. In some ways it is as Greek as Athens, older even than Rome.'

'Yes, when my neck is not on the line one day, perhaps I will waste my time with old maps and cities. How long to march your legions into Macedonia?'

'They are already marching. Come the spring, you and I will have an army to face anything the triumvirate has left after the crossing. We can put nineteen legions into battle, Brutus – more than ninety thousand men and most of them veterans. Whatever half-drowned rabble lands in Greece when Sextus is finished with them will not last long against such a host.'

'I will command, of course,' Brutus said.

Cassius came to a sudden stop in the street and the others paused with him, so that the crowd was forced to go around them, like a rock in a river. There were curses thrown their way in Greek, but the Romans ignored them.

'I believe I have the greater number of legions, Brutus. We do not want to lose the war before it has even begun by squabbling over this.'

Brutus weighed the determination in the sinewy man who faced him.

'I have more experience than you or any five of your legates,' he said. 'I fought in Gaul and Spain *and* Egypt, for years on end. I do not dispute their loyalty to you, Cassius, but I have been wasted before by Caesar. I will not be wasted here.'

In turn, Cassius judged how far he could resist and gave up.

'Joint command then,' he said. 'The numbers are too great for just one man to give orders. Will that satisfy you? Each to his own legions?'

'I'll have eight to your eleven, Cassius, but, yes, I think I can make them dance when the time comes. I'll want the horsemen, though, under my own command. I know how to use extraordinarii.'

'Very well,' Cassius replied. 'I have eight thousand. As a gesture of friendship, they are yours.'

As they walked on, Suetonius shook his head, his irritation growing as they discussed the future with no acknowledgement of the part he and Bibilus had played.

'You think this is all about a war?' he said with a sneer. 'Or a few coins, with boastful words on them?'

Brutus and Cassius stopped again as he spoke. Both men glared at him, but he continued, refusing to be cowed.

'So which of you will be emperor when this is over? Which of you will rule Rome as king?'

'Suetonius, I don't think you . . .' Cassius began. To his surprise, Suetonius held up a flat palm, cutting him off.

'I knew you when you were just a boy, Brutus; do you remember?'

'Oh, I remember,' Brutus said.

A warning had crept into his tone, but Suetonius ignored it. The crowd continued to flow around them.

'You and I believed in the Republic then, not just as a fantasy but as something real, something worth dying for. Julius never did. The Republic is worth a life, remember? It was also worth a death. That is what we were trying to save, but the way you talk, it's almost as if you have forgotten it. Do you recall how you once hated men like Pompey and Cornelius Sulla? Generals like Marius who would do anything if it brought them power? Caesar was one of those, part of the same miserable illness – and his adopted son is another. If Octavian is killed, if he is defeated, it must not be just to put another like him in his place. The old Republic depends on the goodwill of those strong enough to tear it apart, but it is worth more than a few men. I have given my life to this cause and I *will* die for it if I have to. Those are the stakes – more than a war, or a fleet, or another dictator. After this, we will either have emperors or we will have free men. That is why we resist Octavian: not for revenge, or to protect ourselves, but because *we* believe in the Republic – and he does not.'

Brutus had been going to speak for a time, but he closed his mouth. Cassius looked at him in surprise.

'I think you have silenced our general, Senator!' He chuckled to lighten the moment, but no one joined him.

'I think at least one of us should think about what happens when we win, Cassius, don't you?' Suetonius replied coldly. 'This is a chance to restore the old liberties, the compact between free citizens and the state, the great freedom. Or we can be just another branch of the vine that has been strangling Rome for fifty years.'

He reached into his pouch and brought out the coin Brutus had given him, holding it up.

'"Saviour of the Republic,"' he read aloud. 'Well, why not, Brutus? Why *not*?'

CHAPTER TWENTY-TWO

The heel of Italy was lost in the mist and gloom as the fleet of galleys struggled around it in rough, grey seas. Sextus wiped salt water from his eyes as it sprayed over him. He knew better than most how poorly his crews handled a storm. So that they could skip across shallow waters, the galleys had no deep keels, but that great speed brought instability and in rough seas the oars had to be used to prevent the galleys from turning over.

Sextus could see the storm coming in fast on the horizon, a bank of dark cloud with distant threads of rainfall spilling from it. The entire cloud flashed and the sea seemed to respond, the swell surging and showing white foam.

His legion captain was vomiting over the side and Sextus shuddered as he felt flecks of it blown back on the wind, striking his face and neck.

'By Mars, go downwind, would you?' he shouted angrily.

The miserable man shuffled to the stern without taking his

hands from the rail. Sextus walked up the rolling deck to the prow, staring out over the grey vastness. All around him, he could see dozens of galleys plunging through the waves. They were at their most vulnerable when the oars had to be brought in, the openings sealed with tar-cloth so that the rowing decks didn't become swamped. Some of his galleys had already given the order and raised a tiny storm sail, while many more laboured on with the oars out and freezing water pouring through the gaps in the wooden walls. The men inside would be baling for their lives, but at least the galleys could be controlled. For the others, only a scrap of cloth, steering oars and rare glimpses of the southern coast guided them around the mainland.

Sextus swallowed nervously, waiting for the crash that would tell him one of them had struck a rock, or perhaps each other. There was always danger, but galleys were safe enough when they could head for shore and beach themselves. It was only when a madman like him ordered them into deep water that they became vulnerable.

A wave rushed over the bow, drenching him and making him shiver. Rain began to pound the flat deck, reducing visibility even further. Sextus peered out to the distant coast, just a dim line in the grey. He needed to reach shelter before the full storm struck, but the way it looked, his crews would have to endure a battering before they were around the point. When he caught glimpses of the other ships, he saw more and more of them had been forced to pull the oars in or sink. Only the huge double steering oars at the stern could guide them then. Through the spray and mist, he could see galleys wandering away over the sea, soldiers climbing the masts to shout sightings to those below. He groaned, knowing he'd be lucky not to lose a few crews. He wished Vedius were there, but his second in command had been the only man he could trust with the other half of his fleet. Vedius would not betray him, he was certain. He had also left instructions with two others for him to be quietly murdered if he did.

Sextus felt an itch at the back of his neck and when he turned, he was not surprised to see Lavinia there, holding on to the main mast. One hand shaded her eyes as she stared into the distance and he thought she looked like a ghost, with her cloak whipping around her in the wind and her features unnaturally pale. He left his place on the prow and walked back to her, staggering slightly on the heaving deck.

'I can't be worrying about you as well as the ship,' he said. 'What's wrong with your cabin?'

Lavinia raised her eyes to him.

'I needed to breathe, that's all. There's no air down below and the ship is rolling and jumping about like a mad thing.'

Despite his concern, he smiled at her martyred tone. He reached out with his free hand to push back a lock of her sodden hair where it had fallen over her face.

'It won't last much longer, I promise. We'll be round the point soon and the sea will be calmer after that.'

He glanced again at the storm clouds and she read the worry in his expression, her nervousness increasing.

'It's going to get *worse*?' she said.

He grinned to reassure her. 'We are the lucky ones, remember? We'll come through.'

It was an old and bitter joke between them. Their family had suffered far more than its fair share of misfortune. If any luck still clung to the Pompey name, it would surely fall on Sextus and Lavinia. She rolled her eyes at the feeble attempt to cheer her up. Her brother saw her shivering and realised her cloak was wet through with spray.

'You'll freeze if you stay up here,' he said.

'No more than you will,' she retorted. 'At least I am away from the smell of sweat and vomit. It is . . . unpleasant down below.'

'You'll survive,' he said, without sympathy. 'Don't we always? I told you I'd look after you and here I have a fine fleet at my command.'

As he spoke, the galley gave a great lurch as it missed the peak of a wave and crashed down into the trough. Lavinia yelped and he wrapped his arm around his sister and the mast, holding on to them both.

'I think I preferred it when you were a pirate,' she said. 'At least you brought me jewels then.'

'Which you sold and invested! I gave you those to enjoy, not to be sensible.'

'One of us has to be,' she said. 'When this is over, I'll need a dowry. And you'll need funds for a house if you're ever to have a family of your own.'

He hugged her tighter then, recalling a thousand conversations in harder times. As children, they had lost everything but their father's name and a few loyal servants who still honoured Gnaeus Pompey. At the darkest moments, they had talked of the lives they would have one day, with a house and servants and peace: just silence and peace, with no one threatening them or hunting them down.

'I'm glad to know you are still looking out for me,' he said. 'But it would please me more if you'd go down and find a good cloak I can wear – as well as a dry one for you.'

She could not resist such an appeal and it was true that he shivered just as violently as she did.

'Very well,' she said. 'But I'm coming back.'

He guided her to the hatch and held it open long enough for Lavinia to climb down the ladder before closing it. He was still smiling as he walked back to the prow and looked over the grey ocean, taking in everything he had missed.

At least the captains from Syria knew what they were doing, Sextus had to admit, as his ship followed them. The group of ten weatherbeaten galleys held their positions well in regard to each other, a flotilla moving with something like skill. To reach him from Syria they'd crossed open ocean, the wear showing on their galleys and men. Sextus told himself he'd made the right decision letting Cassius' captains lead the way east around the heel.

Sextus jerked as he heard a great crash somewhere on his left. He squinted out through the pouring rain, but he couldn't see what had caused it. The southern coast of Italy was faintly visible and he took heart from that. It would not be long before they were round the point and back into more sheltered waters. He only wished he could take the fleet in closer, but even if they could see his flags, the rocks would rip the bottom right out of a galley.

The wind began to howl around the mast and the prow seemed to dive under another enormous wave, so that Sextus had to grip the prow in a lurch or be swept away. He gasped and coughed as freezing seawater entered his lungs. As the green bronze ram came up once more, Sextus felt exhausted, but the storm was still coming and they were only at the edge of it. With a glance behind him, he saw the Roman captain was still there, bent over. The man looked like a corpse, but he still hung on, swearing weakly. Sextus grinned at the sight, reminding himself to mention it if they both survived.

Ahead of him, the Syrian galleys were still forcing their way through. There was no safe place to wait out the storm. All he could do was continue the insane dash around the heel of Italy and turn for Brundisium once more. He told himself over and over that Cassius was right. He had enough ships to blockade the entire country if he used them in two fleets, like the jaws of a pair of blacksmith's pincers. No one else had a hundred galleys, never mind the two hundred and twelve at his command. He had the forces to squeeze Rome into starvation.

His mood darkened with the storm and he felt a coldness inside to match his half-frozen flesh. His father could have ruled the Republic. Sextus and Lavinia would have grown up with every comfort. All of that had been stolen away from him on an Egyptian dock, his father murdered by foreign slaves just to please Julius Caesar.

For years, Sextus knew he had been no more than a biting fly on the flank of Roman power. Men loyal to his father still sent him reports from the city and he'd seen his chance and risked execution by returning there to make a personal appeal. Vedius had argued against it, telling him never to trust the noble old men of the Senate. The tavern wolf had not understood that Sextus knew those men well. His father had been one of them. Even then, he had been afraid they would look first at his piracy and his youth, but somehow, with the threat of Octavian and his legions, it had worked. Sextus had been given a fleet unmatched in those waters and the moment when the Senate had voted had eased a pain that had been with him ever since his father died.

Now Cassius had called him and he had answered. His fleet was a weapon to bring the Caesarians to a battle they could not win. Sextus wiped salt from his eyes once more, showing his teeth as the wind bit at him. He had learned from a young age that there was no such thing as justice. It was not justice that his father had been taken from him. It was not justice that a man like Caesar had been given Rome to rule as a king. Sextus had lived with despair and bitterness for years, surviving by being more ruthless and more ready to kill than any of his men. It had been a brutal school and he knew he would never be able to go back to the innocent child he had once been with Lavinia. His smile widened into the gale, showing his canines as his lips pulled back. None of that mattered. Cassius and Brutus had killed the tyrant and at last he had a chance to ravage and burn Octavian's forces. One day he would restore everything the family of Caesar had taken from him and that was all he cared about, all he needed to know. His father's shade watched him. The old man's honour was worth a run through a storm.

Driven by some strange joy he did not understand, Sextus began to sing into the wind, a sailor's work tune. He sang badly but with great volume and it was loud enough to cause the captain to look up from his misery, staring in disbelief. Others in the crew grinned at the sight and sound of their young leader roaring and stamping his feet at the prow.

He felt the weight of the cloak as Lavinia came back, looking at him as if he had gone mad as she draped it over his wet shoulders.

'They are saying some sea monster is wailing up here,' she said. 'Shall I tell them it's just your singing?'

He grinned at her, pulling the cloak around him. The storm was tossing the sea into froth and vicious spray that stung his face as the galley crashed on.

'Hold on to the prow with me,' he shouted back. 'The ship needs a little of our luck.'

They stayed there together, arm in arm, until the fleet rounded the point and the storm was left to grumble and flash behind them.

Agrippa scratched at a smear of mud on his forehead as it dried and itched. He could hardly remember when he had managed to snatch more than a few hours' sleep and he was exhausted. It was done. Two thousand men with shovels and wheeled carts had dug a trench just over a mile long and only the final section waited to be breached. He had more than thirty surveyors working with them, checking the depth with long rods as the men toiled. It had to be twenty-four feet wide to accommodate the narrow galleys, even with the oars pulled right in and stacked on the decks, but the width had not caused as many problems as the depth. Agrippa had spent a day having the surveyors go over their figures again and again, but the shallow galleys had to float free or the entire enterprise would be worthless. He looked at the huge gates that held the lake waters back. They had been a tale in themselves, with expert builders driving wooden beams into the clay with enormous weights suspended above them, lifted and dropped a hundred times by teams of sweating labourers. They'd dug out foundations a short distance from the lake, sinking a trench back to the water. His carpenters had worked day and night and when the first short length breached and filled, the massive gates held, forming a short spur. None of the trench men had enjoyed standing close to them as they dug away from the gates towards the sea. The wood groaned occasionally and water sprayed from tiny holes, dribbling along the trench and making the earth sticky and wet. It had been hard, but as the surveyors had promised him, two thousand men could build almost anything and the thing was done at last.

On the lake, his galleys still flitted and lunged at each other, each new crew building the stamina they needed while they practised boarding. He'd had archery targets set up all along the shore of the lake for them to use and one of the top-heavy corvus ships anchored on the water, which now resembled a porcupine for the number of shafts sticking out of its timbers. He scowled at the sight of it, wondering who had failed to give the order to collect the arrows. Every one was precious, though entire industries had grown up around Neapolis to supply him. He had all his carts sent north as obviously as possible for a hundred miles before cutting west and back south, but even so Agrippa suspected his secrecy was a complete farce. His men had to chase local boys away almost every day as they crept along the shore and stole tools or simply gaped at the darting galleys. A city's worth of men had descended on Lake Avernus and Agrippa had been forced to hang two of his carpenters for murdering a local during a botched theft. He had guards on the only road east, yet there were constant attempts by Neapolis officials to come out and demand things from him, either justice or compensation for something his people had done. If it hadn't been for the sight of new galleys growing by the day, he thought he would have despaired, but Octavian's silver poured out and ships were made and rested. The green wood would warp and twist over the winter, needing constant care and repair, but he had teams for that work as well.

The surveyors were waiting for him to give the signal and Agrippa only stared wearily, checking a thousand things in his mind to be sure he had not missed some crucial aspect of the canal that could not be redone once he had opened it. He looked along its length, seeing the smooth lime concrete that covered the clay beneath. It would hold water as well as any bridge pile, he had been assured, but still he worried that the entire length would drain away, leaving him with a lake that was suddenly too low to bring his galleys out.

Agrippa took a deep breath and prayed to Minerva. The goddess of artisans would surely look kindly on such a project as a canal to the sea. That thought brought another prayer to Neptune and finally Agrippa made the horned hand to ward off ill-luck. He could not think of another god or goddess worth asking, so he raised his arm and dropped it.

'Come on,' he murmured. 'Go well.'

The gates had been made with immense beams of wood standing out from each side and locked in place with iron bars set into stone. As the bars were pulled out, he had a dozen men on each one, but the pressure from behind would be with them. He watched as one brave builder climbed down into the trench and used a hammer to knock out a main strut. The teams took the strain, holding the waters back while the builder rushed out again. As soon as he stepped clear, they reversed their pull and water began to roar through, the noise indescribable. The teams were forced back step by step, despite their best efforts. The line of rushing water became a cataract, spraying water high into the air.

The gates came right back into their slots against the walls of the canal and the teams stood panting, their job done. Agrippa began to jog, then ran along the length as fast as he could go. The waters outpaced him and he saw a great wave rise above the final blocking gate, lifting twenty feet or more into the air, so that all the men there were drenched and laughing. He arrived as the water settled back into a placid surface, with mud and torn plants swirling. The sea was on his left shoulder and he only wished he could have driven the canal right out to it in one go. Barely fifty feet of sandy soil remained, but his surveyors had insisted on another gate before the final breakthrough, in case something went wrong with the levels or, worse, they were seen from the sea and attacked before they were ready. Sextus Pompey had ships somewhere out there on the dark water and he could land ten thousand men if he saw something interesting on the coast.

A great cheer went up as the labourers saw the canal fill and hold, the level equalising with the lake. Agrippa grinned at last, wishing Maecenas and Octavian were there to see it. Pride swelled his chest and he laughed aloud, enjoying the smell of salt and seaweed that was strong in the air. When they finished the last section, they'd have the same routine to do again, but he'd have the new galleys waiting in line for a mile, backing up onto the lake. They'd come out in a rush of brown water and Octavian would have his fleet to hunt down the galleys of Sextus Pompey.

Mark Antony was walking the cliffs with Lepidus, looking down on the port city. When he had last been to Brundisium, six mutinous legions waited for him to take command and pronounce punishment. Now that vast assemblage looked small in memory. Twelve legions had camped on every piece of spare ground for miles around the central town, a gathering

large enough to ruin the economy for years as they comman-
deered everything useful from the region, from horses and
food to iron, bronze and leather.

'I'm to have dinner tonight with Buccio and Liburnius,' Mark
Antony said, smiling wryly. 'I think the legates would like to
make amends for the small matter of mutinying under my
command.'

He chuckled at the thought, amused at how fate had swung
them apart and then together again. The movements of the
Republic made a mockery of all his plans. A year before, he
could not have imagined standing on those sea cliffs with
the Senate in hand and an alliance with a young man he had
barely remembered. His mood darkened as he realised Julius
had been alive at that time. No one could have predicted the
events after the assassination. Mark Antony only counted
himself lucky that he had survived and risen, no matter who
else had risen with him.

'They seem to have the ear of Caesar,' Lepidus said. 'Perhaps
you should question them about crossing the sea to Greece.
How long can we stay here without ships?'

'As long as we must, to keep Rome safe from invasion,' Mark
Antony replied uncomfortably. He did not enjoy hearing the
name of Caesar used for Octavian, but it was becoming a hard
reality and he assumed it would jar less and less in time. 'But I
agree, it is not enough to stay here and wait. I can wish for a
new fleet, but then I might as well wish for the men to be given
wings. I do not know all his plans, Lepidus. As it is, we are the
block that prevents Brutus or Cassius landing on this coast. While
we remain in such strength, they too cannot cross by sea. Who
would have thought that galleys would ever be so important?
The future of Rome rests on fleets, while legions remain idle.'

'Then we should build new ships,' Lepidus said irritably. 'Yet
whenever I ask, that friend of his, Maecenas, tells me I shouldn't
concern myself. Have you broached the subject with Caesar? I

would be happier if I knew we were at least beginning the task. I don't want to spend years on this coast waiting to be attacked.'

Mark Antony grinned to himself, turning away to hide his amusement. He had only arrived from Rome the day before, while Lepidus had been stationed at Brundisium for almost three months. Mark Antony was satisfied with the way the triumvirate was working, though he could appreciate Lepidus might not feel the same. It would not be useful to remind the man he had only been included to give Mark Antony a casting vote in any disagreement. Apart from that, he was not concerned with what Lepidus thought.

The wind gusted around them as they walked the cliffs, looking down to the dark blue sea. Both men felt the energy of it raising their spirits as their togas whipped and fluttered. Even from such a height, Mark Antony could not see Greece in the distance, though he imagined Brutus and Cassius there. The vagaries of fate had thrown him onto this shore and Rome would remember only the victors when it was done.

As he stared out over the vastness of the white-capped ocean, Mark Antony felt his attention dragged towards movement on his right side. He turned his head and froze, his good mood curdling like old milk in his stomach.

'By the gods, do you see that?' Lepidus said a moment later.

Mark Antony nodded. Around the bay, a host of galleys rowed into view, sleek and fast and dangerous. Many of them had broken stubs where fine oars had been before and, to his experienced eye, the ships looked battered. Yet they kept coming and his heart sank further.

'Sixty . . . no, eighty . . .' Lepidus was muttering.

There were at least a hundred galleys, fully half the fleet Sextus Pompey led. Mark Antony found himself making the horned hand instinctively. It was more than enough to blockade the east coast of Italy, preventing even the small boats that carried messages and kept trade alive.

'It seems Sextus Pompey has heard about our legions gathering here,' Mark Antony said. 'By Jupiter, what I wouldn't give for a fleet! I'll send a rider to Rome, but we cannot cross now, even if Octavian found me a dozen ships tomorrow.'

CHAPTER TWENTY-THREE

There was no moon as Agrippa's galleys eased out into the black sea. For three nights after finishing the canal, he had waited for perfect conditions to open the final gates, unable to move while a storm whipped the waves too high for his redesigned galleys. Stability had proved the biggest danger, with every one of his innovations adding to the top weight. Time and again, he'd had to abandon some scheme when he found it either slowed the ships or made them a death trap for those inside. The months of building around Lake Avernus had been the most frustrating and fascinating of his life, but he was ready, and even if he had not been, Octavian had sent Maecenas down again to order him out.

For once, his friend was silent as the ships slipped away from the coast. Agrippa sensed Maecenas wanted to be anywhere but there, but his pride had not allowed him to refuse. They would face the enemy fleet together, with just forty-eight galleys. Everything depended on timing and surprise – and luck, which grated on Agrippa when the stakes were so high.

In the darkness, the small fleet communicated with shuttered lamps, sending dim beams across the darkness to mark their positions as they formed up. It had taken most of the afternoon and evening for them to creep down the canal, oars in and silent as men on the ground heaved them forward on ropes. The moment when they were all out on deep water brought a surge of excitement.

Agrippa could not help feeling pride at Roman achievement. His men had built a path to the ocean where none had existed before. They'd crafted immense ships and when ideas had failed or proved too unwieldy, they'd dismantled and begun again without complaint. Agrippa told himself he'd make sure the crews and officers were rewarded, if any of them survived.

The dark swell stretched in all directions, easily capable of hiding a vast host of raptor galleys waiting for them. Agrippa swallowed nervously, clenching and unclenching his big fists as he paced the deck. To the south, the island of Sicily lay across his course, a mass of land and tiny coves that was said to shelter the enemy fleet. His hope was only to come as close as possible before dawn. After that, his new weapons and tactics would succeed or fail. His men had trained continuously, but Agrippa knew they could not yet manoeuvre as easily as veteran crews. He wiped sweat from his forehead as the new ships raised sails into the breeze. His galley eased forward with the rest, the only noise the hiss of water passing under the prow. Sicily cupped the toe of Italy at the far south and they had almost two hundred miles to go. Agrippa continued to pace, picturing his maps in his mind. For all his hopes, he'd been tempted to refuse battle and take his fleet to the east coast where Octavian was crying out for ships. With just a little luck, Agrippa knew he could have beached the fleet further south for a day, then passed the heel of Italy the following night, perhaps before Sextus Pompey even knew he was in those waters. It would have been the right decision if Pompey hadn't split his fleet and taken a hundred galleys of his own around the heel. The news Maecenas had brought had changed everything.

Under twin blockades, both the major coasts of Italy were closed to trade. Rome was already close to starving and the siege could no longer be endured. It had to be broken. Agrippa felt the responsibility weighing heavily on him. If he failed, Octavian would be bottled up in Rome for years, forced to negotiate or even surrender to the forces of the Liberatores. There was no second chance, Agrippa knew. It all came down to Octavian's faith in him.

Forty-eight galleys raised sails into the night wind, but Agrippa could hardly see them. The danger of white sails being spotted had led to his men colouring the sheets with the madder herb, dipping them again and again in huge vats until they were a rusty brown that would not reveal their position to anyone with half an eye out to sea. The sails were the colour of dried blood, but they served their purpose.

'I have a good jug here,' Maecenas said, clinking it against a clay cup to make his point.

Agrippa shook his head, then realised Maecenas could not see the gesture.

'Not for me. I need to be sharp now we're out.'

'You should have been a Spartan, Agrippa,' Maecenas said. 'I find good red wine merely relaxes me.' He poured a cup, cursing softly as some of it spilled onto the deck. 'That's for good luck, I suppose,' he said, drinking. 'You should get some sleep, if sharpness is important. At least the sea is calm tonight. I'd rather not face a watery grave while heaving my guts out over the railing.'

Agrippa did not reply, his thoughts on the galleys all around him. Maecenas did not seem to understand how much of the venture rested on him. Every modification he had made, every new tactic, was his. If it failed, he would have wasted half a year of hard work and a fortune that beggared belief – as well as his own life. His ships were well enough hidden in the night, but the dawn would reveal them to hostile eyes. He did not know whether to dread or welcome the moment they caught sight of the first hostile galley surging towards them.

Vedius was shaken from sleep by Menas, his second in command. He came awake with a grunt, trying to roll over on his bunk and flailing at the man's hand on his shoulder.

'What is it?' he said blearily.

He'd spent so long sleeping on deck that the tiny cabin reserved for a captain seemed an incredible luxury. The mattress may have been lumpy and thin, but it was much better than stretching out under a tarpaulin in the wind and rain.

'Signal light, sir,' Menas said, still shaking him.

The man was a legion officer and Vedius sensed scorn behind his carefully neutral manner. Yet he was at Vedius' command, for all his pretensions and legion honour. Vedius slapped the hand away. He sat up fast and struck his head on a beam, cursing.

'Right, I'm up,' he said, rubbing his crown as he clambered out of the tiny alcove.

In the darkness he followed Menas, climbing a short ladder to the deck and the light of a dim lamp. Vedius stared into the distance to where his subordinate was pointing. Far off, on the peak of a mountain, Vedius saw a gleam. The system was that their watchers lit a bonfire at night when they saw anything moving at sea.

'Someone's making a night run,' Vedius said with grim pleasure.

It had to be a valuable cargo if the captains and owners were willing to risk losing their ships on some unseen rock. He rubbed his callused hands together at the thought, making a whispering sound. Visions of gold or chests of legion silver filled his imagination, or better still, the young daughters of some fat senator. With Lavinia on board, Sextus held women only briefly for ransom, but he was not there. Vedius had been without female companionship for a long time and he grinned into the breeze. Willing or not, the whores of Sicily were nowhere near as exciting as the thought of a Roman virgin in his cabin for a few days.

'Take us out, Menas. Let's pluck a few fat Roman birds for the pot.'

Menas smiled uncomfortably. The coarse tavern fighter repelled him, but the Senate had given men like Vedius the fleet, the true eagle of Rome, and he could only obey and hide his disgust.

There was no need to be cautious, with the western coast sewn tight. Menas took hold of a horn on his belt and blew a long note across the waters. Eight galleys formed their small group and they were moving almost as soon as they heard the note, their captains ready as soon as the bonfire light had appeared on the peak. In turn, they blew their own horns, a droning chorus that would carry to the next cove and alert the crews there to follow them out.

Vedius felt the wind freshen against his face as the rowers below dipped their oars and the galley began to accelerate. There was nothing like the feeling of speed and power and he could only bless Sextus Pompey for introducing him to it. He rubbed his jaw, feeling an old ache. He owed Sextus everything since the young man had rescued him and given him a purpose when Vedius had been little better than a fighting drunk. He told himself Sextus would never have beaten him if he'd been sober, but the broken jaw had never healed right and Vedius had lived with pain ever since, every meal a misery as it crunched and clicked. The Roman noble had been at his back for years, but for this night, Vedius was alone in command. It was a heady feeling and he loved it.

'Half-speed!' he shouted, then he called for a drink to help him shrug off the last of his sleep. One of the Roman legionaries offered water and Vedius laughed at him.

'I never touch it. Wine feeds the blood, lad. Fetch me a skin!'

Below his feet, the rowing master heard and the drumbeat grew faster. The rowers who had been asleep on their benches shortly before put their backs into it with expert ease. The galleys headed out to sea in tight formation, lunging faster and faster to be first at the prizes ranging on the deep water. They left the island of Capri behind them, a hundred miles north of Sicily.

Agrippa was squinting into the darkness, seeing and losing again the point of light that had appeared in the distance. The night sky had turned around the Pole Star, but dawn was still hours away and he could not understand who might be lighting fires on the hills of Capri as his fleet sailed past in the dark.

'I need information, Maecenas!' he said. He thought his friend shrugged, but in the darkness, he could not be sure.

'No one knows where the enemy fleet is,' Maecenas said. 'We have clients on Sicily and every island along this coast, but they can't keep us informed with no link back to land. You're running blind, my friend, though I think you have to assume that fire is not just some herdsman warding off the cold.'

Agrippa didn't reply, his own frustration rendering him mute. The island of Capri was a great dark mass on his right shoulder as he came south, with just one point of light on the highest peak. He strained his eyes into the distant dark for any sign of galleys coming out to hit them.

'I didn't plan for an attack at night,' he muttered. 'My crews can't use the grapnels if they can't see the enemy.'

'Sometimes the gods play games,' Maecenas replied lightly.

He sounded supremely unworried and his confidence helped Agrippa to find calm. He would have replied, but he saw something out on the deep water and leaned right over the rail, turning his head back and forth as he tried to make sense of the blurring shadows.

'Don't fall,' Maecenas said, reaching out to grab his shoulder. 'I don't want to find myself in command tonight. You're the only one who understands how it all works.'

'By all the hells, I *see* them!' Agrippa said. He was certain of it: the vague shapes of long galley hulls.

'Cornicen! Blow three short!'

It was the signal to form up on the flagship and he had to trust that the galley crews knew it meant to follow him. Agrippa snapped half a dozen new orders. The sea was like glass, but he needed light for everything he had planned to do.

Maecenas watched with studied calm as the sails came down and the great oars were lowered into the water. Agrippa's galley slowed and wallowed, then picked up speed once more as the oars bit and began the rhythmic movement that would push them much faster through the waves. He felt the increase and despite himself he smiled. Around them, the small fleet did the same, all pretence at subterfuge forgotten as the captains yelled their orders.

The lull had brought the enemy galleys closer, though Maecenas could see the white foam from their strokes better than the ships themselves. His throat seemed to have gone dry and he filled another cup for himself, tossing it back.

'We'll run south along the coast until dawn,' Agrippa said. 'Gods, where is the sun? I need light.'

In the distance, he could hear drums pounding as the galleys came lunging in, faster and faster. His own crews moved to half-speed and then the captain ordered it higher, notch by notch, as they tried to stay clear.

'They can't keep going like that, not for long,' Maecenas said, though it was half a question.

Agrippa nodded unseen in the dark, hoping it was true. He'd

had his crews running miles around the lake for months. They were as lean and fit as hunting dogs, but the labour of heaving on oars was exhausting even for men in the peak of condition. He had no idea if the hardened legion galleys Sextus Pompey commanded could simply run his fleet down and ram them.

'So why are you here?' Agrippa said. He spoke to break the tension before it suffocated him. 'I mean, here on the ships.'

'You know why,' Maecenas said. 'I don't trust you on your own.'

Even in the gloom, they could both see the other man's teeth as they grinned together. The sound of oars and drums seemed to grow every minute and Agrippa found his heart was racing like prey running from a wolf pack. The wind roared around his ears, making him turn his head back and forth to hear the enemy.

'Why *really*?' he said louder, almost shouting.

As far as he could tell, the enemy galleys were almost on them and he tensed for the first crash of bronze rams into wood. There was no pretence of navigation any longer. The rowers below just heaved and pulled, putting every ounce of strength into each sweep.

'The same reason you are risking your neck in complete darkness!' Maecenas shouted back. 'For him. It's *always* for him.'

'I know,' Agrippa called back. 'Do you think he knows how you feel?'

'How I *what*?' Maecenas yelled incredulously. 'How I *feel*? Are you seriously choosing this moment, with our lives in the balance, to tell me you think I'm in love with Octavian? You pompous *bastard*! I can't *believe* this!'

'I just thought . . .'

'You thought wrong, you ignorant great ape! Gods, I come out here to face brutal enemies with you – on the sea, no less – and *this* is what I get? Octavian and I are friends, you great hairy shit-pot. *Friends*.'

Maecenas broke off as a thunderous crack sounded

somewhere close. Men screamed and splashes followed, but the night was like black ink and they could hardly tell where the sounds had come from or whether it was one of their own crews drowning in the dark.

'You and I will have words about this when it's over!' Maecenas snapped. 'I'd call you out with blades right now if I could see you, if you weren't the only one who knows how these galleys fight.'

In the face of his appalled indignation, he heard Agrippa laugh. Maecenas almost struck him.

'You're a good man, Maecenas,' Agrippa said, his white teeth still visible in the darkness.

If Maecenas could have seen him, he'd have been worried at the great cords standing out on Agrippa's neck and chest, every muscle and sinew drawn tight in fear and rage at the enemy. Agrippa was manic, unable to act with enemies all around him and no way of knowing if he'd be drowning at any moment. Talking to Maecenas had helped a little.

'I *am* a good man, ape. And so are you. Now please tell me we can outrun these galleys.'

Agrippa looked east, praying for the first light of the sun to appear. He could feel the galley creaking and stretching under him, a thing alive. Salt droplets sprayed across the deck, stinging his face with cold.

'I don't know,' he muttered.

Vedius stepped back from the prow of the galley, trying to see into the plunging blackness. Whoever was out there, they had a lot of ships. There had been a moment when he thought he'd fallen into some sort of trap, but then they'd run, their oars scything through the sea and churning it into white froth. He'd ordered full attack speed and closed the gap quickly on the strange, dark vessels running free before him. For a brief time, he called for ram speed. The galleys skimmed across the calm waters, driven as fast as they could go. He knew the rowers could not keep the brutal pace for long. Ram speed was the final surge of acceleration before striking an enemy, a hundred heartbeats at most before they had to fall back. His head came round in a jerk when he heard some sort of crash, but he could see nothing and the men below were already failing.

'Ease back to half!' he roared. He heard the falling horn note drone out, but there was still a bellow of fear behind him as one of his ships came close to ripping the oars off another.

Vedius turned to one of his archers.

'Do you have pitch arrows?' he shouted.

'Yes, sir,' the man replied.

Fire was not the tool it might have been at sea. The lumps of pitch and tar-cloth on the points robbed the arrows of decent range. In a close battle, Vedius had used them before against merchant ships, but mostly when the fighting was over and he had orders to burn them to the waterline. Wooden galleys moving at speed were soaked in sea spray from one end to the other and the arrows often extinguished themselves in flight or were quickly smothered when they hit an enemy deck. Even so, he gave the order and watched as two men brought up a small brazier filled with hot coals. They treated it like a precious child, terrified of spilling the coals on a wooden ship. The arrow flickered yellow at the tip when the archer touched it to the brazier. In the red glow, Vedius watched in fascination as the man bent his bow and sent it soaring up and forward.

They all watched the path of the shaft. For an instant, Vedius thought he saw oars moving in the dark like the limbs of a crab or spider before the arrow hissed into the black sea.

'Another. Use a dozen or so, one at a time. And vary the direction. I need to see.'

The bright points rose and fell again and again, giving just enough light for Vedius to make a picture in his mind. There were dozens of galleys out there, though he still could not count them. They too had eased back to half-speed, enough to keep them out of range of anything he could send in their direction. Vedius looked east, searching for the wolf-light that came before the dawn. For a time, he had wished Sextus were there to see this great prize, but in his absence Vedius' confidence had grown and now he was content to be in command. When Sextus heard, he would know his friend had not let him down when it mattered. His galleys had spread out in a great net of ships, chasing down the prey at speed.

Vedius felt his ship lurch and cursed aloud as they lost way. He could hear urgent shouting down below and growled to himself. One of the rowers had burst his heart or simply collapsed, fouling the oar and knocking the rest out of sequence. It happened occasionally and he knew the oar-master would be quickly among them, heaving the body out while the oar lolled and shoving in one of the soldiers to take his place.

The galley slowed as the other oarsmen took the chance to rest, pleased at even a moment's respite. Vedius let out a short bark of laughter when he felt the oars bite again and the speed increased. He had never ridden a horse into battle, but he assumed it felt much the same, with the enemy fleeing before him and the sun about to rise. His fleet plunged on through the wine-dark sea and he felt the excitement rise in him as he realised he could make out the prow under his hand. The sun was coming and he was ready.

CHAPTER TWENTY-FOUR

Dawn came quickly out at sea, with no mountains or hills to block the first rays. The sun appeared first as a burning thread on the horizon, gilding the waves and revealing the two fleets to each other. Neither found much to please them. Agrippa swallowed nervously when he saw how badly outnumbered he was, while Vedius had not expected anywhere near that number of ships.

As soon as the sun's light cast away the dark, Agrippa was roaring new orders to his ships and running up flags. His captains had been forced to memorise a new system so that the enemy galleys would not be able to read his signals. It was with a grim satisfaction that he squinted north and watched the enemy commander send up flags he knew very well. It was another edge, that he could see what they intended and react just as fast as they could. Against so many galleys he needed every advantage he could get.

The larger fleet responded with all the legion discipline

311

Agrippa had expected, widening the line and forming a great curve on the sea as they rowed forward. They had the numbers. He could see only the closest sixty of the galleys facing him, but there were many more behind, blocked from view by their own ships. Agrippa took a deep breath, forcing himself to be calm. He had planned for this and lost sleep for this. He could not shake the sense of cold dread that gripped him, but he had done everything he could to give himself a chance against such a host.

'Signaller, ready the "attack" flag. Put "prepare" up on the mast.'

Agrippa stared at the great arc of ships coming for him. They were no more than a mile away and he could read the flags flashing between them. He nodded as the order for 'Attack speed' went up on what must be their flagship. There. Whoever commanded them was in the very centre.

'That one is ours,' he yelled. 'Signal "back oars", "turn" and "attack"!'

It took time to send, but Agrippa's galleys had seen his signal to prepare and reacted at great speed. In just moments, they went from running before the enemy to a dead stop in the water and then began the slow turn, where they were most vulnerable. If the enemy could reach them as they presented their flanks, they would be near helpless. Agrippa saw the enemy galleys accelerate like birds taking flight, churning up the sea. They were too late. Agrippa's galleys faced them head-on, leaping forward as the oars swept down and back once more.

The two fleets came together at a terrifying pace.

'Gods, there are so *many* of them!' Maecenas said, gripping the rail with his knuckles showing white.

Agrippa did not respond, his eyes taking in every detail against the glare of the sun. It was not as simple as each of his ships taking two of the enemy. He knew that if he could destroy their command ship and scatter the others, if he could just survive the first clash, he had a chance.

He called over one of the helmsmen, who passed control of the galley to another while Agrippa pointed out the ship he wanted. The man squinted into the sunlight and took a bearing, then raced back to the stern to guide them in. Agrippa could have just roared his orders from the prow back to him – the galleys were short enough – but he wanted to be accurate.

His small fleet would strike up the centre; they had no other choice. The enemy would flank them immediately, but galleys were not as responsive as legion manoeuvres. To sink his ships, they had to ram at speed or lock the galleys together with a corvus bridge and get on board.

The fleets raced closer and Agrippa could only hope he had prepared his men well enough. The first test at sea was one of nerve, with opposing captains shouting orders left and right to guide them in and outguess the other man. Agrippa swallowed hard. The first weapon was his own ship, which could strip the oars from an enemy as it ripped past, killing half the rowers on one side – if he guessed correctly. If he got it wrong, a head-on collision, prow to prow, could sink them both before a single sword was drawn.

He found himself panting in fear and exhilaration as he saw the enemy captain with an arm wrapped around the prow. Agrippa could see the oars plunging back and forth. He knew legion commanders preferred to dip left from instinct, presenting their right side and their strongest arm to an enemy. Yet he did not know if the galley was commanded by a legion man or one of Sextus Pompey's pirates.

'Ready corvus bridge!' he roared. 'Ready harpax!' The grapnel teams exulted in the name they had chosen for his new weapon. The 'robbers' would steal whole ships if they could make them work in the chaos of a battle.

All around, his fleet was meeting the enemy, but Agrippa had to focus on just one galley as it soared towards him. If his

313

nerve went and he turned too early, the other captain would have a clear shot at his side and the ram would smash through, holing him below the waterline. Agrippa counted down in his head as the ships raced in without slowing. At fifty paces apart, the other galley had not deviated an inch and Agrippa knew suddenly that the man in command would not move off course, arrogantly certain that his opponent would turn and run. He could not have said how he knew, except for the rock-steady course he followed.

'Agrippa?' Maecenas said quietly, watching the approaching galley with sick fascination.

'Not yet,' Agrippa muttered.

He made his decision in the last instant, leaving it as late as he could.

'Oars in port side! Now! Oars up on the free!'

On the left side, where a ship unloaded in a port, the oars came in smartly, heaved across the knees of the rowers. On the free side opposite, the oars came out of the water so the galley could stay on course. The helmsmen pushed the steering oars against the wooden stops, so the galley began to swing right, its speed hardly dropping.

Agrippa tensed, grabbing the rail as his galley sheared along the enemy ship, the sharp prow crashing through dozens of oars. He heard screaming pass him as the great beams of wood crushed men in the oar-benches, snapping their backs and cutting across them. Splinters flew in a deadly hail below their deck as the two galleys passed, leaving the enemy ship torn open.

Agrippa's crew gave a roar of triumph as they dipped their oars back to the sea on both sides. They wanted to finish off the wounded vessel, but another was coming at them and to turn and present a flank would have been suicide.

Agrippa saw one galley ahead and another slightly further back on his right side.

'Ready harpax! Target on the free side!'

All around him, ships were locked in battle. Many had lost their oars on both sides, rendered completely helpless. More than one had been ripped right open in the impact, so that they were heeling over, already beginning to sink. Even as he risked a glance around, he saw two hulls turn over and ease beneath the surface, with bodies studding the waves and thrashing in a stream of silver bubbles.

The opposing galley was pouring on speed to repay him for his first attack, but as the second one began to pass, Agrippa bellowed an order to his harpax crews. The grapnels soared out and the enemy crews watched with open mouths as they reached and gripped. His legionaries made the capstans spin and the rest of his fighting men raced to the port side to prevent their ship going over as they were dragged sideways across the waves.

The galley he had been facing head-on seemed to slide left. Agrippa's crew staggered as the galley they had latched on to tipped and capsized. It started to sink as the hold filled with water and Agrippa felt his own galley tipping over as the grapnels remained lodged.

'Axes! By Mars, cut the ropes!' he roared, a note of panic entering his voice.

He cursed the copper wires woven into the cables. They resisted the first blows while his ship continued to tilt, dragged over by the vanishing galley. The first rope parted with a twang that could be heard by all those around. The second of three went with two men hacking frenziedly at it, then the third, which whipped across the face of one of the soldiers, sending him spinning into the water with his face a mass of blood.

Agrippa's galley crashed back, raising a wave of spray that drenched half the men on the slippery deck.

'Harpax crews!' he shouted, already hoarse. 'Fit more ropes and grapnels.'

They had a second set, but while they had been locked

315

together, another galley had slid up to his side at full speed. Agrippa barely had time to order the port oars in once more before the ships grated together, a long, groaning sound. He showed his teeth as he saw the enemy corvus bridge lifted up by sweating soldiers.

'Corvus teams! Up and over! Repel boarders!'

He would not leave his post at the prow, but he saw Maecenas draw a gladius and pick up a shield from where they were stowed in a wooden rack. With the first wave of soldiers, Maecenas raced to the spot where the enemy must come, while their own corvus bridges were thrown up. The enemy ship had come in at an angle, so that the one closest to the stern could not reach. It stuck out into the breeze like a wooden tongue, men standing uselessly behind it. The one closest to the prow slammed down into the enemy deck, the great iron spike at its head lodging immovably in the wood.

Agrippa's soldiers poured over the narrow bridge, while still more of them defended those trying to gain their own deck. Agrippa could see a century of legion soldiers on the enemy galley, but his second advantage showed itself immediately. Each of his rowers had won his place in sword tourneys. They left their benches and raced up onto the deck, three times as many fighting men as the enemy legionaries and each one a veteran and a skilled swordsman. Maecenas went with them over the corvus bridge, battering men back with his shield as his group fought to make space for more to come over.

It was slaughter. For a brief moment, both sides fought their way onto the opposing ship, but the ones that reached Agrippa's galley were cut down in moments, their bodies thrown over the side to sink. His own soldiers hacked and killed their way through the enemy crew and went down into the hold to threaten the rowers there.

A cheer went up as they dragged the captain to the deck, a

man in a plumed helmet who had tried to hide himself below
when he saw his ship was taken. Still alive, he was thrown
overboard to drown in his armour – and Agrippa's men had
another ship. He was tempted to take it for his own, but the
enemy fleet still swarmed all around.

'Set fires and get back quickly,' he ordered, watching the
sea in all directions for a new threat until black smoke rose
over the screaming of oarsmen. Agrippa closed his ears to the
sound. There was no justice in such a battle. He knew they
had not chosen to attack him, but there was no help for it
and he could not show mercy. His soldiers came back on
board and the corvus bridges were levered out of the decks
with fallen swords.

The galleys eased apart and the pillar of smoke thickened
quickly, roaring yellow in the hold. Agrippa shouted encouragement to his men as they took their positions once again at the
oars, dropping red blades at their feet and placing their blistered
hands on the wooden beams. All around him his small fleet
was still fighting.

It was a strange lull. The battle had spread over a vast
distance as the galleys ran each other down. The water was
covered in a slick of oil and splinters and floating bodies,
some of them still moving. Agrippa could see any number
of upturned hulls and had no way of knowing if they were
his own or those of the enemy. For those still fighting, he
knew every ship he'd built, with just a glance. He was pleased
at the numbers. He turned at the cracking thump of catapults
and saw threads leap out again from one of his ships, dragging another of the enemy galleys close enough to kill.
Whether by luck or because they had learned not to rush a
single rail, it remained upright, and then his swordsmen
came charging over two corvus bridges and that ship too
was taken.

Maecenas returned to his side, panting from his exertions.

317

He looked around him in wonder, having never seen a battle at sea before.

'Are we winning?' he said, resting his sword on the rail.

Agrippa shook his head. 'Not yet. Half the ships you see are disabled. We could take those, but there's no point.'

He signalled quarter-speed to the oar-master and the galley eased between burning vessels. They could all hear crying, screaming men in the infernos they passed and the black smoke choked them. The breeze had begun to freshen, driving the smoke away to the east. To Maecenas' shock, the sun was still low in the morning sky, though he thought they had been fighting for many hours.

As they moved through the devastation of the battle, Agrippa sighted the first ship they had struck. The captain's crew had worked hard to transfer oars to the broken side and restore some movement to his battered ship. Agrippa saw new signals fluttering on its mast and he watched to see how many ships could still respond. It seemed to take an age for them to answer, but he saw flags go up on galleys in the distance as they began to come back.

He sent up his own signal to regroup on his flag and then there was nothing to do but wait.

'Now we will see,' he said grimly. He sought out the closest galley that looked undamaged but carried the colours of the Roman fleet on its mast. Agrippa raised his voice to carry to his crew. 'That one. There's no point waiting for them to come to us.'

His men were exhausted after rowing all night and then fighting after that, but Maecenas could see the savage delight in the harpax crews as they coiled ropes and wound back the catapults. They were in no mood to lose after coming so far.

*   *   *

Vedius felt a dim red fury as he watched the enemy flagship run up new signals. They made no sense, even to the experienced legion signallers he commanded. Whoever the man was, he was a cunning bastard, Vedius thought to himself. Those flying grapnels had devastated his galleys. He'd seen three of them turned over before his very eyes while he struggled to restore something like order to the oar crew below his feet.

He shuddered briefly as pictures flashed in his mind. There had been a time when Vedius had believed nothing could ever turn his stomach. He'd witnessed murder and rape with utter calm. Yet on the deck below, bodies and limbs were jammed obscenely together, crushed by the oars and the impact with the other ship. He did not want to go back down there, to the stench of open bowels and more blood than he could believe, so that it pooled and gathered with the roll of the ship. More than sixty men had died as their own oars cut them to pieces. He had been helpless then, waiting for the impact of a ram to send the rest to the bottom. Yet he had not panicked and his legion crew had gone to work with hard faces and Roman discipline, clearing the slippery corpses and moving oars over at good speed. One or two had lost the contents of their stomachs as they worked, but they'd just wiped their mouths and moved on. Menas had been one of those and Vedius had formed something like respect for the Roman officer. Menas had not shirked the labour, pitching in with the others and coming away so covered in blood he might have been working in a slaughterhouse.

For a time, all Vedius could do was watch and give signals to keep his fleet together as the enemy cut through them. Every last one of the bastards had been armed with those appalling grapnels and when the ships came together, they went through good legion soldiers like a scythe through wheat. He had seen four of the enemy ships rammed and sunk, and his men cheered each one, but Vedius knew he had lost many more.

Even now, with some way on his galley once more, he could see a great part of his fleet listing or burning, or simply drifting helplessly, with oars sheared away and dead men lying still on the deck.

With narrowed eyes, he saw the enemy commander's galley come easing back, its prow pushing splinters and bodies aside as it came. As he stared, it accelerated in a new direction, like a wasp attacking one of the ships he had called back to him. Vedius swore impotently. With half his oarsmen dead, he could not keep up with them, never mind stage a ramming action that would do serious damage. For the first time he considered saving as many ships as he could and simply getting away. Sextus would want to hear about these new weapons and tactics.

He held back from giving the order, wanting to see first how many of his ships survived. For all he knew, he still outnumbered the enemy and could yet turn disaster into a victory, no matter what it cost.

From all sides, ships rowed back to him as soon as they saw the flags. With each one returning, Vedius' heart sank further. They were battered and broken, their sides running with blood or gashed open so that he could see through to rowers sitting just feet above the waves. Many would be lucky to make it back to shore. He could see only three that had come through unscathed, their crews staring out at the rest in shock as they took in the scale of destruction. Vedius shook his head. He knew they were not used to losing, but that did not change the reality of it. That small fleet of forty or fifty ships had torn them apart.

Twenty-nine galleys came limping back to his position and by then the enemy commander was engaged in a corvus battle with one of them. Vedius watched with hope until he saw smoke billow out from the oar-benches and the enemy move on, seeking out fresh targets. It too had sent up a new signal, though he could not read it. Vedius saw other ships come rowing in, forming up on their command galley in good order. Staring into the sun, Vedius did his best to count the enemy ships and did not enjoy the result.

'Menas! Count them again! The sun is throwing shadows on my eyes.'

His second in command muttered numbers aloud, though the ships shifted position all the time as they gathered.

'Twenty-three . . . twenty-five . . . twenty . . . eight. I think that's it. Shall I order an attack, sir?'

Vedius closed his eyes for a moment, rubbing weariness out of them with his thumbs. He could not say it had been a good life, not really. He'd had some good days, that was all.

'Stop thinking like a legionary, Menas. It's time to run for the coves we know.'

Menas nodded. 'Very well, sir,' he said.

He gave the orders and the battered galleys began to row south towards Sicily.

Maecenas was staring into the distance as the two fleets formed up. Agrippa knew by then that they'd lost only twenty galleys, though it still weighed on him like a failure. His harpax weapons had proved both deadly and effective in the battle and the double corvus bridges and expert sword crews had done the rest.

'They are retreating . . . that way,' Maecenas said.

Agrippa came to stand by his shoulder.

'South, it's south,' he said. His voice was drained of any pride by then, almost too weary to speak at all.

'Will you follow?' Maecenas asked.

'I have to. They are heading the way I want to go. I don't mind losing another day to chase them down and burn the rest of them. They can't outrun us now.'

'You think we can do it again, against Sextus Pompey?' Maecenas asked.

Agrippa looked around him. A dozen ships nearby were burning, avoided by his galleys as they feared burning sparks and ashes setting their own craft on fire. Others had turned over and could not be salvaged, but there were many more waiting to be taken, their crews slaughtered.

'Given a month to make repairs and to gather new crews for the ships we haven't burned, yes, Maecenas, I think we can do it again. We have to.'

CHAPTER TWENTY-FIVE

Brutus smiled. It was one of the many benefits of a young wife, he'd found. Not only did he feel a greater urge to keep lean and fit rather than surrender to age, but Portia lacked the cynicism that had been battered into him over the years of his life. She laughed more easily than he did and, in doing so, infected him with it, so that when he thought of her, his dark moods eased.

'You are mocking me,' Portia said. She pouted at him, knowing he loved the expression. In the nights together, he would sometimes bite gently at her lower lip, delighting in its fullness.

'I would not dare,' he replied. 'I salute your Roman spirit in wanting to care for your husband on campaign. I only say that I have tasted your cooking before and this is one chore best left to the servants.'

She gasped in mock outrage, gesturing with the kettle she held as if she might throw it at him. She had dressed herself in the manner of the rustic Greeks, with a simple white tunic tied with a wide sash belt and a dark red cloak over all. As she spoke, she wound her hands through the rich cloth so that it seemed almost alive and part of her, always in movement. Brutus looked on his wife fondly, standing before him in jewelled sandals that cost more than the peasant houses they passed each day. Her feet were small and she wriggled the toes as she stood there. Her dark hair was bound in silver threads and already the fashion she had begun was being copied by Roman women in the camp, affecting simpler make-up and cloth, as if they too could look as beautiful as she did.

'*I* will tend to my husband!' she said.

He stepped close to her and his arm slid around her waist.

'You know I would like nothing more, but perhaps your husband's blood has enough charcoal for the moment.'

Portia gasped and pushed him away.

'You have never tasted my herb chicken, husband. If you had, you would not mock me so.'

'I believe you,' he said dubiously. 'If you want to, I will not complain. Each mouthful will be nectar to me and I will smile as I chew each leathery piece.'

'Oh! You will see! You will be sorry you said that when you sleep alone tonight!'

She stalked away, brandishing her kettle and calling for servants. Brutus looked affectionately after her, his gaze taking in the vast camp all around him. He saw some of the legionaries smile as they caught sight of her, staring wistfully at the young wife of their commander. Brutus watched them carefully for a moment, his expression darkening. That was the disadvantage, of course. He could never be certain some young buck wasn't risking his neck to court her, affected by lust or romance until his common sense was drowned like a puppy in wine.

Brutus took a deep breath, letting the warm air fill his lungs and hiss out through his nose. He loved Greece. As a young soldier, he had travelled through the very land where his legions now gathered. His companion had been a grizzled old soldier named Renius, a bad-tempered and ruthless son of Rome who was many years in the grave. For a moment, Brutus could picture the two of them making their way to his first legion appointment. He found himself shaking his head in happy memory. He had been so young then. All those he loved had still been alive and he and Julius had been friends, determined to make their mark on the world.

Brutus looked back through the years, hardly able to recognise the young man he had been when he first crossed Greece. Julius had been rising in Rome, but he had needed military power. Brutus had been determined then to be his general, his greatest support. He could not have imagined there would ever be a day when he struck to kill his friend.

With the sun hot overhead, he sat down on a fallen tree that made the boundary of a farmhouse garden he had taken for the night. He could see all his youth and he was lost in it. He recalled Tubruk, the manager of Julius' estate outside Rome. Brutus would not want to see the disappointment in that man's eyes if he still lived. Tubruk would never understand how they had been driven apart. For some, it was better they were dead, so they could not have their hearts broken by everything that came after.

His mother Servilia was still alive, an old woman with white hair now, who yet maintained a stiff back and upright carriage that belied her years. Julius had loved her, Brutus had to admit, though it had eaten at him for years to see his own mother fawn on his friend. In the end, Julius had thrown her aside for his Egyptian queen, the one woman able to bear him a son.

Brutus sighed to himself. He had seen his mother age almost overnight as she abandoned the last pretences of youth. He had thought she might even pine away and die, but there had never been weakness in Servilia. The years only hardened her, like teak or leather. He vowed to visit her when he returned to Rome, perhaps with his young wife on his arm, though he knew they would squabble like cats.

'What are you thinking?' Portia said suddenly from behind him.

He had not heard her come back and he started, irritated that anyone could get so close without him knowing it. Age stole away all that made him who he was, he thought. Even so, he smiled at her.

'Nothing. Nothing important.'

Portia frowned prettily. 'Shall I show you my scar? My proof that I can be trusted?'

Before he could reply, she flicked back her cloak to reveal a long, sun-browned thigh. With one hand, she lifted the hem of the Greek tunic, showing him a deep pink ridge almost as long as his hand. Brutus looked around him, but there was no one watching. He leaned forward and kissed the mark, making her sigh and run her hands through his hair.

'You should not have done that to yourself,' he said, his voice slightly hoarse. 'I have seen men die from fever after wounds less serious.'

'It showed you I was not some empty-headed courtesan to be ignored. I am a Roman lady, husband, with Roman fortitude – and a marvellous cook. So I can be trusted with your thoughts, with all things. You were very far away just now.'

'I was thinking of Julius,' he admitted.

She nodded, taking a seat on the log next to him.

'I thought you were. You always have that look on your face when you do. Sadness mostly.'

'Well, I have seen sad things,' he said. 'And I have given too much of my life to seeking out the right path to follow.' He gestured to the legions encamped all around them, spreading over miles in formal array. 'I only hope I have found it now. I would like to return to Rome, Portia. Though I love this land, it is not my home. I want to walk through the forum again, perhaps to serve as a consul for a time.'

'I would like that – for you, but not for me, husband, do

you understand? I am happy wherever you are. You have wealth enough for comfort and you are respected and loved.' She hesitated, unsure how far she should go with an argument they had been through before, many times. 'I do not want to lose you. You know I would die on the same day.'

Brutus turned to her and gathered her to him. She felt small against his side and he could feel the heat of her skin through the thin cloth as he breathed in the scent of her hair.

'You are a little mad, you know,' he muttered. 'But I love you anyway. And I will not lose, Portia. I have thrown down a tyrant, a king. Should I now bend my knee to some boy calling himself by the same name? I knew the *real* Caesar. Octavian has no right to it. No right at all.'

Portia reached up and took his face in her hands, the touch surprisingly cool on his skin.

'You cannot unbreak all that is broken, my love. You cannot fix the entire world. I think that, of all of them, you have done enough and hurt yourself enough for one lifetime. Is it such a terrible thing to enjoy the fruits of your life now? To have slaves wait on you hand and foot while you enjoy the summers? To spend those years with me in some fine villa by the sea? My father has a place in Herculaneum that is very beautiful. He writes letters every day and runs his estates. Is there shame in that? I don't think there is.'

He looked down at her. It could not be said that she didn't understand what drove him. He had told her everything of his past and his failures as well as his triumphs. She had married him in the full knowledge of who he had been and who he still wanted to be, but that did not stop her arguing for peace and retirement. He was only sorry their son had died in childhood. Raising a growing boy might have turned her attentions away from her husband. Yet since then, she had not quickened again, as if her womb had died with the child. The thought upset him and he shook his head.

'I am not an old man like your father, Portia, not this year anyway. I have another battle in me. If I don't fight it, or if we lose, they will say of me only that I was a murderer, not that I freed Rome. They will talk of Marcus Brutus as just some petty traitor and they will write the histories to suit them. I have seen it done, Portia. I will not let them do it to me. I *cannot* let them do it to me!' He reached up to hold her wrists and brought her hands down to his chest, over his heart.

'I know you are a good man, Marcus,' she said, softly. 'I know you are the best of them, better than that scrawny Cassius, or Suetonius, or any of them. I know it hurt you to be part of their plots, just as it hurts you now to be fighting still. I think you care too much about how they see you, my love. What does it matter if small men live in ignorance of who you were, who you still are? Is your dignity so fragile that the meanest beggar on the street cannot laugh like a fool when you pass? Will you answer all insults, even from men who are not worthy to tie your sandals? You *did* free Rome, husband. You restored the Republic, or at least you gave them the chance to see a way through without dictators and kings ruling them as slaves. That's what you've said a dozen times. Isn't that enough for you? You have done more than most men would manage in a dozen lifetimes and I love you for it, but the seasons change and there has to come a time when you put down the sword.'

'I will, I swear it, after this. Just after this, Portia. The gods have given me all the lions of Rome as my enemies. If they can be beaten, there is no one else who can make an empire out of the ashes. The Republic will go on and there will be peace for a thousand years. I have that in my grasp, just as I have you in my grasp.'

He accompanied the last words with his hands slipping down and tickling her so that she shrieked and squirmed. He went on regardless, ignoring her protests and struggles until there were tears in her eyes.

'You are a monster!' she said, laughing. 'And you do not listen to me.'

He shook his head. 'I do, you know. There is a part of me that wants nothing more than to walk as a free man, with his freedom bought and earned for Rome. I want that, but I will not be ruled by kings, not again. Not by Mark Antony and certainly not by Octavian. I will stand against them one last time and, if the gods smile on me, I will walk with you on my arm in Rome while all the younger men stare at your beauty. And I will be content.'

There was sadness in her eyes as she responded, though she tried to smile.

'I hope so, my love. I will pray for it.'

She rested her head against his chest, easing into him so that for a time they sat together in silence, staring out over the plain where his legions were preparing the evening meal.

'I loved him too, you know,' Brutus said. 'He was my greatest friend.'

'I know,' she replied drowsily.

'I fought once against him, Portia. Here in Greece, at Pharsalus. I wish you could have seen it. He was incredible.' He breathed out slowly, the memories bright before his eyes. 'He broke the forces of Gnaeus Pompey and after the battle he came to find me on the field. He held me in his arms, as I am holding you – and he forgave me my betrayal.'

His voice caught as he spoke, the memory bringing back old griefs and a half-buried anger. From that moment, Brutus had been the man forgiven for his treachery by the noble Caesar. His place had been set in tales and poems of Rome: the weak traitor blessed by a better man. Brutus shuddered slightly, feeling goosebumps rise on his arms as he held his wife. He had not admitted to Portia how he felt on that day in Greece, years before. He had told her he feared for the Republic when Caesar brought Cleopatra and his son to Rome.

He had spoken of his belief that they had begun a dynasty to rule the world.

It was all true, yet only part of the truth. Caesar's fate had been written on that day at Pharsalus, when he had broken and tortured his friend by forgiving Brutus in front of them all.

Portia seemed to be dozing in his arms and he raised her up, kissing her forehead.

'Come on, love. Let me experience this herb chicken of yours.'

She stirred, yawning and stretching like a cat while he looked fondly down at her.

'The day is very warm,' she said. 'Is there much further to go now?'

'Not so far, though I will send you back to Athens when I meet Cassius' legions.'

'I would prefer to stay with the camp,' she said.

'So you've said a hundred times, but a legion camp is no place for you, I know that much. I'll see you safe before we march to the coast.'

'I don't know why you have to march to meet his men when the coast is in the opposite direction.'

'He's bringing more than half the army, Portia. It makes sense to let them see each other before the horns start blowing. And there aren't too many plains where ninety thousand men can form up, not in these hills.'

'What was the name of the place where we're going?' she said.

'Philippi,' he replied with a shrug. 'It's just a town, like any other.'

Octavian let the breeze fill his lungs. Standing on the cliffs at Brundisium, he could see for miles out to sea. The sun was strong on his back and yet he could not relax, especially in the company of Mark Antony. Separated by a gulf of more than thirty years, he had to struggle not to be intimidated by a man who had known a very different Rome, before Caesar had risen to command the city and the world beyond it.

Even from the height of the rocky path, he could not see the coast of Greece, somewhere across the haze. His attention was on the stretch of dark blue sea outside the port, where two fleets of galleys battled it out. They were like toy ships, too far away for him to hear the orders roared and the crack of catapults sending grapnels and stones soaring into the air.

Agrippa had rounded the heel of Italy the night before, taking advantage of a calm sea with little wind. Octavian had learned they were coming only that morning, when an exhausted messenger had reached him after crossing the peninsula at breakneck speed. Octavian and Mark Antony had had to climb to the highest point on the coast before they could even see Agrippa's galleys, but it had been clear from the first moments that Sextus Pompey had also been warned. His fleet was already in formation when Agrippa's ships came into view at first light. Well rested, Pompey's galleys had sprung into attack immediately, knowing Agrippa's oarsmen would be tired after a night rowing along the coast.

'Gods, did you see that?' Mark Antony called.

He had walked further down the path, following the motion of the fleet battle with grim fascination. He knew as well as Octavian that Agrippa held their own futures in his hands. If Octavian's friend failed, the legions could not cross a sea of raptor galleys and survive. It still rankled with Mark Antony that he had not been told of the secret fleet at Avernus.

'Where?' Octavian replied without looking up.

'Next to the closest one on fire, by the rock there, two ships to the left. The one that turned right over. Your friend is doing well, despite the numbers against him.'

Octavian clenched his jaw at the reminder. Agrippa's fleet was still badly outnumbered, though they had come round the coast with almost fifty galleys. He suspected some of those were almost for show, or to decoy the forces under Sextus Pompey. Certainly, some of the ships fought with full crews, while others only tried to ram, dodging and racing among the rest at full speed. As he watched, Octavian saw one ship crash its prow into another, staving in the side so that it began to sink. Yet the attacker could not free itself and the two galleys remained jammed together. Their crews were fighting on the decks, not just to win, but to decide who would stay on the ship that wasn't sinking. Octavian saw oars sweeping backwards and knew the attacker was one of Pompey's captains. Agrippa's oarsmen poured up and out of his ships whenever they attacked, their oars pulled in or left to droop on chains. It was a dangerous tactic, as they were instantly vulnerable to any other ship coming in hard, but the additional numbers made a vital difference, as far as Octavian could tell.

Even with the knowledge that Agrippa's ships had red sails, it was almost impossible to be certain who was winning. Some of Agrippa's ships wallowed like fat old women in the slightest breeze and Octavian could only imagine the constant terror of the men in them as they waited for the lurch that would send them right over and into the cold sea. They were safe enough while the rowers moved them, but as soon as those men left to fight, the ships became dangerously unstable. At least one had already been sunk with only a light impact from a ram.

'Can you say who has the advantage?' Mark Antony said.

His voice sounded tight and Octavian glanced at him before shaking his head. The older man was feeling the strain, as well he might, given the stakes and with no way to influence the outcome.

'Not from here,' Octavian said loudly. His voice dropped to a mutter as he went on. 'I can't do anything from here.'

He glanced at the sun and saw that he had been there all morning. The noon point had passed and the two fleets were still fighting, with more and more ships set ablaze or sunk or turned right over to become a fouling danger to the rest. Thousands of men were already dead by fire or sword or water. The mass action of the beginning had turned into a weary battering, a test of endurance and will, as each captain took their chances with one more enemy, or just held themselves clear to let rowers recover their wind. There was nothing beautiful in it, Octavian realised. He had somehow expected there would be. The reality was like two old prizefighters smashing away at each other through blinded eyes, already bloody and yet unable to fall as they hung on each other. His future lay in the balance and he sent a prayer to Julius and Mars that Agrippa would come through.

Octavian was not naive. He knew some crimes went unpunished. Thieves and murderers sometimes went on with their lives and did well, dying happy and old in their family homes. Julius had once told him of a man who had robbed a friend, then used the money to begin a successful business. The friend had died in poverty while the thief thrived and stood as a senator. Yet a man could seek to make his own justice, even if it did not come on its own or through the will of the gods. It was not given to him; he had to take it. Octavian could not rest while the Liberatores lived, while they continued to parade their crimes as good works.

Octavian had seen a coin with the head of Brutus and the title on the reverse that proclaimed him 'Saviour of the Republic'. He clenched his jaw at the image in his mind. He would not let them steal the history from more deserving men. He would not let them turn what they had done into a noble thing.

Sextus Pompey saw only despair all around him. His crew had been fighting for hours. They had survived three attacks by boarders, barely pulling the ships apart each time before they were overwhelmed. Few of his men were unwounded and many more were simply gasping for fresh water or a moment to rest.

The life they led had made them fit, but they lacked the endless well of energy his youth gave him. His nineteenth birthday had come and gone over the previous months, with a celebration thrown for him by his Roman legion captains. They had toasted him in wine and those who remembered his father had made fine speeches. The brothers Casca had declaimed a new poem sweeping through the cities, written by Horace, that praised the Republic as a jewel among the works of men.

It was a happy, distant memory as he looked at the detritus and bodies floating all around him. No one in Rome had known he had a string of horses across the narrowest point of the mainland so that he and Vedius could communicate. He had done *everything* right and it had still not been enough. The message had come in time for him to form up and wait for the enemy fleet and he had been confident at dawn. Yet the few lines scrawled on parchment had not prepared him for the suicidal tactics of the galleys he faced, nor the terror of clattering, whirring grapnels soaring over his head. Twice his crew had escaped by hacking at ropes as they drew tight over his ship. The cables were still there on his deck, with copper wires shining. There had not been a moment of peace to dislodge them and put them over the side.

He had only been able to watch as the enemy galleys smashed and sank half his fleet. His ships had started well, ramming and shearing oars with discipline, but they lost three or more for every ship they sank. The enemy galleys moved like hornets, stinging with fire arrows at close range, then boarding as the crews were forced to douse the flames before they could catch hold. It had taken Sextus too long to discover that half the ships he faced were manned only by rowers and were no real threat. They all wore red sails, whether furled or filled with the wind. The dangerous ones hid amongst the greater number, pouring men over twin corvus bridges and slaughtering his crews before setting fires and moving on.

The sea was covered in thick smoke and he could hear the

creak and splash of oars all around him. He did not know if he was surrounded by the enemy or whether he could risk a signal to his own ships. He gave a sharp order for his oarsmen to stroke at half-speed, though they too were failing and more than one body had been cleared in the hours since dawn. The darts and strikes of a war galley had been reduced to a slow creeping progress.

The wind strengthened in a gust, blowing part of the smoke away so that he could see further across the waves. It did not bring him comfort as the expanding horizon revealed dozens of sunken hulls, drifting like pale fish at the surface, with bodies all around. Many more ships still burned and as the air cleared he saw three galleys cruising in close formation, hunting through the wreckage. One of them had grapnels ready on the deck and Sextus knew he was taken as soon as they spotted him and began to turn. He thought of his sister Lavinia, safe in the hold. He could not let them capture her.

'Turn for the coast and beach her hard!' he yelled to his oar-master. 'Give me ram speed for the last quarter-mile. One last time and we will be on land to scatter.'

The exhausted rowers heard his voice and they increased the stroke once again, lost in a world of misery and torn muscles. His galley surged away and he heard cries behind him as the enemy captains poured on speed in response.

The battle had taken him miles along the coast from Brundisium. He could see a sandy cove not too far away and he pointed to it, his helmsmen keeping the ship on its final course with dogged determination.

Lavinia came up from the hold, looking green from the hours she had spent in the foetid gloom. She saw the galleys chasing them and the shore ahead and her heart broke for her brother. He was a beautiful figure as he stood on the prow and watched the shallows with desperate concentration. Even then, he smiled at her when she touched his arm.

'Hold on to me,' he said. 'If we hit a rock, it will be a hard blow at this speed. I do not know the coast here.'

She gripped his arm as the ship shuddered suddenly, the long shallow keel rubbing along a shelving shore. Sextus swore under his breath, terrified his galley would grind to a halt on a sandbank, leaving him stranded with land so close. His oar-master bellowed orders and the rowers cried out in agony, but the shuddering ceased and the galley lurched and dropped into deeper water.

'Nearly there!' Sextus yelled back.

In the same moment, one of the rowers fell dead and the man's oar fouled those around it, so that the galley began to turn in the surf.

'Close enough,' Sextus said to Lavinia.

He had hoped for a landing that would put the galley right up onto the beach, but instead it bobbed and lurched in the surf, splintering oars on one side. He extended a hand to his sister.

'Come on, you'll have to get your skirts wet.'

Together, they climbed down, jumping the last part into white-frothed waves. There was sand under his feet and he felt some of his fear lift as he saw the enemy galleys sweeping back and forth out at sea. They had seen him almost ground on the sandbank and they could only stare and send arrows that fell short.

The galley rocked in a swell that would eventually batter her into pieces. Yet he had brought his crew safely to land and they clambered down, jumping into deeper water as the ship bobbed back and forth. In the lower deck, the rowers sat like dead men, panting and limp. Slowly, they left their oars and came out, red-eyed and exhausted. More than one stepped into the sea and simply vanished, too tired even to make the few paces to shore. Others helped their oar-mates, dragging each other until they collapsed on the burning sand.

As they gathered in exhausted silence, Sextus and Lavinia

looked up at a sea that was becoming choppy and white-flecked. Burning and overturned hulls stretched into the distance, the ashes of all his hopes.

His captain, Quintus, had survived. The legion officer had fallen into the surf as he made landfall and he looked bedraggled and weary.

'Do you have further orders, sir?' he said.

Sextus almost laughed at the absurdity of it.

'Could you carry them out, Quintus, if I did? The fleet has gone. We are landsmen once again.' He thought for a moment and went on. 'But there could be other survivors. Take the men up to a high point and search the coast. My sister and I will head for the closest town.'

Quintus saluted stiffly, calling to the men to follow him. They staggered off to find a way up the cliffs and for a time Sextus was content just to sit on the hot yellow sand and look out to sea. Lavinia watched him, unable to find words that could begin to comfort her brother. Gulls called overhead and the galley creaked as it rolled and shuddered in the surf. After a long time, he smiled at his sister.

'Come on,' he said, taking her hand. He guided Lavinia over the dunes to the bottom of the cliffs, looking for any sort of path that would take them away from the bitter sea at his back.

'What will happen now?' Lavinia asked.

He shrugged, shaking his head.

'Caesar and Mark Antony will cross,' he said. 'I can't stop them.'

'No, Sextus. I mean, what will happen to us?'

In response, he showed her a small pouch from his belt.

'I won't let anything happen to you. I have a few gems and gold coins. If we can reach a town, we'll be safe enough. From there, we'll go back to Spain. There are still men there who remember our father, Lavinia. They will keep us safe.'

Though there were goat paths, the going was very steep. He

and his sister had to climb steadily, struggling for handholds in withered scrub bushes. The shadows moved as they went and for a time both of them recalled climbing hills as children. They were panting as they reached the top of the cliffs and Sextus raced Lavinia over the crest. He came to a shocked halt at what he saw ahead, giving out a groan that was halfway between anger and utter despair. Behind him, Lavinia looked up fearfully at the sound.

Quintus was there with those of the crew who had gone with him. Their hands were bound and they had no fight left in them. A line of legionary soldiers was watching with interest, standing in formation.

A plumed centurion stepped forward. He had watched the flagship beach and he stared at the young man and his sister as they approached, brushing sand and dirt from their hands.

'Sextus Pompey? I have orders from the triumvirs Caesar and Antony for your arrest. Your name is on the list of proscriptions.'

Sextus turned to his sister, passing her the pouch out of sight of the men at his back.

'Thank you for showing me the path,' he said, stepping away from her.

The centurion's eyes flicked between Lavinia and Sextus, seeing the same blond hair in them both. The girl was clearly terrified. The centurion cleared his throat, making a quick decision. He was a father to daughters himself and his orders had said nothing about a sister.

'If you'll come quietly, sir, I'll have one of my men escort the . . . local girl back to town.'

Sextus sagged slightly, struggling to hide the fear that had smothered him since sighting the men. He knew what the proscription list meant. He could see it in the delighted expressions of the soldiers waiting for him as they wondered how they would spend the bounty on his head.

'Thank you, Centurion,' he said, closing his eyes for a moment and swaying as tiredness finally caught up to him. 'I would appreciate it if you chose a . . . trustworthy man as an escort.'

'Don't worry about that, sir. We don't make war on women.'

Sextus saw Lavinia look back at him with wide, horrified eyes as a burly legionary took her gently by the arm and guided her away.

CHAPTER TWENTY-SIX

Octavian was not exhausted. He suspected he needed a new word to describe what he was and he had certainly passed 'exhausted' weeks before. It was not that he did not sleep or eat. He did both and sometimes slept like a dead man before rising again after a few hours. He ate with mindless precision, tasting nothing as he forced his body to go on. Yet each day brought so many tasks and demands on him that he found himself sweating constantly from the first moment he came awake before dawn to the last collapse into his bed, usually still clothed. The sheer complexity of moving and supplying twenty legions and all their auxiliaries required a staff of thousands, an entire legion of clerks and factors. They worked under his orders and yet at times they were apparently unable to do anything unless he had signed it off.

It was one area where Mark Antony showed no particular talent, though Octavian suspected the older man was happy enough to let him take the burden. Whenever the responsibility was left to the ex-consul, Octavian found the work remained undone until he was forced to take over. He could not shake the suspicion that he was being subtly manipulated, but a thousand tasks would have been unfinished if he had ignored them in turn – and the legions would still be waiting to cross to Greece.

Keeping Rome secure from attack while he was away for a campaign had proved to be a logistical nightmare. His co-consul Pedius was content to rule the Senate and they offered no resistance in the city, but the rest of it! Simply moving tens of thousands of men across country, while always securing food and water for them, had been a mountain to climb on its own. After months of blockades, diverting a third of Rome's remaining grain stores to feed hungry soldiers had hardly reduced tension in the capital. Yet Octavian knew supply would play a major part in the campaign against Brutus and Cassius in Greece. Starving men did not fight well.

He doubted Cassius and Brutus had such worries. They could strip the east of food and fighting men and deal with the consequences later. There were times when Octavian wondered if he might triumph in Greece only to spend a dozen years putting down uprisings on Roman lands.

The legions he had left behind looked presentable enough, but for anyone who knew, their training had barely begun. Again, Mark Antony had seemed blithely uninterested. It had been Octavian who'd raised three new legions on the mainland, paying a bounty to a generation of young men to join, then marching them off to barrack towns while they were still half-drunk and dazed with the change in fortunes.

He could feel the galley moving under his feet in a gentle swell, waiting for the sun to rise before they landed. It was Octavian's fifth crossing in a month. Every hour of daylight had been used to launch galleys crammed with soldiers, but they had lost two ships and almost six hundred men in the early landings. The galleys had struck each other, turning over just far enough from shore to make survival almost impossible for those on board. After that, the captains had been more cautious, but the crossing had slowed further and the entire operation had lost another week from the original plans.

Octavian stared east as the sky lightened. The early sun cast a pale gleam over the Greek coast, where the army was assembling and marching inland. He shook his head in awe at the thought. Twenty legions were a greater force than had ever been brought together in one place. As well as a hundred thousand soldiers, there were another forty thousand camp followers and staff and thirteen thousand cavalry taking up space on the galleys Agrippa had managed to salvage after his battles. The coast of Greece had been ravaged for miles, with new roads driven inland just to accommodate the mass of equipment and men coming in each day.

Octavian groaned when he thought of the costs. The coffers of Rome were empty; he had seen to that himself as he toured the treasure houses of the argentarii and the Senate. He had orders out to every mine and coin house in Roman possession to increase production, but without new workers it would be years before they had enough even for the dips and peaks of normal production. He knew there was still wealth in Rome – some of the senators had made fortunes from the estates of those proscribed and from lending gold at high rates during the crisis. Octavian carried notes from more than a dozen of them, for tens of millions of aurei. The debts would be a burden on the state for a generation, but he had not had a choice and had sealed his name to them all as the needs increased. For a time, he had held back the fortunes he had inherited, but then he plunged those too into the war chest for the campaign. He tried not to think of how quickly they had vanished.

As the sun's light increased, the galley captain picked his spot on new docks built for the landings, easing his craft safely in. Octavian waited for the corvus to be raised and dropped to the port side and stepped ashore.

A dozen men waited for him and he forced a smile for them, which became real when he saw Maecenas and Agrippa were there. He felt as if he had been swallowed up in the group as soon as he stepped away from the galley. The small crowd surrounded him and as each man tried to claim his attention, he felt a nauseating lethargy dull his responses. He shook his head and tried to crush the feeling yet again, to make himself think and work at high speed just one more time.

He could not understand what was happening to him. He was young and fit, but sleep and food no longer seemed to restore his spirit or his flesh. Each morning he would surface in confusion, batting away at unseen horrors before realising he was awake once more. As soon as he had washed and dressed, he would be back at work, cudgelling his brain into thinking of clever answers and solutions.

'Give the consul a little room, would you?' Agrippa snapped suddenly.

Octavian shook his head, his senses sharpening. He had been walking away from the docks, with men on all sides calling questions and trying to show him sheaves of documents. He understood he had been answering them, but for the life of him he could not recall what he'd said. Agrippa had sensed something was wrong in his friend's blank eyes and used his size to push a few of the men aside despite their outrage.

'No, Pentias, nothing is that important,' Octavian heard Maecenas reply to another man's demand. 'Now why don't you give us a moment without your noise? The army isn't going to collapse because you had to wait, is it?'

Octavian had no idea who the other speaker was, but whatever he said in reply was a mistake, as Maecenas stepped hard into him and the pair were left behind for a while in furious argument.

Over the previous month the port of Dyrrhachium had

changed so much as to be unrecognisable. That was one thing about legions, Octavian thought dully. They could build anything. He looked up as he reached a main road leading back into what was now a major town. Huge warehouses loomed on both sides, well guarded for the wealth of food and gear they contained. The legions had felled trees and sawed planks to be nailed and pegged together until they had made entire streets. Stores and smithies were working night and day and the stink of leather-workers' vats lay thick in the air. It would all be left behind when they marched, but they would go with new nails in their sandals and the right tack for the extraordinarii, patched or replaced. He had seen a thousand orders for requisition and cargo and the details swam before his eyes as he walked on.

In theory, there was no reason why the clerks and factors couldn't accompany him anywhere on the vast coastal camp. Yet as the group began to pass through the tents of soldiers, Maecenas and Agrippa managed to dissuade the others from clamouring too loudly for his attention. On the previous trip, Octavian had stopped Agrippa throwing a man into the sea as he pressed too close on the docks, but this time the strange lethargy that overcame him made it difficult to object and he merely stared as the big man held another back and told him in sharp, short words what he could do with his requisitions.

The three of them went on alone after that, with Agrippa glaring back to make sure they did not dare to follow.

'Thank the gods this is the last time,' Agrippa said.

The sun was still rising and the road ahead was filled with its glare and the promise of another hot day under an empty blue sky. They passed through the oldest camps, the places claimed by the first men to land six weeks before. Legionaries were early risers by instinct and order, so there were already thousands of men moving around, scraping bowls of warm oats into themselves, or sipping at hot tisanes. Many more were sparring lightly, keeping limber and loosening muscles made

344

tight by sleeping on the stony ground. There was a friendly air to the camp and more than a few called out as they spotted Agrippa, recognising the big man and pointing him out to their tent-mates. He had become famous for a brief time: the man who had smashed the Roman fleet and won the chance to cross.

Octavian felt a weight pressing behind his eyes as he reached the top of the coastal hills and looked out onto the plains beyond. In the morning light, he could not see an end to the vast camp that stretched in all directions. It took a better eye than his to see the line of demarcation between the two forces, but it was there. Mark Antony had sole command of his own legions and Octavian felt a sullen anger at the reminder of another irritation. His colleague had insisted on crossing first. As a result, his legions had taken the very best spots near water and shade. The ex-consul then had the gall to complain at every lost day after that, while Octavian brought his own legions to Greece. Away from Rome, Mark Antony had been able to ignore the host of problems at home and concentrate only on deploying his forces and scouting the land ahead. It had seemed a small thing at the time, but allowing Mark Antony to land first had established the man's legions as the vanguard without any formal decision. Octavian found himself biting his inside lip and gave a weary smile as he thought of Pedius back in Rome, no doubt doing the same thing.

'Have you eaten?' Maecenas said.

Octavian looked up, his eyes blank as he tried to think back. He remembered a bowl of oats and honey, but it might have been the previous day. Little details such as meals had sunk into the mass of things he was too tired to consider or remember.

'I'm not hungry,' he said, though he changed his mind as he spoke and realised he was. Some gleam of energy returned to him then and his gaze sharpened. 'The last of the horses will be over by noon. I have the personal oath of the harbour master at Brundisium, for whatever that's worth. It's done at last, Maecenas. We'll march today.'

Maecenas saw Octavian's hands were shaking and his expression changed to one of concern as his eyes flicked back to Agrippa and then down once more, drawing the big man's attention.

'I think you should try to eat,' he said. 'Even if Mark Antony moves at this moment, we won't be marching for hours yet. Get something hot and take a nap or something. Gods, Octavian, you look exhausted. You've done enough for the moment.'

'Not exhausted,' Octavian mumbled. 'Need a new word.' With an effort, he summoned his will and stood a little straighter, forcing his muddled thoughts back to clarity. 'Yes, I'll eat something,' he said. 'But, Agrippa, would you go back and fetch those clerks for me? I can't just ignore them.'

'You can; I keep telling you,' Agrippa replied. 'I'll have a word with them and see if anything really can't keep. I doubt there's much at this point.'

'All right,' Octavian replied, unable to hide his relief. He was sick of the details. Like the soldiers in camp all around him, he wanted to get moving and he wanted to fight. Putting his seal to some legion arrangement to buy a thousand saddles from some Greek merchant was no longer on his list of priorities.

The three of them approached the command tent and Octavian's heart sank as he saw another dozen men waiting for him, their faces lighting up as they spotted him.

Mark Antony was in a fine mood as he dismounted. His command post was right up at the leading edge of the host of legions that had landed in Greece. He'd made it a habit to ride along the outer perimeter each morning as the sun came up, knowing the men would see him in his polished armour and cloak and take heart from it. He liked as many of his men as possible to see him each day, to be reminded that they fought for an individual rather than a faceless Senate. He had long suspected such things mattered when it came to the morale of individual legions, and those he commanded were, for the most part, strangers to him. A few remembered him from campaigning with Julius and when they greeted him, he made a point of stopping and spending a moment with them that he knew they would remember for the rest of their lives. It was not much to ask of a commander and they were thrilled that he bothered to speak to common soldiers, especially when he truly recalled a name or a place from the distant past. Men who had been young when they fought Vercingetorix were now senior soldiers, many earning a higher rank in the intervening years. When his memory sparked a scene from those days, Mark Antony could hardly believe so much time had passed. It made him feel old.

'Legates,' he said in greeting to the men waiting for him. 'What a beautiful morning. Have you news from the coast?'

He asked the same question each day and in all honesty he could not believe it was taking Octavian so long to land his forces. There had been times when he'd been tempted to take his legions inland and let Octavian catch him up, but good sense had overridden each impulse. He had spies and informers enough among the population to know that Brutus and Cassius had assembled a huge army. He would need every legion he had – and perhaps more than he had.

The thought of Rome in the hands of men like Consul Pedius had worried him enough to leave Lepidus behind in the city. His co-triumvir would sit out the conflict in relative safety, but at least Mark Antony would not come home to find he had lost Rome while fighting his enemies. There had been too many surprises since the assassination and he trusted Lepidus to lack the ambition he would need to reach beyond his grasp.

As a result, Mark Antony had been forced to appoint another to command his left wing. He was uncertain as to whether

Pontius Fabius was the ablest of his generals, but he was the most senior, with almost twenty-five years of service in every post from senator to legion tribune. Mark Antony noted how, as his new second in command, the man stood subtly apart, and he was not surprised when it was Pontius who spoke for the other legates.

'The word is that the last ships are in, Triumvir,' Pontius said. 'We are expecting to move today.' He smiled as he spoke, knowing the news had been a long time coming.

Mark Antony raised his eyes briefly to the heavens.

'I might wonder why that news wasn't brought over last night, so I could be already on the way. Still, that is good to know.'

With a noble effort, he held back from criticising Octavian, unaware that he actually did so regularly. As a result, almost every man there considered themselves to belong to the main army, with a subsidiary force lagging behind.

'Are the legions ready to march?' he asked the assembled group.

They responded with stiff courtesy, nodding. The triumvir was a head taller than all of them and he seemed to have twice the life in his frame, a figure of endless energy. He clapped Pontius on the shoulder as he passed, calling for breakfast and making his servants scurry to provide it.

'Today is the day then, gentlemen. Come and break your fasts with me. I have a little fresh bread, though don't ask me where I found it. My factor is a genius or a thief; I have not decided which.'

They smiled at that, taking their places in the command post and accepting cups of water brought fresh from a stream nearby. As the other legates were already seating themselves, Pontius stayed out long enough to pass on the orders. Around that single point, twelve legions began to pack up to leave the coast behind.

'Send a runner to Caesar when we have finished here,' Mark Antony called out to his subordinate. 'I'm heading east this morning. I'll see him at the first camp.' He took a cup of water to wash the bread down and idly picked through a plate of boiled vegetables, looking for something worth eating. 'If he can catch up, of course.'

The men around the table chuckled dutifully, though they were already thinking of the campaign ahead. The problem did not lie in finding the enemy forces. All the reports carried the same information, that the army of Brutus and Cassius had found a good position and had been fortifying it for months. It was every legion commander's worst scenario – facing quality soldiers on land they had prepared and chosen well in advance. None of them saw any special significance in the name the scouts reported. The town of Philippi may have been named for Philip of Macedon, father to Alexander, but to the stolid Romans sitting and munching that morning, it was just another Greek town. It lay some two hundred and fifty miles to the east and they would reach it in twelve days or less. Like hunting dogs, the march would harden their legs and improve their fitness as they went. They would arrive ready to break the back of anyone who dared to oppose the will of Rome.

Mark Antony's words were reported back to the legions of Caesar gathered on the coast. Even if Pontius Fabius had not been a cousin of Maecenas, there would have been half a dozen other reports before the day was out, keeping Octavian informed of every detail of his colleague's movements and intentions. Octavian had found it useful to have a few trusted men around the other two members of the triumvirate, on the advice of Pedius months before. It was not a matter of trust, or its lack. He had accepted Agrippa's dictum long before, that a commander needed information above all else. A man could never be blind with a thousand eyes reporting to him each day.

When Mark Antony's legions moved at noon, horns blared and the men roared as they felt the excitement of moving at last, after months of preparations. Mark Antony jerked in surprise when that blare and roar was answered behind him and the legions of Caesar set off at the same time, in perfect step.

CHAPTER TWENTY-SEVEN

The city of Philippi had been built as a simple fortress in the mountains, but three hundred years is a long time to stare north for marauding tribes. As well as stone walls and the open space of an agora, the original stronghold was still there, swallowed in a hundred other buildings that had crept out to make narrow streets along the ridge. Cassius had enjoyed seeing a small temple to Philip of Macedon, hidden away in a street of merchants. He had known another man who claimed divinity and it made him smile. If it had not been for a good road leading to the coast, the small town would have withered long before with the glories of its founder, or perhaps his son.

Cassius had not intended it to be anything but a gathering point for his legions and those of Brutus while they waited for Sextus Pompey to smash the forces trying to land in Greece. When news filtered back of the disastrous battles at sea, they had changed their plans and begun to look around them for the best place to stand and fight. Viewed in that light, Brutus was the first to spot the possibilities of making Philippi the centre of their formation. They had access to the sea along the Via Egnatia, a Roman road built on one much older and capable of bearing any amount of men and equipment. Philippi itself sat on a high ridge which was almost unassailable from the west, as the father of Alexander the Great had intended. Even better from Cassius' point of view, the southern approach was guarded by a steep hill and a vast, sucking marsh of reeds and standing water at its foot. The rains had been heavy the previous winter and it was surely an obstacle no legion could slog through.

When Cassius and Brutus agreed to make the town their command, their soldiers had set to work building a massive wooden palisade all along the edge of the marsh. Natural geography and Roman skill meant the town could not be attacked from that direction, while mountains protected the north and the sea lay to the east. The enemy could approach only from the west and be funnelled into the war machines of twenty Roman legions. Everything from sharpened wooden stakes to scorpion bows and even heavy catapults awaited them.

More than a month had gone by since the first reports of landings at Dyrrhachium. The two commanders had been kept busy hunting down increasing numbers of extraordinarii scouting the area. Cassius had brought Parthian mounted archers from Syria and they were brutally effective, accurate even at a gallop across rough ground. Even so, the constant small clashes were proof the legions were coming, their commanders seeking to know everything they could about the forces and terrain they would face.

Cassius belched softly into his fist as he stared across the marshes. He was on the same rations as the men and not enjoying them particularly. At least the weeks of waiting had allowed them to stockpile supplies. He knew there was every chance the galleys taken from Sextus would be blockading the Greek coast before too long. There had been no news of the brothers Casca. Cassius assumed they had been drowned or slaughtered with the broken fleet.

Cassius suspected he spent too much time thinking about his co-commander rather than the men he faced. Yet Brutus had such an odd mixture of qualities that he never quite knew how he would be received when they met. The man came alive like a memory of his youth when he was training the extraordinarii cavalry. The officer in charge of the Parthian archers followed Brutus around like a lost pup, delighting in the Roman's praise. Cassius felt his mood darken further at the thought. Brutus somehow inspired respect from those around them without seeming to try. It had never been his own gift and it irritated Cassius to have conversations with senior men while their eyes followed Brutus. They looked for just a word or a nod of approval from him, while Cassius stood forgotten. As he belched again, Cassius thought sourly of the way the legions had cheered Brutus' wife as she left for the coast.

He wondered if he should have made more of an issue about commanding the right wing. The legions tended to accept the commander of that position as the man in charge and Brutus had drawn up his legions on the wide ridge without bothering to consult his colleague. They would face the worst of the fighting there, Cassius had no doubt, yet the men seemed pleased and honoured even so.

He kept all sign of unease from his expression as he mounted and rode along the ridge of Philippi, projecting, at least to his own mind, a mood of goodwill and confidence to anyone who saw him. To his left, birds wheeled and dived for insects above the marshes, while ahead the huge ripple in the land tapered down to the western plain. It was there that he and Brutus had positioned their legions to await the enemy. Cassius could only nod to himself as he trotted his horse through the Syrian legions he commanded. They were in the process of eating and he saw men stiffen and salute when they saw him. Hundreds more upset their wooden plates as they scrambled up. He waved them back to their food with only half his attention, trying to think of anything that could still be improved.

'This is a good place to stand,' he murmured to himself. He knew Philip of Macedon had chosen the spot to hold off hordes of Thracian tribesmen, but as far as Cassius knew, the walled town had never been attacked. No blood had ever been shed into the marshes of Philippi or the dry ground above it. That would change, he thought, with mingled satisfaction and dread. The very best of Rome would bleed and die on the land he could see all around him. There was no help for it, not any longer.

As he rode, he reached a group of legionaries sitting in the shade of an olive tree ancient enough to have been planted by Philip himself. They saw him approach and rose to their feet before he could wave them down.

'We're ready, sir,' one of them called as he passed.

Cassius inclined his head in response. He knew they were ready. They all were. They had done everything they could and all he needed now was for men like Mark Antony and Caesar to overreach themselves, to believe just a little too much in their own abilities, then break their backs against the best fortified position he had ever known.

Octavian squinted up at the sun, his head aching in a steady thump that seemed to mimic his heartbeat. He had grown used to thirst during the previous eight days, accepting that he had it easier on horseback than the legions marching east. They had to wait for a formal stop before they could line up to refill the lead flasks with water. The most experienced of them drank sparingly, judging the time between stops so that they would have just a little left at each one.

They had marched a solid twenty miles from the coast on the first day and almost twenty-four on the second. That had remained their average pace, as the legions found their stride and muscles strengthened. It was a favourite activity amongst the men to while away the days, taking the length of their pace as three feet, then multiplying the number of paces and counting off the miles as they went. Even without maps, legions had a pretty good idea of how far they'd come at any time.

As they stopped at noon, Octavian found a spot in the shade of a tree by the road and wiped sweat from his face. He considered his own polished iron bottle, soldered with tin and bound in a strap of brass. He knew he should get it refilled, but he could still taste the metal in his mouth and the thought of more of that blood-warm water made him nauseous. It would be hours until the next stop and he either had to get up and fill the thing from the barrels trundling along behind the legions or call someone else to do it for him. Neither appealed. The water-carriers would be along in a moment, he told himself. Yet the sun seemed to have intensified, so that it beat against his skin like a metalworker's hammer.

He shook his head groggily, trying to clear the stinging sweat from his eyes. None of the men around him seemed to be suffering particularly. Maecenas and Agrippa still looked fresh and relaxed as they stood talking nearby, as fit as the horses they rode.

Octavian opened his mouth as wide as it would go, feeling his jaw crack and trying to clear his senses. He hadn't done much sparring or running with Maecenas and Agrippa recently. Perhaps that was it. He was out of condition and feeling it. It was nothing hard work and cool water couldn't cure. The taste of metal in his mouth intensified, making him dry-heave.

'Caesar?' he heard a voice call.

Maecenas, he thought. He opened his mouth again to reply and the headache jabbed, making him groan. Octavian slumped, slipping away from the trunk of the tree and falling sideways

355

onto the dry ground. His sweat sank into it, vanishing instantly as it fell in fat drops from his skin.

'Shit! Caesar?'

He heard more words but he could feel a flood of vomit building in his throat. He could not stop it. Octavian had a sense of strong hands holding him down as he slipped off a ledge into a roaring blackness.

Maecenas shaded his eyes as he watched the legions with Mark Antony trudge over the hills into the distance. He'd sent messengers forward with the news that Caesar had been taken ill. There was no way to keep it secret. Whatever public declarations of brotherhood the triumvirs made to each other, a man like Mark Antony would be suspicious at his ally calling a halt while he marched towards hostile forces.

The legions gave no sign of stopping and Maecenas breathed in relief. The last thing he wanted was the triumvir's booming voice offering to help. The best legion healers were already working on Octavian, though Maecenas didn't allow himself to hope. They could cut a mangled limb free well enough, sealing the blood flow with hot irons. Injured soldiers sometimes lived through such operations and a few even survived the fevers that followed. Yet there was no wound on Octavian's body to be treated, not beyond the numerous red bites they had all picked up in the sand dunes. Maecenas scratched idly at his own, wondering how long it would be before they were ordered forward, with or without their commander.

Each of the eight legates had come to the healers' tent as the day wore on, while the men camped anywhere they could find a scrap of shade. It was a relief when the sun began to sink into the west behind them, though it only reminded them all of wasted time.

Agrippa came out of the tent, looking subdued.

'How's he doing?' Maecenas asked.

'Still burning up. He started speaking a while ago, but it was just gibberish. He's not awake yet.'

Maecenas looked around to see if they could be overheard. The legates Buccio, Silva and Liburnius were standing in a small group nearby, so he bent his head closer to his friend.

'Do you think it's the falling sickness? The same thing we saw before?'

Agrippa shrugged. 'What do I know about medicine? His bladder didn't go, thank the gods. Good idea putting that horse blanket on him by the way. I . . . told the healers about the first time.'

Maecenas looked sharply at him.

'Did you have to? He never said he wanted anyone else to know.'

'I thought they might have more chance of healing him if they knew. We have to explain it, Maecenas, unless you think we can stay here for a few days with no one asking questions. It's done, anyway. I think it won't hurt him with the men. They know Caesar had it – and Alexander.'

Maecenas considered for a moment.

'That works,' he said. 'I'll spread the word tonight, maybe get a little drunk with a few of the officers. I'll say being in the land of Alexander has brought it on.'

'That is ridiculous,' Agrippa said, snorting.

'But believable. The noble ailment of Caesar's. It means he's a Caesar in blood as well as name. Telling them that won't do him any harm.'

Silence fell between them as they stood there, waiting helplessly for some news or change in Octavian's condition.

'We need him, Agrippa,' Maecenas said. 'He's the only one holding all this together.'

'The name of Caesar . . .' Agrippa began.

'Not the name! Or the bloodline. It's him. The men look to *him*. Gods, he took to this as if he was born to it. There's never been an army this size, except the one we face. If it had been left to Mark Antony, we'd still be in Rome and you know it.'

Maecenas kicked idly at a loose stone by his foot.

'He took command of legions in the Campus – and they accepted it. If he'd been willing to slaughter the Senate, he could have had it *all*, right then and there. His sense of honour is all that stopped him becoming an emperor in one night. By the gods, Agrippa, think of that! He faced down legates from Rome when the consuls were killed and they *joined* him. Octavian chose you to make a fleet. Who else would have done that? Perhaps there *is* something in the blood! But we need him now, or this army becomes Mark Antony's and everything Octavian has done will end up in his hands.'

'He came out of it quickly last time,' Agrippa said at last.

Maecenas only looked tired.

'He wasn't running a fever then. This looks worse. I'll pray he rises fresh tomorrow, but if he doesn't, we're going to have to move anyway. Mark Antony will insist on it.'

'I can make a litter easily enough,' Agrippa replied. 'Maybe string it between two horses . . .' He trailed off as he considered the problem. 'It's possible.'

By dawn the following morning, Mark Antony had already sent riders back to find out where his rearguard had gone. As if he already knew Octavian was still senseless, he sent accompanying orders to catch him up at their best speed.

Agrippa worked quickly with the planks of a water cart and his own tools. The sun was barely over the horizon by the time he was satisfied. It was rough work, but he'd rigged an awning stretched tight over the litter and Octavian's limp form was strapped down with instructions to dribble water between his lips as they went.

There was no sign of life from his friend as the litter poles were tied to a saddle. Agrippa brought his own horse to take the other end, but the litter swayed so dangerously between the horses that he gave up and arranged for legionaries to take shifts carrying the litter in pairs. He and Maecenas took the poles for the first few hours, able to watch over their friend as they marched east with the others.

It was a long, hard day, under a sun that burned. Agrippa and Maecenas were ready to hand over to another pair at the noon rest. They were not surprised to see two of the legates ride across the face of the legions to their position. Buccio had been one of those who mutinied rather than attack a Caesar in the forum. He had gambled his entire future on Octavian and the worry showed in every line of his face. Flavius Silva had given his honour into the hands of the younger man when he swore an oath to him in the Campus. Neither man wanted to see him fail, having come so far.

Maecenas saw an opportunity as the two men stood with Agrippa, blocking the view of many of those around.

'Stand just there for a moment,' he said.

With care, he untied the straps holding Octavian to the litter and reached under the thin sheet of linen, pulling out a wineskin that sloshed half-full. Buccio looked confused for an instant, before his face cleared.

'That's clever,' he said.

'Agrippa thought of it,' Maecenas said. He walked away to empty the urine into a bush, then returned. 'The tricky bit is putting it back on. Would you like to have a go?'

'No . . . no, thank you. Some things are for close friends.'

Maecenas sighed. 'I never thought I'd . . . ah well. He *is* my friend. I suggest you block the view of the men as best you can. Oh, and I'd never mention this to him, if I were you.'

He shoved the empty skin back under the blanket and rummaged about with a strained expression before bringing his empty hands out and retying the straps.

'That should hold him until this evening at least. I'm half tempted to give it to Mark Antony the next time he calls for wine.'

Buccio gave a snort of laughter, but as he looked at the other three, he saw only worry in their faces for the man lying senseless. He made a decision.

'I think I'll take a turn with the litter. Will you join me, Legate Silva?'

His colleague nodded, spitting on his hands and taking a grip on the closest pole.

'Have someone lead my horse, would you?' Silva said to Maecenas.

Maecenas was surprised at how the simple gesture touched him. The two legates lifted the litter together and as the legionaries around them saw what they were doing, they smiled in genuine appreciation.

'Onward, then,' Buccio said. 'One way or another, he will reach Philippi.'

He clicked his tongue to start the horse on its way and they set off once more, moving through the legions as they formed to march. To the pleasure of Maecenas and Agrippa, a great cheer went up at the sight of their legates carrying Caesar to battle.

Mark Antony was in a dark mood as he assessed the maps before him. They had not been properly surveyed, but instead had been collated over the previous week from the efforts of hundreds of scouts and extraordinarii. Though the Parthian horse archers had taken a terrible toll, enough men had survived to crawl or ride back and describe the land to his clerks. The best of them had even made their own quick drawings with charcoal, scratching lines on vellum as they hid in the marshes or looked down from the hills.

The result had cost thirty-seven lives, as well as another dozen or so men being treated for arrow wounds. Mark Antony looked at the lack of detail and wondered if the best scouts were the ones who had been killed. There was certainly no obvious weakness in the place Brutus and Cassius had chosen.

'What do you think, Pontius?' he said. 'Cast your eye on this and tell me you can see something I can't.'

His second in command approached the table, where the great sheet was held with lead weights. He could see the massive ridge above the marshes, as well as a broken, jagged line to indicate the wooden palisades protecting the walled town from the south. On the ridge itself, blocks had been marked to indicate the position of the enemy forces. Numbers were hard to judge at the best of times, but Mark Antony had hoped to outnumber the enemy and had been disappointed.

When Pontius did not reply immediately, Mark Antony went on, his voice hard.

'Show me a place I can attack that isn't from the west. Gods, where did they find this place? The sea and mountains on two sides, marshes on the other? You can be sure they've prepared the only approach, Pontius. If we come from the west, it will be bloody work and with no guarantee of victory, none at all.'

He had begun to think the campaign was suffering from a surfeit of ill-luck. First Caesar had been brought low with some ailment – carried into battle on a litter, no less! Mark Antony had been to see when Octavian arrived in the camp, but it had not raised his spirits. Of all men, he had known the power of having Caesar on his side. Had he not lost two legions to him? It should have been a massive advantage, but if the young man died before battle was even joined, it would be taken as a terrible omen by the men. Mark Antony firmed his jaw. It would be easier to bear if he could see a way to break through the legions on the ridge of Philippi.

Cassius was a cunning old man, he acknowledged. He knew

Brutus was capable enough in a field battle, especially with extraordinarii, but this! This had the marks of Cassius all over it. With good Roman legions, there wouldn't *be* a mistake in the preparations. Cassius and Brutus would be happy to defend a strong position while Mark Antony bloodied his head against their walls.

'You have scouted the marshes, I take it?' Pontius said suddenly.

Mark Antony came back with a start from his trance of dark thoughts.

'Of course. The water is neck-deep in places and the mud is thick, black muck that could swallow a horse. There's no way through there. I'm surprised they wasted time building that wooden barrier against the hill, in all honesty. The marsh is enough of an obstacle . . .' He broke off. Julius Caesar had crossed wide rivers in Gaul. Mark Antony had seen it. What was a marsh compared to that? It was no deeper than a river and he just needed a path through it.

'I think . . .' Pontius said.

Mark Antony held up a hand to silence him.

'Wait. Just . . . wait. If I *could* lay a path across that marsh, perhaps something narrow, the reeds would prevent anyone seeing my men, yes?' He barely hesitated long enough for Pontius to nod before going on with a growing excitement. 'They *know* we have to come up that cursed ridge, so I must come from the south. My men can break their palisade – whatever one man has built, another can take down. All I need to do is work out how to cross that marsh. They'll never see me coming.'

He clapped Pontius on the back and strode out of the tent, leaving the other man staring after him.

CHAPTER TWENTY-EIGHT

Brutus watched grimly, shading his eyes to stare into the distance as Antony's extraordinarii rode up the ridge as close as they dared and launched spears and lead balls high into the air. The balls flew further and could do terrible damage, though the spears caused more fear in the packed ranks. They plunged into the men standing or crouching on the ridge and Brutus could not see if anyone had been injured or killed. He knew the intention was to irritate a defending force to the point where they might boil out of their safe position. His men had enough discipline to resist, but it rankled with them not to be able to respond. One or two spears and scorpion bolts had been sent flying back on the first day, but against wide-spaced horsemen they were wasted. The weapons worked best against a massed charge. Until that time, Brutus knew his men had to endure the hail and remember they would get their chance to pay it all back.

Mark Antony's riders had kept up the stinging attacks for

the best part of two days, delighting in every yell of pain they caused. Brutus glowered at the thought of that man taking pride in the tactic. Eventually the legions from Rome would have to attack or go home with their tails between their legs. Brutus knew very well how much they were eating each day, as the same amount was consumed from the stores in Philippi.

As the sun set, Brutus had climbed to the town's walls and looked out on his legions in battle array, reaching halfway down the western slope. If Mark Antony and Octavian attacked, they would have to come uphill in the face of spears, lead shot, iron bolts and a few other treats he had prepared for them. It should have brought him a feeling of contentment, but the disadvantage of such a strong position was that they were free to manoeuvre and he was not. They could roam the land all around, looking for weaknesses, while he could only sit and wait for the real killing to begin.

From the height of the town wall and with the ground dropping away, he could see for miles to the west, easily as far as the massive camp Octavian and Mark Antony had created. It was an odd thing to see for a man of his experience: the high earth ramps studded with stakes, the gates and sentries that were the signs of Rome in the field – yet on a side he faced as an enemy. It was strange to be in the position so many other nations had known since his people had first come out of the seven hills armed with iron.

When he'd seen Mark Antony had placed himself on the opposite right wing, Brutus was obscurely disappointed. Each side had two commanders and two armies, but Cassius would face Mark Antony, while Brutus would see the boy again. He cleared his throat and spat on the dry stone at his feet. He remembered Octavian very well. He had taught him to ride, or at least to ride with cavalry. His mouth quirked as he realised he felt some sense of betrayal at facing that young man in battle. Perhaps Octavian would be feeling the same way when the time came.

All his memories were of a boy, but Brutus knew he would meet a man when the killing started. He told himself not to underestimate the new Caesar. Brutus could still remember being that young, without the painful joints or the terrible slowness that seemed to have drifted over him in recent years. He remembered when his body worked as it was meant to, and if it hurt, it healed as fast as a young dog. He stretched his back at the thought, wincing as it clicked and ached.

'If you remember me at all, boy, you'll be afraid of facing me.'

He muttered the words staring into the distance, as if Octavian could hear him. One of his guards looked up, but Brutus ignored the unspoken question. He had yet to see Octavian's men in any kind of action. The extraordinarii who galloped across his lines carried the legion standards of Gaul, making sure the defenders knew who were harassing them. Brutus felt the simmering anger on behalf of his own men, forced to sit and wait while their enemies hooted and jeered and tried to leave a few dead with every attack.

The biggest armies ever fielded by Rome stood less than a mile apart. The sun was dipping towards the horizon and even the long summer day would end in a few hours. He cleared his throat and spat again, tired of waiting for the dark.

Cassius looked up as the runner came racing down the hill to his position. He saw the man's flushed face and braced himself against a spike of worry.

'What is it?' he said, too impatient to wait through formalities.

'You need to come, sir. The men in the town think they've seen movement in the marshes.'

Cassius cursed as he mounted his horse and dug in his heels

to ride up the hill. He looked back over his shoulder as he went, seeing Mark Antony's extraordinarii gallop back across the front line for yet another sweep through their own dust. He could see specks of black lead rising from whirring slings and he ducked in unconscious reaction. The men under their path raised shields over their heads once more.

Cassius trotted his mount after the runner. They passed through waiting legionaries the whole way, the ground completely hidden by soldiers sitting or standing idle, as they had been all that day and the one before.

As he reached the town itself, Cassius saw one of his tribunes gesturing to him from a set of steps that led up to the wall. Grim-faced, Cassius jogged up and followed him to the top. He saw Brutus further along, already moving in his direction. Cassius raised a hand to greet him.

The tribune found the spot he wanted and pointed into the marshes that stretched into the distance. At his shoulder, Cassius and Brutus stared out across the broken land of water and reeds higher than a man.

'There, sir. Can you see? Beyond that twisted tree.'

Cassius leaned forward to squint, but his eyes were not as sharp as they had once been and the marsh was just a blur of brown and green to him.

'I can't see *anything* at that distance,' he snapped in frustration. 'Describe it to me.'

'I see it,' Brutus said. 'There's movement, wait . . . yes. There.'

'I was told those marshes cannot be crossed,' Cassius said.

Brutus shrugged. 'I sent men to try it and they almost drowned before they made it halfway and had to come back. But anything can be crossed with enough wood and time. It occurs to me that Mark Antony has been keeping us busy watching his extraordinarii while he sneaks up to flank us.'

'Flank us, or come up behind,' Cassius said bitterly. 'I'll have to bring men back to guard the walls here and the Via Egnatia. This town is like an island. I can hold it for ever with the legions we have.'

'Give the orders then,' Brutus said. 'I can hold the ridge.'

Both men looked up suddenly at a great roar, turning their heads.

'What was that?' Cassius demanded.

He spoke to empty air. Brutus was already running back along the wall and vanishing down the steps to the town. Cassius turned to the tribune, picturing the ridge forces in his mind.

'Legions Thirty-Six and Twenty-Seven to this spot to defend the palisades. I want . . .'

He hesitated, unable to recall which of his legions were closest, before losing patience.

'Pick three more to march through the town and guard the eastern road. We cannot allow them to land soldiers from the sea.'

It would be enough, he told himself. No matter what Mark Antony was planning, he would find Roman legions waiting for him. Cassius cracked his knuckles, showing his worry as the tribune ran to deliver the orders. A man of his position should not have to pelt about the walls like a boy, but he was desperate to know what had caused the great roar from the front.

The noise went on, growing louder and louder. Cassius blanched. He summoned calm with an effort and walked back down the steps to the street below, mounting his horse and trotting towards the ridge.

The summer had been hot and there had been no rain for weeks around Philippi. As Mark Antony's extraordinarii raced along the front, a great cloud of dust had lifted and followed them, hanging in the windless air and thickening as they wove back and forth, launching their spears and shot. To get in range, they galloped in hard to barely thirty paces off the front ranks, close enough to see the faces of those glowering at them. The legions of Cassius and Brutus stood straight, with their shields resting on the dry ground and their swords and spears ready. They *hated* those horsemen and there were more than a few men fingering sword hilts in anticipation, longing for the order to rush forward and gut the vainglorious cavalry who jeered and mocked them.

Almost two hundred riders cantered up and down the front ranks, masking the great care they took over range and demonstrating their courage to the standing men. Even when their spears and balls of lead were gone, they remained, making sudden darts and lunges at the impassive ranks to see if anyone would flinch or try a spear-shot they could mock. The dust continued to rise until they were dashing through an orange-yellow haze and the dry particles covered every inch of exposed skin.

A new century of horsemen rode up from the main camp, each man carrying a spear in his right hand and a sling with a bag of shot dangling by his knee. The officers yelled parade-ground orders at the riders, making their mounts prance back and forth in complicated patterns that could only contrast with the sullen soldiers watching them. The entire century came back together when they had launched spears, following the flights with their eyes as they went. At full gallop, they wheeled together to head along the line. At the same time, the riders already there turned to race back through the dust.

When it came, the crash was thunderous. In the haze of dust the two groups had lost sight of each other for vital moments and crossed each other's paths. Horses tumbled over as they tangled at terrific speed, their riders thrown. Some of them struck and rolled, getting dazedly to their feet, while others lay stunned.

The legionaries saw thirty or forty horsemen lying helpless, victims of their own over-confidence. It was too much after another day of stinging blows and insults. The centurions and optios saw the danger and roared orders, but the front ranks were already moving, drawing swords as they bore down on the wounded men with savage expressions. Nothing could hold them back and they broke into a run. Thousands poured over the invisible line where they had stood for two days, a horde of delighted soldiers bellowing a challenge as they came.

The men behind responded, jumping up and racing forward even as their officers hesitated. Had an attack been ordered? They had heard no horns, nor the command word: liberty. The more cautious yelled at their units to stand down, while others thought they had missed the signal and helped to sweep the line forward. They were moving at last. They had waited weeks to fight and it was happening.

Like a roaring avalanche of men, the entire right wing of Brutus' legions surged down the ridge, overwhelming the fallen cavalry in the first hundred paces as men stabbed anything on the ground and went on. They could see the legions of Caesar ahead of them, milling in panic.

The officers higher up the ridge wasted precious moments trying to call a general halt, orders flowing down the lines of command. By then, the first two legions had seen that the enemy were not ready and had not expected an attack of any kind. The legates at the front countermanded the order to halt as the opportunity to do real damage presented itself. They could see a chance and they took it on their own authority, knowing those behind did not have all the facts. They ordered a charge while the legions of Caesar were still running to form lines and yelling orders in complete chaos.

The moment hung in the air. The legions streaming off the ridge broke into a fast jog as they readied spears. The forces behind saw they were committed and were left with no more choices.

Brutus was still high above his moving ranks when he worked out what was happening. He could see his legions spilling out onto the flatter ground, driven faster by the slope. At first he was black-faced with fury. He had seventeen thousand horses on the wings of the ridge and the sudden surge of men had left them next to useless, unable to reach clear ground and accelerate. He stared in frustration as his first two legions crossed the empty mile over the bodies of dead men and horses, swallowing them up in a tide of red and grey.

Brutus felt his heart hammering in his chest. In an instant, he understood his legions had gone too far to call back. He had to throw the rest in support or see them slaughtered by overwhelming numbers. He took a deep breath and roared new orders to advance. Furious officers looked up to see who was interfering. When they realised it was Brutus, they added their voices to the rest. Horns blared across the ridge of Philippi.

There was confusion in the middle of the ridge as opposing orders met, but Brutus bellowed his command over and over, and gradually, slowly, the massed legions turned and formed up and marched towards the enemy.

On the left, the legions of Cassius marched back to defend against the attack from the marshes and Brutus had a vision of two snakes writhing against each other. He stood up on his saddle, his horse standing perfectly still in the press of men as it had been trained to do. In the distance, through the dust that rose with every step and every sandal, he could see his legions crashing into the Caesarian wing.

Brutus bared his teeth in an expression that lacked either amusement or pity. He wanted to be down there on the plain and he dropped back into the saddle, kicking in and urging the animal past sweating, swearing soldiers.

*   *   *

Mark Antony could see very little of the chaos on the ridge, though the sounds of battle drifted to him over the stinking marshes. For two days, he'd had a full legion working in the black filth that mired every step, while thousands more of his men felled trees well away from Philippi and sawed them into planks as thick as a clenched fist for the carts to bring in.

It had been brutal work, beset by flies and snakes lurking in the shallows, as well as the stench of gas released with every sucking step. Yet they had made themselves a path wide enough for two men to walk abreast. It stretched from the edge of the marshy ground to the centre, then across towards the palisade. His task that day had been to bring the legions up as close as he dared, relying on the reeds and rushes to keep them hidden.

They'd crept along, hunched over, until there were thousands of them on the planks and thousands more waiting to come after them. He'd gone himself to the head of the path, to see the last fifty feet and the wooden barricade Cassius' men had built.

Anything one man had built, another could break, Mark Antony reminded himself. Under the shade of the ridge, he'd had men out all night gently sawing at the key beams, muffling the sound with cloths in great bundles. The town had slept peacefully above their heads and there had been no cries of alarm.

When they were ready, he had sent orders for his extraordinarii to keep the enemy attention focused on the front and then simply waited for the sun to set. His men would be vulnerable to missiles from the town. He needed poor light to spoil the aim of those defending, but enough for his men to scramble up the rough earth and stones and breach the walls.

Before that moment came, before the sun had even touched the horizon, he heard a great roar and he froze, certain they had been seen. If his men had been spotted, reinforcements would be running to the walls above his head. He had to move or withdraw and do either one quickly. Mark Antony made his decision and stood up straight, feeling his stiff knees protest.

'Advance and attack!' he roared.

His men lunged forward and those closest to the barricade heaved on ropes they pulled up from the muck, black and stinking in the light. For a few breathless moments, the beams groaned and then cracked, bringing down half of the construction. Slithering wooden stakes fell all around the closest men and they ran over them, clambering up the slope towards the walls above.

Mark Antony looked up at the fortress. The walls of Philippi were centuries old, but then his men were not wild tribesmen. Hundreds carried ropes with grapnels on their backs; others had hammers with long handles that they used to help them climb. They went up the hill in a surge and he soon saw the first men on the walls themselves, climbing up a hundred broken footholds, or smashing them out with heavy blows so that other men could ascend.

As he began to climb after his men he heard the sounds of fighting above. With just a little luck, he would see Cassius and Brutus dead before the sun set. He breathed hard as he climbed, sinking his hands into soft earth and spitting against dust drifting in all directions. His heart pounded, his body drenched in sweat before he was halfway up to the walls. It didn't matter, he told himself. The pain was just something to ignore.

The Seventh Victrix were the first to come under assault, as the legions of Brutus swarmed down the ridge at them. They were caught completely by surprise and could not form a fighting line before the forces met and the killing began.

Hundreds died in the initial contact, the marching machine of Rome cutting through Octavian's forces. More and more raced down off the ridge, but Mark Antony's wing was at half strength or less, with so many of his men down in the marsh. All they could do was hold position in a solid shield line, jamming the boards into the ground and crouching behind them. Rather than be flanked, they too began a slow withdrawal, step by step into the northern plain.

In his command tent in the twin camp, Octavian stirred sluggishly, unaware of the disaster unfolding for his legions. He did not see the initial rout, as Legate Silva was cut down from his horse by a spear and then torn apart. The men with Silva ran to get out of the way and it infected the rest, so that they broke suddenly and without warning. In the time it took the legate to die, his legion had been forced back into the next and they too had felt the impossibility of standing against a wave of Roman legionaries with their blood up and victory in their grasp. The Eighth Gemina fought a solid retreat as the Seventh Victrix broke, unable to do anything but hold lines and step back with locked shields.

They reached the edge of the massive twin camp and tried to steady the men there, but by then, all of Brutus' legions had been turned in their direction and they could see the widest and deepest line of fighting men any of them had ever witnessed coming to tear them to pieces in savage rage. They fell back from the camp, abandoning the equipment and supplies of a hundred thousand men – and the commander lying unconscious within.

Brutus' men charged into the camp, eager for loot and plunder. Somewhere in that perimeter was a war chest of gold and silver, and even those covered in blood looked for it as they stalked in and stabbed anyone who stood against them.

The command tents were at the centre of the camp, laid out according to rules the invading legionaries knew as well as anyone. They yelled in excitement as they saw them, racing forward, loping in like wolves.

CHAPTER TWENTY-NINE

Maecenas cursed as he sank into black mud to the knee. Each step into the marsh was an effort. He had to strain to pull his feet out, the unnatural motion making his knees ache. As he turned to speak to Agrippa, he slipped on some buried log and fell, clutching at the high reeds and wincing as cold muck slapped along his side.

The man they carried fell with him, so that Octavian's body was spattered.

'Get up, Maecenas,' Agrippa snapped. 'We need to get further in.'

They could hear the noise of the battle behind them, as well as the voices of Mark Antony's men somewhere over on their left. The marsh stretched far enough and deep enough to hide them all from sight, so that he and Maecenas had entered a world of stillness. Things slithered away from them and they could see ripples in the standing water as they dipped as low as they could and dragged their senseless friend deeper into the marsh, constantly expecting the shout that would tell them they had been spotted.

Heading away from the town, they reached a wide pool and both men had to give up any idea of keeping clear of the black sludge. Agrippa and Maecenas stepped down into it, swearing in low voices as they supported Octavian between them. They could feel his searing skin on theirs, an unpleasant fever heat. Their friend murmured at times, seeming almost to come awake as they struggled with his weight and his body hung limp.

'That's far enough, I think,' Maecenas said. 'By Mars, what are we going to do now? We can't stay here.'

They had placed Octavian on a raised hillock of the reeds, leaving him face up into the setting sun with his legs still in the water. He was in no danger of drowning, at least. Agrippa prodded another dense patch and decided to risk sitting down, lowering his weight carefully and groaning as the water reached him even through the dead plants. He rested his hands on his knees as Maecenas found a similar spot.

'If you had a better idea, you should have said so,' Agrippa snapped. His eyes caught a sinuous movement and he jerked his leg close as something slid through the water. 'I hope that isn't a snake. I should think even a scratch will turn to fever in this place, never mind a bite.'

Both men fell silent as they considered the prospect of spending the night in the marshes. They would not be able to sleep while things crawled over their feet and legs. Maecenas slapped his neck where something bit him.

'You are the one who is meant to understand strategy,' he said. 'So if you have any ideas, this is the time to mention them.'

'One of us has to get out and see how things lie,' Agrippa said. 'If the legions have been slaughtered, the best we can do is stay here for a few days and then try for the coast.'

'On foot? Carrying Octavian? We'd have more chance surrendering now. By the gods, Brutus had a bit of luck today. I don't think he ordered that attack. I didn't hear any horns when it started, did you?'

Agrippa shook his head. With eight legions, he and Maecenas had watched in horror as the soldiers on the ridge came pouring down with no warning whatsoever. They'd looked at each other and come to the same conclusion in a moment, running for the command tent where Octavian lay helpless and carrying him out even as Brutus' legions continued their mad rush down the ridge. For a time, they had found sanctuary among Mark Antony's remaining forces, but those legions too had begun to retreat and Agrippa had seen the edge of the marsh nearby. He still didn't know if he'd made the right decision.

Octavian twisted suddenly and began to slip into the black water. Maecenas was up first to grab him under the armpits and pull him back onto the crushed reeds. His friend opened his eyes for a moment and said something Maecenas could not understand before his eyes rolled up.

'He's burning,' Maecenas said.

The water was freezing, untouched by the sun in the murky world of shade and reeds. He wondered if Octavian could feel the cold leaching into him and whether it might help smother the fever he was suffering.

'Why hasn't he woken? It wasn't like this before,' Agrippa said.

'He didn't have a fever before. I think he drove himself too hard over the last month or so. I had to make him eat a few times and it's not as if there is much spare flesh on him.' Something whined in Maecenas' ear and he slapped at it, suddenly furious. 'Gods, if I ever get Brutus or Cassius within the reach of a sword, I'll take the chance, I swear it.'

The sun was setting and darkness was stealing across the marsh, seeming to rise from the ground like a mist. Maecenas and Agrippa were tortured by stinging flies that settled on their exposed limbs, attracted to the crusting black mud on their skin. With grim expressions, both of them tried to make themselves comfortable as best they could. Sleep was impossible in such a place, at least while Octavian could slip into the water and drown. It would be a long, long night.

Cassius spat into a cup of water to clear his mouth as more yellow bile came into his throat. It was thick, bright stuff, pooling like soup below the surface of the clear liquid and hanging from a long thread as he coughed. He wiped his lips with a cloth, irritated that his body should betray him at such a time. His stomach roiled and ached and he told himself it was not fear.

Mark Antony's men had breached his palisade as if the thing was no obstacle at all. They'd come over the walls of Philippi and slaughtered hundreds of his men, pushing them back while more and more climbed in.

To save his own life, he'd pulled back to the northern edge of the town, where he had his command, but in doing so he'd lost contact with his officers. He had no idea where his legions were or whether they were still following his last orders to defend the marsh side. He'd sent fifteen thousand men east to guard the Via Egnatia, though he thought now that it was a mistake. All he'd done was weaken the ranks of defenders where they were most needed.

He handed his cup to his servant, Pindarus, who made it vanish discreetly. The only other man still with him was a legate, Titinius, who was clearly uncomfortable at being away from his legion. The man paced back and forth in the small stone building, his hands clenched behind his back.

'I need to see, Titinius,' Cassius said, irritated at the man's agitation as much as anything else. 'Is there a way up to the roof?'

'Yes, sir. Around the back. I'll show you.'

They left the building and found a short flight of steps

against the outer wall. Cassius climbed them quickly, stepping out onto the flat surface and staring all around him. His eyes were not good and the frustration only built. He could see legions swarming on the ridge, disappearing into the distance like storm clouds.

'Tell me what you can see, Titinius,' he ordered.

'It looks like the legions of Brutus have taken the enemy camp,' Titinius said, squinting. 'I think the enemy have pulled back and formed up beyond it, though it's too far for details.'

'And here, on the ridge? Who can you see moving?'

Titinius swallowed uncomfortably. The town was a mile across and he could see huge numbers of men and extraordinarii on the marsh side of the ridge. Even when they were fighting, it was hard to see who they were, or which side had the upper hand. He shaded his eyes to look at the sun as it touched the western horizon. Darkness would come soon and the night would be full of clashes and alarms. He shook his head.

'I can't tell if we still hold the town, sir, but . . .' His attention was caught by a century of extraordinarii riding through the streets towards his position. 'Riders coming, sir. No banners or standards.'

'Are they mine?' Cassius demanded, narrowing his eyes. He could see where Titinius was pointing, but the distant riders were just a blur to him. He tasted bile once again at the thought of being taken. If Mark Antony had won the town, he would not give his enemy an easy death. 'Are they *mine*, Titinius? I need to know.'

His voice had risen almost to a shout and the legate flinched.

'I'll go out to them, sir, and meet them before they reach us. You'll see then.'

Cassius stared at him, aware that the man was offering his life, if the approaching cavalry were under the command of Mark Antony. He almost refused. There was still time to run, but if the riders were his own and they had repelled the attack from the marshes, he would be back in control. Cassius reached out to grip the man's shoulder.

'Very well, Titinius. Thank you.'

The legate saluted stiffly, heading down to the street at a good pace while Cassius stared after him.

'I doubt I deserve that kind of loyalty,' he muttered.

'Sir?' his servant Pindarus said.

The young man looked concerned for him and Cassius shook his head. He was a lion of Rome. He needed no one's pity, no matter how it turned out.

'Nothing, lad. Now, you can be my eyes.'

He looked towards the sun, frowning as he saw it had dipped to just a line of gold in the west. The sky was aflame with colour and the air was warm. He took deep breaths, trying to show Roman fortitude as he waited to hear his fate.

Titinius kicked in his heels, making his horse canter along the stone streets, so that the noise of its hooves echoed back from the houses on either side. The animal snorted in discomfort as it skidded on the stones, but he urged it on along a street he knew should bring him to the horsemen trotting through the town. He could hear them coming long before he was able to see anything and his stomach clenched in fear. If it was the enemy, they would take delight in killing a legate. As soon as they recognised his rank from his armour, they would cut him to pieces. He looked back briefly, catching a glimpse of the distant figures of Cassius and his servant waiting on the roof. Titinius set his jaw. He was a servant of Rome and he would not shirk his duty.

He passed into a small square that caught the last of the sun's light and as he looked across he saw the first lines of horsemen on the other side. Titinius reined in hard, dragging his mount's head in close to its neck. It whinnied and stamped as he stared at them. They had spotted the lone horsemen and a dozen or so kicked their own mounts into a canter out of instinct, drawing swords to face any possible threat.

His hammering heart leapt when he recognised one of them. Titinius found himself panting and blowing in relief, suddenly aware of the tightness of terror in his chest even as it began to ease.

'Thank the gods, Matius,' he said as they reached him. 'I thought you were Mark Antony's men.'

'I thought the same when I saw you waiting for us,' his friend replied. 'It's good to see you alive after all that, you old dog. I should have known you'd find a safe spot.'

Both men dismounted and clasped hands in the legionary grip.

'I've come from Cassius,' Titinius said. 'He'll want to know the news. How is it going out there?'

'It's a mess, that's how it's going. The last I heard, we'd taken their camp, but they've pulled back in reasonable order and we'll fight again tomorrow.'

'What about the attack here?' Titinius said. The riders didn't look as if they'd been fighting and he took hope from that. His friend's expression warned him the news wasn't good before he spoke.

'We couldn't hold them. They've dug in on the ridge and the marsh end of town. It will be vicious work getting them out again, but there are fresh legions polishing their pretty helmets on the sea road. When they come back in tomorrow, we'll retake the position, I don't doubt it.'

Titinius clapped Matius on the shoulder, taking heart from the mixed report.

'I'll take the news to the old man. This part of town has been quiet so far. I haven't seen anyone else before you.' After the mounting fear as he'd ridden in, Titinius was sweating heavily and he wiped his face. 'I really thought I was done when I saw you,' he said.

'I can see,' Matius replied with a grin. 'I think you owe me a few drinks tonight.'

On the roof, the setting sun was casting the houses all around in dark gold and orange. The servant Pindarus called out everything he could see as Titinius reached the horsemen.

'He's pulled up, sir,' he said, straining his eyes. 'Gods, he's . . . off his horse. They have surrounded him. I'm sorry, sir.'

Cassius closed his eyes for a moment, letting the tension bleed out of him.

'Come with me then, Pindarus. I have a last task for you before you find a place of safety. I won't hold you here now.'

'I'll stay, sir, with you. I don't mind.'

Cassius paused at the head of the steps, touched by the offer. He shook his head.

'Thank you, lad, but it won't be necessary. Come on.'

They went down together and the gloom suited Cassius' mood. He had always loved the grey light before darkness, especially in summer, when it stretched for ever and the night eased through the last of the day.

In the main room below, Cassius crossed to where a gladius lay on a table. The sheath was a work of art in stiff leather and a gold crest. He drew the sword, placing the sheath back down as he tested the edge with his thumb.

Pindarus looked at his master in growing dismay as Cassius turned to face him. The older man saw the pain in his servant's eyes and he smiled wearily.

'If they come for me, they'll make my death a performance, Pindarus. Do you understand? I have no wish to be impaled, or ripped apart for their entertainment. Don't worry, I am not afraid of what comes next. Just make it clean.'

He gave the sword hilt first to Pindarus. The young man took it with a shaking hand.

'Sir, I don't want to do this . . .'

'You'd rather see me paraded for the common soldiers? Humiliated? Don't worry, lad. I'm at peace. I lived well and I brought down a *Caesar*. That is enough, I think. The rest is just . . . the screeching of children.'

'Please, sir . . .'

'I gave my life for the Republic, Pindarus. Tell them that, if they ask. There's a pouch of coins with my cloak. When it's done, take it and run as far as you can.'

He stood straight before the young man with a sword. Both of them looked up as they heard hoof-beats growing closer.

'Do it now,' Cassius ordered. 'They mustn't take me.'

'Would you turn away, sir? I can't . . .' Pindarus said, his voice breaking. He was breathing hard as Cassius nodded, smiling again.

'Of course. Quickly, then,' he said. 'Don't make me wait.'

He faced a window into the twilit town and he took a long slow breath, smelling the scent of wild lavender on the air. He raised his head to it, closing his eyes. The first blow knocked him to his knees and a groaning sound came from his torn throat. Pindarus sobbed and swung again, cutting the head free.

Titinius was cheerful as he threw a leg over his horse and dismounted. He hadn't been able to see anyone on the roof as he rode back with Matius and the extraordinarii.

'Come in with me,' he called over his shoulder. 'He'll want to hear everything you've seen.'

He strode in through the door and stopped on the threshold, frozen. Matius paused behind him.

'What is it?' he asked.

Titinius shook his head, his mouth open. He could see the thin body of the commander lying in a pool of blood, its head off to one side.

'Pindarus! Where are you?' Titinius shouted suddenly, striding in.

There was no reply and he paled further as he stood over the body, trying to understand what had happened. Could the servant have been a traitor? Nothing made sense! He heard Matius gasp as he stared in from the doorway. Titinius looked back at him in sudden understanding.

'He believed you were the enemy,' he said. Titinius gathered his thoughts before they could spool away into uselessness. 'I'll look after things here. You need to find Marcus Brutus now. Tell him what happened.'

'I don't understand,' Matius began.

Titinius flushed. 'The old man thought he was captured, Matius. He had his servant take his life rather than fall into the hands of Mark Antony and Caesar. Just get through to Brutus. He has sole command now. There is no one else.'

In the darkness, Octavian woke and stirred. He could not understand why his legs were so bitterly cold or why the air stank and things rustled around his head whenever he moved. He lay still for a time, staring up at a clear sky and a billion stars shining across the dark. He remembered stopping on the march and the dreadful taste of metal filling his mouth, but after that there was only confusion. Moments came to him, of being carried, of men cheering he knew not what, of the sounds of clashing iron coming closer and panic all around him.

He struggled to sit up, his legs skidding in the sludge that had settled around them as he lay there. To his shock, he felt an arm reach out to steady him, then jerk back as Agrippa found him moving, rather than just slipping from his seat into the marsh.

'Octavian?' Agrippa hissed.

'*Caesar*,' Octavian murmured. His head hurt and he could not understand where he was. 'Do I have to tell you again?'

'Maecenas? Wake up.'

'I'm not asleep!' came Maecenas' voice from nearby. 'You were *asleep*? How could you sleep in this place? It's impossible!'

'I was dozing, not fully asleep,' Agrippa replied. 'Keep your voice down. We don't know who's out here with us.'

'How long was I sick?' Octavian said, trying to sit up. 'And where am I, exactly?'

'You've been unconscious for days, Caesar,' Agrippa replied. 'You're at Philippi, but it isn't going well.'

He passed over a canteen to Octavian, who removed the top and sucked gratefully at the warm water within.

'Tell me everything,' Octavian replied. He felt as if his body had been battered all over. Every joint ached and tendrils of pain spread out from his stomach to his limbs, but he was awake and the fever had broken.

CHAPTER THIRTY

In the night Brutus had found sleep for a few brief moments before a unit of extraordinarii reached him with news that Cassius had taken his own life. His first response had been anger at the old man's loss of faith, in their cause and in him. It was not over. They had *not* lost.

In the cool darkness, he'd drunk water and chewed on a piece of dried meat, while the cavalry officer watched him in the dim light of an oil lamp. Finally, Brutus made his decision.

'Send your men out to every legion under Cassius. My orders are to form up on the plain below.'

The man went running for his horse, disappearing into the night as he passed on the order and his men scattered.

Brutus stood at the bottom of the ridge. He knew he could not command two separate armies of that size, not without Cassius. Orders took too long on different fronts, arriving after the situation had changed and causing chaos. His only choice was to bring them together into one host, or see them cut apart separately.

Under the stars, vast forces marched past each other on the ridge and around the marshes. They moved in deliberate silence, not knowing whether they passed friends or foes in the dark and with no particular desire to find out. It was true Brutus left Mark Antony in control of Philippi, but he thought the man would gain no benefit from the walled town. Mark Antony and Octavian had come to Greece to attack, not to remain behind defences. With Cassius already dead, Brutus knew they would want to complete the victory and take revenge for their losses the day before. He smiled grimly at the thought. Let them come. He had waited his whole life.

As the sun rose, his legions drew up on the great plain at the foot of Philippi. Brutus spoke to each of the legates, one by one or in groups as they came to him. He was ready to fight again, legion against legion, pitting his ability to lead against the talents of Mark Antony and Caesar.

When there was light enough to see, Brutus rode along his ranks, judging the numbers left to him. His army had lost thousands, but they had taken the main camp of Mark Antony and Caesar and driven their legions back with many more dead. Bodies still littered the great ridge, glittering like dead wasps in the dawn.

In Philippi, Mark Antony had seen the vast array on the plain and begun to march his legions down. Brutus could see them coming, accepting the challenge. Mark Antony had always been arrogant, he recalled. He doubted the man had much choice, even so. His legates would pressure him even if he tried to hold back.

Brutus had seen the vast, deserted camp on the plain. Everything valuable had already been taken, though Brutus was sorry none of his men had reported the death of Caesar. It would have been somehow fitting if Octavian and Cassius had both fallen on the same day, leaving the two old lions of Rome to fight it out. Brutus could still hardly believe he was in sole command, but the thought did not displease him. He was at the head of a Roman army. There was no Gnaeus Pompey, no Julius Caesar there to gainsay his orders. This battle would be his alone. Brutus exulted in the rightness of it. For this, he had killed Caesar in Pompey's theatre. He was out of the shadow of others at last.

He looked up as a great cheer went up from Octavian's legions, less than a mile from his ranks. He could see a distant figure riding up and down the lines there. Brutus gripped his sword hilt tightly, understanding it had to be Octavian, that the young man had survived to fight again. He told himself it didn't matter to him. Seeing the pretender fall would only add to the sweetness of the day to come. It was a strange thought to know he had only two enemies left in the world and they would both face him that day across the plain of Philippi. Mark Antony would be confident, he thought. His men had done well, though Cassius had denied them the chance to capture him. Brutus gave silent thanks for the old man's courage. At least the day would not begin with the spectacle of a public execution.

Octavian had yet to prove himself. His legions had run the day before and they would be seething with that humiliation, determined to restore their honour. Brutus smiled coldly at the thought. His men fought for liberty. It would do just as well.

Octavian was sweating, his body wet with it, though he had ridden barely a mile up and down the lines. He knew he had to let the men see him, to remind them they fought for Caesar, but he felt as if only his armour held him up, his body as weak as a child's.

He saw a messenger galloping across his ranks with dash, a young man delighting in his own speed. When the rider reined in, he was panting and flushed.

'Discens Artorius reporting, Consul.'

'*Tell* me Mark Antony hasn't found something else to delay him,' Octavian replied.

The extraordinarii rider blinked and shook his head. 'No, sir. He sent me to let you know Senator Cassius is dead. They found his body last night, up in the town.'

Octavian looked over his shoulder at the legions opposing him. There was no sign of Cassius' banners in the cluster around the command position. He wiped sweat from his eyes.

'Thank you. That is . . . most welcome.'

Those around him had overheard the rider and the news spread quickly. A ripple of thin cheering followed, though in the main the men were indifferent. They hardly knew Cassius beyond his name. Yet Brutus still lived and his legions were the ones who had forced the rout the day before. His legions were the ones they wanted to break. Octavian could see the determination in every face as he looked down the ranks. They surely knew the fighting would be hard, but they were more than ready for it to begin.

The two Roman armies faced each other over a mile while the remaining legions came down from Philippi. As Mark Antony was coming in from the east, Octavian had to give him the right wing. He knew the man would expect it and he could hardly make him march through his ranks to take position on the left. Octavian sat and sipped from a canteen, feeling the breeze dry the sweat on his face. Mark Antony seemed to be taking his time, as if he sensed the armies would stand all day until he arrived.

While he waited, Octavian half expected a sudden attack from the legions under Brutus. His men were certainly tense, waiting for it, but it seemed Brutus preferred not to leave a flank open to fresh legions coming off the ridge halfway through the battle.

The morning wore on, the sun moving slowly up to noon.

Octavian tossed the empty canteen back to Agrippa and accepted another as the right wing formed piece by piece and the military powers of Rome faced each other on a foreign field. It would be brutal when it began, Octavian realised. No matter what the outcome, Rome would lose much of her strength for years to come. A generation would be cut down on the plains of Philippi.

On both sides, the extraordinarii gathered on the furthest point of the wings. Their peacetime roles as message-carriers and scouts were only to keep them occupied when they were not fighting. Octavian watched as the cloaked cavalrymen drew long swords and shields for their true purpose, their horses milling and snorting as the animals felt the growing excitement in their riders. He looked to his right, where Mark Antony had taken position at last in the third rank. The town and ridge were empty of men. They were ready.

Octavian trotted his mount back to his own position behind the first and second fighting lines. The sun crept over the noon point as both sides prepared, emptying bladders where they stood and sipping at waterskins or canteens they would try to ration through the day's heat. Against so many, a battle could not be over quickly and they had to prepare to fight all day. In the end, it would come down to stamina and will.

Octavian checked his lines of command to his legates one last time, asking for confirmation that they were ready. Seven of them still lived, with Silva's body somewhere among the carrion meat from the previous day. He did not know the man who had replaced him, but he knew the others. He knew their strengths and weaknesses; the ones who were rash and the ones who were cautious. Brutus would have no such personal knowledge of the legions he commanded, especially not those he had gained from Cassius. It was an edge and Octavian intended to use it.

The responses came back quickly and Octavian made what

plans he could beyond the first clash. The left wing was his to command.

The men were looking to him, waiting for the order. Agrippa and Maecenas were there at his side, steady and solemn. They had saved his life when he was senseless with fever. It seemed another lifetime somehow and he felt the cares and trials of months fall away as he sat his horse and stared across the plain. His body was weak, but it was just a tool. He was still strong where it mattered.

Octavian took a deep breath and a mile away the legions of Brutus began to move. He raised and dropped his hand and his own ranks began to march, the release of tension palpable as they strode towards the enemy. On his right, Mark Antony gave the same order. Out on the wings of both armies, extraordinarii dug in their heels, holding back their mounts as they eased forward, forming slight horns past the marching legionaries. Cornicens blew long notes across the lines, sounding the advance.

The two armies walked over dry ground, raising great clouds behind the front ranks as the gap between them shrank down to a thread that was suddenly made black with thousands of spears in the air. Arrows came from the Parthian horsemen, cutting holes in the extraordinarii. The thread wavered as both sides soaked up dead and wounded men, stepping over and around them and breaking into a run. They crashed into each other with a noise like thunder on the plain.

Brutus felt a deadly calm settle on him, a coldness at the centre of his chest as the armies came together. He was not a young man to be carried away on a tide of excitement and fear, and he gave orders with cool detachment. He frowned slightly to himself as he saw how long it took for them to be carried out, but he had not given complete freedom to his legates. This was *his* battle, though he began to learn how hard it is to command the best part of ninety thousand in the field. It was a larger army than Pompey had ever commanded, or Sulla, or Marius, or Caesar.

He saw his Parthian archers do well on the right wing, surging forward almost a mile away from his position in the centre. He sent a command across the marching lines for them to go wide and empty their quivers into the enemy extraordinarii from a safe distance before closing with swords. It was the right order, but by the time it reached them, they had already pulled back and the moment was lost.

At first, his legions pushed against both wings of the enemy and he felt a glittering pleasure as his men cut their way through thousands of Mark Antony's men. The shade of Cassius would be watching and he wanted the old man to see.

It didn't last long. Where his lines grew weak, the enemy legions advanced before he could shore them up with reinforcements. When his men won a temporary advantage and cut into the forces with Octavian, they found fast-moving legions thickening the ranks against them and brief chances vanished like frost in the sun. Having two commanders halved the time it took for them to control their chains of command and though the difference was subtle, it began to tell more and more as the afternoon crept past in blood and pain.

Brutus felt it happening. He could see the battlefield in his head as if from above, a trick of perspective he had learned from his tutors years before. When he saw the unwieldy lines of command were hampering his legions, he grew afraid. He sent fresh orders to cast his legates loose from overall control for a time, in the hope that they would respond faster on their own. It made no difference. One of Cassius' Syrian legates staged a wild attack, forming an immense wedge formation that cut past Octavian's front rank. Ten thousand men shifted right in saw orders against them, bolstering the lines and slaughtering the Syrian legionaries on two sides. None of his legates had moved fast enough to support the attack and the numbers of dead were terrible. The wedge fell apart inside Octavian's ranks, engulfed in a flood.

Brutus sent an order to rotate his own front line. For the length of a legion, two panting ranks moved back in tight formation with shields up, allowing fresh men to the fore. Beyond that distance, the front two ranks fought on, the order getting lost somewhere on the way. It was infuriating, but Brutus had to roar for extraordinarii messengers and send them out to the legates a second time.

He took full command once more and the entire front line eased back and then forward as unblooded soldiers came through with harsh voices bellowing. They pushed on for a few brief moments, hacking down men who were panting and growing weary. Then the orders were mirrored and they faced fresh men in turn, all along the clashing front.

Brutus found he had to move his horse back a step as the men in front of him were driven in on themselves. He cursed, shouting encouragement. He saw his Parthian archers had been cut to pieces, caught by swordsmen while they still held bows. His entire right wing was in danger of being flanked as Octavian's legions began to spill around it.

Calmly, Brutus ordered two of his legions to saw into them, then waited with his heart pounding for the orders to take effect across a mile of land. Mark Antony was pressing forward on the other flank at the same time. Brutus responded to that, bawling new orders and sending out riders and runners. When he looked back, the right flank had crumpled and he could see his legions falling back, shields raised as they stumbled into their own forces to get away.

'Where are you?' Brutus said loudly. 'Come *on*! Where *are* you?'

Only then did he see the legions he had ordered to support

the wing begin to move sideways through their own ranks. It was a difficult manoeuvre in a marching line and he felt a wave of disgust and dread, seeing they were already too late. The flank was collapsing and the men falling back only hampered the attempt to support them in a clot of struggling soldiers. The enemy came in hard, using extraordinarii well as they swung out and back in at a gallop. It was butchery and Brutus began to feel a black despair. He needed Cassius, and Cassius was dead. It was like acid in his throat to know he could not command so many alone.

With his heart in his mouth, he sent new orders to disengage, to come back a hundred paces and re-form. It was the only way to save his right wing before the enemy routed half a dozen of his Syrian legions. He thanked his gods that it was one command he could give by horn, and the droning notes sounded across the plain.

Octavian's legions also knew what the signal meant. They pressed forward to take advantage, even as his centurions tried to withdraw in good order. Brutus sensed his front line wavering as the horns blared. For tiring men, it was a dangerous distraction. Hundreds died as Brutus made his horse walk backwards, unwilling to turn from the enemy. For an instant, he saw a gap between the armies, then it was filled as Octavian's legions charged forward, roaring and clashing their swords on their shields as they came in again.

Step by step, his army came back with him, furious that they had been ordered away. Brutus saw the right wing sort themselves out as they went, so that the danger of a complete rout on that side began to pass. In the crush, he found himself in the front rank for a moment. He cut down at a helmet and grunted with the impact and satisfaction as a man fell. His ranks re-formed in front of him and he shouted to the cornicens to sound the halt and break off the slow retreat.

The horns moaned again across the battlefield, but his right wing continued to fall back. Brutus cursed as he saw his position. He needed to send fresh legions in to hold it, but Mark Antony chose that moment to begin tearing into his left flank once more.

Octavian cursed as the enemy legions pulled back before he could roll them up from the wing. His extraordinarii were down to a few thousand horses and their spears and lead shot were gone. All they could do was follow the wing's retreat and then cut back in wild dashes, slicing throats as they went. More of the horses fell with kicking legs and the high screams of dying animals. Octavian clenched his jaw, letting anger give him the strength to endure.

His mouth was dry, his tongue and lips a gummed mass. He shouted to Agrippa for water and his friend passed him another canteen. He sucked at it, freeing his mouth and clearing his throat. The sweat still poured off him and it took all his control to hand back the bottle while there was still a little sloshing at the bottom.

He'd seen that the legions under Brutus were slow to respond to any new situation and he'd worked like a madman to make that weakness count. His legions swarmed, moving left and right as they advanced, threatening one spot to test the enemy response, then surging forward in another when the lines grew thin. Octavian felt the first sense of victory when the wing crumpled without support, but then Brutus pulled back in good order and battle joined again with renewed ferocity.

When he moved forward, it was over dead and wounded men, some of them crying out in such pitiful agony that their own friends finished them with quick gashes to the throat. Octavian passed one soldier with his stomach ripped open, his armour torn and broken. The man was sitting hunched over, holding his guts in bloody hands and weeping, until a careless stranger knocked him onto his back. Octavian lost sight of the man in the press, but he could still see his terror.

The fighting had gone on for hours and they had moved barely two hundred paces from where they began, even with the withdrawal Brutus had pulled off in the teeth of the enemy. Octavian was gasping once more, sick of an enemy that seemed never to shrink or falter. He was in no mood to appreciate Roman courage as he sent two almost fresh legions up the centre, using their shields to bow back the lines facing them.

Brutus drew men in to block the advance and Octavian immediately snapped orders to launch the Seventh Victrix and Eighth Gemina at the wing, pulling back his extraordinarii into formation. The two legions chanted 'Caesar!' as they went, the name that had created panic in enemies for a generation.

Brutus was caught by the sudden move, with too many of his forces committed in the centre. Octavian thought he heard the man yelling orders, though the noise of battle hammered his ears on all sides and he could not be sure. The wing crumpled again and the carnage went on and on before there was a sign of new men rushing to the position.

The legion on Brutus' right wing had almost broken once, saved only by the steady withdrawal. They were exhausted from the constant attacks by extraordinarii. As Victrix and Gemina came at them, roaring the name of Caesar, they turned and tried to retreat again. It had worked once.

Octavian watched as the lurching retreat turned into a sudden rout, with thousands of soldiers turning away from the fighting and breaking into a run. He sent new orders to his extraordinarii and they swept back in as the wing disentegrated and the rout began to spread.

More than fifty thousand soldiers still stood with Brutus, panting and bloodied. When the right wing was slaughtered before their eyes, the will to fight went out of them. Brutus could do nothing to stop them falling back, though he bawled until he was hoarse and his messengers raced away in all directions once more, as exhausted as the men fighting. They had ridden fifty miles or more on mounts lathered in sweat, so that his commands slowed even further each time.

Octavian could see the panic in the legions facing him as they felt the wing go. They knew his next move was to get behind them and cut off their retreat. It was the ultimate fear for a foot soldier, to be attacked before and behind and have nowhere left to run. They fell back, further and further. A huge roar went up from the legions under Octavian and Mark Antony as they pressed forward, sensing they would actually survive it all, seeing their triumph in every step against a fleeing enemy.

Brutus looked desperately around him, seeking some ruse, some factor he had not seen that could yet influence the outcome. There was nothing. His legions were falling away in full rout on the right wing and the left was in retreat. He could do nothing but come back with the battered centre, his front ranks fending off blows as they tried to save themselves from an enemy given new strength by the prospect of victory.

His legates were sending riders to him every few moments, pleading for new orders. For a time, he had nothing for them and despair ate at his will. He could not bear the thought of Mark Antony's smug pleasure, or the humiliation of being taken by Octavian.

He took deep breaths, trying to force life back into limbs that seemed suddenly leaden. The closest legions still looked to him, thousands of men knowing he held their lives in his hands. He ordered them back, retreating further and further away from the bloody slash of dead soldiers that marked where the armies had met. When he turned his horse to leave the battlefield, it was over. He saw the confusion and fear in his men as they retreated with him.

Brutus looked further into the distance. The hills behind Philippi were not too far off. The sun was setting and many of his men would survive the slaughter if he could just reach the slopes. He told himself he could scatter the legions through the mountains and perhaps he would even see his wife again in Athens.

The army of Octavian and Mark Antony pressed hard as they retreated, but the light was failing and the cool grey twilight was on them by the time he reached the foothills. Brutus led his legions up the rough ground, leaving a trail of dead the whole way as his men were cut down.

He turned at the tree line, seeing with dull anger that only four legions had come with him. Many more had surrendered on the plain or been butchered. Even those with him were reduced in number, so he doubted more than twelve thousand made it to the slopes.

The legions of Octavian and Mark Antony roared victory until they were so hoarse their voices failed. Then they clashed their swords on shields, spattering blood across themselves as they gave thanks for surviving the battle.

Brutus climbed until his horse could carry him no further. He left the animal to run free, walking with the rest as the gloom darkened across the plain. He could still see for miles as he looked back. The bright lines of everything he had dreamed lay in bloody heaps on the dry soil of Philippi.

In the darkness, Octavian and Mark Antony met. They were both weary and dirty with blood and dust, but they clasped hands, wrist to wrist, each man knowing only too well how close it had been. For that night, the triumvirs had the victory and all they had risked had paid off.

'He won't get away, not now,' Mark Antony said. His legions had been closest to the foothills and he'd sent them up to stay close to the defeated soldiers trudging away from the battlefield. 'When he stops, I'll have him surrounded.'

'Good. I haven't come so far to let him escape,' Octavian replied. His eyes were cold as he regarded his fellow triumvir and Mark Antony's smile became strained.

'I found some of the Liberatores hiding in the town last night,' Mark Antony said. It was a peace offering between allies and he was pleased to see life come back to Octavian's expression as he stood there.

'Have them brought to me.'

Mark Antony hesitated, disliking the tone that sounded so much like an order. Yet Octavian was consul as well as triumvir. More importantly, he was the blood and heir of Caesar. Mark Antony nodded stiffly, conceding his right.

CHAPTER THIRTY-ONE

Brutus couldn't sleep. He had driven himself to the edge of endurance for two days and his mind kept scrabbling away like a rat trapped in a box. High in the hills, he sat on a clump of scrub grass with his hands in his lap and his sword unstrapped and lying at his feet. He watched the moon rise above him and took pleasure in air so clear that he could almost reach out and take the white disc in his hand.

He could smell the sourness of his own sweat and his body ached in every joint and muscle. Some part of him knew he should still be looking for an escape, but the night was stealing through him and he recognised it as the numbness of acceptance, too strong to resist. He was too tired to run, even if there had been a way through the mountains at his back. Perhaps Cassius had felt the same at the end – no anger or bitterness, just peace descending on him like a cloak. He hoped so.

In the moonlight, Brutus watched the dark masses of men moving to surround the tattered remnants of his army. There was no way back to the plain, no way back even to the man he had once been. He could see lights on the ridge of Philippi and he tried to blot out the mental images of Octavian and Mark Antony toasting his failure and their success. He had rejoiced at being alone in command as the sun rose that morning, but it was not a fine thing at the end. He would have taken comfort from the dry wit of Cassius or one of his old friends with him one last time. He would have taken comfort from his wife embracing him.

As he sat there, under the stars, his men sat in groups on the hillside, talking to each other in low voices. He had heard their fear and he understood their hopelessness. He knew they would not stand with him when the sun came up again. Why should they when they could surrender to noble Caesar and be saved? There would be no last great stand on the mountains by Philippi, not for Brutus. All he could do was die. He knew the coldness in his bones was his mind preparing for the end and he did not care. It was over. He had killed the first man in Rome and the dark rush of blood had carried him over the sea to this place, with a breeze tugging at his cloak and his lungs filled with cold, sweet-scented air.

He did not know if the shades of the dead could truly see the living. If they could, he imagined Julius would be there with him. Brutus looked up into the stillness of the night and closed his eyes, trying to feel some presence. The dark pressed in instantly, too close to bear. He opened them again, shivering at the soft blackness that was so much like death. For just a little while, he had held the future of Rome in his hands. He had believed he had the strength to alter the passage of a people and a city as it moved into the centuries ahead. It had been a fool's dream; he knew that now. One man could only do so much and they would go on without him and never know he had lived. He smiled wryly to himself then. He had been the best of a generation, but it had not been enough.

A memory came back to him in fragments, a conversation from too many years before. He had sat in the shop of a jeweller named Tabbic and talked about making his mark on the world. He had told the old man that he wished only to be remembered, that nothing else mattered. He had been so young! He shook his head. There was no point recalling his failures. He had worked for something more than himself and age had crept up on him while he was blinded by the sun.

Alone on the hill, Brutus laughed aloud at the mistakes he had made, at the dreams and the great men he had known. They were ashes and bones, all of them.

In the town of Philippi, Octavian stared coldly as four men were dragged into the room and thrown to the floor before him. They had been badly beaten, he saw. Suetonius lowered his head and stared wonderingly at the bright blood that dripped from his scalp to the floor. Gaius Trebonius was bone-white with terror, visibly trembling as he sat sprawled and did not try to rise. Octavian did not know the other two as men. Ligarius and Galba were simply names on the list of proscriptions to him. Yet they had been part of the group of assassins, stabbing knives into Caesar just a year and a dozen lifetimes before. They stared around themselves through swollen eyes and, with his hands bound, Galba could only sniff at the blood dribbling from his nose.

The man who rose to peer down at them was young and strong, showing no sign that he had fought a battle that day. Suetonius raised his head under that interested gaze, turning aside for a moment to spit blood onto the wooden floor.

'So will you be emperor now, Caesar?' Suetonius said. 'I wonder what Mark Antony will say about that.' He smiled bitterly, showing bloody teeth. 'Or will he too fall to your ambition?'

Octavian cocked his head, assuming a puzzled expression.

'I am the champion of the people of Rome, Senator. You see no emperor here, not in me. You *do* see Caesar, and the vengeance that you have brought down on your own head.'

Suetonius laughed, a wheezing sound from his battered frame. His lips bled fresh as the scabs cracked, so that he winced even as he chuckled.

'I have known Caesars to lie before,' he said. 'You have *never* understood the Republic, that fragile thing. You are nothing more than a man with a burning brand, Octavian, looking at the scrolls of greater men. You see only heat and light and you will not understand what you have burned until it is all gone.'

Octavian smiled, his eyes glittering.

'I will be there to see it, even so,' he said softly. 'You will not.'

He gestured to a soldier standing behind Suetonius and the man reached down with a knife in his hand. Suetonius tried to jerk away, but his hands were tied and he could not escape the blade as it cut across his throat. The sound he made was terrible as he looked up at Octavian, in hatred and disbelief. Octavian watched until he fell forward and looked away only when Gaius Trebonius gave a broken cry of grief.

'Will you ask for mercy?' Octavian said to him. 'Will you call on the gods? You did not wield a blade on the Ides of March. Perhaps I could offer a reprieve to one such as you.'

'*Yes*, I ask for mercy!' Trebonius said, his eyes wide with fear. 'I was not there on the Ides. Grant me my life; it is in your power.'

Octavian shook his head in regret.

'You were part of it,' he said. 'You fought with my enemies and I have discovered I am not a merciful man.'

Once again he nodded to the executioner and Gaius Trebonius gave a great yell of anguish that choked into gurgling as his throat was opened. He fell twitching and scrabbling onto the floor by Suetonius. The smell of urine and opened bowels filled the room, bitter and pungent.

The remaining pair knew better than to plead for their lives. Ligarius and Galba watched Octavian in sick fascination, but they did not speak and prepared themselves to die.

'Nothing?' Octavian asked them. 'You are almost the last of those brave men, those *Liberatores* who murdered the Father of Rome. You have nothing to say to me?'

Galba looked at Ligarius and shrugged, spitting out a final curse before kneeling straight and waiting for the knife. Octavian gestured in sharp anger and the knife was dragged across two more throats, making the air heavy with the smell of blood and death.

Octavian took a deep breath, weary but satisfied. He knew he would sleep well and be up before the dawn. There was just Brutus left. There was just one more day.

The sky was clear as the sun rose and Brutus was still awake after a night that had seemed to last for ever. He watched the spreading colours of dawn in peace and when he stood at last, he felt somehow refreshed, as if the long hours had been years and he had slept after all. With care, he removed his armoured breastplate, untying the thongs and letting it fall away so the cold could reach his skin. He shivered, taking pleasure in the small sensations of being alive on that morning. Every breath was sweeter than the last.

When he could see the faces of his men, he knew what they would say before they said it. The legates came to him as soon as it was light enough and they would not meet his eyes, though he smiled at them and told them they had done all they could and that they had not failed him.

'There is nowhere left to go,' one of them murmured. 'The men would like to surrender, before they come for us.'

Brutus nodded. He found he was breathing harder as he drew his sword. They stared at him as he checked the blade for imperfections and when he looked up, he laughed to see their sorrow.

'I have lived a long time,' he said. 'And I have friends I want to see again. This is just another step, for me.'

He placed the tip of the blade against his chest, holding the hilt tight in both hands. He took one last breath and then threw himself forward, so that the blade punched between his ribs and into the heart. The men with him flinched as the metal stood out from his back and life went out of him like a sigh.

The soldiers of Mark Antony began to march up the hill towards them and the legates readied themselves to offer formal surrender. Two of their number went out to those climbing and word spread quickly that they would not resist, that Brutus was already dead by his own hand.

While the sun still rose, Mark Antony came striding through the scrub bushes with a century of men. The legates laid down their swords and knelt, but he looked past them to where Brutus lay dead. He approached the body, then undid the clasp that held his cloak, draping the cloth over the still form.

'Carry him gently, gentlemen,' he said to the kneeling legates. 'He was a son of Rome, for all his faults.'

They bore the body down the hill to where Octavian waited. The news that they would not have to fight had spread to his men like fire on a dry hill and the mood was sombre as they watched the red-draped figure brought back to the plain of Philippi.

Octavian walked to the legates as they laid the body down. They had taken the sword out of the still flesh and Octavian looked at a face that was strong, even in death.

'You were his friend,' Octavian murmured. 'He loved you more than all the rest.'

When he looked up, his eyes were red with weeping. Agrippa and Maecenas had come to stand by him.

'There's an end to it,' Agrippa said, almost in wonder.

'It's not an ending,' Octavian said, wiping his eyes. 'It is a beginning.' Before his friends could reply, he gestured to one of Mark Antony's men. 'Remove the head for me,' he said, his voice hardening as he spoke. 'Put it with the heads of Cassius and the other Liberatores who fell here. I will have them sent to Rome to be thrown at the feet of the statue of Julius Caesar. I want the people to know I kept my promises.'

He watched as the legates hacked Brutus' head from his body and bound it in a cloth bag to be taken home. Octavian had hoped for joy when the last of them fell – and it was there, a brightness in him that swelled as he breathed in the warm air.

Mark Antony felt old and tired as he watched the hacking blades fall. There would be triumphal processions to come and he knew he should feel satisfaction. Yet he had seen the bodies of the last Liberatores, left to rot in a room in Philippi. The odour of death was in his hair and clothes and he could not escape it. The crows were gathering already, he saw, settling on the faces of men who had walked and laughed only days before.

He was unable to explain the sadness that gripped him. He looked into the rising sun and thought of the east and the Egyptian queen who was raising the son of Caesar. Mark Antony wondered if the boy would look like his old friend or show some sign of the greatness he had inherited with his blood. He nodded to himself. Perhaps in the spring he would leave Lepidus to handle his affairs in Rome for a time. When Rome was settled, he would visit Cleopatra and see the Nile and the son who would one day own the world. It was a fine promise to make to himself and he felt his weariness lift at the prospect. Philippi would be a place of the dead for years, but Mark

Antony was alive and he knew good red wine and redder meat would help him recover his strength. He was the last general of his generation, he realised. He had surely earned the peace to come.

EPILOGUE

Mark Antony checked himself one last time as he stood waiting on the docks at Tarsus. There was a breeze coming off the water and he was cool, his uniform polished. He could almost laugh at his nervous sense of anticipation as he looked down the river with a hundred officials from the Roman town. None of them had predicted that the Egyptian queen would come herself, but her barge had been sighted off the coast of Damascus days before.

Mark Antony leaned forward yet again, staring down the river at the huge barge coming slowly up to the port. He saw the description had been no exaggeration. The oars shone blindingly in the sun, each blade covered in polished silver. Purple sails fluttered above the craft, catching the breeze and easing the strain on the slaves working below. Mark Antony grinned. Or perhaps it was just for the effect, the glorious splash of colour that already made the Roman port look drab in comparison.

He watched in pleasure at the spectacle as the enormous

vessel came up to the piers and the crew snapped orders in a tongue he did not know, easing their charge in as the oars were shipped and ropes flung to waiting dockmen to tie them off fore and aft. Mark Antony could see a figure on the deck, reclining under an awning amidst a sea of coloured cushions. His breath caught as she rose like a dancer to her feet, her gaze passing lightly over the men waiting and then settling on him. It was surely no accident that she was wearing the formal dress of Aphrodite, with her shoulders bare. The pale pink cloth looked well against her tanned skin and Mark Antony recalled the woman's Greek ancestry, visible in the curling black hair bound in tiny golden seashells. For a moment, he envied Julius.

Mark Antony told himself not to forget that she was the joint ruler of Egypt with her son. It had been Cleopatra who led the negotiations with her estranged court when Caesar had come to her lands. It was because of her that Cyprus was Egyptian once more and no longer an island of Rome. Her barge would have passed it on the journey around the coast and he wondered if she had thought of Julius then, or pointed out her possession to his son.

A wooden ramp was laid to the docks and, to Mark Antony's surprise, a troupe of beautiful women came up from the hold, singing as they went. A dozen black soldiers took their position as an honour guard on the docks, perhaps aware of how splendid they looked with their dark skin set against armour of polished bronze.

Through them all, the queen of Egypt walked, guiding a young boy with her hand resting on his shoulder. Mark Antony stared, entranced as they came towards him. The women walked with her, so that she moved in song.

He cleared his throat, deliberately bluff and composed. He was a triumvir of Rome! He told himself to get a grip on his awe as she came to stand before him, looking up into his face.

'I have heard about you, Mark Antony,' she said, smiling. 'I have been told you are a good man.'

Mark Antony found himself flushing and he nodded, collecting wits which seemed to have deserted him.

'You are . . . welcome in Tarsus, your majesty. It is a pleasure I did not expect.'

She did not seem to blink as she listened, though her smile widened. By the gods, she was still beautiful, Mark Antony thought to himself. His eyes drank her in and he did not want to look away.

'Let me introduce my son, Ptolemy Caesar.'

The boy stepped forward with her hand still on his shoulder. He was dark-haired and serious, a boy of only six years. He glowered at Mark Antony, looking up at the man with no sign of being impressed.

'We call him Caesarion – little Caesar,' Cleopatra said. He could hear the affection in her voice. 'I believe you knew his father.'

'Yes, I knew him,' Mark Antony replied, searching the boy's features in fascination. 'He was the greatest man I have ever known.'

Cleopatra cocked her head slightly as she listened to him, all her attention focused on the big Roman welcoming her to his lands. She smiled a little wider at that, seeing honesty in his response.

'I know Caesarion would like to hear about his father, Mark Antony, if you are willing to talk about him.'

She held out her hand and he took it formally, leading her away from the docks and breaking the trance that had settled on him since she set foot on land.

'It would be my pleasure,' he said. 'It is a fine tale.'

HISTORICAL NOTE

No other writer can equal Mark Antony's funeral oration as written by William Shakespeare, though the playwright didn't use the detail of a wax effigy, a matter of historical record. It is true that the rioting crowds burned the senate house down for the second time, along with an impromptu cremation of Caesar's body. Nicolaus of Damascus gave the number of assassins as 80, whereas the first-century historian Suetonius mentions 60. Plutarch mentions 23 wounds, which suggests a core group, with many more who did not actually strike. Of those core conspirators, the names of nineteen are known: Gaius Cassius Longinus, Marcus Brutus, Publius Casca (who actually struck the first blow), Gaius Casca, Tillius Cimber, Gaius Trebonius (who distracted Mark Antony during the assassination), Lucius Minucius Basilus, Rubrius Ruga, Marcus Favonius, Marcus Spurius, Decimus Junius Brutus Albinus, Servius Sulpicius Galba, Quintus Ligarius, Lucius Pella, Sextius Naso, Pontius Aquila, Turullius, Hortensius, Bucolianus.

For those who are interested in details, Publius Casca had his estate and possessions sold in a proscription auction, which included a table bought by a wealthy Roman and then transported to a provincial town in the south: Pompeii. Preserved in the ash of the Vesuvius eruption, the lionhead legs of that table can be viewed there today, still marked with his name.

Though I have made him a little older to fit the chronology of previous books, Octavian was around nineteen when Caesar was assassinated in 44 BC. He was in Greece/Albania when the news came and he returned to Brundisium by ship. On his return to Rome and learning of his adoption by Caesar, he changed his name to Gaius Julius Caesar Octavianus, though he dropped the final part shortly afterwards and never used it.

Caesar's will had been written at an earlier stage of his life, though it is not known exactly when. It is true that he gave 300 sesterces to each citizen – a total somewhere in the region of 150 *million* silver coins in all, as well as a huge garden estate on the banks of the Tiber. Even then, Octavian received around three-quarters of the total after bequests and legacies. Although it was lodged at the temple of Vesta, as I have it, it was in fact read publicly by Caesar's last father-in-law: Lucius Calpurnius.

The most important part of the will was that it named Octavian as Caesar's son, so catapulting him instantly to a status and influence mere wealth could never have brought. With the adoption came the 'clientela' – tens of thousands of citizens, soldiers and noble families sworn to Caesar. There is no modern equivalent of this bond, which is closer to a feudal retainer or family tie than a business relationship. It can be fairly said that without that bequest, it is unlikely Octavian would have survived his baptism of fire in Roman politics.

* * *

Mark Antony had a number of children before Cleopatra, most of whom are lost to history. With Fulvia, he had two sons: Marcus Antonius Antyllus and Jullus Antonius. I changed the name of the second son to Paulus as Jullus was just too similar to Julius. Anytllus was a nickname. In later years, he was sent to Octavian with a vast sum offering peace, but Octavian kept the gold and sent him back to his father.

In a similar way to Jullus Antonius, I changed the name of Decimus Brutus to Decimus Junius, as I didn't want another Brutus to cause confusion. That assassin of Caesar was in fact a distant relative of Marcus Brutus. It is true that he was given an area of northern Italy as a reward for his part in the assassination. It is also true that Mark Antony decided to take it from him with the Brundisium legions, and that Octavian was given the task of stopping him. What an irony it must have been for Octavian to be ordered north by his enemies to stop the one man who had supported Caesar!

Note on cowardice. It has become the fashion in recent years to consider Octavian as some sort of weakling. He was neither weak nor a coward. There are well-attested historical accounts of him walking into a hostile camp unarmed to address a mutinous legion – with the body of the last man to try it still on the ground before him. It is true that he was prone to a peculiar collapse at moments of stress. Some modern writers have suggested asthma or dropsy, though the Roman historian Suetonius described him as deeply asleep and senseless, which does not fit those ailments at all. Given that epilepsy ran in his family, the likelihood is that he suffered 'grand mal' fits, which left him helpless whenever they struck. His enemies certainly crowed about his absences, but he showed courage in every other aspect of his life. After a wasted day where he was absent and sick, he went on to lead from the front at the battle of Philippi. On other occasions, he stood his ground in riots, with missiles flying all around him. He once went first across over an unsteady gangway and was badly injured when it collapsed. In short, claims of his cowardice sit on weak foundations.

The death of consuls Hirtius and Pansa in the same campaign against Mark Antony was incredibly fortunate for Octavian. I have simplified the events, which actually took place in two major battles a week apart. Pansa fell in the first and Hirtius in the second, leaving Octavian in sole command. There is no evidence that Octavian colluded with Mark Antony, though I suggest that does not mean there was no collusion. It is one of those historical moments when the extraordinary outcome should be considered a little *too* fortunate, without someone having jogged fate's elbow. Octavian was not present at the first battle and fought personally at the second, securing a Roman eagle on his own as he withdrew.

Having accepted Senate authority and the position of propraetor – equivalent to a governorship of a province – Octavian found himself in sole command of eight legions. There are one or two interesting rumours that spread after the battle. Pansa survived his wounds for a time before dying, which led to gossip that his own doctor had poisoned him on Octavian's orders. It was even said that Octavian had struck Hirtius down himself, though this is almost certainly untrue.

While in exile in Athens, Brutus was a regular patron of debates and philosophical discussions, like many other Romans in Greece before him. The small training scene is fictional, though he was fit at the time of Philippi and must have trained regularly. The detail of the second man moving faster is a little-known truth from studies of gunfighters in the American west that I could not resist including. The man who draws first sparks an unconscious response from a trained opponent, who tends to draw more smoothly and with greater speed. It is counterintuitive, but as Japanese kendo fighters will affirm, the instinctive reaction after thousands of hours of training is often faster than a blow resulting from a controlled decision.

On coins: Both Brutus and Cassius had coins minted after the assassination of Caesar. The most famous is the one with the head of Brutus on one side and the words 'Eid Mar' on the reverse, with two daggers around the skullcap of a newly freed man. Others linked Brutus with the words 'liberty' and 'victory' – an early example of propaganda in an age before mass communication.

Note on fleet construction: Agrippa's secret fleet was based near modern-day Naples at the lake of Avernus. The lake has the benefit of being only a mile from the sea and at roughly the same level. Roman surveyors will have confirmed this for him, but it was still a relatively minor project compared to, say, bringing an aqueduct for a hundred miles, or laying road for thousands. Bearing in mind that 25,000 men working with spades on the Panama canal could shift a million cubic yards a day, the Avernus canal could have been dug in just three or four days with a thousand men. Add in complications such as canal gates to hold back the lake, and a figure of start-to-finish in a month is reasonable.

Agrippa's catapult grapnel, named the harpax or 'robber', is part of the historical record, though not well known. The description of bronze bearings comes from a similar project at a lake by Genzano, near Rome, where Roman ships were rescued from the bottom in the nineteen thirties. In Genzano, the Romans built a tunnel from the lake to the sea. I didn't know the ancient Romans had ball bearings before that trip and it is well worth a visit.

With those sorts of innovations, and despite being badly outnumbered, Agrippa was able to destroy the Roman fleet under Sextus Pompey. It is one of those key moments in history where a single man influenced the entire future of a nation and yet it is almost unknown today.

It is occasionally necessary, for reasons of plot, to alter the main line of history. I have followed the true history for most of this book, but the events concerning Sextus Pompey took place *after* Philippi and not before as I have them here. Octavian agreed to meet him at sea for a failed peace accord, where Sextus' admiral Menas offered to cut the ship adrift and effectively hand Rome to Sextus. Sextus had given his oath of truce. He was furious with Menas, not for offering, but for not just doing it and thereby allowing Sextus to preserve his oath.

The second wife of Brutus was an interesting character. Her actual name was Porcia Catonis, which I changed to Portia because it didn't sound like the slender beauty she actually was. According to the histories, she came upon her husband when he was considering the assassination of Julius Caesar. Porcia was very young and famously beautiful. He said he couldn't trust a woman with such a secret, so to prove her loyalty, she wounded her thigh with a knife, then bore the pain and fever for a full day before showing him what she had done. He trusted her after that, though when he went to Athens, he left her in Rome, rather than bring her with him, as I have it here. Instead of showing a relationship through letters, I preferred to put her in the scenes in Greece. Though the exact manner is disputed, she committed suicide after the death of Brutus at Philippi.

On poets: It is an odd coincidence that the two best-known poets of the Roman world, Quintus Horatius Flaccus (Horace) and Publius Vergilius Maro (Virgil), should have known each other. History sometimes throws up clusters of great names in the same generation, just as Michelangelo and Da Vinci knew and loathed each other in a later century.

Octavian's noble friend Maecenas was in the habit of collecting poets among his wide group of friends. He knew Virgil well when they were in their twenties. Horace actually met Brutus first when he was in Athens and was present at the battle of Philippi, though Horace was forced to flee in the general chaos.

Philippi was indeed created by King Philip of Macedon as a walled city to stand against marauding Thracian tribes. It is in ruins today and was rebuilt at least twice even in the time of Augustus. At the time of the battles there, it was a walled stronghold built on a wide hill and overlooking a marsh that Cassius did think was impassable, especially once his men had built wooden palisades along the base.

When Octavian collapsed, he remained lucid enough to give orders that he be carried to Philippi on a litter. He was in the twin camp when the unplanned attack started. Brutus' legions rushed forward without warning after days of being stung by skirmishes and raids against their lines. I have compressed the timeline here, as the battles took place after many days where little happened.

While Mark Antony led his legions in an attack across marshes, taking Cassius' camp, Brutus' legions captured his own camp – but Octavian had vanished. We cannot be certain where he went, but he is said to have hidden in a marsh and there was only one around Philippi. Agrippa and Maecenas were almost certainly with him.

The first day of battle was utterly chaotic, with vast numbers of men passing each other in poor light and not knowing whether they were surrounded by friends or enemies. It is true that Cassius thought he was taken and asked his servant Pindarus to kill him. By the time Titinius returned with news that the approaching horsemen were on their side, Cassius was dead and Brutus was in sole command of the legions against Mark Antony and Caesar.

Octavian had recovered enough to take part on 23 October 42 BC, when Brutus led out his forces alone for the second battle of Philippi. The Caesarian forces fought bravely, perhaps with the motivation to repay their rout in the first clash. Octavian and Mark Antony worked well together. They broke Brutus' legions and Mark Antony led the pursuit as Brutus retreated into the wooded hills above Philippi with four battered legions.

It was Mark Antony who surrounded that exhausted force. Word came to Brutus that his men were considering surrender and the following morning he said goodbye to his companions and threw himself on a sword.

Mark Antony treated the body with respect, laying his own cloak over it. When Octavian came to see, he had the head removed and sent to Rome to be thrown at the feet of Caesar's statue.

It is true that Octavian executed many of the captured men after Philippi, including almost all of the Liberatores still alive. He had his revenge in the end, surviving illness and disasters, setbacks and betrayals to find himself consul and triumvir, in command of Rome.

Mark Antony travelled to the east to oversee and restore Roman rule to states driven to near bankruptcy by Cassius as he prepared for war. It was Antony who installed King Herod as ruler of Judaea, a man best known for the slaughter of innocents as he tried to defeat a prophecy foretelling the birth of Christ.

Famously, Mark Antony met Cleopatra when she came to him at Tarsus in her royal barge, rowed by silver oars and with purple sails. She was in her early thirties and still renowned for her beauty and intelligence. It is said that she dressed as Aphrodite to meet the Roman. The relationship that followed would be the great love of his life. When years of argument and strain between Antony and Octavian finally led to conflict in 31 BC, Mark Antony lost the sea battle of Actium and another at Alexandria. He and Cleopatra both committed suicide when it was clear they had lost. The son she had with Julius Caesar, Ptolemy Caesarion, was killed in Alexandria on the orders of Octavian. He was just seventeen years old.

Octavian ruled for decades as Augustus Caesar, a title meaning 'noble' or 'illustrious'. He was first in Rome for a golden age of expansion, until his death in AD 14. Yet in his long life, he never called himself emperor. Historians refer to him as the first emperor, but that title would not be used until his successor, Tiberius. Octavian's long rule was exactly what was needed for Rome to consolidate after decades of internal wars. It can honestly be said that his legacy *was* the Roman empire, his period of stable rule saving Rome from destruction and chaos. It is because of Augustus as well as Julius that Rome survived longer than any other empire in history and the name of Caesar came to mean king.

As a writer of historical fiction, I like to travel to the lands in question wherever possible, but I also need the best histories for the details. As well as older sources such as Plutarch and Cassius Dio, I am indebted to Anthony Everitt, for his wonderful book *Augustus: The Life of Rome's First Emperor*. I recommend it to anyone interested in the period. Thanks are also due to Shelagh Broughton, who moved heaven and earth to research the list of Caesar's assassins for me.

It would be possible to write another two or three books on